THE CAVERNS OF THE DARK

Sickened and exhausted, Rudy holstered his flame thrower and prepared himself for the long, ugly journey through the caverns of the Dark back to the surface.

Wind struck him, chill and sudden—the swirling, directionless breath of the Dark Ones. From deep in the cavern he had left, he heard the thud of running feet and a man's hoarse, labored gasps. Before Rudy could move from the niche where he was hidden, the fugitive captive blundered through the entrance and stumbled into his arms.

The Dark were instants behind. They poured down from the top of the tunnel as the runner and Rudy fell in a blundering tangle. Rudy gasped in shock and despair, trying to twist himself free.

Then the swarming, horrible bodies of the Dark descended on them. Slimy coils of clawed tentacles began unfurling . . .

By Barbara Hambly
Published by Ballantine Books:

THE DARWATH TRILOGY
The Time of the Dark
The Walls of Air
The Armies of Daylight

The Armies Of Daylight

Barbara Hambly

A Del Rey Book

BALLANTINE BOOKS • NEW YORK

A Del Rey Book

Published by Ballantine Books

Library of Congress Catalog Card Number: 82-90936

ISBN 0-345-29671-0

Manufactured in the United States of America

First Edition: July 1983

Cover art by David B. Mattingly

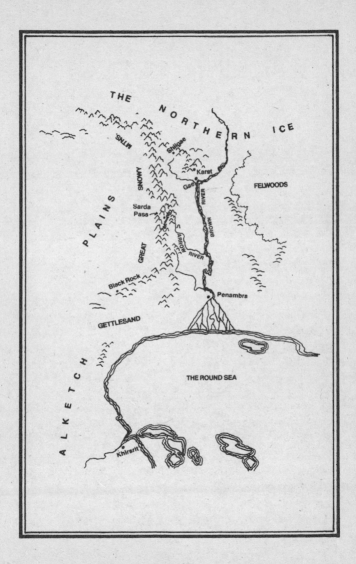

PROLOGUE

When the wizard Ingold crossed the Void between worlds to save the infant Prince Tir from the destruction of Gae, Gil Patterson and Rudy Solis tried to help him. But one of the monstrous, evil Dark crossed behind him, and they were all forced to flee back to the world of magic from which the wizard came.

It was a world where magic worked and where the loathsome Dark were destroying humanity, after having lain almost forgotten in underground lairs for three thousand years. And it was a world where the only hope for mankind lay in the distant, ancient stone Keep of Dare, built to resist the previous ravages of the Dark.

The King had fallen in Gae. Now Chancellor Alwir was the Regent, as brother to young Queen Minalde. Vying for power was the Bishop Govannin, fanatic leader of the Straight Faith. And both Alwir and the Bishop feared Ingold.

The road to the Keep was a hell of cold and danger, with both the Dark and the barbarian White Raiders taking toll on those who struggled through the freezing mud. But Gil found herself accepted as one of the Guards. Rudy won the love of Minalde and discovered that he had wizard powers. He became a student of Ingold.

Once the remnant of humanity was established precariously in the Keep, Ingold and Rudy set out for Quo, the city where the wizards ruled and protected all their ancient lore. There had been no word from that city, and no magic of Ingold's could reach through the veils of illusion guarding it. But when they reached Quo, after two thousand miles of marching through hardship and danger, they found the city in ruins—the Dark had been there. Of the wizards, only Lohiro remained to meet them. And Lohiro was possessed by the Dark. In a bitter struggle, Ingold managed to destroy Lohiro.

Ingold sent out a desperate mental summons for any wizards of any degree of ability. Then he and Rudy began the long struggle back to the Keep.

During their absence, Gil had used her training as a scholar to investigate the old records, looking for some clue as to how the ancient Dare of Renweth had defeated the Dark. Together with Minalde, who had a touch of the mysterious memory of past events that was supposedly inherited by only a few men, she found the ancient workshops of the wizard-engineers who had built the Keep. And she found artifacts of all kinds, most without apparent use.

When Ingold and Rudy returned, they found a ragtag assembly of wizards, half-trained witches, and village healers waiting to become the Wizards' Corps under them. Ingold realized that the crystals Gil had found were the ancient source of artificial light. And Rudy seized upon a collection of parts which he assembled into a flame thrower, a possible weapon against the Dark.

Alwir used the discovery as an excuse to determine that the wizards must spy out the Nest of the Dark at Gae. Ingold, knowing the folly of the plan but unable to deter Alwir, began trying to create a cloaking-spell that might protect the wizards against the Dark.

Part One

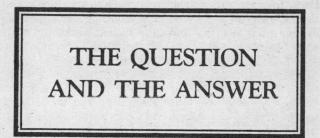

THE QUESTION
AND THE ANSWER

CHAPTER ONE

The night was still. The wind that had beaten with such violence down the ice-locked mountains to the north had fallen at about sunset to an uneasy murmuring in the dark pines that filled the twisting Vale of Renweth. By midnight, even that had ceased. The black branches hung motionless from one end of the Vale to the other, slowly furring with frost in the deepening cold. A man's breath, barely visible in the soulless glimmer of the few remote and haughty stars, would hang like a diamond cloud about his face or freeze in white hoarfrost to his lips. In that piercing cold, not even the wolves were abroad; the silence ran from cliff to lightless cliff, an almost tangible property in that frozen and desolate world.

Yet beneath the dark trees, something had stirred.

Rudy Solis was sure of it. He glanced behind him for the fourth time in as many minutes, fear creeping along his spine and prickling at the nape of his neck like tiny teeth. Yet he saw nothing there, only the thin sheen of starlight frosting the unmarked snow.

He looked back to the darkness of the trees. He stood some fifty feet from the forest's edge, his shadow a misty blur on the old broken snow around his feet, his breath a tiny smear of steam against the darkness. Even wrapped in the thickness of his buffalohide coat, he shivered, though not entirely with cold. He knew that it would be warmer in the protection of the forest and, look as he would, he could sense no movement there. It was undoubtedly perfectly safe, and sheltering there would be a damnsight more intelli-

5

gent than standing in the open listening to the ice crystallize in his lungs.

But neither hope of Heaven nor fear of Hell would have induced him to seek the shelter of those shadowed woods.

A wind touched his face like a clammy, seeking hand. It took all his strength not to whirl, to face the unseen foe. But he had been told not to run. In the open ground of a still mountain night, flight would mean instant death. The cloaking-spell that covered him, like all cloaking-spells, depended upon diverted attention; the wizard who used one must do nothing to call attention to himself, lest the illusion fail. And in any case, Rudy knew that no human being could ever hope to outrun the Dark.

This is stupid, he told himself desperately. *What if Lohiro was wrong? Or worse, what if he was lying? The Dark possessed his mind for weeks. How the hell do we know he was telling the truth when he said they'd let him go? This spell of Ingold's is to cloak against a collective, rather than an individual, intelligence—but how do we know that will overcome the reason human magic never worked against the Dark Ones? What if it was all a trap?*

The unbearable terror returned again, as if some vast, dark bulk were creeping slowly toward his back. But he could see nothing there, no movement in the stark white emptiness of the snow-covered meadow, and could hear no sounds but the hiss of his own breath in his lungs and the hot, too-swift pounding of his heart. The years he'd spent on the fringes of the motorcycle gangs, among the tough guys and would-be tough guys of smog-bound Southern California, had given him a kind of bar-fight courage sufficient for his survival. But the waiting in terror for an unknown danger was different. His every perception, sharpened by wizardry to detect what others found invisible, was keyed to a fever pitch for the warning of danger. And in his heart, he was sure that no warning would save him.

Cold, directionless winds breathed upon him, like the draught from a primordial abyss of darkness which had never seen light. At the touch of it, his heart seemed to lurch, then hammer chokingly. His intelligence screamed at his instinct to run, telling him that, even if he ran, even if he made the half-mile dash through the ice-locked drifts of the buried meadow to the windowless Keep of Dare, they would never let him in. Once the cyclopean doors were sealed at sunset, Keep Law forbade that any should open them before dawn.

So he drew the veils of alien illusion more firmly about him and prayed that they all were right—Lohiro, Ingold, and Thoth—when they said that this kind of spell would guard his body from the inhuman hungers of the Dark.

He could feel the Dark Ones coming closer; he sensed their coming in the change of the air. Close by him a little skiff of snow whirled up, as if stirred by wind, but no wind riffled now in the fur of his collar. In all directions the snowy landscape rolled like a frozen, silver sea; yet from the corner of his eye, he glimpsed movement, a sudden flurry that vanished, as things did in dreams. In the shadows of the trees before him, he thought he saw something shift, though not a branch stirred.

They were all around him—he knew it, but their illusions screened them from his eyes as he prayed that his own covered him. He felt their stirring, though there was nothing that he could fix his eye upon—just a gleam of starlight on something that pulsed wetly and the sudden glitter of acid on chitinous claws. There was a buzzing, humming sensation in his brain . . . a drift of wind that stank of rotten blood . . .

Then suddenly it was above him, a delirium-vision of an obscene, squamous bulk, fifteen feet from the tucked, slobbering tentacles of that drooling mouth to the wriggling tip of the spined cable of tail. Huge, clawed legs dangled down, like the feet of a wasp; from them, acid dripped to smoke on the snow.

Rudy shut his teeth hard on a scream. Sweat was freezing on his face, and every muscle in his body fought to remain still against the instincts that shrieked at him to run. The effort and the revulsion at the nearness of that filthy dripping thing brought nausea burning to his throat. More than its evil, more than the terrible danger that breathed like smoke over him, he was filled with sickened loathing of its *otherness*—its utter alienness to the world of the visible, the material . . . the sane.

7

Then it was gone. The wind of its departure kicked a stinging gust of snow over him as he slowly folded to his knees in the drifts.

How long he knelt there in the darkness he didn't know. He was trembling uncontrollably, his eyes shut, as if to blot out the memory of that hideous, slobbering bulk swimming against the stars. Stupidly, he recalled a night last spring, a warm California evening, when he and his sister had been headed down the Harbor Freeway in downtown Los Angeles, and the old Chevy had a blowout in the fast lane of the interchange. His sister had managed to pull the veering car under control, to force it out of the hammering madhouse of sixty-mile-an-hour traffic and over onto the shoulder. Then she'd gotten out, calmly checked to see if the rim had been damaged, asked him if he was okay—and folded up on the car's steaming hood and gone into violent hysterics.

Rudy suddenly found himself in sympathy with how she had felt.

Something brushed his face, and he swung around, the cold searing his gasping lungs.

Behind him stood Ingold Inglorion, looking quizzically down at him in the faint blue starlight.

"Are you all right?"

Rudy collapsed slowly back to a sitting position, his gloved hands pressed tightly together to lessen their shaking. He managed to stammer, "Yeah, fantastic. Just give me a minute, then I'll go leap a tall building at a single bound."

The wizard knelt beside him, the full sleeves of his patched brown mantle brushing against him again, warm and rough and oddly reassuring. In spite of the cold, Ingold had pushed the mantle's hood back from his face, and his white hair and scrubby, close-clipped white beard gleamed like frost in the ghostly light. "You did very nicely," the old man said, in a voice whose mellow beauty was overlaid by a grainy quality, scratchy without being harsh, and pitched, as a wizard's voice could be, for Rudy's ears alone.

"Thanks," Rudy croaked shakily. "But next time I think I'll let *you* test out your own new spells."

The white eyebrows quirked. Ingold's face as a whole was

totally nondescript, redeemed only by the heavy erosion of years and by the curious, uncannily youthful appearance of his eyes.

"Well, I'm certainly not out here because it's the proper phase of the moon for harvesting slippery elm."

Rudy colored a little. "Scratch that," he mumbled. "You shouldn't be out here at all, man. You're the one the Dark Ones have been after."

"All the more reason for me to come," the old man said. "I can't remain walled in the Keep forever. And if it is true, as I suspect, that somehow I hold the key to the defeat of the Dark Ones, at some time or another I shall have to come forth and meet them. I had best assure myself of the efficacy of my cloaking-spells before that time."

Rudy shivered, awed at that matter-of-fact calm in Ingold's tone. Rudy feared the Dark Ones, as all humankind must fear them: the eaters of the flesh and of the mind, the eldritch spawn of the hideous night below the ground; and arcane intelligence beyond human magic or human comprehension. But at least he was reasonably certain that they did not know him—his name, his essence. He knew that he was not the target of their specific malice. It was not his personal flesh they sought. He stammered, "But Christ, Ingold, you didn't have to come and check out the spell yourself. I mean, hell, if it works for me, it should work for you."

"Possibly," Ingold agreed. "But that is something that no one can ever wholly know." He drew his mantle closer about him. In the dim light, Rudy could see that the wizard was armed; the billowing folds of his outer garment broke over the long, hard line of the sword that he wore belted underneath. His right hand in its faded blue mitten was never far from the sword's grip-smoothed hilt.

"Do you remember how," he went on in his mild voice, "in the mazes of illusion that surrounded the City of Quo, you asked me once for a spell to break the wall of fog?"

"You told me the one I was using already would work just fine," Rudy recalled. "I can't say I was real pleased."

Calmly, the old man removed a speck of snow from his frayed sleeve. "If it is ever my aim to please you, Rudy, I shall certainly ask you what methods I should employ." The gleam of mischief in his eyes turned his bearded face absurdly young. "But what I told you then was true. The strength of any spell is the strength of your magic—your spirit. Your power is shaped by your essence. You are your spells."

Rudy was silent, understanding this for the truth as he had not understood it in the mazes of the trackless Seaward Mountains. It was the key to human magic—perhaps the key to all things human.

"Do you feel sure of this spell, Rudy?" the wizard asked quietly. "Could you use it again?"

"Yeah," Rudy said slowly, after long thought. "Yeah, I think so. I was scared to death, but . . ."

"But you kept your head," Ingold said. "And you kept your hold over the spell." Crusted frost gleamed in his scrubby beard as he nodded his head. "Do you think you could do so in the Nest of the Dark itself?"

The thought was like a hypo filled with ice water, injected directly into Rudy's heart. "Christ, I don't know! It's . . ." Then he saw the intentness, the calculation, in those crystal-blue eyes. "Hey, you mean—*really* in the Nest of the Dark? I mean, that wasn't just a—a hypothetical question?"

The frost crackled a little as Ingold smiled. "Really, Rudy, you should know me well enough by this time to know that I seldom deal in hypotheses."

"Yeah," Rudy agreed warily. "And that's probably the scariest thing about you."

"It is the most frightening thing about any wizard. A hypothesis to anyone else is merely an overwhelming temptation to a wizard. Do you think you would be able to handle yourself in the Nest of the Dark?"

Rudy swallowed hard. "I think so." The vivid imagination which was the mainspring and curse of the mageborn sent a series of chills scampering up his spine. "That's what this is all about, isn't it?"

Ingold's eyes returned to focus from some private, inner reverie. In the starlight, they seemed bright and preternaturally clear. "The Chancellor Alwir cannot hope to reconquer

Gae from the Dark without reconnaissance of their Nest there," he said quietly. "He has chosen Gae, partly because of its importance as the capital of the Realm and partly because it lies at the center of communications.

"But time is short. Our allies, from the Empire of Alketch and from the various landchiefs of the Realm, will be assembling here in the not-too-distant future. You will be leaving for Gae within a day or so."

"Okay," Rudy agreed shakily, with valiant mental adjustments. "Uh—just me?"

Ingold snorted. "Yes, just you, all by yourself," he snapped gruffly. "Of course not! For one thing, Gae is a flooded ruin—you could never hope to find your way through its streets to reach the Nest."

A drift of wind stirred his mantle and ruffled Rudy's long hair. Rudy's muscles locked at the touch of it, but he made no move. A moment later he saw the flickering shadow of a little whirlwind dancing away over the snow. He let his breath out in a shimmer of silvery smoke.

"Of the mages who survived the coming of the Dark Ones," the wizard continued quietly, "less than a dozen have powers strong enough for me to have made this test on them. They, too, are abroad in the Vale tonight. Of those, only two hail from Gae—Saerlinn, who was a healer in the lower part of town, and me."

Rudy nodded. He'd become acquainted in the last week with the other survivors of the world's wizardry. Saerlinn was a fair-haired, rather nervous young man, a few years older than his own twenty-five. He was unusual not only in the fact that he wore spectacles—uncommon enough among mages, who could generally adjust their own senses and faculties—but also because he'd managed to preserve them unbroken on the long and desperate trek from Gae to the Vale of Renweth.

"At one time I considered leading the Gae reconnaissance myself," the old man went on, and Rudy cast him a startled, protesting glance. "But aside from the fact that, as the head of the Wizards' Corps, I could ill be spared, I do take a rather academic and refined interest in the preservation of

11

my own skin. Since the Dark are hunting me—for whatever reason—I would be in twice the danger of detection within the Nest. It would be folly to tempt them."

"It would be sort of pointless to get yourself killed on a routine mission," Rudy admitted.

Ingold smiled. "Precisely," he agreed. "I'm sending Thoth to head the reconnaissance of Penambra—he knows that city from his early days as a healer there. And I'm having the Raider shaman, Shadow of the Moon, take a couple of scouts to the Nest in the Vale of the Dark, some twenty miles north of here. She knows woodcraft—among other things."

In the black wall of woods to their right, branches stirred suddenly, rustling in dark, aimless winds. Clouds were moving down from the glacier-locked mountains that loomed above them to the west, swallowing the few remaining stars. Cold cut through Rudy's coat like a skinning knife.

"Kara of Ippit will go with you and Saerlinn to Gae," Ingold went on. "She's had the most formal training as a mage. Unless one counts the Chancellor Alwir's Court Mage Bektis, of course."

Rudy sniffed. He did not like Bektis. "If he's out here tonight, I'll eat my boots without even scraping the mud off 'em."

"If that's the case, I regret to inform you that you're going to miss a meal." Ingold sighed. "Bektis knows Gae, too. But I'm sure that his ever-pressing duties will not permit . . ."

He looked up suddenly, the words dying on his lips. A scream split the mountain stillness, a hopeless, echoing shriek that scaled up to a frenzied pitch of horror, then jarred and broke. Rudy sprang to his feet, the hair prickling on his neck, and was instantly arrested by the iron grip on his arm.

"Be still, you fool."

A figure broke from the edge of the woods on the far side of the valley, black and tiny against the hoarfrost landscape. *A man,* Rudy thought, watching the way he ran, young and slender, stumbling over his own cloak in his terrified haste.

A swirl of darkness passed like a whirlwind over the snow. The fugitive screamed again as he ran, his arms outstretched, plunging blindly down the hill toward the black

12

monolith of the Keep of Dare. Darkness swelled from the trees behind him, a strange shifting of images that even the dark-sight of a wizard could not pierce. Something flashed, wet and sticky, and a last piercing cry rang out, as if ripped from the dissolving flesh. Then there was silence, and something scattered over the half-melted snow.

Even at this distance, Rudy could smell the blood on the backwash of the erratic winds.

"Who was it?" Rudy asked.

His voice was pitched low, audible only to certain beasts, or to another wizard. But still his words sounded sacrilegiously loud in the horrible stillness of the hillside.

Ingold straightened up from the sodden, stinking mess in the torn snow. Even the bones they had found had not only been stripped of flesh but seemed strangely deformed, as if the bone tissue itself had been melted. Nauseated, Rudy looked away from the black, half-liquefied remains, to Ingold's impassive face. Darkness masked the wizard's features, but mageborn eyes could penetrate ordinary night; Rudy could see no change of expression in that lined, nondescript countenance.

But then, he supposed, after what had taken place in the ruins of the City of Wizards, it was not likely that the old man would ever be shaken up by much of anything again.

"We shall come out with the others, when the sun is in the sky, to burn what remains," Ingold said quietly. "To do so now would only bring the Dark Ones once more upon us."

He dropped what he held in his hand back onto the fetid little heap. Round, discolored lenses flashed in the starlight in their twisted frames. Ingold said, "It seems that I shall be visiting the Dark Ones at Gae, after all."

Dawn was just thinning the stygian overcast of the night when Rudy and Ingold again reached the gates of the Keep. Against a charcoal sky, the ebony mass reared like a small mountain, close to a hundred feet from the top of the rock knoll on which it stood to its flat, snow-powdered roof and nearly half a mile in length. Its black, windowless walls faintly mirrored the trampled snow and dark trees that lay below it. Only its western face was broken by a gate and a short flight of broad steps. From a distance, the torchlight flickering in the square opening gave it the appearance of a single, small, baleful eye in the midst of an otherwise utterly featureless face.

As Rudy climbed the muddy path past the goat pens and ramshackle workshops that surrounded the Keep in a vast zone of trash, he could see most of the Wizards' Corps assembled on the icy steps. He could pick out those who, like himself, had spent the night outside. Kara of Ippit, tall and homely, in her threadbare mantle and the two cardigans her mother had recently knitted for her. Thoth the Scribe, called the serpentmage, sole survivor of the massacre at Quo, austere as a bald vulture-god of antiquity, his topaz eyes illuminating his narrow white face like a jack-o-lantern's. Dakis the Minstrel. A little fourteen-year-old witch-child from the north called Ilae, her dark eyes peering from behind a mane of red tangles. Others, a pitiful few, it seemed, huddling in the shadows like refugees in an old photograph of Ellis Island. And behind them stood those survivors of the massacre by the Dark who had been judged too lacking in power to participate in this trial of spells: itinerant conjurers, spellweavers, weatherwitches, and goodywives, the lower end of the spectrum of power that had not answered the dead Archmage's fatal summons to the City of Quo.

Rudy's heart sank at the sight of them. *So few,* he thought. *And what the hell can we do, anyway, against the might of the Dark?*

Other shadows appeared in the firelit tunnel that pierced the wall, leading from the outer gates to the inner, their forms ghostlike in the steam where the warmer air within came in contact with the outer cold—the day watch of the Guards, rubbing their bruises from the morning's weapons practice and cursing one another and their deceptively elfin instructor good-naturedly. The Keep herdkids went tearing out in an enthusiastic boiling of infant energy to throw snowballs and milk goats. Soap boilers, hunters, woodcutters, and tanners emerged, men and women plying what trades they could from the scanty resources of this bitter and isolated valley.

And among them were a dark-haired girl in a black fur cloak and a peasant woman's rainbow skirts and a tall, rather gawky woman some five years older, dressed in an outsize black uniform and white quatrefoil emblem of the Guards.

Minalde brushed the sable hood from her dark hair as she ran down the steps to meet Rudy, the rich fur of her cloak rippling glossily in the gray light. In sunlight, her eyes were the unearthly blue of a volcanic lake on a midsummer afternoon; shadowed as they were now, they were velvet-blue, almost black, and wide with anxiety. She caught Rudy's hands. "They told me they'd heard a scream," she said.

Rudy fought the urge to put a comforting arm around her shoulders, as he would have done had they met alone. *She's the Queen,* he told himself, *the Regent and the mother of the heir, for all she's nineteen years old and scared. There are too many people watching.*

"Glad to see it wasn't you, punk," Gil Patterson added, bringing up the rear, her long sword tapping at her ankles as she walked. Since she had joined the Guards of Gae, her former shy defensiveness had been gradually replaced by a toughness that, Rudy reflected, wasn't any easier to see through. Those pale schoolmarm's eyes still forbade any inquiries into the true state of her feelings, but she did look pleased that he'd survived.

At his side, Alde whispered, "Who was it?"

"Saerlinn. I don't know if you knew him."

She nodded, tears starting in her eyes. Alde knew, and was friends with, almost everyone in the Keep. Again Rudy struggled with his instinct to hold her, to offer her silent reassurance. "It puts us in a bad place," he admitted quietly. "When we go to scout the Nest at Gae . . ."

"You?" Fear widened her eyes. "But you can't—" She bit off her words, and a slow flush rose to her cheeks. "That is—it isn't just for that," she added with a soft-voiced dignity that made Rudy smile. "What about your experiments with the flame throwers, Rudy? You said you'd be able to create weapons to hurl fire from the things that Gil and I found in the old laboratories. You can't . . ."

"They'll just have to wait," Rudy said quietly. "I'll put one together for myself to take to Gae; the rest can wait till I return." He put his hands on her shoulders and smiled at her frightened, woebegone face. "And I will return," he promised her.

She looked down, her eyes veiled, and she nodded.

Gil's voice cut sharply into the silence between them. "You think you'll really be able to put working flame throwers together, then?"

He looked up, startled at her tactlessness, and saw what she had seen—the tall form of the Chancellor of the Realm, Alwir, Minalde's brother, standing watching them in the mist and firelight of the gates. Rudy backed quickly away from Alde and took a few steps up the path toward the Keep.

"You bet," he bragged in his best Madison Avenue voice. "Hell, in a month we'll make swords obsolete."

"That would be to your advantage," Gil commented, "since you can't pick one up without cutting yourself."

But in spite of the banter, Rudy was acutely conscious of Alwir's cold gaze on him as he rejoined Ingold among the mages at the foot of the Keep steps.

Alwir came down toward them, "a gleaming edifice of sartorial splendor," as Alde had once joked, dominating those around him with his size, his elegance, and his haughty, unbending will. Like his sister, he was cloaked in black, a velvet mantle that billowed like wings behind him. The chain of sapphires that lay over his broad shoulders and breast were not bluer or harder than his eyes. He was trailed by the obsequious Bektis, his Court Mage, who alternately rubbed his long white hands together or stroked his waist-length, blue-silver beard as if in a self-congratulatory caress.

The Chancellor came to a halt on the lowest step and looked down at Ingold with an impassive face. "So your information was correct," he said, in his rich, well-modulated voice. "The thing can be done."

"By those with the strength," Ingold returned quietly. "Yes."

"And the reconnaissance?"

"We shall leave this time tomorrow morning."

Alwir gave a satisfied little nod. Beyond them, the rising of the cloud-veiled sun had cast a kind of sickly, diffuse light upon the snowy wastes of the Vale, bringing forth from shadows the tangled grubbiness of the barricaded food compounds and the chain-hung pillars on the hill of execution across the road from the Keep.

"And these?" The Chancellor's careless gesture took in the other mages—old women, young men, solemn black Southerners, and ice-white shamans from the plains.

"Believe me, my lord," Ingold said, and there was a flicker of anger in his shadowed eyes, "whether or not it is decided to undertake this invasion, these people constitute your chief defense against the Dark Ones. Do not treat them lightly."

Alwir's eyebrows went up. "An unprepossessing lot," he commented, scanning them, and Rudy felt that those enigmatic, speedwell-blue eyes lingered for a moment on where he had returned again to Alde's side. "But perhaps more dangerous than they look."

"Far more dangerous, my lord." The new voice drew Rudy's eyes and, half against his will, Alwir's as well. In the suffused pallor of the dawn, the Guards on the steps had doused their torches in the snow, but within the gate passage above them fires still reflected redly on the polished walls. Against that reflection stood the red-robed shape of the Bishop of Gae, Govannin Narmenlion, her bald head and narrow, delicately jointed hands giving her the appearance of a skeleton wrapped in a crimson billow of flame.

"If you undertake your invasion using the Devil's tools, my lord," she warned, in a voice as dry and deadly as famine winds, "they will be its downfall. They are excommunicates, who have traded their souls to Evil for the powers they possess."

Anger stained the big man's cheeks, but he kept the melodious calm of his voice. "Perhaps if the Straight Faith were as dependent upon a centralized government as the Realm is, you would be even at this moment showering them with blessings," he commented sardonically.

17

The fine-chiseled nostrils flared in amused scorn. "Such words tell more about the speaker than they do about their subject," she remarked, and Alwir's flushed face reddened further. "Better your precious invasion should fail than that you should bring yourself under the wrath of the Church by harboring such as these. Having commerce with the mage-born—the magedamned!—fouls the soul like clinging mud, until all the Faithful can see it, and cast you out. Even to converse with them taints you."

Rudy felt Alde's icy fingers close over his and, glancing sidelong at her, he saw the shame struggling in her taut face. She had been a good daughter of the Faith until the rainy night on the road from Karst when he had found his power—and they had become lovers.

Alwir grated, "That didn't prevent you from coming out to see how they had fared!"

The Bishop's dry voice was silky with menace. "It pays to count one's enemies, my lord Alwir."

There was silence on the steps, save for the rising whine of the icy wind in the trees. The Guards watched this confrontation uneasily. They had long grown used to the swift, vicious arguments between Bishop and Chancellor, but there was never any telling when one might suddenly escalate into civil war.

Then Alwir's eyebrow canted mockingly. "And do you count me so, my lady?"

"You?" The gray light slipped along the curve of her shaven skull as she looked him up and down, austere scorn in the curve of her delicate lips. "You care not whether you are numbered among the godly or the wicked, my lord, as long as you can command what you call your niceties of life. You would sup in Hell with the Devil, were the food good."

So saying, she turned in a swirl of scarlet and vanished into the darkness of the gate passage, her ringing footfalls dying away across the vast, empty spaces of the Aisle beyond toward the dark mazes where the Church kept unsleeping domain.

Alde whispered, "Rudy, I'm afraid of her."

Hidden by the folds of her heavy cloak, his hand pressed hers. Talk had surged up again around them. Two of the

18

junior weatherwitches had been offering to send the coming snowstorm elsewhere until Saerlinn's body could be burned, and Thoth's harsh, academic voice was saying, "To do so is to presume upon the laws of the Cosmos that bid the winds blow where they will." There was some argument, but all of them, with the exception of Ingold and a withered little hermit named Kta, were terrified of the Scribe of Quo.

Under cover of the talk, Rudy said softly, "What can she do, babe? You're the Queen. Even if she knew about us—which she doesn't—we aren't doing anyone any harm."

"No," she murmured. But her fingers trembled in his.

CHAPTER TWO

"Ingold?"

Gil paused in the narrow doorway, all but invisible in the harlequin shadows that spangled the room. One of the other mages, the wizened little guru Kta, had told her that he was here, in a tiny chamber hidden deep within the secret levels of the Keep—the subterranean levels of whose very existence nine Keep dwellers out of ten were ignorant. Looking into the room, Gil saw that it was a miniature version of the "observation chamber" up on the second 'level, in whose stone and crystal table Rudy had once seen the possessed Archmage from afar.

Ingold was sitting on the edge of the circular, black stone table, looking into the changeable brightness that flowed upward from its heart. He raised his head at the sound of her voice, his face checkered with light and shadow; then he held out his hand to her, and the white light faded.

"I was on the point of sending for you," he said quietly as she took a seat on the table's edge beside him. Then, seeing the tautness of her mouth and the way her long, hilt-blistered fingers fidgeted with the buckle of her sword belt, he asked, "What is it, my dear?"

"Is it true what Rudy said?" she demanded. "That you're going to lead the reconnaissance to Gae?"

For a moment he studied her in silence. It seemed to Gil that, as the cold brightness of the light faded, the lines of his battered face deepened momentarily. "After Saerlinn's death, I am the only one who can lead it," he replied.

She cried in despair, "You're going to be killed!"

At that the blue eyes lightened. Ingold's smile was a curious thing, for it transformed him as sunlight could transform a Highland landscape, making what was grim and angular suddenly young and wild. "You wound me, Gil," he chided. "My very own cloaking-spell . . ."

"This isn't a joking matter." In Gil, concern for others had always taken the form of anger. Her voice was rough and harsh as she spoke. "The Dark Ones took Lohiro, and he was the goddam Archmage."

"Lohiro went to them willingly," pointed out the man who had loved the Archmage as a son. Against the chill, shifting luminosity of the crystal's light, the scar he'd taken in killing Lohiro stood out jaggedly raw on the flattened corner of his cheekbone.

"Well, if they could hold him as their prisoner," Gil snapped, "they sure as hell won't have any problems killing *you*."

An echo of that wild lightness still lingered in his eyes. "They'll have to catch me first."

Gil looked across the flickering fountain of light at him for a moment, struggling with anger and caring. Then she sighed, disarmed. "Well, all I've got to say is, you have the flakiest way of hiding out from them that I've ever seen, but that isn't any of my business."

" Ah." Ingold smiled regretfully. "But it is your business, Gil. I have rather effectively made it your business, by bringing you to this world against your will and by getting you trapped here."

Gil shook her head. "That wasn't your fault. You couldn't have known the Dark Ones would try to get through the gap in the Void."

"It's kind of you to say so. But I should have reasoned it out earlier than I did." Amid the darkness of the wall, his huge shadow stooped forward like a giant as he took her hand and drew her to his side. "I knew of the possibility. But at the time I rescued Prince Tir, flight into your world seemed to be my only recourse, and I needed a confederate on the other side of the Void. And believe me, it has been a grim lesson to me about the inadvisability of tampering with worlds beyond my own."

21

Gil shrugged. "If you hadn't tampered, Rudy would still be painting bikes for the Hell's Angels. You can't say that was just coincidence."

"I don't believe that there is such a thing as coincidence," Ingold said, and for a moment their eyes met. "And in any case," he went on, "if I had not tampered, you would not have been dragged from the life you were working to build for yourself at the university, your research, and your friends. If it had not been for the danger that the Dark could follow you back across the Void and devastate your world as it has destroyed ours, you would have returned to all that long ago. And that, my dear," he concluded quietly, "is why I came here tonight." He drew her forward. Light pulsed suddenly in the crystal inset in the table's center, bathing them in a white kaleidoscope of brightness. "Look into the crystal, Gil."

She obeyed him, bending over it and blinking against that coruscating glare. "I— I don't understand," she stammered.

The brightness drew her sight, blinding her to the room, the shadows, and the robed figure at her side. Though there was a silence, she felt as if she were looking at music; only the faint buzzing throb of the machinery in the nearby pump rooms broke the utter stillness of the vision in which she was caught.

"It is—not easy to explain," that deep, grainy voice at her side said. "This observation chamber, like the one up on the second level, was originally built to monitor the defenses of the Keep—a logical expedient, considering the miles of corridor involved. But, as Rudy learned, magic crystals have many uses. What you are seeing now is a construct, a simple visible expression of ideas too vast to be comprehended by ordinary means."

Gil frowned, as her eyes slowly adjusted to the brilliance of that river of light that seemed to pour up around her.

For a time she was not certain that she even saw what she thought she saw, for she had no consciousness of the crystal itself. She thought that she looked down through an infinity of space, bathed in burning whiteness, and that, like bubbles in shining solution, gold spheres were moving, circling one

22

another in the slow patterns of an unknowable dance. Their opalescent surfaces swam with colors that she neither recognized nor comprehended, revealing stars, galaxies, ages—cosmic vistas of something that was neither space nor time. The spheres grew infinitely smaller with distance, though there was neither horizon nor wall to break her line of sight; as far as she could see in that blazing ether, they were moving, merging, parting, and drifting around one another in endless patterns whose meaning whispered at the verges of her understanding. They shimmered like oiled gold as they touched, pressed together like the hands of joining dancers in those veils of light, and then, with infinite slowness, parted.

Ingold spoke again, his words seeming to her to come from some great distance. "What you see is the Void, Gil, the Void between universes—the Void that you crossed to come here. The spheres are worlds—universes—eons of time—each one a limitless cosmos of matter and energy, entropy and life. This is the closest I can come to explaining it to you, and it bears about as much relationship to reality as a child's five-point drawing bears to the wonder and complexity that is an actual star. Do you see the joined spheres that lie closest to us?"

She nodded. "Are they—? They look as if they're moving apart."

"So they are," he murmured. "They are your world and mine, Gil. Last summer they had been drifting together, until they lay so close that the curtain between them thinned. It is possible for one who understands the nature of the Void as I do to travel from this world to any other. But on the night that I first spoke to you, in the courtyards of Gae at the first quarter moon of autumn, they lay so close that a sleeper, a dreamer, could be drawn across unknowingly, as you were. It is this closeness that has prevented me from sending you back, for any rent in the tenuous fabric that divides your world from mine would set off a series of gaps through which the Dark Ones could find their way—as, in fact, one did.

"But our worlds are parting, drifting out of their cosmic conjunction. In six weeks or so, at the time of the Winter

Feast, it will be safe for me to open the gate in the Void and return you to your world, without endangering the civilization that gave you birth."

When he spoke of her return, she looked quickly up from that shining well to meet his eyes.

"And that, my dear, is why I am here tonight," he repeated, as gently as he could. "For you are right. I do not know what awaits me in Gae. Danger, certainly, and perhaps my death. I had hoped to return you to your own world tonight, lest you should be trapped here forever."

Gil whispered, "Tonight?" She was shocked at the suddenness of it, the fact that she might eat her dinner in the bleak Vale of Renweth and finish the evening with a midnight snack at a cafe on Westwood Boulevard. Indefinable emotions beat upon her, and she could only stare at him with blank, startled, stinging eyes.

Ingold took her hands gently and said, "I am sorry, Gil. Was that why you sought me out?"

She could not reply. Beside her, his voice went on. "Since the night the Dark Ones tried and failed to break the gates of the Keep, you know that they have haunted the Vale of Renweth. It may be that they are waiting for our guard to slacken or that they look for the opportunity to trap me outside the walls. But it could be that they are waiting for me to tamper again with the fabric of the universe, to open a gate through the Void. And that I dare not do."

Still she remained silent. Below her, the crystal had gone dark, and the room was drowned in shadow. But it seemed to her that she still could see vague infinities of dark spheres and the suggestion of slow, turning movement through blackness. Quietly, she said, "It's all right."

His hands rested upon her shoulders, warm and comforting, banishing fear as they always had the power to do. "I am sorry," he said again.

"It isn't that."

Out of the darkness that surrounded them, a faint thread of bluish light flickered into being. As Ingold helped her to her feet, the gleam widened and strengthened, showing the room small, black, and Spartan, the crystal plug set in the center of the table opaque and sparkling, a faint and frosted gray. The light drifted along above Ingold's head, and their shadows lumbered, black and sprawling, about their feet as they went through the narrow door. It illuminated the gray fog of dust stirred by their feet as they passed through the deserted corridors of the empty hydroponics chambers. It winked on the disassembled components of flame throwers beyond the shadowed doorway of Rudy's laboratory. Like a vagrant ball of foxfire, it preceded them up the narrow stair to the inhabited levels of the Keep and through the dark succession of closets, doorways, and interconnecting halls that made up the headquarters of the Wizards' Corps.

The Corps common room was deserted, its only light the dim apricot glow that pulsed from the embers that lay, like a heap of jewels, on the wide hearth. Their two shadows moved clumsily through the greater darkness of that long room, passing, like the shadows of clouds, over the paraphernalia of habitation there: the jewel-bound books, salvaged from the wreck of Quo or shamelessly stolen from the archives of the Church; Kara of Ippit's satin pincushion, sparkling like a diamond hedgehog among a great tumble of homespun cloth; the knuckly, knobby braids of herbs and onions hanging above the hearth; and the silver rainfall that was the strings of Rudy's harp. The round, gold eyes of the headquarters cats flashed at them from every gloomy corner.

Ingold sighed, breaking his bitter silence, and there was a note in his voice which she had never heard before. "I had never meant to put you in such peril, Gil. It is said that wizards, among their many faults, have a horrible way of endangering their friends. I only hope to get you safely away from here, back to your own world, before disaster strikes. Those who are close to me seem to have a shocking rate of mortality."

The beaten regret in his voice shocked her. "That isn't true," she said.

In the darkness he was only a darker shape, edged with the tawny colors of the fire. "You think not?" With his face hidden, the pain and irony of his words sounded all the clearer. "Rudy has inherited the staff of one of my dearest friends, child, and the widow of another."

25

"That had nothing to do with you."

"No?" Like a spark rising, his eyebrow was tipped with reflected gold. "One of them I deserted in the hour of his death; another I killed with my own hands. I don't see how much more I *could* have had to do with it."

"Either of them would have commanded you to do what you did, and you know it." When he tried to turn away from her, she caught at his robe, the rough homespun bunched in her fist. "You were all trapped together by forces you couldn't control," she whispered savagely. "Don't torture yourself because you were the survivor."

Still he was silent, except for the thick draw of his breath. In the fading ember light, he was only a dim shape to her, but she was aware of him as she had never been aware of anyone or anything in her life. The touch of the patched wool clenched in her hand, the scent of sweet herbs and soap and woodsmoke that permeated the cloth, the stippling of fire outlining the edge of his white hair—with a heightened consciousness, she felt that she would have known him anywhere, without sight or hearing, merely by his nearness alone. When he raised his fingers to touch her wrist, she felt it like an electric shock.

In a softer voice, she said, "Quit tearing at yourself, Ingold. None of it was your fault."

"But your death here would be."

"Do you think that matters to me?"

"It matters to *me*." Then suddenly her hand was empty. She heard the dry swishing of the curtain that covered the door of the alcove where he slept, but her eyes could not pierce the gloom at that end of the room. His grainy voice came to her as a disembodied murmur from the shadows. "Good night, Gil. And good-by. Forgive me, if I should not return from Gae."

Elsewhere in the Keep, other good-bys had been said.

The hour was late. Rudy thought he had heard the changing of the deep-night watch some time ago; but though he was more aware than most people of the span of time that had elapsed since then, it cost him conscious effort to translate it mentally into hours and minutes. He knew, in one sense, that it was two-thirty or so in the morning. But this was something that had lost its importance. He had lost his impulse to check the time, just as he no longer automatically felt for a light switch when he walked through a door.

The calling of light was an easy matter, like whistling. Seeing in the dark was easier still.

He trod the lightless corridors of the second level soundlessly, taking his memorized turnings as surely as he had once known that you got off the San Bernardino Freeway at Waterman Avenue, and two right turns got you to Wild David Wilde's Paint and Body Shop. He threaded his way along a black, dusty passage between the cells that housed Alwir's private guards and a storeroom where he was sure the Chancellor was illegally storing undeclared food for one of his merchant buddies. He passed through a closetlike cell that had been partitioned off an old scriptorium and turned down a cutoff through a dark, disused latrine.

Alde had shown him this route after he'd returned from Quo. It was the quickest way from the Wizards' Corps commons to her rooms, allowing for a detour to avoid Church territory. Alde and Gil had spent weeks exploring the Keep, digging out the mysteries of its building, and either of them could get through the stygian warrens of jerry-built walls, spiraling mazes of old brick and grimy plaster and up and down the drunken spiderweb stairways with the swift, unthinking ease of a second-grader getting through the Pledge of Allegiance. As for the mysteries whose answers they had sought, they had uncovered no answers, but only more mysteries.

They had found fuelless, everlasting lamps and the component parts of flame throwers; they had found the ancient machinery that the Keep's builders, the wizard-engineers, had used to power the air and water pumps; they had found riddles as enigmatic as the frosted gray polyhedron crystals that littered the lower labs in such useless numbers. But they had discovered no evidence that the vast hydroponics gardens had ever been used, no records of the early days of the Keep, and no sign of how the wizard-engineers had so suddenly vanished.

There was no evidence of how Dare of Renweth, builder of the Keep and founder of the line of High Kings, had defeated the Dark—nothing at all as to why the Dark Ones had ceased their ancient depredations upon humankind and returned to the black abysses that had spawned them.

Rudy stepped cautiously around an oblique corner and through a dark complex of cells where, even at this late hour, a soft flicker of greasy yellow lamplight winked through a crack in a door and quarreling voices brushed his awareness like wind as he passed. Rodent eyes sparked redly at him from the murk; somewhere a chicken clucked loudly, followed by the sodden thump of a thrown boot.

Had it been the flame throwers that defeated the Dark?

He didn't think so; the pieces he'd found in the labs were few and incomplete. Besides, the Dark had been around for centuries after Dare's time. Had some other champion of humankind arisen, some other warrior who had dealt the Dark Ones so crippling a blow as to render them unwilling to continue the attack?

How had humankind defeated the Dark?

The question is the answer, Ingold always said.

The question is always the answer.

But Rudy had cudgeled his brains over all possible answers and had found himself faced with only that question.

Maybe Tir would remember how. Maybe his father Eldor would have remembered eventually, had he not perished in the blazing ruin of the Palace at Gae. Though Tir was yet too young to speak, the baby prince gave evidence of having inherited that terrible and mysterious legacy common among the descendants of Dare of Renweth, not only from his father, but—by carrier, as it were—from Minalde as well. Her memories were vague—recognition rather than recall— but if the flame throwers were the answer, wouldn't she have known it?

And if not the flame throwers, what?

White light gleamed palely before Rudy, reflecting against the slick, black stone of the walls. He passed the head of one of the main stairways of the Keep, its smooth construction announcing that it had been built at the time of the founding of that colossal maze itself. In a cage over it hung a single glowstone, a warning to the unwary.

How else had humankind defeated the Dark? Had the wizard-engineers stood at the top of those hellish stairways that led down to their hideous domains and dumped barrels of glowstones into that chasm?

Unlikely. Early experiment had shown that sufficient numbers of the Dark Ones could damp the light of glowstones, just as they killed fires or sucked the strength from a wizard's spell of light.

Some other weapon, buried in the deeps of time? Something Ingold might have learned of in his years of study and wandering? Some piece of knowledge that lay like an unexploded bomb in the depths of that complex mind?

Rudy would have swapped several of his younger siblings for the answer to that one.

A drift of warmer air rose from the stairway, stirring his long hair. It bore on it the soft, musical chanting of the night offices of the Church, and Rudy turned away, uneasy at the thought of the minor empire that filled the first-level warrens around that fluted Sanctuary. He had heard too many tales from the other mages in the Corps—rumors of rooms where magic would not operate and where a wizard could be imprisoned, as Ingold had been imprisoned in the doorless cell of Karst. There were whispers of black magic or such things as the Rune of the Chain, which bound and crippled a wizard's power and left him helpless to his ancient, ecclesiastical foes.

Rudy had seen the Rune of the Chain. The memory was not a pleasant one.

He turned down another corridor, past a guardroom where voices hummed above the rattle of a dice cup. For a moment the haughty, intolerant face of Bishop Govannin floated through his memory, as he had seen her in the dawn light on the steps. *It pays to count one's enemies.*

There was one he sure as hell didn't need a magnifying glass to find. But what, after all, could she do?

He found what he'd been seeking—a jury-rigged, ladder-like stairway leading down to a back corridor of the level

29

below, at a healthy distance from the Church. Not even a glowstone marked it, for few people came this way; below lay only a chasm of darkness, stinking of dust and mice. The crazy rungs creaked under his weight. Steadying himself against the splintery wood, he jumped the last few feet to the floor.

It was only when he landed that he saw movement. His wizard's sight caught the glint of velvet and jewels; then, as faint as a whiff of the orris root perfume, he heard the unmistakable clink of a sword hilt on a belt buckle and the slurring whisper of a heavy cloak.

A rich, mellow voice spoke from the shadows. "Don't be so apprehensive, my dear boy. I have no intention of doing you harm."

Rudy let his breath out slowly. "That's nice to know," he remarked. "I mean, you know, halfway through the deep-night watch, you kind of wonder about the people you meet wandering around the back corridors."

"Indeed you do." Alwir opened a single pane of the lantern he bore, and dim, dappled white light filtered through the fretwork slides that surrounded the enchanted stone within. "You have let Ingold make you suspicious." He set the lantern on a ledge of projecting bricks and turned back to face Rudy, his handsome, fleshy face very white within the raven masses of his hair. "Yes," he continued, "one cannot but wonder about those who walk in the night."

Rudy realized, with a sudden chill in the pit of his stomach, that Alwir had been waiting for him. There was nothing that he could possibly reply; the smell of Minalde's perfume clung to his clothes. *On the last night before we split,* he thought, *Alwir knew he'd be able to intercept me. Not that he'd have had much problem any other night since we got back from Quo.* Rudy wiped his clammy hands on his breeches and waited in silence for what Alde's brother would say.

"They tell me you've made excellent progress in the arts of magic," Alwir went on in a conversational tone. "Your work on the flame throwers will, of course, be invaluable to us when we march against the Dark. Is it your belief that

Dare of Renweth used something of the kind to invade the Nests?"

Rudy swallowed, put off balance by the small talk but unable to do anything except play along. "Uh—I don't know. We've never even found evidence that Dare did invade the Nests."

"Oh, come," Alwir chided patronizingly. "We both know he must have done so. The Dark were defeated somehow. I feel sure that your reconnaissance to Gae will reveal to us exactly how it was done—and how we, allied with the armies of Alketch, may do likewise."

"Yeah," Rudy said warily, still trying to understand this cat-and-mouse game. "There are good odds, anyway."

Alwir's smile was wide and false and cold, like something he'd stapled on. "And afterward?"

"If I'm alive afterward," Rudy replied, picking his words carefully, "we'll see."

"Indeed." Alwir was still smiling, but the lobelia-blue eyes would have scratched diamonds. As if to change the subject, he said, "I assume your liaison with my sister is a well-kept secret? Not that I don't understand her feelings," he hastened to add, cutting off Rudy's flaring words. "After all, she is young and lonely. She was grateful to you for saving her son's life—as were we all, of course. And she could hardly have fallen in love with Gil or Ingold." He sighed. "I would have prevented this if I could have. But the affair seems to have begun behind my back and was, I believe, well advanced by the time we arrived here. Was it not?"

His voice strained, Rudy asked, "What do you want?"

"My dear young friend." The Chancellor sighed, his face never losing that determined smile. "I am not trying to trap you. But a man has a right to do a little plain speaking with the man who is lying with his sister. I wonder if you have considered the consequences to her?"

When Rudy made no reply, Alwir shook his head with mingled patience and disappointment. "Presumably, as a wizard, you can prevent her conceiving by you—or if that hasn't occurred to you, I assume that she can get advice

31

from her women friends among the Guards. And as far as I know, my sister was quite faithful to poor Eldor, and Altir is indeed the late King's child."

"As far as you know!" Rudy lashed, furious at the insult. "She worshipped him, dammit!"

"And mourned him intensely, I'm sure," Alwir purred. Rudy felt his face redden. Alwir went on. "It would be putting it mildly indeed to say that her reputation would suffer, were the news to come out among the people that their Queen was less than two weeks replacing their—worshipped—lord in her bed. I could probably protect her from actual harm," he mused, "but without a doubt she would be excommunicated."

Govannin's fanatic eyes seemed to glitter before Rudy. He swallowed, "You couldn't . . ."

Alwir's curved eyebrows lifted. "For lying with a wizard? In the South she would be burned for it."

Rudy stared at him in shock. "You're kidding."

"Don't treat yourself to false comfort at her expense," the Chancellor told him mildly. "If the scandal became open, she would certainly be excommunicated and, as such, would no longer be able to hold the Regency or to have custody of her son."

The words fell on Rudy's ears without meaning at first; then understanding came and the slow kindling of fury deep within him. He was surprised at how steady his own voice sounded. "Which you would get."

"Of course." Alwir sounded amazed that there would be any question. He laid a patronizing hand on Rudy's shoulder. "But believe me," he went on, his voice low and grave, "I have no desire to create such a scandal."

Through his teeth, Rudy said, "That's nice."

"I am quite fond of Minalde, you know. She's a dear child, for all she's headstrong; and I admit to a certain weakness for pretty young girls."

Rudy remembered the agonies of remorse Alde had passed through, fighting her instinctive loyalty to her brother, and the disillusionment that stemmed from the strength of her love for him. He found himself literally trembling with rage, overwhelmed with a primal urge to

32

smash the smirking big man's teeth down his throat—not that that would help Alde any.

Alwir continued pleasantly, "But, you see, it is in my own best interests to protect her reputation, as well as her son's creditability, which scandal would certainly damage. I hope you appreciate my position."

What Rudy appreciated, at the moment, was how someone could see red and do murder in blind passion. He fought for calm, then asked, "And what is your position?"

Alwir raised his brows. "Why, to offer you my protection, of course," he said, as if the matter were self-evident. But his calculating eyes were on Rudy's face, gauging that startled break in his anger. "To 'cover' for you, as I believe the vulgar say," the Chancellor went on in a friendly voice, "until you depart from here to return to your own world."

Rudy looked stupidly at him, like a man looking at his own spilled guts before it dawned on him that he was dead. Numbed, Rudy could only listen to that smooth, casual voice run on.

"I can countenance my sister's passion for you, since it harms no one. It does not affect the succession and will in any case soon be at an end. Indeed, I think it good for a woman to have something to occupy her. Though I cannot approve of her actions, of course, it is better than mourning and brooding. And you did, in fact, always intend to make your stay among us temporary, did you not?"

"Yeah," Rudy whispered helplessly. *Before Quo,* he thought. *Before the desert. Before I knew what I was, and called fire from cold wood and darkness.*

"Then it is well," the Chancellor said contentedly. "And when Minalde marries again . . ."

"Marries?"

"She is, after all, only nineteen," Alwir pointed out suavely. "I should hope, for the sake of your relationship, that you know her well enough to know that she cannot hold power by herself, particularly not in the sort of world which we are now entering. Even after the Dark are defeated, we will face a long war against them. It will be a time when the strong take what they can get. She cannot hold power under those circumstances—but a man could hold it through her."

33

"As you do," Rudy said bitterly.

Alwir shrugged. "I am her brother. Naturally, I would prefer that she remain single, but it is hardly fair to her. And I have no intention of letting her develop an affair with someone—wholly unsuitable."

Or strong enough to make trouble for you, Rudy thought through a daze of misery. *Oh, Christ, Alde, what have I done to put you in his power like this?* In helpless rage, he cried, "Why can't you just let her alone?"

"My dear Rudy." Alwir chuckled softly. "You must know by this time that those who by their very existence hold power are never let alone by anyone. What have you to lose? I understand that your little affair is temporary and I have no objections to its continuing as such. But what happens after you have left her is no concern of yours. So what will you have lost?"

Only everything, Rudy thought, the stunned, empty numbness beginning to give way to a cold despair, like the touch of death upon his bones. *Magic and love. Hope. Things that I found after never thinking I would have them.* Like a well of inconceivable grief, the future yawned at his feet, the bleak, desolate world of car paint and barflies made a thousand times worse by the awareness of what he would lose. Since he had come to this world, he had often been in fear of death, but this was a fate that he had never even imagined—to be raped of the only two things that mattered in his life and condemned to live on without them in a world where they did not exist, and never had existed.

CHAPTER THREE

The most beautiful city in the West of the World—that was how Minalde had spoken of Gae.

A garden, the Icefalcon had called it.

But the Icefalcon was said to be dead, murdered by the representative of the Empire of Alketch, Alwir's prospective ally. Minalde . . . Rudy did not want to think of Alde, though he had done little else for seven wretched days. And Gae sprawled, like the maggot-riddled corpse of a beautiful woman, with the bones starting to work up through discolored and falling flesh.

The wizards had entered the city at dawn, shadows in the dark mists that rose from the ice-scummed marshes. The swollen loops of the Great Brown River had engulfed the lower town, and even the upper, landward quarters bore foul evidence of the winter's floods. Fungi and mosses slimed the fallen walls; the square below the shadows of the crumbling turrets of the gate was a steaming, knee-deep slough, stretching as far as Rudy's eyes could penetrate the chill, pearlescent fog. In all that filthy, shrouded world, the only sounds seemed to be the distant drip of water and the cries of unseen rooks, quarreling over horrid prey.

Alde loved this town, he thought, surveying the leprous desolation before him. *She was raised here; it was part of the life she loved, before the Dark . . . and before me.*

Rudy hoped she would never have to see it as it was now.

He shifted his staff to his other hand—the six-foot, crescent-pronged staff that had once belonged to the Archmage Lohiro—and checked the weapon that hung holstered at his side. It was the only one of its kind, like a glass and gold Flash Gordon zap-gun—a hand flame thrower that could spit a thirty-foot column of fire. If he must enter the realm of the Dark, Rudy had resolved to enter it prepared.

The silence that hung over the town was frightening. Fog covered it like pewter darkness, masking the broken walls and fallen columns in opal veils of mystery. But it was not a dead silence that prickled Rudy's hair and made him strain his eyes to pierce the mists. It was a silence that lived and watched.

Like a thickening of smoke, Ingold faded into being at his side. "This way," he murmured, his voice scarcely louder than the skittering of rats' feet on the broken stones before them. "Kara tells me the main path to the Palace is blocked. We can go by way of the Street of Oleanders."

Other forms materialized—Kara of Ippit and the withered little hermit Kta, who had included himself, over Ingold's protests, in the expedition at the last minute. Kara whispered, "I didn't like the look of that street. It looked almost as if—as if a wall had been built across it out of rubble."

Ingold nodded. "It could be that it had." The wraith of his breath drifted for a moment like smoke about his head, then dissipated into the cloudy whiteness that surrounded the group. Within the shadows of his hood, his eyes had an over-bright, fagged look to them, the look of a man living on his nerve endings. Then he turned away, and chill, smoky darkness once more enveloped the wizards.

As they moved through the ruined town, Rudy came to understand the old man's insistence that the party be accompanied by one who knew Gae. No map could have gotten them through the back-doubling alleys that avoided the open ground of the fog-locked marketplace or could have guided them through the leaden darkness to the weed-hung colonnades and shopping arcades whose denser shadows lent the wizards cover from seeking eyes. Ingold led them easily through ruined courtyards where tangled mats of vines ran riot over the charred commingling of stones and human bones, down half-flooded alleys whose walls were thick with pullulant green-black moss, and through the frost-furred muck of empty mews that skirted the wealthier parts of the town. Twice, as the milky vapors around them lightened toward dawn, Rudy glimpsed little bands of dooic, slipping through the vine-tangled side streets, half-obscured by fog. And once, as they passed the hoared bowl of a frozen fountain in what had been a fashionable square, he heard a baby cry somewhere close by, a fitful, helpless wailing that filled him with horror.

He reached to touch the wizard's mantle. "Do you hear that?"

The sound had been quenched as suddenly as it had begun.

Kara glanced behind her nervously, her big hands tightening over the long-bladed halberd that she carried instead of the customary staff; Kta's bright little bird-black eyes were sharp with interest. In the cold pewter light, Ingold's face was impassive, but Rudy thought he looked rather white around the lips.

"Did you think that Gae was deserted, Rudy?" he asked softly. The steam curling from the fetid pool of ice-crusted brown water in the court blew between them, blurring him momentarily to a flat gray shape, featureless but for the glitter of his eyes.

Rudy whispered, "Dooic babies don't cry like that. I've heard them, out in the plains." When Ingold did not reply, he asked, "Do you know who it is? I thought there was nobody alive in Gae."

"Nobody?" The wizard's voice was soft; behind it, Rudy detected other sounds, distorted by the fog—squishing footfalls and the wet drag of something heavy over stone. He sensed the sudden change in the air and felt the fog condense around them, drawn by Ingold to shield them from hostile eyes. The pinprickle sensation of a cloaking-spell tingled on his skin. "Nobody whom we would recognize as human, perhaps."

"You mean—the ones whose minds the Dark have eaten?" Rudy's hand felt clammy on his staff; he groped for the flame thrower at his belt. "But I thought they became zombies and died—of exposure or starvation . . ."

"They do." Ingold's voice was a flicker of breath, blurring into the scritch of the vines on the wall at their backs. "Less innocent than that, I'm afraid. These, Rudy, will be ghouls."

They came into sight out of the mists near the broken fountain bowl—slumped, repulsive, stinking. It was more than the putrid stench of corruption that clung to their gaudy, tattered clothes; the reek of what they were loured about them like a fog of filth. There were five of them, two men and three women. One of the women was swollen-bellied with child; another was hardly more than a girl. Their hair was matted with scum and old blood; their clothes—brocades and velvets, stitched with gold and tipped with ermine—were filthy and wrinkled, as if they had been slept in, eaten in, fornicated in, and worn to slaughter some small and violently struggling animal. The ghouls moved at a furtive trot, glancing constantly over their shoulders; two of them were armed with cleavers, and the leader carried a jewel-encrusted sword.

They passed within a few feet of the wizards, murmuring among themselves, their glances flitting here, there, and everywhere but toward the spot where the wizards stood. Rudy heard the leader whisper, "That mothereating scout said the downriver people had moved up into this neighborhood someplace." The pregnant woman enlarged on the subject of the scout in terms that would have brought blushes to the cheeks of some Hell's Angels Rudy had known. Close to them, holding his breath against their reek, he could see that none of them looked very healthy. The youngest girl's face was blotched all over with savage scars—like huge vaccination marks, he thought stupidly, then realized that they must be from smallpox. The smaller of the two men sniffled and blew his nose on his already dripping sleeve; the other cursed him and told him to shut up if he didn't want to end up in the pot himself.

As the white vapors swallowed them once again, Rudy grasped who these must be.

They were the citizens of Gae who had not followed Alwir's convoy to the south—who had remained in Gae to loot the empty houses and live in wealth among the ruins. They'd taken the weapons from the charred hands of corpses buried under the wreck of the Palace—weapons that, as in the case of King Eldor, had proved the only means of identifying the burned bodies—and robbed the clothes from the backs of those dead in the cellars and streets. They'd clung to the city rather than trade it for the hardships of the road, making rats' burrows of homes in the majestic remains of the villas of the rich and fighting the former dooic slaves and one another for the dwindling supplies of food that were left.

It occurred to Rudy, as the mists swirled suddenly around Ingold's abrupt departure, that, if the old man had known the town in its heyday, he might just have recognized one of the ghouls as someone he had once known.

Rudy moved off after him, torn between revulsion and pity.

They crossed another court and turned down an alley that was so choked with the vines that seemed to have overtaken whole districts of the city that it was only with difficulty they could move through the persistently tangling mat at all. Elsewhere they had to cut through a veritable wall of them, and Rudy found himself wondering, as he struggled with the clinging, knotty stems, what this place would be like when darkness fell, with these ubiquitous snares slowing their flight. Then Ingold halted at the mouth of a narrow street beyond which could be seen only a wall of opal mist. In the growing light, his face was a harsh medley of planes and shadows; as in a certain type of art, the only spark of color lay in his eyes. He touched Rudy's sleeve, pointed across the court before them, and whispered, "There."

Rudy blinked, frowning into the mists. After a moment he realized that what he had taken for a darkening in the fog was the opaque bulk of some vast building, a suggestion of broken roof lines and sagging towers, of charred rafters, and of decay. Winds stirred at the billowing veils, smelling of water, corruption, and wet earth. The fogs were infused with the sudden, weak light of the sun; watery colors became slowly visible through the shimmering gauze. Edges seemed to step forth from obscurity. Piece by piece, pillar and pavement and pierced frieze of stone, the Palace of Gae manifested itself to them, like the many-colored corpse of a dead dragon, its bare ribs arching high into the milky air.

So this, Rudy thought, was where Eldor had left his bones

in the flaming ruins. Where the Dark Ones had dragged Alde away, captive, and the Guards of Gae had rescued her on the edge of the chasm. Where Ingold had deserted the last battle, to carry Eldor and Minalde's infant son Tir across the cosmic Void and into the temporary safety of the mild and sunny realm of California.

This was where it all started.

And this, he realized with a foreboding chill, was where, somehow, now or later, it was destined to end.

The court lay bare and empty before them, a mud-smeared expanse of broken green and scarlet inlays, half-sheeted with ice and already infected by the long, searching runners of the vines. Ingold shifted the weight of the coiled rope he carried over his shoulder and whispered, "We'll cross one at a time. Kara, keep an eye on Kta." He gripped the staff in his hand and stepped into the open ground of the court.

A movement caught Rudy's attention, along the wall to his left. He whirled, his hand going to his flame thrower, but all he saw was a huge rat, sliding insolently among the matted compost of dirt and vines and bones. When he looked back to the court, Ingold was gone.

There was no sign of him in all that bleached expanse. Not even a footprint marked the frost-fuzzed moss of the broken pavement.

Then he saw the wizard in the dense shade of the arch at the far side of the courtyard, barely visible in the dappling shadows of filigreed marble and dead vines. Ingold moved a hand, signaling Rudy to follow.

He obeyed, with a hopeless sense of nakedness in the open ground. But though he half-expected Ingold to greet him with a mild query about whether he intended to send out a crier to announce his presence as well, the wizard said nothing. It was borne upon Rudy that the time for his education in wizardry was past. He was what he was, and it was up to him to keep himself out of trouble.

Kara followed. Rudy had a quick impression of the gray ripple of a homespun cloak and the touch of a skirt hem on frozen vines. Once, where the tessellated pavements were cracked, he saw the brief shadow of a tall woman and the glint of wan daylight on the blade of a halberd. Then Kara was beside him, her face pale under her hood.

Ingold had moved off, scouting the porch. The mists held thicker here, stirring faintly about his feet like pallid ground fog; sometimes it was only that vague shifting movement that allowed him to be seen at all. His brown cloak seemed to blend with the gloom, melting indistinguishably into the thicker shadows of the broken archways. Rudy glanced back across the moss-splotched court, seeing its smeared and dirty pavements with their brave colors all but hidden beneath the soupy scum of mud and ash and leaves.

"Where did Kta go?"

Kara, who was likewise looking out across the court, shook her head. "He was going to follow me," she whispered.

Rudy cursed his own stupidity. "One of us should have gone after him," he whispered back. "He may be tough as an old sagebrush root, but I don't think he was mageborn. If he was, I've certainly never seen him work anything resembling a spell." Which was true; as far as anyone could tell, the withered little mummy was totally illiterate and untaught, though he took a childlike joy in the spells of the younger mages. Most of the other wizards in the Corps tended to regard him as a curiosity, rather than an asset to the Corps. But Rudy had tried to keep up with the little fossil's untiring footsteps for seven days' hard slogging through the foul, flooded river valleys that lay between Gae and Renweth, and had come to the conclusion that not only did Kta neither eat nor sleep, but that he only sat down to rest at night out of consideration for the frailty of his companions.

Kara murmured, "Should one of us go back for him? Ingold would never forgive us if we lost . . ."

Her voice trailed off. Ingold and Kta materialized from the shadows behind them, Ingold whispering in an exasperated voice, ". . . and since you insisted upon including yourself in this expedition to begin with, the least you can do is accept my judgment as its leader."

"Ah?" the little hermit said, not at all concerned. He was hopping along at Ingold's side with a birdlike gait, tiny and incredibly fragile-looking, like some worn macramé made of rags.

"You have to admit you're too old for active fieldwork. I've permitted you to come this far, but you will not go down with us into the Nest."

The older man straightened his back as much as was possible and peered up at Ingold with bright little black eyes. "I will be unseen," he replied in his piping voice.

"I'm only concerned for your safety, Kta," Ingold insisted. "You know—"

The tiny creature rounded upon him, almost tripping him with the quickness of his movement, and jabbed a skinny pink forefinger up at him. "Always this concern for others' safety," he accused shrilly, "whether they wish to hold safe or not."

"You know you couldn't fight your way out of a trap," Ingold told him gently.

"Neither could you, for all your skill with that fearsome meatchopper you carry."

Ingold looked miffed, and Kta turned and hobbled ahead, toward the vast, broken doorway that opened into the darkness of the vaults. As he clambered up the weed-choked rubble of stone and shattered bronze, he half-turned and flung smugly over his shoulder, "And it is not me whom the Dark Ones pursue from one end of the world to the other."

Ingold opened his mouth to retort, but Kta was gone, hopping calmly into the terrible shadows below. Rudy and Kara fell into step beside Ingold as he hurried to catch up with Kta, where he waited in that anteroom of Hell. Rudy said softly as they passed into the clustered shadows of the vault doors, "He's got you there." It was the first time he'd ever seen Ingold lose an argument with anyone.

The wizard glanced over at him sharply. "Nonsense," he snapped. "He's too old to undertake the exploration of the Nest with us and too stubborn to admit it."

And you love him too much, Rudy thought, *to want to see him killed trying.* But he wisely refrained from tackling the issue of stubbornness with Ingold and walked after him in silence through the wan, dappled grayness of the broken upper levels.

Here the ruin was greater, as if this semisubterrene ante-chamber to the vaults had been transformed into a kind of borderland of darkness. The vines here grew thicker, festooning the burned rafters in impenetrable curtains, insolently forcing apart the very stones of the walls. Darkness seemed to lurk in every corner; the walls and floor had a slimy glitter, and the fetid stink of netherworld vegetation clogged in the nostrils and collected like a film on the tongue. Rudy found himself prey to a growing uneasiness, a feeling of being snared; the vines and the paving-stones they had tilted seemed to snag at his feet deliberately. He wondered how quickly a man could run from this place.

"There," Ingold said quietly. Half-hidden by the mats of vegetation, another doorway gaped, black and terrible, over a bone-littered threshold. "That leads down to the lower vaults, where we will find the stairway to the Darkness itself. You all know the spell that will cloak you against the awareness of the Dark—" He vouchsafed not a glance at Kta. "—but remember also that you must use a double spell and avoid likewise the notice of their herds. Also," he went on, glancing sharply from Rudy's face to Kara's, "we must not let ourselves be seen by any human prisoners. The Dark have been taking prisoners from the beginning of their rising. It is not our business to free them, no matter how much compassion we may feel. To do so would jeopardize not only our mission but also our lives. There is just so much that a cloaking-spell will cover; if we do anything to bring ourselves to the attention of the Dark, we are lost."

Easy for you to tell us that, Rudy thought as he followed the dark, cloaked form down the red porphyry stairs that led to the vault. *None of us knew Gae. You're the only one likely to see anyone you know.*

Afterward, he read the wax tablets he had sketched with the maps of the Nest, registering the various tunnels and caverns he had wandered through, and what he saw surprised him, for he did not remember most of them singly. The greater part of his memories of the Nest he forced down below the levels of consciousness, only to have them surface, like bloated corpses from black waters, in his dreams. The hours he spent below the ground had a surreal quality;

in that unending night, time became meaningless. Terror, shock, and disgust further clouded his sense of the passage of hours. He lost even his own sense of self, for he walked hidden in his wreaths of illusion, invisible to all around him.

After they parted in the topmost cavern with an agreement and a common spell to mark the limits of their time, he walked alone, like a ghost haunting a world as alien and incomprehensible as it was revolting and horrifying. It was a world of darkness, of slimy moisture and ever-present, hideous danger, a world whose existence he had never even imagined possible and which would never, he feared, be wholly eradicated from his mind.

The Dark Ones were everywhere. They crowded the walls and ceilings of measureless caverns of darkness, the clicking of their claws on the slick-polished limestone a constant chattering background to his sickness and dread. His wizard's sight showed him the wet gleam of their massed backs and the glitter of the foul fluid that dripped continually from those gelid surfaces. The stink of them, sharp and somehow metallic, clogged his nostrils, and he felt a mounting horror of being discovered and buried alive under those squirming, slithering beings.

That first enormous cavern, where he parted from the other wizards at the foot of the drop-off and the spelled rope, was the worst, for the Dark Ones crawled not only over ceiling and walls but across the floor as well, scurrying like monster roaches through the dry and crumbling brown moss, their long whiplike tails hissing through the withered vegetation and leaving trails of sticky wetness behind. Elsewhere they seemed to travel mostly on the ceilings of the tunnels, crawling among the stalactites and folded veils of stone as cavern succeeded cavern, the drip of their noisome slime tapping viscously on the mossy floors. Never having been subject to the terror and loathing of spiders and snakes, Rudy had not understood that morbid dread of simply being touched by something abominable. He understood it now.

He had thought that custom would acclimate him to their presence in time, so that he could have confidence in the spells that guarded him and walk more easily. But it never did. Nor did it dull the smothering horror of the darkness itself or the unreasonable sensation of the weight of all those miles of earth and stone pressing down upon him. Only those who had never been trapped in the darkness below the ground could compare the mazes of the lightless Keep of Dare with the realms of the Dark. For all its pressing darkness, its weight of enchanted steel and stone, the Keep was finite. But the darkness here was infinite. The weight was the weight of the earth. The crawling horrors populating this place were likewise infinite, as inescapable as this darkness that had never seen light.

Only now did he understand Ingold's warnings and conviction that an invasion of the Nests could never succeed. The tunnels were endless, twisting down and back into the black bowels of the earth, incomprehensible mazes that could swallow a dozen armies. Nauseated despair took him, as he wandered farther and farther in that sightless realm, along with a sense of black hopelessness. He wondered how any army, even with the technology such as Dare of Renweth had had at his disposal, could have made so much as a dent against the numbers and power of the Dark.

But he had been sent to observe. Through the panic, the loathing, and the numbing despair, certain details stood out absurdly clear. Rudy noticed that the Nests were warm, and a flow of warmer air marked the downward-leading tunnels, even where the Dark Ones did not come crawling forth like round-headed, filthy beetles from holes in the putrefying moss. He saw that different kinds of moss grew in different places. Heavy carpets of velvet green-black in many places—whole caverns, sometimes—were crumbling to brown and withered dust. In other places, clubbed, knobby growths infested the floors like stumpy, unspeakable forests. Whitish mosses hung like curtains of slimy seaweed down the dripping walls. The herds of the Dark fed greedily upon them all.

The herds of the Dark affected Rudy strangely. He found his loathing of those bandy-legged, bulge-eyed humanoids almost as intense as his horror of the Dark Ones themselves. He had known they were close to human, but had expected creatures like the dooic of the plains—hairy and apelike, trapped Neanderthals. But the creatures that shuffled through the withering beds of moss or squatted to lap at the bottomless pools of onyx waters were smaller, more delicate, and larger of skull; their chittering squeals as they fled, blinking, from any movement in the air sounded horribly analogous to speech.

They were not the only ones chewing bits of moss in their soft little teeth and staring about in the darkness with huge, terror-stricken eyes. In a cavern so vast that his eyes could not reach its end, Rudy found herds of men and women in torn and soiled rags, stumbling about and feeding on moss, muttering endlessly in the dark. They did not move like those miserable zombies whose brains the Dark had devoured, but Rudy wondered how many of them could be called sane. This single chamber seemed to house a dozen good-sized bands, whose members had formerly owned shops, raised families, and promenaded the arcaded streets of the broken town above. Maybe they still had relatives up there, Rudy thought in a puzzled confusion of nausea and loathing; maybe they had husbands, or wives, or children in the Keep of Dare.

He drew back to avoid touching a woman who crawled past him on her hands and knees, seeking the edge of the pool by which he stood. She had long blond hair and had probably once been very beautiful, Rudy thought, looking with numbed dispassion at her emaciated face and bloated, sagging belly. She groped for the water in the darkness and mumbled, "Water fifty-five steps from the wall, water fifty-five steps from the wall," in a dulled, mechanical recitation.

It could have been Alde, Rudy thought, and the idea brought nausea burning up into his throat. Maybe it was a friend of hers. Hadn't Janus said that the Dark carried off large numbers of the defenders from that last battle in the Palace? Rudy shut his eyes, his head swimming suddenly; it could just as easily have been any one of them at the Keep.

But, as Ingold had said, it was not to pity or to rescue that they had come. It was to map, and map Rudy did, marking the immense caverns and the endless bowels of black tunnels crawling with filthy life as he followed the windings of the Nest deeper and deeper into the pressing earth. He found caverns flooded with black, oily water, through which stalactites rose like pillars from a floor of glass. He found cavern after cavern filled with bones—ages old and crumbling to dust or fresh and slithering with hideous rodent and insect life. He found the nurseries, the breeding grounds of the Dark, and the sight brought him as close as he had ever come to fainting in his adult life.

If I have to come back myself with a book of matches, he promised himself, hefting the gleaming weight of his flame thrower in his hand, *I will see that place burned out.*

He rested at last in a rock crevice, his sweating face cooled by the rising drift of air. He had marked the wall, tracing upon it with his fingertip a silvery rune that only he could see. The thought of going forward, further into that endless domain of darkness and smothering horror, was almost more than he could bear. He was weary, but he felt no hunger. After the nurseries, he doubted he would ever be hungry again.

Time had no meaning in the realms of the Dark, so it was with a sense of surprise that he glanced at the back of his hand and saw that the red rune Hlal, which Ingold had drawn there before they parted, had darkened almost to black. *Time sure goes fast when you're having fun,* he told himself cynically and got to his feet. Decaying moss crumbled to brittle dust where he put his hand against the wall, filtering into the air to choke him. He holstered his flame thrower, wiped his filthy hand on the skirts of his filthy coat, and prepared himself for the long, ugly journey to the surface.

Wind struck him, chill and sudden. It poured down over him from the tunnel above—the swirling, directionless breath of the Dark. Deep in the cavern he had just left, he heard the thud-thud-thud of running feet and a man's hoarse, labored gasp. *Making for here,* Rudy thought, glancing up from the narrow rock slit where he was hidden toward the tunnel, then back at the cavern again. Winds were flowing from that direction, too, pursuing the man who ran toward him in the darkness.

Fantastic, Rudy thought, and debated which way to flee, for he had no intention of being trapped between the Dark and their prey. But before he could move, the winds rushed over him like a torrent of water, rasping in the dry moss all around him. The running man blundered with arms outstretched through the entrance of the crevice and fell, stumbling almost into Rudy's arms.

The Dark were instants behind. They poured down the top end of the tunnel as the runner and Rudy fell in a blundering tangle of arms and legs. Rudy was cursing, and the fugitive was gasping in surprise and despair. Rudy twisted himself free as the swarming plasmoid bodies descended on them both, soft coils of tentacles unfurling like dripping snakes.

Wyatt Earp himself couldn't have cleared leather faster.

The flame thrower belched light and fire, streamers of chrome-yellow flame pouring from its thick barrel, unbearably brilliant in the eternity of the underground dark. The fire flowed up over those slick backs in a licking torrent of searing gold.

By the first blast of the light, Rudy had a confused glimpse of the fugitive's face, an emaciated skull between hanks of grayed, dirty hair. Then the man screamed, covering his eyes that had not seen light since the fall of Gae, and the Dark were on them again.

But the fire was spreading among them; they blundered into one another like a flock of Hindenburgs in the confined space of the tunnel. Conflicting winds swept up from below, and Rudy whirled, bracing his feet on the slippery floor and firing downward, the noise of the flame a smothering roar. At the same instant, the spiny cable of a lashing tail grabbed at him from above, and he fired as he turned, the leaping column of silken heat brushing the withered moss of the cavern mouth beyond.

It went up like torched paper. Rudy blinked and flinched away in shock as the fires spread, rushing back into the empty cave below with a velocity that was horrifying. Stalactites, columns, twisting alabaster veils, and clumped masses of crystals leaped into ruddy visibility, their colors dazzling—bronze, rose, and cream—all smeared with the ruddy dye of the flame. He had a confused vision of Dark Ones falling in writhing clouds from the unseen ceiling, twisting about in agony at the brightness, splattering acid as they fell and were consumed by the greedy roar of the flame.

Then he fled, all hope of concealment shattered, and felt the winds of the Dark swirling on his back.

He was plunged again into darkness as he hit the wider tunnel beyond, staggering in the noisome muck of the steep floor. His traced, invisible runes beckoned; he turned, and the flame thrower spewed fire at the Dark Ones in his wake. The massed blackness erupted into flames, twisting and thrashing as they blazed, sparks sizzling in the wet, black mosses of the floor. Channeled by the tunnel walls, the winds raged around him, and he ran blindly from mark to mark, turning every now and then to fire at his pursuers or to clear the path before him. Where the sparks fell on the patches of brown and withered moss that blotched the walls like mildew, they exploded into violent flame.

Blind, white semihumans fled shrieking through the fire, covering huge, rudimentary eyes against the light. Men and women in rags ran past him, screaming in terror and confusion. Walls and ceiling were bursting into flame all around him, and he remembered with sudden horror that the last cavern before the one that contained stair and rope was covered in the brown, dried moss. The knowledge was like an electrified spur. It would take only a single spark to set the whole thing off, and if he were halfway across it at the time . . .

The upper caverns were a choked confusion of smoke, darkness, and half-lights. He stumbled where the ground was slippery and fought againt the screaming humans and almost-humans who blundered against him, grabbing at his arm, shrieking unintelligible words. Columns of smoke burned his eyes, thrashed by the winds of the Dark. Rats streamed around his feet, fleeing the inferno below.

In the last cavern, there was nothing but a wild storming of darkness. Rudy could feel the power of the Dark Ones already reaching out, damping the flames as they damped light. He felt the immense might and will that throbbed in the swirling air. Brown moss and old bones crunched under his feet. The light of the fire streamed up from the tunnels behind him, touched the limestone lace with sulfurous glory, and outlined the billows of the smoke. Black, shining bodies poured through the passage that led upward, a torrent of dripping slime and gaping mouths. They streamed like a river toward the fire in the passageway, putting out their power to quench it, to damp it. Rudy flung himself up the rockslide toward the next tunnel just as one of the hapless herd-creatures, burning and shrieking as it ran, fled blindly into the cavern, stumbled, and fell into the crumbling moss.

It seemed to Rudy, shielding his smoke-filled eyes, that the monstrous cavern, which could have swallowed the entire Keep and still had room to spare, was engulfed not so much by spreading flame as by a single explosion, so rapidly did the moss go up. He gasped at the sudden vacuum of oxygen, his head turning light and giddy. For a moment he feared he would pass out and fall backward down the rocks into the roaring hell of the fire. As he ran on, staggering, he felt the flesh of his right cheek blistered and the backs of his hands scorched by the tremendous heat. It seemed to him as if all the Dark Ones in the Nest were streaming past him over his head, putting out their magic to kill the flames, while he fled beneath them, seeking the magic rope, with the weight of his flame thrower dragging at his blistered hand.

Then he was falling, and consciousness left him.

He came to slowly, and in the dark.

He tasted rock and water and smelled slime and stone. Both his hands were empty.

With a cry of despair he sat up, and a strong hand pushed him down again. Something wet and shockingly cold smeared his burned cheek.

"Sit still," Ingold's voice said, not unkindly. "I believe you've caused quite enough trouble for one evening."

Slowly, his dark-sight came into focus.

They were in a small stone room like a vault. Its single entrance looked out onto a tiny garden close where half a dozen apricot trees huddled like crones in a train station, heads down against the bitter cold. Above the stink of acid and the gritty taste of dust and powdered moss in his nostrils, Rudy could smell old snow mixed with dirt and the chill scent of bad weather to come. Just visible, outlined in darkness against the door, Kara of Ippit was making additional notes on one of her tablets, her halberd leaning against

50

the wall at her side. The unscarred profile of her face was turned toward him, and Rudy decided that, if a man were in love with her, and didn't mind cheekbones that made him think of an outcrop of granite on a desert hillside, she'd be almost pretty to him. Rudy's pronged staff, which he had somehow kept hold of during the chaos in the Nest, was propped up nearby, its points glinting dully in what wan light managed to leak from the overcast darkness of the night sky. In a corner of the little chamber, Kta was curled up asleep, like the rag-bound mummy of an Inca child.

Rudy sighed and relaxed into the not uncomfortable bed of old leaves on which he lay. They made a tired mushing sound under the single blanket spread over them and sent up a moldery, melancholy smell. "Christ," he whispered. "I'd hoped to hell you were all three out of the Nest before the fires got out of hand."

Ingold smiled and went back to mixing herbed grease between his hands. In the dim, filtered light from outside, Rudy could make out a broken pot or bowl on the floor beside the wizard, half-filled with ice-cold well water that glittered faintly as it leaked down onto the rough stone floor. "If I hadn't stopped to fight a rearguard action against the Dark," the old man replied mildly, "I would have been in that last cavern when it exploded into flame. You didn't see me?"

Rudy's eyes widened with horror and guilt. "Jesus, no. I'm sorry, man . . ."

"I suppose I should be galvanized with delight that the cloaking-spell works so effectively . . . Hold still, I'm not going to brand you. It's only burn medicine and it's good for you. Fortunately, there was a fairly straightforward tunnel that detoured around the cavern, and I did make it out—though I had to leave the rope at the stairs."

"How come?"

"Because I was carrying you." He sat back, wiping his hands on the corner of Rudy's blanket. His rough brown mantle reeked of smoke and of all the foulness of the Nest. In the shadows of his cowl, his eyes were amused and kind. "I trust your experiment with the flame thrower proved satisfactory?"

Rudy laughed shakily, and Ingold joined in—the first time, now that Rudy thought of it, that he had heard the wizard laugh in quite some time. The driven tension had faded from his eyes, leaving only an elusive, slightly haunted expression, like an echo of what he had seen in the Nest of the Dark. Rudy was later to know that look in the eyes of those who had been a part of the reconnaissance.

The memory of that putrid darkness returned to him, and he sobered. Quietly, he said, "It's going to be rough."

Ingold flashed him a quick, sideways glance. "You believe it can be done at all?"

Rudy frowned. "Of course. We'll need a heavy covering force to get the flame thrower squad to the bottom of the Nest, but once we're there, we can burn our way backward. If we can knock out the nurseries and damage as little as fifty percent of the Nest, we can make Gae safe for human habitation again."

"And you believe that a human force can damage as much as half the Nest?"

"That moss burns like paper, man." Rudy moved a little and winced. His muscles were already stiffening. "You don't think so?"

The old man was silent a moment, staring down at his own cut, blistered hands. Then he glanced toward the doorway. "Kara? Are you taking the first watch?"

"If it's all right," she said in her queer, deep voice.

Rudy struggled to a sitting position, surprised at how sore he was. His hands and face smarted under the sticky paste of Ingold's medicines. "I'll arm-wrestle you for it." he offered. "Or let's have the three of us draw straws. Short straw has to go to sleep. God knows how Kta manages it," he added feelingly.

"Kta's a hundred years old," Ingold reasoned mildly. "If there is anything he hasn't seen, I don't know what it could be."

Kara's smile was brief and hesitant, an expression that flickered out of existence almost before Rudy realized she'd been amused; it was as if at some time in her childhood she had been punished for laughing. She sat forward from the wall and put away the tablets she'd been working on, wrapping them in her old satchel. Like Gil, Rudy saw, she took her note on the wax with a sharpened hairpin, which she now carefully stuck through the lapel of her cloak, its tiny lily of diamonds twinkling like a star against the coarse gray fabric. Even the most precious jewels and trinkets were common coin among those who had survived the massacres of Gae and Karst. "Why couldn't we just pack up and leave the city now?" she asked quietly. "I don't think any of us is in any shape to sleep."

Ingold lay down in the shadows next to Kta and pulled his blanket over his mantle. "No," he decided softly. "We shouldn't be moving about Gae at night. There are other things besides the Dark abroad. And we are all exhausted. It would be fatally easy to make mistakes. It isn't many hours until dawn." He turned his face to the shadows of the wall, but Rudy wasn't going to take any bets on whether he would sleep or not.

Rudy got stiffly to his feet and drank what was left of the water in the leaky pot. It was cold and tasted of stone and of Ingold's herbs, but he felt parched with thirst. Then he limped to the door and settled himself opposite Kara in the broken doorframe. The thought of the dreams that sleep would bring made him wonder if he were in for a lifetime of insomnia. "Scoot over," he said. "You and me can tell each other ghost stories all night for jollies."

Again that fugitive smile appeared, going no farther than her eyes. Wind rattled in the branches of the court trees, a thin clattering, like the dangling bones of hanged men. Little spits of rain scampered over the wet ground and stung Rudy's burned cheek. Over the broken turrets of the city, he thought he heard a child crying again—or perhaps it was only the moaning challenge of a tomcat.

"Rudy?" Kara asked softly. "What did you see in the nurseries?"

"You didn't see them?"

She shook her head, "I explored sideways rather than down. I never reached them."

"Count your blessings." Rudy pulled his old coat a little tighter about him as a tongue of wind licked at his flesh. The curly wool of the collar felt stiff against his jaw.

53

"Were they so horrible?"

He was silent, staring out into the darkness of the frozen court. Kara blew on her knuckles and rubbed them, her dark eyes never leaving his face. Finally he said, "You grew up in the desert."

She nodded, "Yes."

"You know what a tarantula-wasp is?"

"Of course," Kara said, a little surprised at this non sequitur.

"Then don't ask me about what I saw in the nurseries."

He waited for a moment while she thought that one through. She made a dreadful, stifled noise in her throat and relapsed into sickened silence.

CHAPTER FOUR

"It scarcely matters when they return, my lord Chancellor," Bishop Govannin said quietly, looking across the laced fingers of her white, bony hands. "In some ways it might be better if they never did."

Chancellor Alwir did not turn his head; but, from where she sat on the corner of the barracks hearth, Gil could see the white gleam of the glowstones dart across his brocaded shoulders as his muscles stiffened. On the other side of the hearth, the captain of the new-formed firesquad, Melantrys, stopped in the midst of her exposition of flame throwers to a group of her fellow Guards. At the room's long, central table, Minalde, who had been talking with the Keep's other Bishop, the lanky, ragged leader of the Penambran refugees, turned her head sharply. Conversation in the main room of the Guards' barracks was suddenly stilled.

Govannin continued with silky malice. "You cannot pretend that the powers that rule the Empire of Alketch will agree to lend their might to an endeavor led and counseled by wizards."

Slowly and deliberately, Alwir regarded the prelate where she sat in the room's single, carved armchair, with her white hands linked before her and the hearth fires dancing in the purple depths of her episcopal ring. "Ingold Inglorion, my lady," he declared quietly, "neither leads nor counsels in this fortress. I have appointed him chief of the Wizards' Corps, since that is where his talents lie. And I might point out to you that the Church has yet to produce either reconnaissance, protection, or weapons to aid us against the Dark."

Govannin's chin went up. "And of what merit is any wizard's work against the salvation of souls?"

"You know more about the salvation of our souls than I, my lady," Melantrys said in her low, sweet voice. "But these devices are going to be the salvation of our hides, and no mistake." Her small, dainty hand caressed the looping rigs of wire and tubing that festooned the flame thrower's glass bubbles. She shook back her barley-gold hair. Under soot-black, impossibly long lashes, her eyes were as pitiless as a hawk's. Rudy had left two rifle-sized flame throwers with Melantrys, with instructions to organize the firesquad among those born with the lesser magical powers capable of wielding the weapons. The lovely captain had taken him at his word. "The troops of Alketch won't quibble with magic on those terms," she added.

"The ignorant won't," the Bishop replied softly. "The godless won't. But ignorant and godless warriors march in all armies. Sometimes they even command them."

Alwir swung around, bristling, and met only that close-lipped, reptilian smile. With determined cheerfulness, he said, "Surely it would be flying in the face of providence to reject weapons that have come down to us, miraculously preserved, from the Times Before. Exactly how Dare of Renweth's forces defeated the Dark Ones and drove them back underground is a secret regrettably lost to us, for the last scion of his House is an infant, and Tir's father perished in the ruins of Gae. But I am convinced that Dare used weaponry of this kind—and as such, he must have had a trained corps of firebringers to wield them. Their success may be gauged by the centuries of respite humankind had from the Dark."

The Bishop's ivory fingers flicked. "Wizards' work," she snorted disdainfully. "Work that fouls the hands of any who touch it, your precious Dare of Renweth along with the rest." She cast a scornful glance across at Bektis, who sat with the amber colors of the hearth fire gleaming in the white silk of his beard, gravely examining a second flame thrower at the other end of the table. In the middle of the table, the

Guards' Commander Janus and the handful of poker players around him were keeping a wary eye on which way the muzzle was pointing.

Alwir's smile remained resolutely pinned to his mouth. "I think we have heard enough of wizards for one evening, my lady Bishop."

"You will hear enough and more than enough when the representatives of the Lord of Alketch arrive." Her bitter eyes were like starlight on oily black water. "The Emperor of Alketch is a man of true faith."

"He's a priest-ridden bigot who had his own first wife burned for a witch," the Penambran Bishop snapped, looking up from the misshapen knot of his crippled hands.

Govannin's lip curled. "The fact remains, Maia *of Thran*," she said, rolling the peasant form of his surname from her tongue with all the scorn of a descendant of the most ancient of noble Houses, "that in the South, where the Straight Faith is strong and unpolluted, there are no Dark Ones. Only in the North and in the plains where the heathen Raiders roam have the Dark Ones risen to scourge humankind."

"According to Stiarth of Alketch," Janus said. He spoke the name of the Imperial Ambassador as if it were wormwood in his mouth.

"Do you doubt him?" Govannin purred.

As Commander, Janus could say nothing, but Melantrys opened her mouth, and Alwir's rich voice cut across her possibly unseemly reply.

"Of course not. There is an air about a man whose world has collapsed in ruins about him. You know it; you have all seen it. That, if nothing else, should have spoken to you all." The Chancellor turned to survey them, haughty eyes challenging any of those ragged warriors in their frayed surcoats to deny what they all knew in their hearts. "He was clad richly and fed well—too richly and too well for a man whose world is a ruin. No," Alwir went on, "whether it was by virtue of God's will, or the Emperor's merit, or purest chance and the fate of mankind, there are no Dark Ones in Alketch. We would be fools if we did not mold our policies accordingly."

There was a murmuring, unrestful and wary. Melantrys folded her arms over the clumsy length of the weapon in her lap; Minalde, her mouth set at the memory of her battles with her brother over the preliminary negotiations with the Emperor's Ambassador, looked down at her fingertips. Govannin settled back in her chair and tented her fingers again before her, an unpleasant glitter in her narrow eyes.

Alwir continued. "We have sent word to all the landchiefs of the Realm: to Harl Kinghead in the North and Tomec Tirkenson in Gettlesand; to Degedna Marina and her vassals in the Yellow River Country in the East. From none of them have we received a reply. The hand of the Dark lies heavy over the Realm. It may be that none will stir to fight. I have heard that the greatest of the landchiefs, the Prince of Dele, is dead; the others may have set themselves up as independent kinglets, each ruling from his own pitiful fortress, in spite of the vows he made to the High King of Gae.

"Therefore, we must work with our allies of Alketch and hold in check out prejudices and whatever grudges we may have formed in the past." As if by chance, that chill, jewel-blue gaze touched the gaunt form of the Bishop of Penambra, who raised smoldering eyes in return. "We need that alliance," the Chancellor continued grimly. "We need it, as a wounded limb needs a healthy body for its rejuvenation. The Empire of the South has all those things that we now lack—trade and commerce, education, arts, culture, the wherewithal to forge steel weapons, and the civilization to enforce laws."

"Aye," Janus murmured, leaning his great, red-furred forearms on the table. "But whose laws?"

In the momentary silence, Alwir's face seemed to harden in the cross-grained shadows of the scattered glowstones and the leaping redness of the hearth.

Govannin said, "Written laws, my muscular friend. The sort that my lord Alwir has sought from the beginning to purge from the records."

"The useless quibblings of Church legalists whose bones rot in the streets of Gae!" The Church records were a sore point with Alwir. "I swear by the ice in the north, woman, the paper they're written on is of more use!"

58

"To write your own laws upon?"

"To keep census and records of the Keep!" he shouted, losing his temper. He made a move toward her, goaded past endurance, but then he saw her smile and struggled to master himself.

In the shadows of the guardroom, no one moved or spoke. Only Gnift the swordmaster slapped a greasy card on the table and crooned, "And eight lovely hearts for the charming lady in black."

Alwir took a deep breath, his mouth clamping beneath flared nostrils. "I tell you, my lady Bishop—and I tell all of you—that, of all things, this alliance with Alketch is of the greatest importance to the Keep and to everyone within its walls. Without it, we lose our last hope of civilized existence. We will become degenerate villagers, ignorant and brutal, prey to the stronger and the better-armed. And that I will never permit." His eye touched them all: Melantrys, her delicate nostrils flared as if against the stink of Ambassador Stiarth's perfumes; Alde, still looking down at her hands in angry silence; the Bishop of Penambra in his patched red cloak and scavenged brocades. "I will let nothing interfere with it. Believe me, there is nothing—and no one—that I would not sacrifice to bring about a lasting alliance with the Empire."

"Including yourself, my lord?" a new voice inquired, a flawed, mellow voice that spoke from the dense shadows of the barracks door. Gil looked up at the sound of it, warmth kindling in all her veins.

Alwir swung around, recognizing, as they all did, that shabby form in the darkness. "So you've returned," he said.

The firelight glittered on flecks of sleet that clung to Ingold's stained mantle. As he stepped into the light of the room and pushed back his hood, Gil was shocked at how old he looked. Behind him, Rudy and Kara emerged from the darkness and they, too, were mud-splattered and silent, weary past caring about anything. Gil saw Alde look up and Rudy turn his face away, as if he could not bear to meet the joy that shone in her eyes.

"Did you think I would not return, my lord?" Ingold set down the satchel that he carried. From within it, Gil heard the faint click of wax tablets. Janus was already on his feet, his shadow blotting the light of the hearth as he bent to pour a cup of so-called guardroom wine from the small kettle that was warming beside the fire.

"No," Alwir said at last. "No, you have shown yourself proof against most calamities, my lord wizard."

"Or able to avoid them," Govannin remarked acidly.

"It is the secret of my indecently long life," Ingold agreed with a small smile. "Thank you, Janus—this is the other secret of my indecently long life." He sipped the steaming liquid, which was not wine at all, but a horrible compound of hot water and homemade gin.

The Commander of the Guards steered him to a seat on one of the rough benches at the table, and Alde moved her heavy skirts aside so that he might sit. Rudy and Kara took seats on the raised brick hearth beside Melantrys, their thawing garments steaming and dripping unnoticed in the heat. Where Kta had vanished to, none of them could have said, but he was found later, peaceably warming his skinny hands by the kitchen fire in the Wizards' Corps complex, eschewing the councils of the mighty.

"My lord," Ingold said at length, "are you still set upon this invasion?"

The Chancellor's voice was brisk, but there was an edge of wariness in it. "Of course I am still set upon it," he said. "Can it be done?"

The wizard's eyes glinted in their discolored hollows. "Rudy believes that it can."

"Indeed?" Alwir's eyebrows quirked. "And I collect you hold a different opinion, my lord wizard?"

"It is folly," Ingold said simply.

The Chancellor's thin smile broadened, without increasing its warmth by a single degree. "Well," he murmured, "fortunately for us all, you are no longer the sole source of information on the subject, are you? Was it folly that enabled Dare of Renweth to defeat the Dark?"

Ingold made no reply to this baiting. With a sneer, Alwir turned away. "Rudy? Are those magical devices of yours the answer to this riddle, after all?"

Rudy looked up, as if startled out of some private, terrible dream. "I don't know whether they were Dare's solution to the problem or not," he said in a voice thick with fatigue. "But we can damage the Nest badly, maybe so badly they'd have to abandon it completely."

And haltingly, half-numbed with exhaustion, he told them of what he had found in the Nest—the vast complexity of that dark and filthy realm, the ability of the Dark Ones to damp light or fire, and the curiously flammable properties of the dried, leprous brown moss.

"That will be our strength," he concluded. "If we sent a strike force down each of the two main branches of the Nest, to cover the firesquad as far down as the nurseries, the fires would spread in the moss as the army retreated. I think that would do it."

"Especially if the mosses themselves are the nitrogen fixers for the whole ecosystem of the Nests," Gil added unexpectedly. "If that's so—and that's what it sounds like— the whole Nest must be saturated with nitrogen compounds."

Everyone in the guardroom, Rudy included, stared at her with as little comprehension as if she had spoken Etruscan. Tardily reminding herself that she was dealing with a preindustrial world-view, Gil amended, "My studies have shown that this type of moss can be very flammable."

"Indeed," Alwir said thoughtfully. "I had no idea you were a scholar, Gil-Shalos. A curious pastime for a soldier. That is two of your students, my lord Ingold, who disagree with your findings."

He turned back to Rudy. "So you think that, with men to guard the firesquad from the Dark and perhaps the wizards to surround the whole force in an aura of light, it would be feasible to burn out the Nest in the fashion you describe?"

"I think so," Rudy said. "The drawback is that there would be no way of getting the human prisoners of the Dark out of there. Unless they fled in the army's wake . . ."

"It is regrettable." Alwir sighed. "But indeed, it might be better thus. After so long in the realms of the Dark, they can hardly be said to be sane."

"You're very sure of that for a man who has never seen them," Ingold commented, raising his eyes from the gold-bossed rim of his cup. "For myself, I would not even inflict such a death upon the herds of the Dark, who are likewise innocent."

"T'cha!" The Chancellor wrinkled his lip in disgust.

"Beyond that, you might give a thought to what would befall the Keep, should the invasion fail and the army that you send to destroy the Nest of the Dark perish in it. On our way up the road from the valleys, we found the remains of propitiation-sacrifices offered by the White Raiders, not two miles below the old watchtowers at the Tall Gates. And there are those in the valleys who would lay siege to the Keep if they were assured that its defenders were gone—not only brigands, but families banded together, embattled tribes, who would take shelter by force if they had to."

"That," Alwir returned, with a nasty sideways glance at the Bishop of Penambra, "we already know."

"I will not argue with you, Alwir, for you will believe what you choose and act as you will," the wizard said. As he raised his head, the firelight showed his face hollowed with exhaustion and his blue eyes glittering with anger. "I am tired, tired to death—we have fought the Dark for two nights running and I am all but perished with cold. If it is your will to invade the Nest of the Dark, the wizards will aid you, up to and including our lives, so that we may save what survivors we can from the wreck. But I feel in my bones that your plan is death—death for most, and worse than that for some."

With an impatient gesture, he threw what remained of the Blue Ruin in his cup into the fire, and the alcohol exploded in a swift thunderclap of flame as it hit the hearth.

Then he was gone, his footsteps fading down the hall toward the Wizards' Corps common room almost before anyone was aware that he had risen.

Alwir said softly, "The old fool."

There was an uncomfortable silence. Everyone, from the card players to Bishop Govannin, looked uneasily at one another and then at the Chancellor, who stood with his arms folded beside the hearth.

Rudy sighed and rose to go. "He's not a fool, though," he

said tiredly. He picked up his pronged staff from where he had rested it against the doorpost and turned back, all his movements stiff and weary. "Yeah, I think you can retake Gae. But what the hell are you going to do with it when you've got it? Most of the town's under a couple of feet of water, and what isn't is crawling with rats, ghouls, and the dooic slaves that got left behind and turned wild. With the Raiders in the valley and the Dark Ones by night, you'd never be able to keep up lines of communication with the Keep, let alone the rest of the Realm."

Alwir's eyes turned suddenly ugly, though his voice remained suave. "Let that be my affair," he remonstrated. "Since you will, after all, be leaving to return to your own world after the initial invasion of the Nest, the matter hardly concerns you, does it?"

Rudy saw Alde's sudden movement in the shadows; her face had gone white within its frame of crow-black hair. Sour, weary anger filled him as he realized that the blow had been deliberate, to punish him for speaking against the Chancellor's plans.

In a toneless voice, he said, "No, it doesn't." Turning on his heel, he strode away into darkness.

"Rudy!" The desperation in Alde's voice stopped him as he crossed the common room. Looking back, he saw that she had run after him, down shortcuts that only she and Gil could have found. Tears gleamed on her face, and the sight of them broke and drained the anger in him, leaving only grief and pity for her sake. He held out his arms to her without a word.

For a moment they could only hold each other in silence, her face buried in the damp, rough wool of his coatcollar, her scented hair tickling against his lips. Then they kissed, feverishly, as if trying to deny what they both knew to be true. The hot saltiness of her tears burned where they touched his chin.

"I'm sorry," he whispered. "Alde, I'm sorry."

He felt her arms lock tighter about his body, felt through his grip the shuddering draw of her breath. He had not known her long, but already it seemed strange to him that he had ever known the feel of any other woman's body in his arms.

She shook her head. "No," she murmured. "Don't be sorry, Rudy—not for this." Her words were muffled against his chest.

In the hearth a log broke, and the sudden spurt of gold threw their shadows leaping on the opposite wall.

"It was always going to be temporary, wasn't it? And then it seemed as if we both forgot it. But I wanted to forget. It seemed that you'd been here forever—and would be—" She stopped, and against his chest he felt the determined tightening of her jaw and the stifled trembling of her ribs. Then she shook her head again, the red flickering of the ember light tipping her hair with carnelian. She swallowed hard. "This world was never your own. You have no choice, have you?"

"No," Rudy whispered bitterly. "No, I have no choice."

She let out her breath in a long, thick sigh and rested her forehead against his shoulder. "Then there's not much we can say, is there?"she murmured. "Sometimes I think we never have the choice. That no one has the choice. How long do we have?"

His voice was almost inaudible against the fragrance of her hair. "Until the Winter Feast. After the Feast, the army will leave for Gae. And after . . ."

She shook her head, the soft skin of her temple gritting on his unshaven jaw. "There won't be any after," she said. "It was all fate, wasn't it? Fate that you came here, so you could discover how to make the flame throwers to use against the Dark. And after fate is done with you, you must return to your own world. Isn't that how the universe works?"

His arms tightened around her body, feeling the smallness of her bones through gauze and velvet and soft flesh. "Ingold's always saying there's no such thing as chance. But for Chrissake, why did fate decide it had to work out this way?"

She looked up at him, shaking back her hair; the front part was braided, the back fell in a loose cascade over his hands where they rested upon her waist. "It worked out this way because I would have begged it to," she whispered. "Rudy—better this little than nothing at all. I've been happier with you than I have ever been in my life. Do you know, you have spent more time with me between your journeyings with Ingold than Eldor ever did in the thirty months we were husband and wife? And I have never feared you, never felt helpless or stupid or like some gauche, stammering child in your presence. You've never expected me to be other than what I am . . ."

"What did Eldor expect you to be?"

"I don't know!" she cried. The words broke from her like long-pent floodwaters. "But it was in his eyes when he'd look at me and then look away. I gave him all that I was, but since it wasn't what he wanted, it was as if he didn't know, or didn't care, that it was everything. I was sixteen. I loved him. I worshipped him. If I had known you then . . ." She stumbled to a halt, her lashes beaded with tears like diamonds in the firelight.

Rudy bent his lips, kissing the glittering droplets. "Nah," he said softly, "they wouldn't have let you marry some old wizard's apprentice anyway. And besides, when you were sixteen, I bet you were flat-chested and pimply."

"I never had pimples," she argued, choking on tears and unexpected laughter. "Stop it! You make me laugh."

"That's not all I'll make you," he murmured through her lips.

"You all right?"

Ingold nodded without opening his eyes. Against the black fur of the very grubby bearskins on which he lay—the only blankets his narrow cot boasted—his face looked suddenly white under the weatherburning. Gil paused, irresolute, a cupful of smoking tea in her hands. Then she stooped to set it on the floor where he could reach it and turned to go. "You'll have a helluva time falling asleep," she remarked over her shoulder at him, "unless you take off your sword belt and your boots."

Still the wizard did not open his eyes. He merely murmured, "You're wrong about that."

But a flicker of witchlight glimmered into existence over his head and slowly spread and strengthened through the room. It picked out the delicate marquetry of the desk that she and Alde had scrounged for him from a distant store-room on the fifth level, its pearl and pearwood surface invisible under piles of old parchment scrolls, dingy with smudged ink and greasy with lanolin. Jewel-clasped books salvaged from the ruin of Quo lay with their open pages a counterpane of red and blue and shimmering gold leaf. Among and between everything lay wax note tablets, like the tiles of a Brobdingnagian Scrabble game. The mess overflowed the desk to litter the floor; the heaped books, scattered tablets, and twinkling gray glass of those enigmatic crystal polyhedrons surrounded the desk like a pool that spread itself along the wall almost to the foot of the hard, narrow cot. Gil paused, then came back and began to pull off the wizard's boots.

"The other mages will be in for dinner soon," she told him as she did so. "If I wanted to risk an amphibian future, I'd try to talk Kara's mother out of something for you now."

Outside in the common room, the harsh, screechy voice of the little witchwife Dame Nan could be heard, accusing someone—probably Dakis the Minstrel—of being a pestilent food thief, deserving of every ailment from cold sores to piles, and threatening to inflict him with the same if he dared to violate her kitchen again. Kara's reproving "Mother!" sounded faintly from another room.

Ingold smiled and shook his head. "Thank you, child," he said softly as Gil dumped the sodden boots beside the door. Then she thought he had fallen asleep, for he lay unmoving, his eyes closed and his hands resting limply at his sides. But oddly enough, Gil did not leave. She stood in the doorway loking down at him, her wide, chill gray eyes curiously blue in the fading glow of the witchlight.

"Ingold?" Her voice was barely audible against the rising chatter in the common room behind her.

"Yes, child?"

"Did you mean what you said? About its being hopeless?"

His eyes opened. For a moment, he considered her, thin and gawky, like a teen-age boy in her outsize surcoat. "Hopeless or not," he murmured, "you at least will have returned to the safety of your own world by the time the army marches. But no," he added, seeing the look of grief that crossed her face, "there is always hope."

"But you don't think that in this case it lies with Rudy's flame throwers," Gil finished for him. "But, dammit, Ingold, the Dark *were* defeated once and driven back underground. The forces that did it can't have been much more numerous than we are here. And the Dark seem to think that you know the answer."

His eyelids drooped closed again, and he gave a faint, tired chuckle. "The answer to what question?" He sighed. "If the memory of how the Dark Ones were defeated has come down to Tir, it may very well be useless by the time he gets old enough to understand it. The Dark Ones' fear is that I will remember sooner, or that I already know."

He laughed again, a dry, weary sound. "The irony of it all is that I haven't the slightest idea what it is that they believe I know.

"I thought that, like Minalde, I might recognize what I could not remember independently. The memories that she inherited through the House of Bes could only be triggered by something she had seen before, but they were no less true. I have meditated on it; I have cudgeled my brains and combed the records of all things touching upon my research and Lohiro's that I could bring from the library at Quo . . ." His scarred fingers moved toward the heaped books that strewed the desk at Gil's elbow. "And there is nothing. No reason at all for the Dark Ones to fear me."

"If they don't fear you," Gil asked, "why do they want you?"

He lay silent for a long time, and again Gil wondered if he might have fallen asleep. But in the dark, heavy fur of the blankets, his hand clenched suddenly, and for an instant his brow furrowed, as if with pain. Then, just as suddenly, his expression smoothed again, and he said, "I haven't the foggiest idea. Tell me why that one party of mages returned prematurely from exploring the Nest in the Vale of the Dark."

Gil did a mild double take at the swift change of subject. "How did you know about that?"

His mouth moved a little under his beard—he might have

been smiling. "I should be a poor mage indeed if I couldn't follow the doings of my colleagues in my crystal," he said. "Shadow of the Moon—the Raider shaman—was in charge of that party. I expected they should be the first to return to the Keep, since the Vale of the Dark is only a day's journey away, but they returned so quickly that I think they never went down that Nest at all."

"They didn't," Gil said, leaning her bony shoulders against the stone of the doorframe. "But then, I expected they wouldn't be able to. When you look down on the Vale from above, you can see how the outlines of the old city of the Dark there have been changed by the gradual movement of the earth. The pavement in which the stairway is located is so badly displaced that I'm not surprised the stairs themselves will no longer admit humans."

"Indeed?" The blue eyes opened, suddenly sharp and alert. "You guessed that?"

Gil nodded and folded her arms. "It would stand to reason, if these mountains are geologically active enough to have displaced the pavement. Those ruins are old—older than our conceptions of time. The Dark formed and shaped that Vale among the older rocks of the foothills, but they couldn't stop the subsequent lift of the earth enough to keep their stair open."

The wizard considered this for a moment, looking intently into the shadows of the ceiling over his head. Then he rolled painfully up onto one elbow and reached for his cup of tea.

"Interesting," he said quietly. In the half-darkness of the alcove, the witchlight falling on his white hair was like strong moonlight on mountain snow; his face, below it, was plunged in shadow. "You once asked me, child, why you were here—why it had been you, and not someone else, whom circumstances had thrust into exile from all you knew and wanted."

Gil looked down at her knobbed and bony hands, lying on the frayed black homespun of her sleeves, and said nothing, but her lips tightened.

"What do you know about the moss in the Nests?"

She jerked her head up, thoroughly startled by what

68

seemed like a whole new topic of conversation, to meet the old man's intent, curious gaze. "Nothing," she said.

"But you guess something about it," Ingold pursued. "You said as much back in the guardroom."

Ruefully, she chuckled. "Oh, that. It isn't important. It's just that I flashed onto something from my college biology course which would explain why the moss is flammable, that's all. It's nothing that has anything to do with the Dark."

"Isn't it?" the wizard murmured. "I wonder. Do you remember, Gil, when you and I visited the Vale of the Dark, how you looked back from the mountain above and saw by the slant of the evening light the pattern of the ancient walls that told you there had once been a city there? I would never have taken those changes in the colors and thickness of vegetation for anything but a rather curious pattern in the valley floor."

"Well, of course." Gill shrugged. "You didn't sit through three Historiography 10-B lectures on the subject of aerial photography, either."

Ingold smiled. "No. Instead, I devoted a considerable portion of my brilliantly misspent life learning how to cast horoscopes—an interesting pastime, but not much to the point. What I am getting at is this: The answer to the question of how the Dark were defeated—how they might be defeated again—may require, not a wizard, but a scholar. And that could be why you are here."

"Maybe," she agreed wryly. "But the fact remains that no record I've seen—either Govannin's chronicles, the old books you salvaged from Quo, or what Alde and I found here in the storerooms—goes back to the Time of the Dark. Nothing gets within a thousand years of it."

Ingold set his tea down and leaned gingerly back against his blankets. His white brows pulled together in a frown. "Why not?" he asked.

Gil started to reply, then left the words unsaid. *The dog did nothing in the nighttime . . . and that, as Sherlock Holmes had once remarked, was the curious incident.*

She returned to the barracks in a meditative mood.

CHAPTER FIVE

Oddly enough, it was Gil's mother who provided the clue to the unraveling of the riddle of the records of the Times Before.

Gil seldom dreamed about her mother; it had been months, indeed, since she had even thought of her. The two had never been close; Mrs. Patterson's relationship with her daughter had been largely based upon emotional blackmail, from which Gil's morbidly sensitive spirit had never recovered.

Yet she was not really surprised to find herself, dreaming, back in her mother's house, sitting on the sky-blue upholstery of the uncomfortable antique loveseat and listening to her mother chat with a podgy young medical student whom she had invited over ". . . to meet you, dear. I told him I had a daughter, and he said he would be so *interested* to get acquainted with you."

Gil reflected, in her dream, that her mother had not changed much at all. Spa-trim and tennis-golden, dainty and svelte in a designer suit of dusky rose, with not an electrum curl out of place, she did not look like a woman whose elder daughter had vanished without a trace and had been missing for months. As always, she monopolized the conversation with her vast fund of small talk, describing in detail how she had undergone the very newest thing in hypnosis therapy to stop smoking, and what wonders it had done for her—far more than any of the half-dozen other cures she had tried.

Feeling as gauche and tongue-tied as she always did, Gil looked down at her hands, wrapped around the thick crystal of a highball glass. She saw them as she knew them now, skeleton-thin and hard, nicked all over with the scars and blisters of sword practice. She saw that she was wearing her one rather unbecoming blue dress. Because her body had thinned with hardship and training, it fitted her less well than it ever had. Like a smear of dried ocher plastic, the scars she'd taken in her first fight with the Dark Ones showed below the line of her unfashionably short sleeve. She wore stockings and high heels, too; looking at her feet, she saw that one of the hose was developing a run.

". . . of course, I do get tremendously nervous, what with my husband away so much and Gillian at school. What is it you're majoring in, dear?"

"History," Gil said quietly, and her mother's face blossomed into a smile as pretty as an arrangement of silk flowers.

"Of course. Do you know, dear, Dr. Armbruster here uses hypnosis for his psychiatric patients, too? Really, I found it so useful . . ." She lighted a cigarette, the California sunlight flashing off the gold of the lighter and the pink polish of her nails . . .

Gil opened her eyes. Down at the far end of the womens' barracks, the banked embers of the tiny hearth gave out a feeble glow; but other than that, the room was in darkness. In the mazes beyond the thin wall of the long cell, she could hear the measured tread of the deep-night watch going on its rounds.

She supposed, thinking about it later, that she should have felt some yank of sorrow at the sight of her parent and the world that she had lost. But for the moment her mind was preoccupied, and she lay, considering the barracks ceiling above her in the dark.

"Hypnosis?" Ingold said thoughtfully, his tongue unfamiliar on the English word. He leaned an elbow on the workbench in Rudy's lab and scratched one corner of his white mustache meditatively.

"Christ, I never thought of that!" Rudy exclaimed, turning from the mess of tubes, stocks, homemade sticky tape, and glittering glass bubbles that strewed the table before him to regard Gil with awe and delight. "You think it would work?"

"I don't see why it wouldn't." Gil pushed aside the glue pot and four of the odd, crystal-gray polyhedrons that they had found in such numbers in the deserted lab levels and perched herself on the edge of the workbench, her feet in their scarred old boots dangling above the floor. She picked up one of the polyhedrons and angled its frostlike facets to the ball of witchlight that floated over Rudy's head. "You ever find out what these were good for?"

"Sure," Rudy said cheerfully. He daubed some glue on one of the hand-whittled gunstocks, fitted a glass bubble—one of the firing chambers they had found in a deserted storeroom—to the top, and used three of the crystal polyhedrons to prop the whole thing delicately together while the glue dried.

"But what is this—hypnosis?" Alde looked up from her corner of the lab, nearest the brazier that warmed the room. She looked very domestic, with gold embroidery scissors glinting in her hands and rags piled in her lap, which she had been snipping into long strips, to be later painted with glue to make sticky tape. Prince Altir Endorion, last scion of the House of Dare, was solemnly mummifying himself at her feet.

"It's kind of like being put to sleep," Gil began, and Rudy shook his head.

"No," he contradicted quietly. "A girl I knew did age-regression therapy—she said you aren't asleep. It's like—like all your concentration is on the hypnotist's voice. You relax to a point where your mind is open to suggestion. Anything sounds reasonable." He glanced from the wizard to Alde. "And it can be used to uncover things that have been forgotten."

"It sounds like *gnodyrr*," Ingold mused, setting down the slightly egg-shaped firing chamber he had been examining and regarding the three young people with thoughtful, half-shut eyes. "*Gnodyrr* is a type of spell that relaxes and opens the subject's mind—and it is done primarily with the voice."

"Have you done it?" Gil asked.

"Of course."

"Would there be someone else here who could work such a spell on you? Because that's the way we could find out what it is that you have forgotten—the key to the defeat of the Dark. Would Thoth be able to do it?"

The wizard's smile widened. "Oh, I don't think so," he said, his eyes beginning to twinkle impishly. "Thoth would never speak to me again if I so much as suggested that he knew such things. *Gnodyrr* is categorized as black magic—forbidden magic. The teaching of it is punishable by death."

Aghast, Rudy gulped. "Why?"

There was a momentary silence, broken only by the faint throbbing of the pumps, hidden deep in the rock of the walls. Then Gil said, "Think about it."

"Yeah, but you can't get someone to do something he knows is wrong under hypnosis," Rudy argued. "That's been proven."

"But we're not talking about hypnosis," she pointed out quietly. "We're talking about magic—*gnodyrr*."

Rudy was silent. He knew the power of Ingold's flawed velvet voice, the voice that could make all things seem possible, logical—even necessary. In the dusky laboratory, the witchlight that wavered over Ingold's head seemed to halo them both in disturbing brightness—this thin, dark-haired girl in her patched black uniform, sitting on the workbench among the confusion of crystal and steel, and the old man who stood beside her, the sleeves of his pale robe rolled up over his scarred forearms. Now that Rudy thought of it, he wouldnt have been entirely willing to bet that Ingold couldn't get her to do murder, cold sober and in the rational light of day.

"And in any case," the old man went on, "I would hesitate to surrender the control of my mind to anyone, even to someone whom I trusted implicitly—Gil or Kta. I have far too much power to take a risk of that kind, even for the best of causes. If for no other reason, mine are the spells that bind the gates of the Keep against the Dark. And as holder of Master-spells . . ."

"Master-spells?" Rudy frowned, reaching out with one

foot to prevent Tir, who had grown bored with his cocoon, from seeking his fortune among the piled junk under the workbench.

"Certainly."

For an instant Rudy was conscious of what he had seen, one night in the depths of the desert—his own isolated soul, viewed through the bright sea-blue eyes that suddenly held his. Like an image made of crystal, there was nothing in his mind or spirit that the old man could not probe out, if he wanted. Ingold's thoughts, his will, were like a needle of ice and lightning, piercing to the bottom of Rudy's startled brain.

Then, with a shock as palpable as the cutting of a straining rope, he was released, and had to catch his balance on the edge of the table, for all the strength seemed to have gone out of his legs. The shadows in the stark, rectangular lab had deepened. Rudy realized that his own witchlight had been quenched and that the only illumination in the room was that which burned like searing ball lightning above Ingold's uncut, silky white hair. He found his hands were unsteady, his face drenched in sudden, icy sweat.

"Master-spells," the old man explained gently.

"Ingold." Alde straightened up from retrieving a dust-blackened Tir from beneath the workbench. "Could you work this—this *gnodyrr*—on me?" Her voice was halting, as if her own audacity terrified her. "I have no—no Master-spells. But I am descended from the House of Dare.

"We have all talked of the heritable memories of the House of Dare," she went on hesitantly, clasping the grimy and repulsively dirty scion of that House in her arms. "Eldor had them. Maybe Tir has them. My grandfather had them. And I can recognize things that my ancestors must have seen, here in the Keep, though I can't remember independently, as—as Eldor used to. But—why do we remember at all?"

Gil's head came up, her gray eyes suddenly sharp and hard.

"You see," Alde continued, her fingers plucking nervously at the cobwebs trailing from Tir's dress, "Gil and I looked all over the Keep for records. *Anything,* to tell us how the Dark Ones may have been defeated. And there's nothing, nothing at all. But—but maybe the old wizards, the engineers who raised the Keep, knew that records do get lost, especially when, as you said, fire is the principal weapon."

Gil's finger stabbed out like a sword. "They tied the memory to the bloodline, and that was their record! A record that wouldn't get lost and couldn't be destroyed!"

"Could they do that?" Rudy asked doubtfully.

"I wouldn't put it past them."

Rudy glanced through the half-open door of the laboratory, past the blue-white bar of light with its diamond mist of dust motes, and out to the blackness of the hidden levels of the Keep beyond where lay hundreds of thousands of square feet of sunken hydroponics tanks filmed with dust, sealed labs and enigmatic storerooms, and pumps which had operated for a score of centuries on power sources that were still unknown.

When he thought about it, he wouldn't put much of anything past them.

"It seems that women remember these things differently from men," Alde said, gently thwarting Tir's attempts to escape her arms and investigate the frost-gray crystals that twinkled so invitingly on the workbench beside him. "But could what I half-remember be brought to the surface by— by *gnodyrr?*"

"It could," the wizard said slowly, his voice low and very grave. "But at what cost to yourself, my lady? *Gnodyrr* is black magic. But more than that, in certain places, local Church rulings have condemned the subject of the spell as well to imprisonment, banishment, or death."

Alde's eyes seemed to get huge in her pale face.

Indignant, Rudy cried, "How come?"

"Don't speak of it so loudly," Ingold said. He leaned upon the workbench, his blunt, thick hands folded on the dark metal of its shining surface. The witchlight threw a curiously sinister glitter into his eyes. "Suppose I were to use *gnodyrr* on Minalde and instruct her to—oh, three years hence—put

75

ground glass into her brother's food. Then I go away and don't return until Alde has been executed for murdering her brother, leaving the Regency open . . ."

"The Regency!" Gil gasped, as Alde's arms tightened involuntarily around her child's body. Indignant at such treatment and oblivious to the dangers that surrounded him, Tir demanded rather unintelligibly to be released at once to pursue his quest among the litter of the table.

Rudy felt suddenly cold all over.

Alde whispered, "But you wouldn't . . ."

"No," the old man agreed. "But the law is based upon the possibility that I might." His scarred fingers brushed the thick coils of hair that veiled her ashen cheeks. "If Alwir learned of it, the consequences to you would be unthinkable, my child. An expensive risk to run, for something that might not be among your memories at all."

No more was said on the matter that morning, and Rudy returned to his experiments with the flame throwers. Alde and her overly venturesome son remained after Ingold and Gil departed, Alde to help and Tir to prevent either of them from getting anything accomplished in peace for very long.

Prince Altir Endorion, heir to the Realm of Darwath and last Prince of the House of Dare, had been a source of never-ending wonderment to Rudy since the first morning that he had unwillingly aided Ingold in rescuing the child from the pursuit of the Dark Ones. Small and with his mother's air of compact delicacy, Tir had nevertheless survived the sack of cities, the destruction of a civilization, and a succession of dangers that had made Rudy's hair stand on end, with a calm resiliency that would have been awesome if it were not so utterly matter-of-fact.

If I'd gone through all that little rug-rat has, Rudy told himself, watching Alde prevent her son from crawling out the door to lose himself in the endless darkness of the Keep's underground levels, *I'd spend the rest of my natural life in the fetal position. I sure as hell wouldn't have this talent for wandering away toward shadows or high places or any other kind of available danger.*

There were times, looking into the infant's wide, jewel-blue eyes, that he wondered how much of that fearlessness came from the buried memories of his ancestors and how much of it was his own, inherited from a father who had been a warrior King and a mother whose crazy courage Rudy had encountered in only one other woman in his life.

By the end of the afternoon, he had satisfied himself that the optimum range of the flame throwers was about twenty-five feet and that no adjustments of the barrel or barrels would lengthen it much beyond thirty.

"That's still farther than a mage can throw fire from his hands, isn't it?" Alde inquired as she followed him along the teeming corridors of the first level, with her much-soot-blackened son balanced upon her hip. Around them in a hundred jerry-built cells, the voices of men and women could be heard quarreling, gossiping, and making love. Woodsmoke stung Rudy's eyes, and the heavy, ever-present, compound reek of unwashed clothing and greasy cooking assaulted his nostrils.

"I'm not sure," he replied, wiping the stray smut from his hands. "I've seen Ingold throw fire about fifteen feet. I asked Thoth about it once, and he said that if the danger were any more than fifteen feet away you'd be better off to run."

Alde laughed. "That sounds like Thoth." But there was a trace of uneasiness in her laughter. Like everyone else, she was a little afraid of the serpentmage.

By common consent, neither of them had spoken of their coming parting. There was an aura of peace about them, even in its shadow, that they were loath to break.

They turned a corner, and the noise from the Aisle hit them, a vast commotion of sound. Startled, they exchanged a glance; then Rudy put his arm about her shoulders and quickened his stride. They found the great open space at the core of the Keep filled with a crowd of men and women warriors, slapping sleet out of their bedrolls and stomping mud from their boots. At the far end of the Aisle, more and more were entering by the great gates, bringing with them blasts of icy air and the whirling gray snow blown by the storm outside. Torchlight and glowstones threw a restless, flickering illumination over the vast, steaming crowd, picking out ruffianly faces, ragged coats of fleece or buffalohide, and hands and cheeks scarred by recent battles with the Dark.

In the midst of it, hoary with ice and hairy as a werewolf, Tomec Tirkenson, landchief of Gettlesand, stood facing Alwir, Ingold, and Govannin with an ugly expression in his saddle-colored eyes.

"Dammit, I *am* the only landchief between the mountains and the Western Ocean!" he growled in his gravelly bass. "Half the men I brought are from Dele, and they're all you're likely to see from that part of the world. Dele was wiped out. These came to me with Kara of Ippit's folks, after months on the road."

"I would have expected a better showing," Alwir replied dryly, "from the landchief of the whole southwestern half of the Realm." The diamonds sewn in his black gloves caught slivers of light and strewed the dark brocade of his sleeves with fragments of color as he folded his arms. "If that is, indeed, what you claim to be."

"I'm not claiming a thing," the landchief rumbled. "But I've got a Keepful of women and kids—an old Keep, which was half-torn-down way back in the old days and rebuilt as best we could. It's damn stout, but there's no magic in its walls, bar the spells old Ingold put on it five years back and what Kara and her mother could do before they got the summons to come here. If I'd left the place unmanned, I'd have come back to find it gutted, sure as the ice in the north."

"So you made the decision not to fulfill your vows to the High King . . ." Alwir began with a sneer.

"Dammit, I brought all I could!"

"And he has done more than any other landchief in the Realm," Ingold added quietly. "And more than any of the others will."

The Chancellor swung around, an unpleasant curl to his full lips. "And are you party to the counsels of such traitors, my lord wizard?"

"No, my lord." Ingold stepped aside, to give room to a couple of snow-covered brigands who were lugging a groundsheet piled high with sacks of provisions and fodder.

"But I and the other mages have scried in our crystals, north, south, and east. And neither from the Keeps of Harl Kinghead in the North, from the lands of the petty princes of the Eastern Woods, nor from the country of the landchief Degedna Marina have we seen any sign that any other landchief in the Realm is sending you the aid you requested."

"So." Alwir drew himself up, haughty and bitter, his sapphire-dark eyes flashing at this new evidence of the fractioning of the Realm. "All the more reason for my lord Tirkenson not to have stinted the duty that he owes to the Realm."

"An excommunicate such as the Lord of Gettlesand . . ." Govannin began in her thin, vicious voice.

"The Lord of Gettlesand is welcome, with all those whom he could bring." Minalde stepped forward quickly, holding out her hand, heedless of the dust that daubed the hems of her faded peasant skirt and liberally smutched the baby Prince in her arms. "In our time of need we could scarcely ask for a more loyal vassal."

Alwir looked down his nose at her dishevelment, but Tirkenson grinned, the frost glittering on his mustache and unshaven cheeks. The explosion that would have erupted in another instant between Chancellor, Bishop, and landchief faded like a rumble of thunder into the distance and dissipated under Alde's warm smile.

"It is hardly the time or place, my sister, to extend formal welcome to the leader of this—vast legion," Alwir said primly. "If it is true that he is the only landchief to answer our summons, then we shall meet in Council at sunset to determine the time and distribution of the upcoming reconquest of Gae. I trust," he added, his lips pinched, "that you will trouble to comb your hair for the occasion."

Turning on his heel, he strode off through the mob of ragged, gesticulating Gettlesand rangers that filled the Aisle and quickly blotted him from view.

Alde's face was crimson with anger and shame at his last remark. Tirkenson laid a gloved, comforting paw on her shoulder.

"He's put out that we're so few," he rumbled. "Don't trouble yourself over it, my lady. We're few enough and, unless they *have* found the means old Dare used to drive back the Dark, we're going to be hard put to it." He glanced down at her, his yellow-brown eyes sharp. "They haven't, have they?"

In a hushed voice, Alde said, "I don't know."

"My lord Chancellor's precious mages have devoted enough time to it," Govannin remarked spitefully, her coldly beautiful face disdainful in the restless, jerking shadows that surrounded them. "Yet they themselves seem to have doubts about their solutions." She rested her hands on the jeweled buckle of her sword belt in a gesture Rudy found reminiscent of Gil's; like a baleful eye, the amethyst of her episcopal ring flashed in the dimness.

"That reminds me," Tomec Tirkenson said suddenly. "I brought you another mage, Ingold." He raised his head, scanning the bustling confusion whose noise seemed to echo and re-echo from the black, featureless walls around them. Then he caught sight of someone—*God knows how,* Rudy thought, *in that steamy chaos of snow-covered bodies*—and yelled in his foghorn voice, "Wend! *Wend!* Get over here, you little warlock!"

A young man emerged from the crowd and elbowed his way with surprising diffidence to the big landchief's side. Looking at the newcomer, Rudy realized with a start that it was, in fact, the same Brother Wend whom he and Ingold had met in Gettlesand, the village priest who had refused to risk his soul, as he believed, by acknowledging himself a mage.

He looked thinner in the harlequin shadows of the Aisle than he had in the little fire-lit cell in the back of the Church. He had left off shaving his head and face, and both were covered in a uniform black stubble that glistened with flecks of ice. His eyes, as he faced Ingold in silence, were the eyes of a man who had crossed half a continent to seek his own damnation—haunted, weary, empty of all but despair.

Ingold stepped forward, his face filled with compassion. "So you came," he said quietly.

80

After a long moment the priest whispered, "After you spoke with me that night I—I could not stay away. I tried. But if—if mages are needed for the defeat of the Dark, I will become one, though it costs me my soul."

All around them, the Aisle was a jostling sea of weary bodies, lit by crazily bounding torchlight and raucous with soldiers' raillery and quartermasters' curses. But for an instant of time, it seemed to Rudy that these two stood alone, wizard and priest. The silence between them seemed stronger than the noise that rang on all sides.

Then, like a steel file, the voice of Bishop Govannin grated furiously into that silence. "You cannot!" She took a step forward in a billow of flame-colored vestments, her cobra eyes black with hate. "Apostate!" she cried.

Wend flinched, white-faced, from the balefire that seemed to burn in her face.

"Let the damned look to their own! You belong to the Church!" Her voice shook with livid rage—rage that any would desert the ranks of the Faithful, no matter what the stakes involved. She advanced upon Wend like a death-angel, and Ingold quietly stepped between them, meeting her scorching gaze with eyes that were at once utterly mild and utterly immovable.

"I should have known it would come to this!" she spat at him. "That, in your arrogance, you would rob what belongs to the Church! What belongs to me!" She was literally trembling with fury, her knuckles white under the thin skin of her clenched, skeletal hands.

"Well, he is yours, Ingold Inglorion," she whispered in a dry voice that bit like broken glass. "You are his seducer. On your head lies the damnation of his soul."

The little priest looked away, hands fluttering to cover his gray lips, but Ingold did not move. The Bishop's wrath broke over him like a wave on a rock.

"We damn our own souls, my lady," he replied quietly. "Or save them."

"Heretic!" Her rasping whisper was more violent, more terrible, than a shriek. "The time will come when God will judge you for what you have done today."

"God has judged me all my life," the wizard said. "But that is God's privilege, my lady. It is not yours."

For a moment she faced him, her lips drawn back, the aura of her anger consuming her like a terrible heat. Then she turned and swept away into the confusion of the Aisle, leaving Rudy, Alde, and Tirkenson all feeling that they had been scorched by their proximity to her wrath.

Night had fallen. Rudy and Kara of Ippit were standing together in the doorway of the large, square chamber just off the Wizards' Corps common room where the younger mages generally engaged in their more strenuous pastimes like invisible tag or dazzledart, watching Gil and Ingold fence.

The room before them was flooded with soft, brilliant witchlight, which showed every crack and strain on its grimy walls with merciless clarity. In that even, shadowless light, the old man and the girl circled each other, balanced to strike, with long, split-cane practice swords in their hands. Ingold's white robe was blotched with dark patches of sweat, and his silky hair was stringy and dripping, but he moved on his feet as lightly as a dancer. He sideslipped Gil's attack effortlessly, turned to let the hissing blade whine past him, and tapped his way through her guard with neither force nor haste.

"Gently, Gil," he urged and turned the plane of his body a few degrees, so that, without taking a step, he was no longer in the path of her rush. "Why tire yourself out? You care too much about it."

Gil muttered a curse. Rudy knew that she had practiced with the Guards earlier in the evening and he considered this additional training certifiable proof of lunacy. She looked sick with fatigue, her soaked hair straggling around a taut face. But she moved with a deadly lightness before which he personally wouldn't have wanted to find himself on the receiving end.

"Take your own death as a given," Ingold told her. "Forget about it. It's your opponent's death you want." And he attacked her with sudden viciousness, taking her off balance and driving her with brutal force to the wall. Rudy saw the split cane sting her flesh and winced, for he had seen the bruises that the practice swords could leave. The wizard's face never lost its serene expression, but in his eyes was an almost inhuman intensity that Rudy had seen only once before, in the rain-slashed ruins of Quo. Ingold cut his way through Gil's defenses and always seemed to be a step ahead of her dodges. Her back to the wall, she hacked against his greater strength, droplets of sweat flying from the ends of her hair. Finally she faked, parried, and slipped through his guard and past him, out into the center of the room, gasping for breath.

"Good." The old man smiled as if he hadn't been all but bludgeoning her to death a moment before. "But breathe lightly, smoothly; exhale on your cuts and let the inhaling take care of itself. Else your opponent will outwind you." He swept in with a snarling cut that Gil was barely ready for, the blades momentarily tangling, and the tip of Gil's weapon broke through his guard to brush his retreating ribs.

"You're a woman," Ingold chided. "You haven't a man's strength. A woman's attack is in and out, before he has time to touch you . . . So."

"In a way," Kara's voice said softly in Rudy's ear, "I could almost be glad that—all this—came to pass. For I would have remained all my life in Ippit, were it not for the rising of the Dark. I would never have been able to study magic under him, as I have done here."

From the commons behind them, the warm reflection of the firelight woke mosaic fragments of color in the shawl she wore and glimmered like cornsilk in its long fringes. Rudy could not remember having seen that shawl before. Its oddly primitive embroidery looked like Gettlesand work.

"He said something like that once," Rudy remarked quietly. *"Nothing is fortuitous* . . . There's no such thing as coincidence."

"He's right," Kara agreed. Rudy felt and heard, rather than saw, the movement of her gray dress as she leaned against the wall beside him. "Ingold had left Quo by the time I studied there. He was pointed out to me once at a distance, but I never had the nerve in those days to go up and speak to him. But I was always sorry I never had the chance to learn from him."

Rudy was silent, thinking of the learning that he would be leaving. His heart felt sick within him. "Was he a member of the Council, then?" he asked her. "I always thought he was kind of a maverick, but . . . There are times when I don't know what he is." The terrible strength of the Master-spell still lingered like a disquieting echo in his mind.

When she didn't answer, he looked back at her in the gloom and saw that her eyes were wide, startled and half-amused at his ignorance. "Ingold Inglorion," Kara said, "is the greatest wizard and swordsman in this age of the world. He was the Archmage of Quo and Master of the Council for twelve years—he retired in favor of his student Lohiro and turned over the Master-spells to him—oh, five, six years ago now. Even before the destruction of Quo, there was no one alive to equal him; there have been legends about him ever since he came out of the desert. He never told you?"

Rudy shut his mouth, which had unfortunately come open, and felt the hot color rise to his face. He felt like a fool. He had seen the way the others treated Ingold, even the haughty Thoth.

His eyes returned to the lighted room before him—to Gil, pursuing the wizard with genuine battle fury in her pale eyes, and to Ingold, parrying, sidestepping, drawing her on. Below his rolled-up sleeves, the wizard's forearms were heavy with muscle and striped with whitened scars. Rudy remembered the duel at Quo and how, even in the worst of the battle, Ingold had never feared Lohiro's magic.

There was a quick ghost of a smile in Kara's voice. "Believe me, the rest of us are as envious as a parcel of old maids at a wedding that he chose you to be his student. For myself, I can't understand how you could give it up and go back to your own world."

Rudy shut his eyes, feeling suddenly ill. At the thought of it, a black pit of despair seemed to open inside him, draining life and color from all things. He whispered, "Don't ask."

Behind him, Kara was silent.

"And anyhow," he went on, turning from the door and

84

brushing past her to return to the common room hearth, "he didn't choose me. I asked him if I could be his student." He wondered whether he would have had the nerve, if he'd known.

Kara followed him into the dark room, sidestepping, with a wizard's dark-sight, a footstool and one of the Corps cats. She hitched the silken waterfall of her shawl up over her shoulders and bent to poke up the dying fire, the red light outlining the scars that striped her rugged features. "Maybe you did ask him," she assented. "But he picked you, all the same. My guess is that he chose you for his student the first time he met you."

Rudy paused, his hands resting on the dark curve of the harp Tiannin, the one thing that he had salvaged from the ruins of Quo. "He couldn't have done that," he said quietly. "He didn't know I was mageborn when he met me. Hell, *I* didn't even know it."

Kara smiled. "You're very certain about what he knows."

Tawny flame leaped up, chivied to life by Kara's poker. The warm light of it slid through the twining inlays of the harp, then, reaching into the inglenook, picked out the coiled, glossy hair of the girl who sat there so silently, her iris-blue eyes gazing into the glowing hearth.

"Alde," Rudy said softly and reached to take her hands. "What . . . ?" Her fingers were like ice in his, the bones feeling incredibly fragile within the chilled flesh. "Is the Council over?"

She nodded. The play of the firelight showed up the tenseness of her face and the mauve stain of sleeplessness that tinted her eyelids. Looking down into her intent eyes, Rudy barely heard the tactful rustle of Kara's departure.

"Rudy, is Ingold here?" Alde whispered.

"Sure. He and Gil are making chutney of each other in the next room. What . . ."

"I want him to work the spell of *gnodyrr* on me."

Rudy looked quickly around. Though they were alone in the dim, golden room, there was no guarantee they had not been overheard. With the thinness of the jury-rigged walls and the twisting labyrinths of corners and side passages, spying was ridiculously easy in the mazes of the Keep.

"I want to see what I remember of the Time of the Dark."

"No."

Her chin came up, her eyes flashing.

"Alde, it's too risky," he pleaded.

"So was your going to Gae."

He fell back on the old standby. "That's different."

"Is it?" she asked softly. "Rudy, are you so sure that Dare of Renweth defeated the Dark Ones by burning out their Nests with flame throwers? Are you so sure that Alwir's plan will succeed?"

"We can't be sure, babe . . ."

"But we can be a lot surer than we are!" Her wide eyes held the same desperate glint that Rudy had seen on the night of the massacre at Karst, when she plunged back into the haunted galleries in search of her son—a passionate determination as difficult to deflect as a descending sword blade.

"If Alwir found out about it, you could lose your son," he argued, bracing for battle in the last ditch.

"And you could have lost your life at Gae," she replied in her low voice. "Gil could have, on the night that man had his mind taken over by the Dark and tried to open the Keep gates. Ingold could have, the night he got us here under cover of the blizzard. Rudy, Alwir won't admit it, but this invasion is a terrible gamble. We have to know the answer. It doesn't matter what it costs."

Her hands tightened over his, the jeweled rings she wore only on ceremonial occasions digging into his flesh. The saffron light rippled over the dark colors of her brocade gown as she leaned forward, her face as intent as a point of flame. "Get Ingold for me," she whispered. "Please."

So much for the last ditch.

"You're as crazy as Gil is." Rudy sighed, rising. "But all right."

As he moved to go, she caught his hand again. Looking down, he saw alarm in her eyes, the desperate resolve melting suddenly into fears inculcated in her since childhood. He leaned down and kissed her icy lips. "Don't worry," he said softly.

"Ingold won't—won't really take over my mind—will he?"

"As stubborn as you are, I don't see how he could." Rudy helped Alde to her feet and led her toward the moving shadows of the lighted room next door.

CHAPTER SIX

"Minalde?" Ingold's voice was gentle, but, like the shadowy aura of his power, it seemed to fill the tiny room. "Do you hear me?"

In a toneless voice, she replied, "I hear you." In the dim blue phosphorescence that illuminated the underground observation chamber, Alde's face looked white but relaxed; her open eyes were empty.

Sitting with Gil, like a couple of silent watchdogs by the door, Rudy thought how fragile Alde looked and how helpless. Ingold's power seemed to engulf her—the power of the Archmage that Rudy himself had felt through the strength of the Master-spell, bone-shaking for all its quietness. That terrible magic seemed to isolate the two figures, the old man in his patched robe and the girl whose face was like a lily against the smoke of her unbound hair, in a world where the only reality was Ingold's voice and the enchantment that seemed to shiver in the air like a bright cloud about them.

No wonder the Church fears him, Rudy thought. *There are times when I fear him myself.*

"Minalde?" the wizard said softly. "Where are you?"

"Here," she answered him, her eyes staring unseeingly into the circumscribed shadows that pressed so closely upon them. "In this room."

It had been Ingold's idea to undertake the *gnodyrr* in the old observation chamber, hidden in the depths of the subterranean labs. It was as safe a place as could be found within the crowded Keep, and Ingold said that not even a mage with a crystal could spy upon them there.

"You sure about that?" Rudy had asked him as they made their way through the dusty reaches of the abandoned hydroponics chambers.

"Of course," the wizard replied. "Every civilization which involves magic has its countermeasures. It is a relatively easy matter to weave shielding-spells into the stone and mortar of walls, so that what passes within them is hidden from divination. Rudy, you yourself know of the existence of rooms in which no magic can be worked at all—in fact, there are said to be several within the Keep."

Rudy had shivered at the memory of the vaults of Karst and the doorless cell with its queerly null, sterile smell . . . Nervously, he had drawn Alde closer to him, and she had returned the pressure of his arm gratefully, for she walked just then with her own fears. The heavy darkness of the lab levels seemed to press somehow more thickly about them.

"Why is that?" Rudy had asked. "Why would they make rooms like that? I mean, wizards built the Keep, for Chrissake."

Gil, pacing along on Ingold's other side, had said, "It stands to reason. Govannin told me about—about renegade mages, wizards who used their powers for evil. You'd have to have some way to hold them in check. Even the Council of Wizards would have to agree to that."

Rudy thought about that now, watching the old man and the girl who was held in such absolute power. He understood now why *gnodyrr* was a forbidden spell, its teaching ringed around with the most terrible of penalties. The ony thing that protected Alde from utter enslavement to Ingold was Ingold himself—his reverence for the freedom of others and his innate kindliness. *What would Alwir be,* Rudy wondered suddenly, *if he had that kind of power? Or Govannin?*

"Minalde," Ingold's warm, scratchy voice said. "Look beyond the walls of this room. Tell me what you see."

She blinked, her slender brows puckering over those inward-looking cornflower eyes. Then her lips parted and her face flooded with joy, as if at a vision of startling delight. She whispered, "Gardens."

Beside him, Rudy heard the swift hiss of Gil's intaken breath.

"Tell me about these gardens."

In the blue, glimmering light, her eyes were wide, luminous with wonderment. "They're—they're like a floating jungle," she stammered. "Fields planted on the waters. Room after room, filled with leaves—dark leaves, fuzzy like gray-green velvet, or bright and hard and shiny. Everywhere you can smell the growing." Her face tilted upward, as if her eyes followed the thick, trailing vines over walls and ceilings that had for ages been as dry as a rock-cut tomb. "There are nets of glowstones strung over the tanks, and the room glitters with leaf shadows on the water. Vegetables—corn and peas and lentils, squash and melons—climbing up trellises and suspended in nets and on wires. Everything is green, warm, and bright, though the blizzards are raging outside, and the Pass is buried in snow."

"Ah," Ingold said softly. "And how do they grow, these gardens?"

She frowned into the distance, and Rudy had the sudden, uncanny feeling that the expression on her face was no longer her own. It was that of another woman, older than Alde, he thought. The timbre and pitch of her voice altered subtly. "It is—all in the records. I—it was all recorded. How to operate the pumps, how to make the fluid that feeds the plants . . ."

"And where are these records?"

She tried to gesture, but Ingold would not release her hands. Her eyes were still fixed upon vacancy, hundreds of lifetimes distant. "They—people take them, of course. The Central Library is at the east end of the second level, behind the open spaces of the Assembly Room. Mostly the mages in the labs use them, but you need not be a mage to do so. The words alone unlock them."

"What words?"

She repeated them; a short spell in a burring, liquid language to which Ingold listened with the precision of a trained philologist. "The unlocking is the same for all," she added. "There is no secret to it."

Gil murmured, "The east end of the second level is all part of the Royal Sector. The biggest room that's still in its original shape there is behind the upper part of the Sanctuary, which I guess was the old Assembly Room. Alwir uses it these days for his justice hall. There wasn't a thing in it resembling a book when we came to the Keep."

"Not after so long there wouldn't be, of course," Ingold replied softly. "Even if there were not periods of anathemas for the wizards, the records would have been moved as the Keep grew more crowded in the passing centuries."

"Might the wizards themselves have hidden them?" Rudy asked. "If there was some kind of attack against the wizards, could they have stashed them someplace in the labs?"

"They could have done so," Gil agreed. "Except we haven't found a stitch of anything written down here yet."

Rudy sighed. "This reminds me of when I was a little kid, and I'd have something that was really precious to me, and I'd put it in a safe place."

"That was so safe you never found it again," Gil concluded with regret. "I did the same thing."

"Well," Rudy said gloomily, "mine was organic . . . and we found it eventually."

"They said—they said that the records might be lost," Minalde whispered, her forehead suddenly tightening, as if with pain. "Or that the secret of them would be hidden. That was why Dare said that we must remember."

"*Dare* said?" Ingold's white eyebrows went up. "Is it not from Dare, then, that you have these memories?"

She shook her head, and her hands tightened over his. "There were twenty of us. They—the wizards—did not want women to bear the memories. They said that women carry griefs enough of their own; that they bear too many losses, of husbands, of children. My baby died, that first winter. So cold," she whispered hopelessly. "So cold. But many of the men who could have done it refused. Some called it evil; others said only that it was too heavy a thing to bind to the shoulders of their children. But it was a chancy thing, and there were so few of us whose bloodlines the wizards could tie this to." Her voice had changed, stammering, as if seeking words, blurred with an accent at times, like the soft, rolling lilt of the spell that would unlock the vanished records of the Keep.

"Time is so deep," she murmured. "So many things are

lost in its well. Dare said that we must remember." The pallid chill of the magelight glinted on a tear that trickled down, for griefs not her own. Ingold's scarred finger brushed it gently aside.

"What must you remember?" he asked gently.

She began to speak, hesitantly at first, then gaining strength and sureness as grief, fear, and wonderment colored her stammering voice. Now and then she stopped, struggling with concepts and memories that she did not understand—machines that operated by magic and spells that drew the lightning from the sky and ground to fuse the separate stones of the Keep's mighty walls. She spoke of battles fought by the mages against the Dark, who would come sweeping down from the Nest in the Vale to the north, of freezing nights torn by the fire and lightning of these combats, of hopelessness and terror, and of cold.

"The Keep had to be built," she said quietly, staring into the darkness of that shadowy room hidden at the heart of the ancient fortress. "Everything was sacrificed to it—fuel, power, energy, magic. It was a cold and bitter winter. The Dark attacked us, night after night, killing or carrying off prisoners alive." She paused, her lips pressed tight to keep them from trembling and her eyes wide with remembered horrors.

"And then?" Ingold's voice was little more than a breath in that still, dark room. The cold light fragmented his lined face into chips of brightness and darkness. As he leaned forward, his moving shadow woke a single blink of brightness from the gray crystal set in the heart of the stone table. "Tell me, Minalde. What means, what weapon, did Dare of Renweth use to combat the Dark? How did he go against them?"

She sat still for a moment, staring into the darkness. Then her eyes widened, until it seemed that only the black pupils showed, dilated within a thin ring of indigo. She shut her eyes and began to weep, deep, heaving sobs that racked her body like the pains of childbirth.

Rudy sprang to his feet with a startled cry. Ingold waved him back and gathered the weeping girl into his arms, stroking the dark, braided head that he held pressed to his shoulder and murmuring words of comfort. Her sobbing quieted but did not stop. The wizard continued to murmur to her, rocking her like a child, and Rudy sensed the slow withdrawal of the spells that had filled the room. The air seemed to change. The scent, the feel, of power dissipated and the dark aura slipped away until Ingold was nothing but a ragged old vagabond, comforting a frightened girl.

Finally Alde sat up a little, her face blotched and swollen. From somewhere about his person, Ingold produced a clean handkerchief to give her.

"Are you all right?" he asked her kindly.

She nodded, her hands still shaking from the violence of her tears, and blew her nose comprehensively. "Why was I crying?" she whispered.

He brushed the wet tendrils of hair back from her face, a father's gesture. "You don't remember?"

She shook her head. Rudy put a gentle hand on her shoulder; her fingers slid around his, and she looked up at him with a wan smile. "Did you—did you learn what you were looking for?"

"We have learned some things of value," the wizard replied after a moment. "Something of the founding of the Keep." He frowned and got to his feet, helping Alde up with a strong, gentle hand. The soft glimmer of the witchlight in the room coalesced into a floating shred of ball lightning, which drifted out the door before them, showing their dusty route through the whispering darkness of the dry gardens.

"But nothing of how humankind defeated the Dark?"

In the bobbing blue light, Ingold's face seemed suddenly harsh. He said quietly, "Perhaps more than we know."

Minalde's experience with forbidden magic yielded other fruits than that ambiguous dread. In her trance she had spoken of caves, where the refugees from the realms in the valleys had lived through that first brutal winter, during the construction of the Keep itself. "And whereas we cannot, of course, tell Alwir how we came to learn of their existence," Ingold said as they returned to the Corps common room, "considering the border war that has been carried on for generations between Gettlesand and Alketch, were Rudy

93

and I to 'discover' these caves, I think things could be much more peaceable in the Keep when the Army of the South arrives.''

"The caves would have to be fortified, wouldn't they?'' Gil mused, stirring the fire to life and prowling into the dark kitchen in quest of bread and cheese.

"They must have been, if the refugees survived in them until spring.'' Ingold held out his hands to the warmth of the blaze, the saffron light winking off the brass of his belt buckle and the hilts of sword and dagger. "They would provide a protected camp for our allies—protected not only from the Dark Ones but, I think, from the White Raiders as well.''

Rudy shivered. The idle threnody that he had begun to pluck from the strings of his harp fell silent. He had seen too many of the hideous sacrifices that the plains barbarians offered to their ghosts. One would have been too many.

"When Rudy and I go in search of the caves . . .''

"Rudy and you?'' Gil re-emerged from the kitchen and tossed a bannock lightly across the room that the wizard fielded without getting up. "If you plan on meeting the White Raiders, you're going to need me there as well as Rudy. Unless you want another forest fire,'' she added uncharitably.

"And you aren't leaving me behind.'' Alde spoke up unexpectedly from the hearth rug, where she had seated herself at Rudy's feet.

Ingold sighed. "This is not a primrosing expedition . . .''

"Do you really think you could find the place without me?''

So it was that the four of them set out in the morning, searching for a place whose appearance might have shifted radically in the last three thousand years. Ingold chose the cliffs that stretched north of the Keep, on the grounds that the caves that Alde had spoken of seemed to be higher than the rest of the Vale, and both Gil and Alde backed him up. Rudy, who had no opinion on the subject, brought up the rear, his holstered flame thrower slapping at his side, scanning the gloomy woods for any sign of the White Raiders.

Though there was nothing resembling a road from the Keep along the north cliffs, the woods there were not too thick to penetrate, and in places deer trails skirted up the benches and broken ground at the feet of those towering ramparts. The winter woods were silent under the gray, lowering sky. Once Ingold found wolf tracks, several days old; it was the only sign of life, human or animal, that they encountered.

But about a mile from the Keep, Alde stopped and looked through narrowed eyes at a spur of the mountain wall that ended too abruptly and at an irregular rock knoll just beyond. The way they were taking passed between the end of the spur and the knoll, and Rudy searched both in vain for some sign of artificial cutting. He did not have Gil's archaeological training or Minalde's memories—all he saw was trees.

A short way beyond that, Alde stopped again, looking around her. Below the bench on which they stood, a pool was set in a cuplike bay amid the rocks, all but hidden by the gray, tangling branches of a thicket of trees. The cliffs above were low and broken-looking at this point; the bench itself was strewn with boulders and talus spills, dotted with stands of dark-browed pines. It was a desolate-looking place, bleak and sinister, with the black trees of the forest sloping away below them and the beetling rocks shouldering one another above. But Alde looked around her, a slight, puzzled frown on her brow.

"I don't know," she murmured, her breath a faint drift of smoke in the icy air. "But—somehow I think we're here."

"Stands to reason," Gil remarked, tucking her gloved hands into her sword belt and scanning the dreary slopes around them. "There's water here and a break in the geological formation of the cliff that could mean caves underneath."

Minalde's frown deepened and she hugged the thick fur of her cloak more closely around her shoulders. There was a curious expression, both distant and inward, in her cornflower-blue eyes as she followed Gil's gaze along the snow and rock of the jumbled land above them, as if she were

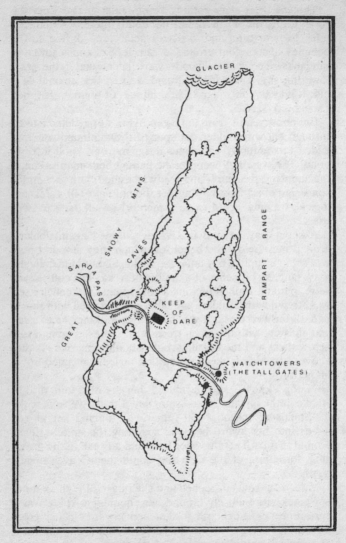

The Vale of Renweth

comparing what she saw with some inner picture that had been carried for generations in her heart. "There should be a stair . . ."

Rudy poked with the iron-shod foot of his staff at the mess of snow and dirt that half-covered the bench. "One good landslide would have taken care of that," he pointed out. "Hell, the cave itself could be buried."

"I don't think so." She turned, her eyes half-shut, tracing the formations of tumbled boulders and jutting, broken cliffs. Then, with sudden decision, she hitched up her heavy cloak and thick skirts and began to climb.

The cave had not been buried, though its single entrance was hidden in a tangled grove of scrub oak and wind-twisted, hoary crabapple trees. "You can see there was a sizable ledge here at one time," Ingold observed as they paused in the low, rounded arch behind the screening trees. "The earthquake that broke it must have carried away the stair." He took his staff by the end and extended it into the darkness of the chamber beyond. Pale light burned off its tip, illuminating curving, water-worn walls and a sandy floor strewn with dead leaves and the frosted bones of some small animal, mauled by foxes. At the far end, the light flashed on the metalwork of a small door, locked as the Keep doors were locked with inner bolts and a ring. The hinges were deep-sunk into the living rock of the walls; the metal was black, hard, and unrusted.

For a moment there was nothing anyone could say. Rudy looked sideways and saw by the wan reflection of the daylight that Alde's eyes were filled with sudden tears.

Then he looked back to that dark door whose memory had faded from all minds but one. The light of Ingold's staff slid coldly over the locking ring as the wizard advanced cautiously into the room and touched the thread-fine runes marked on the black steel that only a wizard could see.

"Well, I'll be damned."

"Govannin certainly thinks so," Gil remarked, following Ingold into the deep, shifting gloom. Alde quickly wiped her eyes and crossed the shadowy threshold, with Rudy bringing up the rear, staff in one hand and flame thrower in the other. Their voices echoed eerily against the low ceiling.

"Sure is lucky for our side," Gil added judiciously, poking at the fox mess in a corner of the cave, "that we didn't find a grizzly holed up here for the winter."

Rudy sniffed scornfully. "If we had, I'da slayed it with mah bowie knife. Then you wimmenfolk coulda skinned it."

"Aaah, you lie like a rug, white man."

"Hey!" he protested, turning. "I'll have you remember I slayed a dragon. Not bad," he added, "for a poor boy who was borned on a mountaintop in Tennessee."

Gil paused in her investigation of the smoke-blackened ceiling and looked at him with new respect. "Even if it is the greenest state in the land of the free," she agreed, nodding gravely. "Was you raised in the woods, then?"

" 'Til I knew every tree," Rudy asserted proudly.

"Do you know what they're talking about?" Alde asked quietly of Ingold, who was listening to this interchange in mystified astonishment.

Bemused, the wizard shook his head.

"It's the ancient lore of our people," Gil explained and came to join them beside the locked door, her feet scuffing in the thin sand of the cave floor. "Is the door spelled shut?"

Ingold's mittened hand caressed the smooth steel ring. "Not unbreakably so." In the half-light his face was grave, the ice crystals glittering in his frosted beard. "But these caves have been sealed for centuries. At the time they were in use, they were presumably proof against entrance by the Dark Ones. But that is no guarantee that they have not been entered since."

Gil glanced nervously around her at the murky twilight of the cave. The light at the tip of Ingold's staff began to burn with a stronger, fiercer glow, throwing their shadows black and harsh against the gleaming door.

"You and Alde go back and stand in the light from the cave mouth. Rudy . . ."

Rudy shook back his long hair from around his face, then bowed his head, standing silently, like something carved of weathered oak, the snow like chips of glass on the bison fur of his collar and cuffs. He had holstered his flame thrower; in his other hand, the razor-edged crescent that tipped his staff began to burn with a white, clear radiance. The brightness drowned the pale daylight, threw sharp blue shadows that outlined Rudy's high cheekbones and broken nose, and cast into prominence the scars and lines that scrawled over Ingold's face like a map of his endless journeyings. In the doubled light of the two staffs, everything had two shadows, darker blue and lighter, midnight and cobalt, and the white glare that beat on those two faces stamped them with sudden, uncanny resemblance.

Ingold reached forward and touched the metal of the door. His blue eyes were half-shut as his hands passed over the shining surface. In the cave's icy cold, the breaths of the two wizards mingled like a dust of diamonds in the searing light. Then with a sudden movement, Ingold's mittened hand closed over the locking ring, twisted it with visible effort, and thrust the door open and inward.

A black hole stared at them, like the eye-pit of Hell. But nothing emerged, neither darkness nor beast not even the cloud of bats that Gil had half-expected. The wizard bent his head to pass the low doorsill and vanished into the room beyond.

They saw his shadow, moving against the streaming brightness of his staff. Then he called out, "Come and see this, my children."

"They *lived* here?" Alde straightened up as she came through the low door and gazed around the wide, smooth-floored chamber. The twofold glare of the lights had scattered the ancient darkness. Eight monstrous shadow shapes lurched and reeled across the frost-crusted walls as the lights of the wizards' staffs moved. Alde's voice, quieter than was even her usual soft-spoken wont, echoed queerly against the walls of that huge, hollow place.

"Evidently." Gil bent down to touch with cautious fingers what looked like a bundle of grayed, dust-covered rags heaped near the wall. They crumbled to powder, but she said, "See underneath here? Broken dishes. And bones of some kind—rabbit or chicken . . ."

"Rabbit," Rudy said, looking over her shoulder. He had spent a good portion of his time crossing the desert in learning to identify bones. He moved off, the glowing crescent of his staff throwing a bobbing black shadow close around his feet. "Look, here's a niche where somebody stored something—old bottles, I think." He dropped to one knee and carefully ran the lighted end of the staff into a water-scooped hollow in the wall near the floor. "Yeah, there's broken glass at the back, under a lot of dust and leaves. You notice there are no signs of animals having lived here?"

"It would be more surprising if we did find such signs," Ingold commented from the far end of the cave. He was standing next to what had been a long fissure in the stone, a fissure that had been sealed with a wall of the same black, glassy material that formed the Keep. The wall was pierced by a single locked metal door. "From the looks of this cave, it was carved by the action of an ancient river. These caves lie in a series, walled and locked from one another—a sensible precaution, if there was no telling where and when the Dark Ones might break in. Any crack to the outside, or even to another cave, must of necessity have been sealed off." He came back to where they knelt, his hair shining like sunlit snow in the white dazzle of his staff.

"They sure didn't leave much," Rudy muttered. He moved a few feet off and looked down at the floor, his forehead creased in a sudden frown. "Is that—oil stains?"

"Sure looks like the floor of my mechanic's," Gil observed, following him to where the floor was blotched with round, dark smears. "Look, there are scratches on the floor, and on the wall as well. They stored some kind of machinery here."

"Yeah, but I thought they lived here . . ."

"They were very crowded," Alde pointed out, tucking her hands for warmth into the rippling black fur of her cloak. Beneath the curve of her braided hair, her eyes had that disquieting remoteness of expression. Rudy felt almost that she might have said, "We were very crowded." She went on. "Thousands made their way up here from the river valleys. There was barely space for them, or food. They lived wherever they could."

"And stored things wherever they could," Gil added thoughtfully, kneeling by another dusty old cache that proved to contain nothing more than crumbling, unrecognizable rags and the broken fragments of several glowstones. "From where the scratches are on the floor, I'd guess this stuff was shoved under a piece of machinery. Look!" she said, turning as she sat on her heels and pointing. "They had something bolted to the ceilings as well." She went back to investigating her dusty midden, clotted with hardened oil and resins, brittle and falling to pieces even under her delicate touch. Ingold came back, holding his staff aloft to illuminate the intermittent double line of bolt-holes in the rock above. Gil went on digging, unearthing stiffened and decayed rags, more broken glowstones, tiny bones, a kettle with holes in its corroded bottom, and, rather surprisingly, two of the frosted gray glass polyhedrons like those they had found in such baffling numbers in the Keep, almost buried under a drift of nameless dust and the mummified sole of a broken sandal.

Rudy traced the stains and scratches along the wall. It was clear that quite a bit of machinery had been stored here. "You know what's funny?" he remarked, turning back to where Ingold, Alde, and Gil remained grouped around Gil's cache. "There's not so much as a scrap of paper."

"Hardly funny," Ingold commented. "It would have taken them a while to get the door built. There was smoke blackening in the fissures of that first cave's roof."

"And what wasn't burned for protection," Minalde added diffidently, "would have been burned later in the winter for warmth."

"With people crowded together like cows in a byre?"

"And besides," Gil tossed out over her shoulder, "didn't you say, Alde, that the records were taken to some kind of Central Library? That means that they weren't all destroyed."

"Not then," Rudy agreed. "But even your toughest paper isn't going to last three thousand years without special treatment, or spells, or something."

Gil sat back on her heels suddenly, speculation sharpening in those frost-gray, crystalline eyes. "Are we talking about paper?"

Rudy paused, frowning, his hands hooked loosely through his gun belt. "What, then? Parchment? Cloth? Plastic?"

"Videotape?" Gil queried softly.

"Videotape?"

"What's videotape?" Alde asked.

Ingold said suddenly, his voice charged with excitement, "Isn't that the—the substance your people record things on and which you put into another machine that calls forth the images from it? You told me about that, Rudy . . ."

Gil turned, still folded together on her heels, holding the gray glass polyhedrons balanced in the palm of her outstretched hand. Her voice was careless, but in the witchlight her face flamed with the brightening ecstasy of purely intellectual delight. "Yeah," she said casually. "Videotape."

Ingold let out a very un-Archmagelike whoop of delight and fell upon her, folding her, polyhedrons and all, into his arms. Rudy said, "Hunh?" Then, as his mind tardily made the connection, he nodded. "Sweet Holy Mother!"

The wizard hauled Gil to her feet. They were hugging each other and laughing like idiots with delight and scholarly triumph. Gil jabbed a gloved and bony finger at Rudy. "And that's why there are those little crystal tables in those observation rooms near where there are labs or machinery. They put them there so they could read the manuals!"

"You're right!" Rudy yelled, swept away by the blaze of their enthusiasm. "Christ, Gil, you're a genius!" He threw his arms around her and kissed her heartily on the mouth. Carried away by delight, he repeated the process on the mystified Alde. "Hell, with all the wizards in the Keep, there's got to be somebody who can figure out how to get them working!"

Then they were all talking at once, as if a time limit had been placed upon their words. In gabbling chorus, Rudy and Gil explained the theory behind videotape to Minalde, Ingold speculated upon the connection between the tables and the crystals, and Gil cursed her own stupidity for not having come to her conclusions sooner. In the dual radiance of the wizards' staffs, her sharp, sensitive face seemed to glow, the glacial reserve breaking to reveal the curious, eager beauty that lurked beneath its deceptive surface. Minalde, catching the fever from the others, was already drawing up plans for assembling and sorting the crystals from the far corners of the Keep and for categorizing them, her white, slender hands sweeping the air as if she would summon them all before her by gesture alone. For a moment it was as if the future's darkness had been wiped away, as if no parting, no danger, no loss, existed beside the triumph and hope they shared. Arms linked around one another's necks in a kind of mutual hug, they trooped, laughing, into the pale grayness of the outer cave.

Then they stopped short, as if they had been stunned. Silhouetted against the latticed light in the cave's mouth, silent as the shadow that, for the moment, was all he seemed, was a White Raider.

Ingold's staff moved to check Gil's sword arm in the same instant that his other hand closed on Rudy's wrist. "No," he told them softly. "If the Raiders had wanted us dead, we would never have seen them."

For a long moment the Raider did not move, an enigmatic blue shape against the matte brightness beyond. The shadows hid his expression, but a cold gleam of reflected daylight slid along the ivory braids as he tilted his head, like a leopard at leisure on a branch, making up its mind about an approaching deer. A little knife of wind rattled the tangled trees outside and ruffled at the wolf pelts he wore.

Then he said, "My people are right," in a light, breathless voice that shocked Gil by its familiarity. "They say that it takes a brave man to befriend a Wise Man; and so it seems."

Gil cried, *"Icefalcon!"*

"Your people are right," Ingold said formally, though a deep delight had begun to dance in his eyes. "It seems that the talisman I gave you, the Rune of the Veil, brought danger rather than safety with it, since Stiarth of Alketch contrived to murder you for it. I am pleased to see that his efforts were attended by the usual degree of success that one has in trying to kill Raiders."

The Icefalcon stepped into the cave. He was as thin as a starved wolf, wind-bronzed, yet that same aloof, faintly arrogant captain of the Guards whom Alwir had sent to bear the messages to the Empire of Alketch.

He looked down his cool nose at Gil. "Do I take this delight to mean that there was money in the barracks on my survival?" he inquired.

She grinned. "Not a copper. We'd given you up."

Feigned concern widened the colorless eyes. "Not reassigned my bunk to someone else?"

Gil shook her head regretfully. "No one would take it. Even after Janus swore by all that's holy that it had been fumigated."

Anyone less haughty would have grinned, but Gil could tell by his eyes that he was pleased to see her. "And what is this thing?" he asked, indicating the flame thrower with a flick of his fingers.

With a flourish, Rudy drew, aimed at the far wall, and let loose a leaping column of fire that splattered from the stone and left a great charred patch.

"Random," was all the Icefalcon said. He turned back to Ingold, leaving Rudy stuttering with indignation.

The wind had turned icy when they emerged from the cave, stinging their faces and blowing brief, hard flurries of sleet down from the darkening sky. It clattered in the small bones that the Icefalcon had braided into his long hair. Boiled and picked clean, Gil thought, but disconcertingly like . . .

"Are those human handbones?"

His enigmatic eyes looked almost silver against the gold windburn of his face. "When I became a Guard," he said inconsequentially, "I vowed that I would become a civilized person and learn to fight honorably in a civilized fashion. These are the bones of a man who came upon me when I lay near death, after our civilized friend Stiarth of Alketch— parted company from me. I begged this man for water and he stole my boots and my cloak." The Icefalcon shrugged. "Later my sisters and brothers, the barbarians of the White Lakes People, found me and healed me, and I rode with them for a time, though their people and mine were enemies in the plains. They helped me to—recover my cloak and boots."

A sleety gust of wind rattled the bones in his hair.

Gil stopped and raised her head to listen, having caught some sound over the growing cry of the wind. The straggling ends of her braided black hair fluttered around her face in the streaming currents of cold air that some trick of the cliffs' geology funneled through the gap between that oddly broken rock spur and the knoll. From here the Keep was visible, stabbing like a fractured bone end through the mucky wound of turned-up dirt, mud, fences, and trash that surrounded it.

"Is that—thunder?" she asked.

The others were also listening now to that faint, deep roar that underlay the keening of the wind like a bass note. The high shriek of the coming storm drowned it; then it sounded again, a throbbing in the air, more felt than heard.

Ingold drew his hood over his head. "At a guess," he said quietly, "it is the drums of the Army of Alketch. They should be on the road up the mountains now, and they will be at the Keep itself tomorrow."

The party in the barracks was long over. Gill wasn't certain how late the Icefalcon's welcome-home festivities had broken up, or even whether it was still last night or this morning. In the darkness of the Keep, time had little meaning, and here, in the hidden lower levels, there was not even the solitary tread of a patrolling Guard to mark the watches of day and night.

On the black stone table before her lay two heaps of crystals—frost-gray polyhedrons the size and shape of the glowstones, of a material identical to that of the table's circular central inset. She wondered why that had never occurred to her before.

From the larger pile she took a crystal at random, sighed, and automatically scratched the number 14 on the wax note tablet that lay at her elbow. Then she set the crystal before her, covering it with both her hands, and repeated in a clear, painstaking voice the words that Minalde had spoken in her trance, the words of unlocking. The sharp edges of the polygon pressed into her palms as she leaned forward to look into the table's faintly glowing core.

For a moment she saw nothing but the edge of her own

huge shadow lying across the table and the dim reflected gleam of the light of the single glowstone she'd brought here with her. Around her, the black walls of the observation chamber formed a narrow circle of darkness. The silence was absolute. She cleared her mind, as Ingold had instructed her, stared into the angles of the crystal's heart, and waited.

Then something glittered deep below her, a flash of brightness that resolved itself into the blinding flicker of sunlight on water. Like dark knife blades, oars broke the blazing wake, and she saw a barge, carved over every inch of its surface and riding low in the smooth water under the weight of its own gilding. The oars stroked again, and the sun smote Gil's eyes. The colors seemed to intensify. Bright-hued birds flew up in startled explosions from the lotus patches that grew thick on the marshy shores. The barge put about, banking neatly before water-stairs of black-veined pink marble.

There was movement on the stairs, eerily silent, of men and women naked to the waist, their bronzed shoulders darkly gleaming under jeweled collars and pectorals. The breeze from across the lagoon rippled in the elaborate frills and tuckings of long gauze skirts and shifted the rainbow-dyed curls of servants who bore a carrying chair whose design Gill half-recognized. The style was sinuous, carved with winding lines of hearts, eyes, and diamonds, like the furniture she and Alde had found in the most ancient storerooms in the Keep.

Gil was not sure whether this was an intelligence report, a documentary, a manual, or the opening chapters of a novel, or what the date was, or the historical context. But she knew that she looked into the Times Before.

A haughty bishop descended from the barge, the Earth Cross of the Faith embroidered in bullion and sardonyx on the edges of his frilled white loincloth. Jewels flashed from white, unworked hands and from the earlobes and nostrils; people moved about, amid a bobbing of ostrich plumes; some kind of rite was clearly in progress. Gil noted that, though the bishop was shaven bald, all the others wore their hair as long as they could, braided into elaborate coiffures such as Minalde wore on ceremonial occasions, plumed, flowered, or jeweled. Beneath the eye paint and rouge, the faces of the audience on the steps looked bored to death, and Gil saw that they flirted among themselves whenever the bishop's head was turned, or else covertly eyed one another's outfits.

Govannin's words came back to her, with the memory of soft chanting among the tiered darkness of the great Sanctuary. *I have heard that the men of the Times Before were evil and that in their pride and their splendor they practiced abominations* . . . One man in a padded, sunshine-yellow silk loincloth produced an ivory eyebrow comb and made minute adjustments with the aid of a mirrored ring on his little finger. A youth with lilies coiled in his blue-dyed hair noticed him and blew him a kiss. Sunlight glittered on the waters of the lagoon; parrots fluttered among the garlands that hung the marble colonnade along the shore. Gold flashed on the bishop's white, upraised hands.

Beyond the pillars, past the myrtle trees and arbors of roses, Gil had a glimpse of mountains, blue and close and shawled with a thin lace of snow . . .

Mountains she had seen before.

Where?

It was difficult to be sure because of the trees and the domes and turrets of the city in the distance. But a sense of familiarity pulled at her—a memory of ruined streets, of fallen and smoke-blackened walls, and of the buzzing, crawling stink of decay. Hadn't she turned to look over her shoulder once, her bones aching with the jarring jog of the exhausted cart horse she rode? Hadn't she glimpsed those mountains, standing just so, above the corpse of a despoiled city?

Those were the mountains that stood above the plain of Gae.

Frowning, Gil turned her eyes from the crystal at the center of the table, and the bright images before her died.

She sat for a long moment, staring into the darkness that seemed to press upon her from the walls of that narrow room.

This isn't how it's supposed to be, she told herself numbly. *We were supposed to find the ancient records of the Times*

Before, and there it would be in black and white or in this case in living color—the Answer. How to Demolish Dark Ones. (See: Secret Weapons, Specs. Appendix A.)

But of course that's stupid. When the Dark Ones hit, civilization probably lost all capability of making record crystals. There won't be any of these made after the coming of the Dark.

She pressed her hands to her head, her fingers tangling in her coarse, unruly hair, her palms cold against her scalp. *Why do I care?* she wondered, rather rhetorically, for she knew perfectly well why she cared. *I'm going to be leaving this bloody universe to its own devices in a little under ten days, and the whole thing should be nothing to me.*

But the thought of leaving, rather than bringing her joy as it once had done, stabbed her with nostalgia and a kind of hurtful, ambiguous grief. She fought a weak longing to bury her face in her arms and weep. Instead, she picked up a stick of charcoal, marked the number 14 on the bottom of the latest crystal, and etched on her tablet, "14-relig. crmny—Gae?"

Hard work is the novocaine of the soul.

"Spook?"

She looked up to see Rudy silhouetted against the darkness of the doorway. He hesitated in the narrow aperture, his Aztec cheekbones and broken nose thrown into curious, craggy shadows by the pallid light of the glowstone, his coarse, homespun shirt sleeves pale against his sheepskin vest. In a fit of annoyance against the multiple layerings of shirt, tunic, breeches, surcoat, doublet, and cloak, Rudy had recently reconstructed a sort of ski vest for himself that would keep him warm but leave his arms free for work in the labs. In a reminiscence of his old Pachuco days, he'd painted on its back his private omen, a child's hand clutching a flowering branch, barbaric yet strangely beautiful, in a circle of stars.

"Did you—did you find anything?" he asked hesitantly.

For an answer, Gil flung her stylus against the opposite wall. "Nothing," she whispered. "Bloody nothing. There wasn't one of these things made after the coming of the Dark."

Rudy was silent, He, too, had expected to find the answer cross-indexed under *World, Saving of*.

"Christ, Rudy, what are we going to do?"

"Do?" His voice was suddenly bitter and grating. "We're going to get the hell out of here before the ax falls. We meant to do that once, remember?"

"And never know?" she asked.

He closed his eyes, fighting pain with cynicism, the only weapon he had ever had. "And never know," he affirmed quietly.

CHAPTER SEVEN

The booming of kettledrums echoed like thunder against the ice-pure silence of the Vale of Renweth. Above it, like the thin cry of wind, Gil could distinguish the high, mellow sweetness of horns.

It seemed to her that every man, woman, and child in the Keep was gathered before those black walls, carpeting the hill of execution with its sinister, chain-hung pillars and blackening the snow of the lower meadow. A shifting lake of humanity spread out beyond the lines of the Guards, the ranked masses of the scarlet troops of Alwir's private corps, the Church regiments, and the long, disorderly row of the Gettlesand rangers. Now and then gusts of talk would swell over that close-packed, uneasy body and spread like wind ripples to its edges—rumor, speculation, and fears. Only at the end of the Guards' rank, where Gil stood on the lowest step of the Keep, was there silence, centered upon the Guards' burly Commander Janus and the old man who sat on the ground at his feet.

At length Ingold stood up and put away the yellowish crystal into whose depths he had been peering. "I make their numbers some three thousand," he said, brushing the snow from his robe.

Janus did some rapid calculation in his head. "We've over half that strength here of fighting men, not counting volunteers. Even with the flame throwers, it will be a near thing."

To that Ingold did not reply.

The drums boomed louder, an insistent, throbbing rhythm that seemed to engulf flesh and bone, and someone in the lower meadows cried out as the first glittering ranks of the Army of Alketch broke through the trees.

Except for the small corps of halberdiers, the Army of the South was composed solely of men; an Imperial Army, gleaned from the half-dozen races that acknowledged the sway of the lord who sat in Khirsrit. It emerged from the woods like a gilded serpent, spined with spears, rank after rank of haggard, grim-faced men who had fought their way here from beyond the swampy ruins of the Penambra Delta through hundreds of miles of freezing, haunted countryside. From the crowd in the meadow a cheer rose, sweeping all the watchers, echoing against the flat walls of the Keep.

Gil had to admit that they were a brave sight, these stern and hard-faced men beneath the gaudy rainbow of banners, and the roar of the drums and wave after breaking wave of the sound of horns would have stirred the coldest blood. But she could see that Ingold was not cheering, and the ranks of Penambra and Gettlesand were silent.

Like the shrill whinny of stallion answering stallion, horns sounded in the passage of the Keep gates. Looking up, Gil saw them emerge, remote and hieratic as chess pieces beneath a black velvet canopy—Alwir, Minalde, Prince Altir Endorion, Maia, and Govannin, scarcely human at all in their formal robes; the cold, brittle daylight sparkled on the bullion embroidery of their pennants, on ivory and ebony, opal, sapphire, and pearl.

The honor guard that surrounded them blew a final blast on its trumpets. Before them, the kettledrums fell silent. Hooves scrunched daintily in the crusted snow as a white horse emerged from the front ranks, and Gil recognized upon its back that graceful young courtier who had tried to murder the Icefalcon—Ambassador Stiarth of Alketch, clothed in primrose satin and gilded chain mail. Dismounting, he bent himself almost double in a deep salaam.

"My lord," he said in his lilting voice, "my lady. I greet you in the name of the Emperor of Alketch."

Minalde stepped forward, opals flickering like chains of misty stars in the coils of her hair. Carefully, but with a grave confidence possibly imparted to him by his stiff-cut brocade gown, Tir toddled at her side, one fat, pink hand clutching hers. Gil was conscious of Rudy standing beside Ingold, his face glowing like a two-hundred-watt bulb with pride.

Alde's voice carried clearly in the silence. "In the name of my son Altir Endorion, Lord of the Keep of Dare and heir to the Realm of Darwath, I greet you, and through you, your Imperial Uncle, the Emperor of the South and the Lord of the Seven Isles. I bid you welcome as guests in this Realm and to this fortress."

Stiarth bowed again. Another man, both taller and stockier than the slender Ambassador, dismounted and handed the reins of his charger to a kneeling groom. Then he, too, stepped forward and made his obeisance. "My gracious thanks for your greetings, my lady Minalde," he said, his voice harsh as unpolished stone under the lisping accent of the South. "I am Vair na Chandros of the Imperial House of Khirsrit, and I greet you in the name of the head of my House, Lirkwis Fardah Ezrikos, Emperor of the South and Lord of the Seven Isles, whose name and ancestors are revered from the White Coasts to the Black and on all the Islands of the Ocean. I am designated Commander of this expedition—and your humble servant."

Straightening up, he surveyed man, woman, and child on the steps before him with eyes that were cold, honey-colored, and anything but humble. Like Stiarth of Alketch, Vair na Chandros was black-skinned, his features haughty and aquiline, more Arabic or Pakistani, Gil thought, than Negroid. His hair reminded her of an Arab's, thick and closely curled, silvered to pewter but still retaining a few streaks of black. His one hand, the left, rested on the turquoise-crusted hilt of his cross-hung sword. His right arm ended in an ivory stump, equipped with two steel hooks inlaid with silver. The metal glinted palely in the cold daylight as he introduced the third of the men who had ridden at the head of the Army.

In contrast to these dark members of the Imperial House, this man was of the ivory-fair race of the Isles, his eyebrows over his green eyes proclaiming that, before he had entered the Church and shaved his head, he had been red-haired. Like Maia and Govannin, he wore the arcane white of the

112

High Church panoply; he was a tall, kindly-faced, elderly man whom Vair introduced as Pinard Tzarion, Inquisitor-General of the Army of Alketch.

"Aye," Gil heard one of the Guards in the back ranks mutter in a thick north-country brogue, "come to make sure we're all in t' Faith proper."

"As long as we fight their battles for them," Gnift's rather hoarse voice replied, "they don't care if we worship sticks and old bottles. So," he added maliciously, "you can breathe easy, Caldern, my pear blossom."

"Garn to your sticks and old bottles. If they'll eat our porridge, they best not squeak over t'grace we says."

"They best not," Melantrys' purring voice agreed, "but what will you bet they do?"

Odds were given—Gil had long ago learned that the Guards would bet on anything—while, on the steps of the Keep, Alwir was continuing his gracious welcome, looking like Lucifer in his Sunday-best. The hook-handed Vair did not seem pleased about bivouacking his men a mile and a half from the Keep, but Stiarth smiled suavely and said, "Of course this excepts our personal bodyguards, servants, and key members of the General Staff—a minor point which you must forgive my even mentioning, since certainly that was your intent."

"Indeed it was," Alwir beamed, with a determined amiability that reminded Gil of the old tale of the Spartan youth and the fox.

Stiarth tested his boundaries. "The way there is not too rocky for you to send the daily rations to the troops? But naturally, it wouldn't be."

"It's a matter that will have to be discussed," the Chancellor informed him affably.

"Ah!" White teeth flashed in his dark face. "But then, so much will."

Vair na Chandros barked a summons, and an officer came hurrying from the ranks, scarlet plumes nodding in the thin, snaking wind. He rasped a string of orders in the singsong tongue of the South; the man bowed deeply and effaced himself. In a moment the drums began again, a deep, hollow booming that vibrated in Gil's bones. The ranks began to move, following the men whom Alwir had appointed as guides. Cold sunlight flashed upon their spears.

"My lord Vair's—incapacity—has ever prevented him from the field generalship that was his chosen career," Stiarth purred, as he and those around him on the steps watched the hook-handed Commander summon the bodyguards forth from the main host. "But his years as Prefect of Khirsrit, and in particular his expeditious handling of the autumn food riots in the city, have given him more than ample experience to head these forces. I'm sure you will find him an able military co-Commander, my lord Alwir." His dark, slender fingers toyed with the ruffles of his extravagant gloves. "But I am nominal head of the Expeditionary Force. It is with me that you will negotiate the final terms of the treaty of alliance with my uncle."

Alwir's sapphire gaze cut sharply sideways at him. "I had thought, my lord Stiarth, that the final terms had already been negotiated."

The Ambassador sighed. "So had I, regretfully. But upon returning to the South, I received new instructions from my Imperial Uncle. It has been a bad winter in the South as in the North. Though we have not, of course, experienced the depredations of the Dark Ones, the harsh weather has caused crop failures, and many troops that my uncle would otherwise gladly have committed to your aid were needed to suppress unrest." He looked up, the diamonds in his earlobes glinting no less brightly than his teeth. "But with good faith on both sides, all things are possible, are they not?"

"Indeed they are."

The last time Gil had seen a smile like that, it had been on the face of the loser of a tennis championship as he'd shaken hands with the winner.

Commander Vair returned to the group at the foot of the steps, the wan sun winking off the polished chain of his gilded mail and the rainbow hues of his brocaded surcoat and cloak, making him appear like some deadly, scintilla:.: tropical fish against the dull, muddy background of dirt and snow. With his hooks he gestured for Inquisitor Pinard, as a prelate of the Church, to preceed him up the Keep steps. But the motion froze in mid-gesture. His expression hardened and his pale eyes gleamed suddenly with the red glint of a hatred long cherished.

He had caught sight of Ingold, standing among the Guards near the bottom of the steps.

"You . . ." he whispered.

He came forward slowly, and the murmur of talk that had risen among the Guards at the mention of the Alketch bodyguard's being admitted to the Keep faded to utter silence. The silver hooks flashed as he lashed out with them. Without any seeming haste, Ingold intercepted them on the iron-hard wood of his staff. The wizard's brows were drawn down, his face puzzled.

The Commander whispered, "So you don't remember, do you?"

With considerably more haste than tact, Alwir intervened. "My lord Vair," he introduced. "Ingold Inglorion, the head of the Wizards' Corps and the Archmage—" His voice flourished almost mockingly over the tattered title. "—of the Wizards of the Western World."

Vair spat the words. "We've met."

And suddenly, Ingold's eyes widened with startled recognition.

The Commander went on bitterly. "So you were a mage all the time." His hooks clattered against the wood of Ingold's staff. "I should have known I lost my hand and all my chance for a life of glory through a wizard's tricks."

Ingold sighed. There was regret in his voice, but he never relaxed his guard against the dragon-bright warrior standing before him. "It was no magic that let me overcome you, my lord Commander," he said quietly. "I was no mage then, and if anything, you had the advantage of me."

"You were never my superior with a sword!" Vair lashed out. "You were a man grown. Fledgling Archmages don't come to their power so late in life." He turned to the discomfitted Alwir, his lip pulling back from his white teeth in scorn. "So this is your—ally," he rasped. "Your weapon against the Dark. See that it doesn't turn and cost you the hand that wields it, my lord."

So saying, the Commander thrust his way past those who

stood on the steps and climbed to the gates, where Stiarth waited with a look of calculation in his eyes and Pinard with one of I-told-you-so. After one glance of bitter hatred at Ingold, Alwir hurried to catch up, and his fluent, melodious voice could be heard drifting placatingly back as they disappeared into the darkness of the Keep.

The sun would set soon. From her position on the high ground, where the track to the caves passed between the rock spur and the knoll in the forest, Gil could see the activity around the Keep. Men and women were coming in from the woods with cut kindling on their backs. Those fortunate enough to be possessors of cows or goats moved about the heavily fenced pens and byres to do their evening milking. The wind stung her cheeks like acid. It was time she returned.

To what? she wondered.

She had spent the day combing the secret levels of the Keep, gathering record crystals. She knew that she would likely spend the night reading them patiently, one by one. Body and bones hurt for sleep, but she was aware that the Winter Feast was less than two weeks away, and after that the army would march, with the riddle of the Dark's former defeat still unsolved. So she had opted for a walk in the freezing air insted, and the promise—which had gotten her through her master's thesis at UCLA last year—that she could sleep when she'd done a little work.

Wolves were howling in the high Vale, and Gil spared a thought for horses of the Alketch and the cattle they had brought as part of their provisions. Well, they'd protected them thus far. But she drew her cloak more closely about her shoulders and hurried down the broad, trampled track that led back toward the Keep. The temperature was dropping—the soupy muck churned up by the feet of the army was already freezing. From somewhere above the gray, constant cloud-cover, winds sneered down from the glaciers.

"Gil-Shalos!"

The gray mists between the trees seemed to thicken, materializing into the Icefalcon's tall form. He fell into step with her, one pale eyebrow lifting. "Strolling?"

"Picking buttercups," she replied, and he grinned.

Clothed once more in the familiar black uniform of the Guards, he seemed to be as Gil had first known him, back in the noisy chaos of Karst. He'd gotten rid of the bones in his hair; his long white braids hung smootly over his back. In fact, the only signs that he'd ridden with the Raiders at all were the slight darkening of his fair skin and the wariness in his eyes.

"I, too, seek buttercups," he said quietly. "Only I have sought them farther along the cliffs, near the pool under the caves."

Gil said, "Stiarth isn't there."

The fine chiseled nostrils flared slightly. "He will be, one day." Like a cat, the Icefalcon picked his way around an ice-scummed puddle in the road, his boots making barely a sound in the decayed snow at the track's edge. "And when he is, believe me, my sister, he will pray for even half the poison that he dumped into my food that night in the river valley."

"I wondered how he'd done it," she said after a time.

The Raider sniffed. "I am not certain whether he meant me to die of the dose, or whether it was only to make me sleep. In the open ground in the valleys, it makes no odds." The colorless eyes glittered suddenly, like dirty ice. "He had been better to make sure of his job."

Gil sighed. She would not say so, for she knew that the Icefalcon had brushed sleeves with death, but it was in her mind that if Stiarth were to die, Vair na Chandros would be the leader of the Alketch troops. *This doesn't concern me,* she told herself despairingly. *I'm getting out of here before the invasion, and what happens afterward is their problem.* But she remembered the hatred in Vair's eyes as he had spoken to Ingold before the doors of the Keep, and she shivered.

"You'd think Stiarth would have made sure you were dead," she remarked. "If he brought poison on the trip in the first place, he must have planned to use it."

"Not necessarily." The Icefalcon skirted a steep place in the track, leaping down a snow-covered boulder to avoid the mud-wallow made by the slipping horses of the Southerners.

"Things are very different in the South. A man in Stiarth's position carries poison as a matter of course."

For some reason, the graceful, bejeweled people of the crystal came to her mind, flirting through the ceremonies on the ancient water-stairs. Had they, too been a race of poisoners? "Tell me about the South," she said.

He shrugged. "You have seen the men. The South is a land of all colors. The people dress like popinjays. There are flowers there, orange ones with stripes or purple ones like something you see in fever dreams. Even the ants are all hues of the rainbow." His light, terse voice formed the images curiously clearly to her mind, against this snowy waste of dreary mud and somber trees.

"The Round Sea is warm; Alketch is a land of jungles, palm trees, and mile after mile of untouched white beaches. There are high mountains, like a wall in the west." His hand sketched their mist-hung skyline. "The people are all colors, too—black and red and gold. They put too much spice in their food, stink of depilatories, and treat their women like cattle. There are no Dark Ones in the South."

"Why is that?"

He shrugged again. "Ask the Dark. Ask Ingold. Ask our lady Govannin, for that matter. She will tell you it is because the Church rules the Empire, where their Straight God is better honored. There are rumors in places—but there are always rumors. Rumors of people who have disappeared, or of matters that someone else saw. But all those I spoke to in the South seem to think of the Dark Ones as a sort of plague that has befallen the North."

Gil was silent as she slopped through the shadowy woods, suddenly troubled by the half-memory of something Ingold had once said. "Yeah," she protested, "but Ungolard—the old scholar from Alketch who joined the Wizards' Corps—says there was what he thought was a Nest buried under the ruins of an old city in the jungle near his home. And he says that historically the earliest records of civilization in his part of the world don't go back much farther than they do in this one."

The pale eyebrows quirked. The Icefalcon had little use for chronicles and books. "How long does parchment last?"

he asked her. "Even words carved on stone can be broken to make way for a king's pleasure garden. The South is a warm land, and records perish easily there."

"How far back do records of your people go?" Gil countered, and he smiled.

"To the days of the gods," he replied softly. In his breathless voice she caught the echo of campfire light and shamans' songs, the taste of tundra and ice fields on the wind. His voice sank, half-chanting the words, as if they came from the distant memories of his wild boyhood among his own people. "To the days when the rain fell upon the grasses, and men stepped forth from the growing seed. To the days when the Long Songs were not made, and the List of Heroes was short. To the days when the Sun Chief fought the Wall of Ice, and drove it back to make the Sea of Grass for his people to dwell on, and caught the birds of the air in his hands, to make the horses for us to ride."

Gil frowned as some thought snagged at the back of her mind. Something in that soft, husky voice . . . something that Tomec Tirkenson had grumbled in the bitter snowfall of Sarda Pass. The hills of Gae above an arbor of tropical flowers . . . the dusty sole of a sandal, found in a midden in a cave.

She felt a stirring in her, a quickening, as images coalesced in her mind—the warm, putrid vapors of the Vale of the Dark and Minalde's night-blue eyes, tear-filled, gazing into the horrors of an earlier life . . .

Gil stopped, staring out into the gray, cold distance with unseeing eyes, as knowledge broke like an exploding star within her.

She saw it whole, a pattern resolving from meaningless shapes, and the understanding smote her like a blow. As surely as she knew her own name, Gil knew why the Dark had risen.

CHAPTER EIGHT

"The ice in the north," Ingold said quietly, folding his scarred fingers together and gazing into the distances beyond the walls of his narrow cell. "Lohiro spoke of it as he lay dying. The bitterest winter in human memory . . ." He glanced up at Gil, the movement of his shadow making the gold-leaf embellishments of his manuscripts flicker like autumn stars. "It is . . . a fantastic explanation. Can you prove it?"

"I don't know!" Gil threw up her hands in despair. Her explanation to him had taken some time, for the old man had not been familiar with the concept involved, but when she finished, his face was grave. "I know it's true. It's the only explanation that covers everything—why the Nests were deserted in the North, why they haven't risen in the South. I can't point to a single source and say, 'This is why.' But—I know."

The muscles of Ingold's jaw grew taut under the white scrub of his beard. She thought that he looked tired these days, driven and vulnerable, as if he lived with some knowledge or dread that he could scarcely endure. "Alwir won't want to hear it," he said at last. "Can you prove it, before the Winter Feast?"

"I can try."

In the days that followed, Gil was little to be seen by anyone in the Keep of Dare. Her friends in the Guards—the Icefalcon, Seya, Melantrys—spoke with her at training, which she still attended, though Janus had given her leave from regular duty. Sometimes Alde came to the little room that Gil had taken for her study in the midst of the Corps complex and spoke to her while she herself waited for Rudy to emerge from his work in the labs. Rudy visited her, too, bringing the slim ration of stew and bread from the Corps kitchen at mealtimes, and reminded her to eat. But they all found her distracted, her mind elsewhere.

Ingold helped her, as much as he was able. He was often to be found in her study, sitting cross-legged on the rug with one of the Quo chronicles on his knees, taking notes by the flickering gleam of St. Elmo's fire that burned above his head. But more often Gil worked alone, hearing the watches change in the corridors outside without much idea of whether they were day or deep-night.

Occasionally she would be seen in the Corps common room, talking to the tall Raider shaman, Shadow of the Moon, or to Ungolard, the diffident, black-skinned professor who had left the University of Khirsrit to answer Ingold's summoning. Once she buttonholed Caldern, a big, brawny north-countryman in the Guards, and asked him questions regarding his childhood; once she spent most of an evening in the fourth-level Church, where Maia ruled his gaudy slums of garlic-eating Penambrans, taking notes and listening while that lanky, gentle prelate told her things without asking why she wished to know.

One evening while the other mages were playing ball-and-ring-toss with moving fireballs in the commons, she took Kta aside, and he told her, in his rambling, piping voice, of certain strange matters that he had seen with his own eyes during the endless years of silence in the Gettlesand deserts, or of things that the dooic had told him.

"I didn't know that dooic could tell anyone anything," Gil said, looking up, startled, from her notes.

"No more can they," Dame Nan's voice crackled from the curtained doorway of the kitchen. The old witch poked her head around the curtain of gray burlap, her pale eyes glittering with malicious challenge. "Dooic are speechless beasts, for all that old faker may clatter on about them. I'd drive them away from my dooryard with a broom, the cowardly, rotten, thieving lizard eaters."

"Do you drive them off with a broom," Kta retorted with shrill indignation, "no wonder they will never speak."

"They've no more speech in their tongues than my donkey," she snapped.

"At least they use not tongues for malicious speech as old women do," the hermit returned, his black-current eyes sparkling with entertainment.

"Pah!"

"Pooh!"

Witch and hermit made ritual spell-throwing gestures at each other, and Dame Nan vanished behind her curtains as suddenly as she had appeared. Sitting on the far corner of the hearth and plying her needle, Kara only sighed. A moment later Dame Nan could be heard cursing her kitchen fire, which had unaccountably gone out.

Other evenings Gil spent in the little observation chamber near Rudy's lab, staring into the crystal table, one hand on the latest of her growing collection of record crystals and the other jotting what notes she could concerning that bright and beautiful world of sunlight, intrigue, and flowers. Upon occasion Rudy came into her study and found her, her feet propped amid the shoals of Church records, borrowed from Govannin, and iron-locked, spell-twined chronicles salvaged from the ruined library of Quo, reading one or the other of the old romantic novels that Minalde had brought from the library at Alwir's villa in Karst in preference to worthier tomes.

Because the books had belonged to the Royal House of Gae, they bore the High King's crest, the gold eagle stamped into the black leather of their well-worn covers.

Gil thought about Eldor while she sat in the silence of her study, listening to the murmur of Thoth's voice instructing the junior mages in the common room or to the haunting, rain-pure music of Rudy's harp. She thought about her one sight of the man, tall and austere, the candlelight flickering from the gold eagle embroidered on his black surcoat as he stook gazing down at his sleeping son. The cold of that miserable night came back to her—how she had shivered in the shadows of the window embrasure and watched the rubies in the hilt of his sword twinkling like stars in the dim light with the movement of his breath. *A King has a right,* he had said, *to die with his country* . . . He had only asked that Ingold save his son.

Ingold *had* saved his son, she thought to herself. The Palace had fallen; the following morning Janus had pried that ruby-hilted sword from the burned hand of an unrecognizable corpse and brought to the refugees at Karst the news that their King was dead.

It had been the night of the Palace's fall that Alde and so many others had been carried off as prisoners to the underground realms of the Dark, the night Alde had been rescued on the brink of those hideous stairs by the Icefalcon and a handful of Guards. *No wonder,* she decided wearily, *Alde was off her head for forty-eight hours with grief and horror.* The wonder of it was that she'd survived at all. But Alde, Gil had long since come to know, had unsuspected reserves of toughness beneath her timid and gentle compassion.

This was an ugly and disquieting time. The rumors relayed to Gil by the Guards were conflicting and largely improbable: the Southerners were planning to return home without risking themselves in the battle for Gae; Vair had a second army waiting to attack the Keep the moment its defenders had departed with the first; Gae would be held in the Emperor's name when it was retaken; Alwir had sworn fealty to the svelte Ambassador; plans were afoot to assassinate the Chancellor and establish Govannin in a theocracy. No sooner was one rumor quashed than three others sprang up in its stead, and all of them, Gil sensed, carried the ugly taint of mistrust and schism.

Alde did what she could to counter the rumors, spending much of her time on the fourth and fifth levels, where Tomec Tirkenson's rangers were bunking on floors, in halls, and in storerooms among the already overcrowded Penambran refugees. But Gil could see that Alde was pushed to the end of her tether. She and Rudy had ceased altogether to meet in her rooms in the Royal Sector; as the days went by she would more and more often wait for him in Gil's study. The strain was telling on her, and there was a fevered desperation in her meetings with Rudy that made Gil's heart ache.

Rumor was not the only evil in the Keep in those days.

123

The bitter animosity felt by all the people of Darwath against the men of Alketch was returned in kind and fourfold. The bodyguards of Stiarth and Vair were always in the Keep, and by day the southern troops, who drilled with Alwir's forces under a joint command, came and went freely.

The hatred was felt particularly among the Gettlesand rangers and among the Penambrans, who had lived along the borderlands of the southern Empire. There were rangers whose families had been butchered or enslaved by the borderlords of Alketch and Penambrans whose houses and goods had been ravaged by Imperial freebooters along the warm, mosquito-ridden coasts of the Round Sea. Bitter fights became common, and revenge was not always taken directly on the instigating parties.

Racial and political hatred was not the sole cause of contention. Few camp followers had dared to accompany the Army north. Ugly stories began to circulate of women or young boys raped, either in the woods or in the back corridors of the Keep itself, so that it was considered dangerous to go about alone. Three flat-faced Delta Islanders ambushed Gil one night as she returned from visiting Alde in the Royal Sector; she told Janus of it only so that everyone's story would be straight when the bodies were finally found.

Enclaves formed. No Southerner, whatever his business, ventured above the third level of the Keep. Ingold was the only wizard who would go into the Church-ruled mazes at the east end of the Keep, where Govannin and the Inquisitor Pinard kept their council among Pinard's shaven, silent warrior-monks, and Gil found herself prey to growing uneasiness every time he did so. Old statutes regarding the spheres of power of Church and civil government were hauled from Govannin's cherished library and debated hotly in Council. Moreover, Gil became aware of a song in circulation among the Guards regarding the sexual proclivities of the Alketch leadership; since she recognized the tune, there was no doubt as to its source. The lilting march was whistled at all hours in the corridors by the deep-night watch and did nothing to remedy matters.

"I don't know how much more of this I can stand," Minalde said one evening, sitting on the ramskin-covered bench by Gil's desk with her child asleep at her side. "It's like waiting for lightning to strike and not knowing where. I know they hold 'informal' Council meetings, Alwir and Stiarth. They present me with things to sign that they've clearly negotiated between themselves, and there's nothing I can do about it." Her fingers curled restlessly at the fleece of her vest—a ski vest Rudy had made for her, like his own, painted with the black and gold eagle of the House of Dare. "I feel so helpless."

Gil was silent. Her idle scratch-pen picked herringbone patterns in the wax of the note tablet before her; the shadows of her fingers were black and bony over the translucent, creamy surface. From outside in the common room, they heard Dame Nan's gibing voice and Tomec Tirkenson's disgusted cry: "Let be, woman! Can't I say hello to your daughter without you scratching at me like a broody hen?"

Gil raised her eyes to meet Alde's. "Your brother's set on this alliance, isn't he?"

Alde sighed and brushed the hair back from her face. Her white, too-slender fingers looked like bones against the thick braids. "He's like a—a man in love, Gil. You know Stiarth came north with gifts, things we haven't had since Gae fell—bolts of velvet and musical instruments, scissors and books. He gave me these . . ."

She drew her dark skirt hem aside, to show beneath her white petticoat the pointed toes of slippers of heliotrope satin, brocaded and stitched with pearls. "Alwir goes on for hours about trade with the South, about renewing the civilization we've lost, once we've taken Gae. Alwir always wanted things to be the best, you know. He loves the fine things, the beauties of civilization. He's an aesthete at heart. The crudities of living here at the Keep rankle him like a sore. You know it. You've seen him."

Gil reflected upon the Chancellor's immaculate tailoring, the fineness with which he surrounded himself, and the scent of soap and perfume. Being this pedestal of perfection had served to set him apart from his increasingly shabby subjects. But she had also noticed that Alde, in her peasant skirts and painted ski vest, had lost none of her subjects' hearts.

"But it isn't only that," Alde went on quietly. "If we're going to try to retake anything from the Dark, it has to be now. Who knows what will happen by spring? Of all the landchiefs of the Realm, only Tomec Tirkenson answered Alwir's call, and we know at least four others survived. Alwir's right in one thing—if we can retake the cornlands around Gae, we can establish some kind of alliance with Alketch based on trade, rather than face them next year as our invaders."

Gil bit back a cynical remark and carefully began to crosshatch the patterns she had scratched in the wax.

Witchlight brightened into the room, twinkling on the grainy edges of the piled record crystals. Rudy entered, disheveled and unshaven, his eyes red from strain, his hands and face marked with soot that he'd washed off without the aid of a mirror.

"Hi, spook," he greeted Gil, then bent to kiss Alde, drawing her up into his arms in a mingled fever of joy and grief.

Waking, Tir raised eager arms and cooed sleepily, " 'Udy! 'Udy!"

With a wry grin, Rudy went to pick him up. "What's your mom been feeding you, Pugsley, rocks? Everybody in the Keep's griping about food and swiping food from each other, and you just keep on getting fatter. How come that, hunh?"

Tir only laughed joyously. The accusation was hardly true, for he was a small baby and gave promise of growing into a boy as slim and compact as his mother. As far as anyone could ascertain, he was absolutely fearless, his increased mobility—he could toddle, after a fashion—simply widening his scope for adventures.

"I think we've just about killed the supply of firing chambers." Rudy sighed, sinking down on the bench beside Alde and rubbing his eyes. "We've come up with a total of fifty-two, and that's by searching the storerooms from top to bottom. There are nearly eighty in the firesquad; we'll have to use the extra people as alternates. This inventor noise is for the birds," he added, as Alde stood behind him and kneaded his shoulders with her fingertips. "I shoulda stayed at Wild David's Paint and Body."

"Is it true the Ambassador has asked for a demonstration of the firesquad?" Alde asked.

"Melantrys is already drilling her people for it," Rudy replied, his eyes closed in ecstasy. "Have you ever thought of going into back rubs as a profession? I'll have something ready for his Nibs in a day or so." He reached up, stilling Alde's hands, and opened his eyes to look up into hers. "He's worried about his troops," he explained unnecessarily. "Christ, I'm worried, too."

With very good reason, Gil thought, *but she held her peace.* After they had gone, she sat for a long time, thinking of Rudy and Alde, of the Winter Feast, and of the Dark. Silence settled upon the black mazes around her. The glowstone on her desk cast her shadow huge and hard on the grimy wall behind her, picked out, as that white light had a way of doing, every splinter and nick in the grain of her wooden table, and edged every parchment in shadow, every crystal in light. It showed up the dirtiness and pokiness of the tiny room, the claustrophobic atmosphere that Gil had begun to grow used to—the lack of furniture, the trestle table, the heaps of furs, the worn straw pallets, and the frayed edge of her surcoat sleeve. A faint odor of cooking grease and unwashed bodies pervaded everything. *No wonder,* she thought, *that Alwir finds himself seduced by purple satin slippers and a steady supply of soap. He's probably the only man with a stock of whole clothes in the Keep. God knows where he came up with the banners he used to greet Vair. But he knows his supplies are limited.*

As a historian, Gil was too familiar with the economic domination of a depressed, underpopulated, and largely rural area by a wealthy manufacturing one. *And what's more,* she thought, *Alwir wouldn't half mind being someone's satrap, if he could do it with comfort and prestige. Better a rich man's house nigger than a starving poor white.*

A sound came to her ears from somewhere in the cells that surrounded her study. It was very late, and the other sounds of the Corps HQ had sunk away into silence and sleep.

Otherwise, distant and muffled as the sound was, Gil would never have heard it. But it came to her, faint yet startling in its harsh violence—the sound of a man crying.

Gil sat for a moment, disquieted and almost ashamed. Like most unmarried women, she had never seen a man weep and she felt a horrible sense of eavesdropping, more shameful than if she had overheard the sounds of lovemaking. It wasn't inconceivable that someone of that enchanted rabble who occupied the surrounding cells would have the horrors and regrets of a destroyed home to mourn. And she had seen for herself the look that lurked behind the eyes of all those who had been down into the Nests.

But the despair and horror of that heartbroken sobbing drove her away, and she abandoned her research and her study to seek the silence of the common room. Such grief was none of her business. She knew that, if ever she were driven to weep as that man wept, she would sure as hell not like to think that she was being overheard.

It was almost pitch-dark in the common room. The muted flicker of writhing embers showed where the hearth lay, but it illuminated nothing. Gil stumbled against a chair, catching herself on its curved back, and spared a curse for wizards who saw so effortlessly in the dark.

The only other light in the room was the marshfire flicker of bluish light that outlined the curtain of Ingold's cubicle. As she approached it, she could hear the soft scratching of his pen.

"My dear." He held out his hands to her as she came in, the frayed brown mantle that he had draped shawlwise about his shoulders sliding down over the back of his intricately carved and much-mended chair. As always, his hands were warm; and as always, his touch seemed to transmit to her some of his buoyant strength. For a moment, he studied the marks of fatigue on her face, the bruised look to the eyelids, and the sharpness of that hard, delicate bone structure, but said nothing; he was too much a night owl himself to comment. But he cleared a place for her to sit in the confusion of the corner of his desk top and went to the narrow hearth to pour her some tea.

Gil looked down at the parchment upon which he was

128

working. Spaghettilike in their intricacy, the tunnels and caverns of a map of the Nest writhed over the page. She looked up at the old man kneeling beside the hearth, the warm light seeming to shine through his extended hands. "You don't think Alwir's going to buy it, do you?"

Ingold glanced up. "Do you?"

Gil was shocked. "He has to," she protested. "I have proof—dammit, I have a truckload of proof! He can't just disregard it!"

The wizard got stiffly to his feet and came back to her, wraiths of steam curling around his face like mephitic smoke. "Perhaps not," he assented. "I hope not. You see, I was not deceived by the Icefalcon's glib nonanswers. He was brought here by a band of White Raiders, and I suspect that band is still somewhere in the Vale. They'll know how many men depart for the Nest at Gae and they'll know how many return."

Gil sat looking up into his face for a moment—the flat, curiously shaped cheekbones and the determined chin outlined by the glow from the hearth. She felt, as she had often felt, that she had known that face forever.

"Ingold," she asked quietly, "why are the Dark Ones after you? I asked you that once before, when you left for Quo last autumn. I think you've found out the answer since then."

He evaded her eyes. "I don't know," he replied, his voice almost inaudible. "I used to think it was because of something that I knew. Now I fear it is because of what I am."

"And what's that?"

"The Archmage," he said in a colorless tone. "The holder of the Master-spells over the others."

Gil frowned, puzzled at the sudden wretchedness in his voice. "I don't understand."

"Good." Ingold smiled suddenly and laid a hand comfortingly over hers. "Good. And in any case, if it did come to an invasion, as a mage I would have a better chance than most to survive it. Moreover, if I did not accompany the army, my alternative would be to remain here at the Keep with the civilians, Govannin, and Inquisitor Pinard."

And to that, Gil realized, there was no reply.

"The Church in the South is different from what it has been in the Realm of Darwath," he continued. "Here the Church has always observed the bounds of laws. But in the South, it *is* the law. It crowns their kings as well as blesses them; in some cases, it has selected them as well. Govannin recognizes the spiritual authority of the Inquisition."

"You mean she'd take orders from Pinard?"

He chuckled. "Govannin Narmenlion has never taken orders from anyone in her life. But she listens to him when he tells her that God's ends justify whatever means His servants choose to employ. And she has never gotten over her anger at me for taking Brother Wend away from the Church. I suppose you could say that Pinard has corrupted her, though both of them feel nothing but the highest of intentions. And because Maia of Penambra will have none of it, he runs the risk of being charged as a schismatic himself."

"Whereas he's nothing but a simple Episcopalian." Gil smiled ironically and then said abruptly, "Did you really whack off Vair's hand in an unfair fight?"

"Of course." The old impishness twinkled suddenly in his eyes. "Considering that he was mounted and armed with a long sword, while all I had was a two-foot short sword and a chain that held me by one wrist to a post—yes, I suppose you could call it unfair. This was, as you may have gathered, back in my days as a slave in the cavalry barracks at Khirsrit. I had no idea that Vair had lost his hand as a result of that fight—I did not wound him that badly, though of course, without magic, the state of the healing arts in Alketch is notorious. In fact, I scarcely gave the matter any thought, once my own wounds were healed, and I did not see Vair again. Looking back on it, I suppose it was he who tried to have me killed shortly afterward, forcing me to escape." The wizard was silent for a moment, his eyes focused on that distant vision of another self.

"Vair was never much of a swordsman," he added, glancing over at Gil. "Despite what he claims. As I remember it, I knocked the sword out of his hand at exercises or did something which earned him a bad mark from his instructor,

130

and, against all rules of the arena, he lost his temper and came back to finish the job."

"Crowning the sin of wrath with the penultimate sin of stupidity," Gil grinned suddenly. And then, with a slight frown, she asked, "Were you a mage then?"

"Do you think that I could have been?"

She shook her head. "But if you were a grown man . . ."

The wizard sighed. "I was twenty-two. And old enough, as our left-handed friend has pointed out, to have come to my powers, which most mages find between the ages of nine and fourteen." He settled back in his chair and drew the mantle once more around his shoulders, as if to ward against a chill.

"But there was a war, you see, after I returned from Quo. My people were borderlords in Gettlesand; my father was the Lord of Gyrfire, a principality near Dele. In the last battle before the doors of my parents' fortress, I took a head blow which all but killed me. When I woke in the slave pens of Alketch, I had no recollection of my name, my powers, or—mercifully—my role in starting the war."

She regarded him in silence for a time, seeing with sudden clarity that brilliant, arrogant, ginger-haired young man who had been Ingold Inglorion at twenty-two. "And when did you remember?" she asked softly.

"After I escaped from Khirsrit. Out in the desert. I had a fever; I nearly died then. Kta found me." Ingold paused, staring into the fire as if through the flames he could contemplate that very distant young man. "After that, I was a hermit for many years. I remembered my power and who I was. But I also remembered that it was I who had started the war, between my use of black magic and my damned meddling in what was essentially none of my business.

"It was a long time before I had the courage so much as to light a fire without flint and steel. I got over their deaths—my parents', my younger brother's—Liardin . . ." He shook his head, as if clearing from it the echoes of half-forgotten voices. "But Gyrfire was never rebuilt. I am probably the only man living who remembers where it stood. We wizards are a dangerous people, Gil," he finished, reaching to take her hand again. "We are hardly safe to know. The Icefalcon was right. Only the brave should befriend the wise."

She dismissed the Icefalcon with a shrug. "I don't believe that."

"Being brave, you wouldn't." He smiled at her.

"So that's why . . ." she began and stopped herself. "There are times when I wonder if you're as wise as you think." To her own surprise as well as his, she bent down and kissed him lightly on the forehead before she turned and hurried from the room.

After the dim firelight of Ingold's quarters, the dark in the common room was like being struck blind. With an automatic caution she had learned from the Icefalcon, Gil did not pause before the curtain to let her eyes adjust, but stepped to the side, her back to the wall, where even the little light that leaked through the weave would not show her up. Thus, when a dark form emerged from the blackness of one of the many hallways that led into the room Gil had only to press back against the wall and freeze to remain unseen.

She knew at once that this intruder was no wizard—a thin, white hand caught at the back of the same chair that she herself had stumbled over in the dark. A shadow passed in front of the winking embers; a cloak whispered against a tableleg. As the form turned, Gil had a vague impression of a white, beardless face and a shaven head showing up briefly against the thicker darkness of the door to the corridors beyond. The skeletal hand groped for the doorframe. For a moment it rested there, and a vagrant glint of a sparking ember called, like a candle in darkness, the answering gleam of purple from an amethyst ring.

CHAPTER NINE

The tensions built within the Keep until one night Minalde failed to come to Rudy's cell, as had been her custom.

He lay awake for hours in the darkness, listening for the sound of her step, the touch of slippered feet on the damp stone of the winding corridors whose mazes she knew so well, and the slurring whisper of the heavy fur of her cloak—sounds that only a wizard could hear. Some two hours had passed since he had heard the far-off, muffled commotion of the deep-night watch leaving the barracks on its rounds.

She had never been so late before.

And yet he knew—*he knew*—that she had planned to come to him.

The firesquad demonstration had taken place that afternoon. Most of the population of the Keep—with the exception of Gil, who, Rudy surmised, was so wound up in the pursuit of her mysterious research that she'd forgotten the day—and virtually all of the Alketch troops had been there. The frozen mud of the drilling ground in the meadow below the Keep walls had been darkened with a lake of humanity, crowding to see this weapon with which, rumor had it, Dare of Renweth had defeated the Dark Ones. A dais had been erected at the south corner of the meadow near the road, and on it the somber black and bloody crimson pennants of Realm and Church alternated with the gaudy, gold-stitched banners of the South.

Lying in the darkness of his cell, Rudy picked over the memories of the day, sorting them like jewel-bright photographs. He remembered how straight the ranks of the firesquad had been, despite the wide range in their ages and origins—boys of ten or twelve on up to one old lady of eighty; the orange oriflamme that was their emblem had blazed brightly on the pale homespun of their uniforms. He remembered the gleam of sun on the looping rigs of their glass and gold weapons and the sharp bark of Melantrys' commands.

Other images came back to him: Vair and Stiarth, like a couple of refulgent tiger lilies in slashed doublets of orange and magenta, jewels twinkling among the extravagant ruffles of their sleeves; Bektis, at the foot of the dais among the other mages, sulking because he had not been given a place with the notables of the Realm—although Govannin would have excommunicated the entire government at the mere suggestion that she and Inquisitor Pinard be asked to share the platform with one who was mageborn; and Alwir's face, and the mingled glitter of wariness and contempt beneath his half-shut eyelids.

Especially, he remembered Minalde, with Tir in her arms.

Ingold had stood at the far end of the meadow, with the heavy folds of his mantle thrown back to reveal the shabby homespun robes and beat-up sword belt underneath, picking little, brightly colored bubbles of illusion from the air with the sweeping gestures of a side-show magician.

Since Rudy was familiar with the rainy-day pastimes of younger wizards, this was nothing much to his eyes. But he heard the uneasy murmur of the crowd as Ingold tossed the small and gleaming colored spheres out into the air, and they grew in a twinkling to some two feet across and bobbed about him, green and purple and electric blue, like monster catfish trawling for garbage in the snow.

The firesquad had moved forward. At Ingold's wave of command, the bubbles had swirled upward like a torrent of blown leaves in autumn. Someone in the crowd gasped in horror; from the dais behind him, Rudy heard Vair whisper, "Devil!" The ludicrous rainbow toys moved in a precise imitation of the gliding, sinuous flight of the Dark Ones.

There was not a person in the meadow who had not seen at firsthand how the Dark attacked. When Melantrys whirled in mid-stride to pick off a quivering globe of scarlet that swooped down upon her from behind and above, there was a gust of applause, which quickly rose to a roar as more targets were hit. Against the drabness of the wintry afternoon, the leaping streaks of fire looked chill and rather pale. The moving targets flashed out of existence as soon as the flames touched them, and the cheering mounted to a thunderous shout, as if it were actually the Dark being destroyed. Up on the dais, Alwir and the peacock lords of Alketch were nodding to one another in grim satisfaction; down below, mages and Guards pounded one another on the back with tooth-jarring verve. Rudy found himself jostled, grabbed, patted, and congratulated by friends and total strangers. Even Thoth unbent enough to admit, "Impressive."

But it was the pride on Alde's face that stayed in Rudy's mind. In all his life, he could never recall anyone who had ever been proud of him.

Why doesn't she come?

There had been that look, that promise, in her eyes as their gazes had crossed, and for a moment they had been alone together in the midst of that ebullient crowd.

And time is so short, Rudy thought despairingly. *The Winter Feast is three days from now! And after that . . .*

He pushed the thought from his mind, as he had resolutely kept it at bay these past weeks, so as not to cloud the halcyon days that they had. In a forlorn hope, he extended his awareness far into the mazes of the Keep, seeking for some sound of her coming in all that damp, inhabited darkness. He heard nothing—nothing but the slumberous murmur of a father soothing a crying child and the drip and trickle of water coursing through the Keep's stone veins.

Rudy was an old friend to the night sounds of the Keep. If nothing else, the Nest had cost him that. In dreams he wandered again in that dark, hideous world where staring, white-faced herds shuffled pathetically through the rotting mosses of endless caverns. He felt the clammy, hairless bodies and the touch of dark winds on his face; he saw the slimy, oozing things that infested the ceilings above. Sometimes he saw the tall, gray-haired prisoner again, running and gasping through that vibrating darkness, running nowhere . . .

Other dreams were more horrible. In them, the faces of the squeaking, pale things that fled his approach were familiar to him—Alde's, Ingold's, his own. The prisoner's eyes returned to him again and again, as he'd seen them for the single instant in the yellow reflection of the fire, wide, blind, and half-mad, the eyes of a beast that had forgotten what it was to be a man.

Then he would awaken and lie listening to the Keep's slumber.

He knew that others had less sleep than he. His own cell lay in the midst of the crowded complex that the mages had taken over. He could sometimes hear a breathing that he knew to be Kara's, when she woke with a cry from similar dreams; he could hear her sobs calm slowly into waking rhythm, but never deepen again into sleep. Occasionally he heard the faint clicking of Gil's wax tablets, or, from another corner of the complex, whispered giggles and the brisk, rhythmical creaking of rope bedsprings. Twice he'd heard a man's weeping, desperately stifled in bedclothes.

Where is Alde?

She could have changed her mind, half of him argued, but the other half remembered that glowing pride in her face. If ever a look said, "I'll come to you when I can . . ."

Did something keep her?

What could? he argued. *Alwir said he'd grant us his protection.*

And then it occurred to Rudy that he could find out by looking in one of the magic crystals.

She has enough spying from Alwir, for Chrissake, he told himself angrily as the idea insinuated itself with overwhelming urgency into his thoughts. *You don't own her!*

But once it was formulated, the notion took hold of him, like a nagging itch. The tiny green crystal that he'd found in one of the labs downstairs seemed to wink at him in the darkness from the crude shelves that housed all of his few possessions. His fingers twitched to touch it, his mind to see.

Knock it off! he commanded himself. *It's none of your goddam business what's keeping her. You have no claim on that lady—it's you who's going to be deserting her. That's a kid's trick, like driving by your girlfriend's house to see whose car is parked out front. If she decided not to come, she doesn't need you peeping on her.*

Miserable with self-hate and frozen feet, he padded across the room, his blanket wrapped around his shoulders. A spark of witchlight brightened into being over his head as he took the greenish crystal from its place. Its facets glinted with tiny explosions of light as he angled it and stared deep into the heart of the jewel.

The candles in Alde's room were all but guttered. Wax dripped in thick, white columns down over the shoulders of the little bronze knights that upbore them and ran in creamy pools on the gleaming inlay of the polished table. The dying light flickered over the white brocade of her gown, danced in the jewels still knotted in her half-unraveled ceremonial coiffure, and winked on the little heap of rings and earrings that lay piled at her elbow. She had been in Council, he thought, and remembered that the first thing she did when she returned from such official functions was to strip off her jewelry and let down her hair.

He could not see her face, for she was asleep, with her head on the table and her face hidden in her arms.

A sheet of paper—the torn-out flyleaf of one of her books—lay beside her, and something was written on it in large, scrawly runes. Rudy had by this time mastered enough of the written language of the Wathe to spell out the message laboriously:

RUDY, HELP, PLEASE COME.

Her door was locked. The cloaking-spell that hid him from the two red-clad troopers at the end of the corridor would be useless if he called out loudly enough to wake her.

He laid his hands on the door. Closing his eyes, he felt for the mechanism of the lock with his mind in a technique that Ingold had shown him. The mechanics were crude and decadent, put in during the bad times, when the state of the lock-making art was low; working the wards with his mind was less difficult than forcing them to operate against the rust that choked them.

He pushed the door ajar and slid silently through.

As he pushed it to behind him, Tir stood up in his cradle, his plump, pink hands grasping the carved footboard for support. He called out gaily, " 'Udy!"

With a startled little cry, Alde raised her head, her hair swinging down over her face in an asymmetrical tangle of braids and gems. Then she gasped, "Rudy!" in a voice choked with tears.

She half-rose, and he crushed her in his arms. Her face had hardly more color in it than her gown, except for the swollen redness of her eyes. He tasted the tears that salted her lips; she was shivering with sobs as she pressed frantically into his embrace. "I thought you'd never come."

"I almost didn't, babe . . . What's the matter? Why's the door locked? What's happening?"

Her voice sank to a desperate whisper. "Rudy, Alwir's going to betroth me to the son of the Emperor of Alketch."

He blinked at her for a moment, not taking it in. "He's what?" he asked, not certain that he'd heard correctly. And then, as rage swept him with fever heat, he cried, *"He's what?"* But he remembered where he was, and his shout was no more than a violent whisper. "He can't do that!"

"The Inquisitor told me," she went on in a low, stifled voice, "after the Council was over—oh, long after! I think the others had gone on with the talks after I left. I—I went to Alwir . . . He said the treaty had already been signed—that it would be announced the night after the Winter Feast, and I would marry by proxy and be sent south with Stiarth and an escort when the army leaves for Gae. Then he locked me in . . ."

Rudy's long acquaintance with the brotherhood of the road had given him considerable powers of self-expression. He wondered how he could possibly have been so naive as to trust Alwir's word. The lengthy tirade upon the Chancellor's ancestry, personal habits, and probable destiny that rose to his lips was partially aimed at his own stupidity as well. But he had been a wizard too long to think that such commentary would do other than waste time.

Instead, he said, "But they can't bring Tir up in Alketch!"

"They're not going to!" she whispered frantically. "Tir's going to stay here to rule the northern realms, with Alwir as

138

the Regent." She pressed her forehead to his shoulder. "Rudy, what are we going to do?"

Damn good question, he thought, with a feeling akin to panic creeping through his heart. What could they do? The Keep was the last sanctuary from the Dark, and there was nowhere in the Keep that Alwir would not have absolute power over them. If her brother repudiated Alde and took Tir from her, she would lose what slender independence she had. Of course, then the heir of Alketch wouldn't marry her . . . or would he? Rudy cudgeled his fumbling brain to think and found only confusion and ignorance, his train of thought circling back on itself, like a man lost in a snowstorm.

What good would it do to escape? he wondered. *Wherever we go in the Keep, we're Alwir's prisoners. And besides, where in the Keep can we go?*

As he asked the question, the answer became immediately obvious to him.

He bent his head and kissed the frightened, upturned face. "Get your cloak, sweetheart," he said grimly. "I don't know what we're going to do, but Ingold sure as hell will."

Despite the lateness of the hour, Ingold was awake when they reached his alcove, seated in his carved chair with a moth-eaten bearskin blanket pulled around his shoulders, staring into the few coals that remained on his hearth fire. Both his white hair and the blankets on his narrow cot in the shadows at the back of the room were rumpled from unquiet sleep, and the litter of scholarship—parchments, books, those unfathomable charts of dates and food prices Gil was compiling—strewed the desk and the floor about his feet. But by the look of them, they had given the wizard no respite from the thoughts that had driven sleep from him. He appeared to have been sitting, staring silently into the fire, for some time.

He looked up as they entered, his glance going from Rudy's face to Minalde's, and his brow darkened when he saw the wrapped bundle of quilted velvet blankets that Alde bore in her arms. "What is it?" he asked quietly. "What's happened?"

Succinctly and profanely, Rudy informed him. While he did so, the wizard got to his feet, magelight brightening over his head as he handed Alde into his own chair by the fire and took Tir to lay upon the bed. Tir promptly started working to unravel himself and go exploring.

While Rudy was speaking, Alde sat, shivering a little under the bearskin that Ingold had drawn up around her shoulders, her eyes downcast, half-hidden among the fallen coils of her hair. Only when he finished did she look up. Her eyes were dry; the fear that had been in them as she'd guided Rudy, masked by the protection of his cloaking-spells, through the frowsty and smoke-stinking back corridors of the Keep to reach the Corps complex in secret was gone. It had been replaced by the look Rudy had seen in her eyes the night she'd submitted to the spell of *gnodyrr*, one of determination to do what must be done.

She asked softly, "Ingold . . . if Alwir agreed to this—this marriage—behind my back, what else might he have agreed to?"

The old man looked down at her consideringly, leaning his wide shoulders against the rounded clay and rubble wall of the chimney, the firelight mottling his robe ocher and rust. "I can think of several things," he replied. "Bishop Maia told me of an earlier attempt to gain control of the Penambra Delta. And there have always, of course, been quarrels over the Gettlesand border."

Her iris-colored eyes seemed to grow darker with bitter and helpless anger; her slender fingers shook as they locked together in the harsh fur. She whispered, "He has gone too far."

Standing half-forgotten in the dim circle of the firelight, Rudy had the sudden impression of having wandered into realms beyond his ken, into politics, power, and matters far above his own troubles and loves. Beside this greater issue, his love for this dark-haired girl seemed suddenly a small thing. Perhaps, he realized, it had always been.

Ingold folded his arms. "How far are you willing to go?"

"How far can I go?" she countered in a taut voice. "Whatever is said, I am still his prisoner, whether in my rooms or here. He'll find a way to bend me to his will . . ."

"Shall he?" the old man inquired mildly. "The fact that he

140

locked you up as soon as you found out tells me that he wasn't as sure of that as you seem to be. He clearly planned to announce it as a *fait accompli* . . . If we can speak to him before he does so, we have a chance to change him."

Her shadow swooped across the broken plaster of the wall as she rose with restless abruptness to her feet. "Do we?" she demanded shakily. The jewels flashed, still caught in the dark knots of her hair. "He has proclaimed he will have an alliance with Alketch, and from that position he will not back down. For that alliance he would sacrifice everything—me, the Keep, his very soul." She turned restlessly, her white gown burnished with honey and flame. Her face in the flickering shadows looked suddenly aged by the grimness of her expression, its beauty tempered by the underlying strength of wrath.

Rudy found himself thinking how much she had changed from being the dead King's frightened child-widow; or perhaps it was simply that she had become what she had never before had the chance to be. Long ago, on the journey down from Karst, she had spoken of a ruler's responsibility to the people, and he had not understood at the time what that meant. It was possible, he thought, that she had not, either.

Ingold shifted his shoulders against the chimney breast, regarding her from beneath half-shut eyelids. "These things that you speak of," he said quietly, "—another's life, the safety of the Keep, the integrity of the soul—are matters of great import to you, my lady. But to my lord Alwir, I suspect that such things yield precedence to power and personal comfort—and those, perhaps, he will not be so willing to endanger, even for the sake of an alliance with Alketch."

She was silent for a long moment, struggling with the unexpected hurt she felt at those words. *For all that's gone down,* Rudy thought, seeing the sudden hotness that flooded her eyes, *he's still her brother; she has loved him and depended on him all her life. That's a helluva thing to know for truth about someone you used to care for.*

Then she sniffled and wiped her cheeks with defiant fingers. In a small, carefully balanced voice, she said, "I don't see how we could be in a position to endanger either of those things, Ingold—or anything else for that matter, except yourself and Rudy for sheltering me. I—I suppose I could go back and try to talk with him . . ."

"Would you believe anything that he assured you?" the wizard inquired.

She was silent, but the mauve-stained lids of her eyes fell.

Ingold turned and fielded Tir just before the baby Prince managed to crawl out the door into the wider world of the dark common room. After setting Tir back on the bed, he bent to take up his sword belt, which lay on the floor. Then he turned to hunt for his boots, his bare feet soundless on the uncarpeted stone of the floor.

"Why should he bother to assure me of anything?" Alde asked after a moment. "Maybe I am, as Gil says, the legal ruler of the Keep, but it is Alwir who holds the power here. I know it. It is only that I never had call to feel it before now. I have no power. Only friends."

Ingold turned back to her, slinging on his heavy mantle and drawing the dark hood over his rough, white hair. His shadow loomed over them, huge and batlike against the stone walls. "Never underestimate our friends, Minalde," he said gently. "In risking your life to visit Maia and the Penambrans and pleading their cause to your brother when he refused to admit them to the Keep, you made a friend; in standing against your brother in his dealings with Alketch, if for no other reason, you made others. And it so happens," he added, retrieving the wandering Prince from under the bed and wrapping him once more in his offensive swad-dlings, "that Tomec Tirkenson and his rangers are staying on the fourth and fifth levels, with Maia's Penambrans. You know the backways of the Keep better than I do, my child. Would you be able to guide us unseen to the fourth level?"

It was barely the start of the day watch when Minalde returned to the Royal Sector, surrounded by her entourage.

In the Aisle, the Guards had thrown wide the gates again, and children had gone running out through the steamy dawn, to do their chores and race to the woods and cut evergreen boughs. Their singing floated back over the rucked snow and drifted faintly throughout the Keep itself. In two days it would be the Winter Feast.

But solstice cheer was hardly evident in the confusion of the lord Chancellor's quarters, and the traditional love and friendliness of the season were the farthest things from the rage-darkened countenance he showed his sister when she entered his audience hall with her train.

The opening of the doors had caught him in mid-gesticulation. He froze, mouth ajar, hand extended; all about the council table, eyes snapped to the dark doorway, now crowded with Maia's ragged guards and buckskinned Gettlesand rangers. In the split second of stopped time before the Chancellor swung around to face them, Rudy identified the others there. Vair was opulent in cut-velvet and pearls, but plain beside the emerald-green intricacies of Stiarth's gorgeous costume. Inquisitor Pinard, his white robes an advertisement of spiritual purity, stood beside the gory crimson costume of Bishop Govannin.

Alwir's face was engorged with rage; the finger that stabbed out at his sister was almost trembling with it. "You—" he began in a strangled voice, across which Govannin's dry, harsh tones cut like a knife.

"Be careful what you say, fool," she warned, and Alwir, turning, seemed to realize that they were in the presence of the ears in service to the Emperor of the South. This checked the rashness of his first words, but there was murder in his eyes as Alde and the outland chiefs stepped into the council chamber.

Against the wealth and elegance of Alwir's power, Alde's supporters did not show up well. Under Bishop Maia's tattered scarlet episcopal cloak, he wore a faded panoply of scavenged rags, topped by a sweater knitted for him by one of the Penambran ladies. Tomec Tirkenson, in his fringed buckskin shirt and fleece moccasins, looked much like the barbarians he fought. Ingold, the best-dressed of the three, might have passed for anything from a genteel beggar to a street-corner harpist, but certainly not for the Archmage of the Wizards of the West. Among them, Alde seemed to blaze, like a slip of white flame in shadows.

When Alwir spoke again, his voice was calmer but no less deadly. "I suppose you have reasons which you believe to be valid, my sister," he spat acidly, "for coming armed into my presence. But if we are to talk, it will not be in the company of these—bravos."

"These bravos, my lord, are the commanders of your outland troops," she returned, and her soft voice easily filled the council chamber.

His lip curled. "And what do military commanders have to do with statecraft and policy?"

"They die for it, my lord."

There was momentary silence. Then Alwir's face softened, and he came around the table, his hands held out to take hers, his voice gentle and beautiful. "Alde—Minalde. There are always those who die, child; always those who must sacrifice to the good of all. You know this—none better than you." He took her hands in a warm clasp, the soft modulations of his voice excluding all others around them, speaking for her ears only, as if they had been alone. "If every soldier were given his vote, no battles would ever be fought. That is why there must be leaders, my child. Without unquestioning unity, we are like a palsied man in a duel, with every limb flailing to no purpose. Sometimes one arm must take a cut so that the other can deliver a killing blow."

He stood close to her. For a moment she looked up at him, once more his little sister, sheltered under the strength of his shadow.

Then she turned her wrists, not violently, but sharply, something Gil had taught her, breaking his hold before he could tighten it to draw her close. She stepped back from him, between her tall, ragged allies.

"Nevertheless, my lord, they are your subjects. The lives they put in your hands are the only ones they have. The least you owe their dignity is to invite their opinions and not hold secret councils to seek the advice of foreigners before you ask it of your own."

Alwir's voice hardened, as if edged in metal. "Worthy as these lords are, my sister, they are the servants of one House who have fought the servants of another. Their

144

bravery and sacrifice are not the less for being, perhaps, overzealous . . ."

Tirkenson's lynx eyes narrowed. "It's damn difficult not to get a little overzealous when you find your sister gone and your brother gutted and their kids speared through the belly with Alketch pikes."

"If we sank to a discussion of every personal grievance that ever existed between the men of Alketch and ourselves, my lord Tirkenson, we would sit in this miserable fortress until we all starved or were devoured by the Dark," the Chancellor flashed haughtily. "And if we continue to be interrupted by these—friends—whom you have chosen to bring with you into my Councils, my sister, we might just as well abandon discussion here and now. If you will seek the company of these ruffians whose blind prejudices would prevent the union of the Houses which they serve—"

"I will not marry the heir of Alketch!"

"You sang a different tune last night," he reminded her softly.

"I was prisoner last night!"

Alwir's upper lip seemed to lengthen, his mouth hardening into a single dark line. "Things have changed in the Realm, Minalde, since you sat on the water terraces of Gae and fanned yourself with peacock plumes. We need the alliance with Alketch. They alone can help us reconquer the Realm from the Dark; they alone can help us rebuild it; they alone have not been scourged with this plague that has washed like a tide of death and ruination across the lands of Darwath. We have suffered, and without their aid we will continue to suffer. We can no longer afford the kind of warlike pride that once kept us from uniting in a single federation for the good of all humankind."

Alde flinched from this accusation of vanity and luxury— *not an unlikely one, either,* Rudy thought, *since the kid was married at sixteen.* But her voice was unwavering as she replied, "I will not leave my son, nor will I permit the heir of Darwath to be brought up in a foreign court."

"Not even one that is safe from the Dark?"

Alde swallowed; Rudy could see the struggle in her face.

Alwir must have noticed Tir's absence and known its meaning—that she would not put both of them into his power again. But this was a low blow, Rudy thought. Offhand, he couldn't think of anyone, including himself, whom Alde wouldn't kill to protect her child.

Her voice was unsteady as she said, "I would rather he shared his people's dangers than grow up a stranger to them."

"Don't be a fool," Alwir snapped roughly. "You'd kill the child for the sake of your silly pride?"

Tears flooded her eyes. She started to stammer a reply, but Ingold laid a gentle hand on her shoulder.

"For a northern-bred boy, like the legal heir to the Realm of Darwath and the last scion of the House of Dare, it is possible that the warmer climate of the court of the Emperor of Alketch might itself prove unhealthy," the wizard said, his deep, slow voice almost, but not quite, laying emphasis on certain words. "A fever or a change of food, perhaps, might carry him off as surely as the Dark Ones, against whom this fortress and the presence of men loyal to his interests would in some measure protect him."

It took Rudy a moment to unravel the implications of the seemingly innocuous words, but Alde gasped and turned pale. Alwir's brow grew thunderous with anger.

"You *dare* . . ." he rasped.

With a grinding clatter of his thrust-back chair, Vair na Chandros jerked to his feet. "Are you hinting that aught would happen to the child under the Emperor's care, you devil?"

Stiarth reached up to catch Vair's sleeve and pulled him down once more. The Ambassador's eyes glinted with light, cynical amusement. "In what danger could the Emperor's stepgrandson stand?" he inquired silkily. He looked across the table at Alde, his fine, slender hands echoing, in graceful gestures, the music of his voice. "In time, my lady, you might find yourself the most revered woman in the West of the World, you know. You would be the mother of the rulers of both Darwath and Alketch—the Golden Mother, in fact, of a union of humankind that stretches from the ice in the north to the impenetrable cataracts of the southern wall.

146

Your love, your motherhood, would unite what has never been united in all the days of the world."

He tossed the sparkling vision of it to her, like a sugarplum cast to a child. But the child did not grasp for it. In a clear, glass-hard voice, she said, "I have been chided for my pride once already, my lord. I cannot see myself with an elder son upon one throne and a younger upon another."

Not if that younger son's Imperial Grandpa has anything to do with the preparation of Number One Son's baby food, Rudy thought bitterly. *And leaving him at the Keep for Alwir to raise might just as easily amount to the same thing.* The anger that surged through him was not for Alde alone or for himself, banished to the slow death of emptiness and grief. He felt a flash of anger for the child he had grown to love, robbed of birthright and mother and life.

The despair at his banishment turned to rage, rage that he would be unable to protect his own. *And if the Inquisition's come to the Keep, Ingold may not be able to stick around to protect the little rug-rat, either.* Looking up, he saw Alwir's eyes upon him, and what was in them seemed to slice into his flesh like a dagger of ice.

"And is your—natural grief—so much," the Chancellor continued, his jeweled gaze moving from Rudy's face to Alde's, "that you cannot by any means overcome your understandable aversion to replacing your dead lord so quickly in your bed, my sister . . ."

Alde's expression did not change, but her chin came up.

". . . especially when so much is at stake?"

There was a deadly silence.

For perhaps the time that it might take to draw and release three long breaths, they waited—for Alwir to speak, for Alde to break, for Rudy to give them both away. But as Alwir drew in breath to speak, Ingold stepped into that fraught hush with uncanny timing and every appearance of unconcern.

"In that regard my lady's choice is her own, as you know by Church law. It has been the ruling of every Church Council that has ever convened that no marriage entered into under coercion or force is valid. Indeed, I believe that many years ago my lady Govannin herself fought—successfully—such coercion by her family to make her wed instead of enter the Church. Is that not correct, my lady?"

Govannin's black slits of eyes gleamed as she turned her head. "It is, my lord wizard."

"And the same Councils have ruled," Ingold continued in that mild, scholarly tone, "that the act of love itself, as long as it is between parties of full age and responsibility, is always lawful, be it between the same sex or opposite, mageborn or not, faithful, heathen, or excommunicate, as long as the rights of contract or person are not violated. There is a certain amount of controversy over this ruling, but is that not, at base, the law?"

Govannin's dry, bitter voice sounded stiff. "It is."

Rudy had enough sense left to stifle his gasp of outrage at the lie Alwir had told him. Then a heat went through him, a raging misery. He had no doubt that Alwir would banish him anyway—the Chancellor held too much power over his sister and could hurt her too much if Rudy stayed. But he now saw the full extent of what would happen after he was gone.

Alwir was pale, his nostrils two black, flared slashes, bracketed by the ugly lines graven around his mouth. "It is the law, my lady Govannin," he grated, "but the opinions and good will of the people are another law entirely. For a Queen to—disregard the good of the Keep—" Rudy let his breath out in a shaky sigh. "—would certainly risk creating a scandal. And scandal, as we know, can be extremely expensive."

He loomed over them like a cloud, black and lambent with evil; the rage seemed to burn out of him like thunder heat. Before the threat of his power, Alde looked suddenly very small and young, and Ingold seemed old and ragged.

Except for his eyes; they were bright and fierce under their white brows and met Alwir's unafraid.

"Prohibitively expensive, in fact," the wizard said. "For who knows which way the die will fall, my lord?" Like a fencer disengaging, he turned his deceptively mild gaze to Stiarth and inquired, "Would your lord the Emperor press his demand for this term of alliance at the risk of losing the alliance itself?"

"I cannot in truth . . ." the Imperial Nephew began deprecatingly.

Alwir rasped, "Nothing will make me forgo the alliance!"

"For indeed," Ingold continued, as if the Chancellor had not spoken, "if there is a conflict and a schism in the Keep, who knows who would hold the power afterward?"

The Chancellor gasped, taken for one instant utterly off balance, as if he could not conceive another coming to power in the Keep. Then his black brows dived over his nose, his face clotting with rage. "And who speaks of that, pray?" He would have reached out and shaken the old man, had not Ingold without apparent effort turned aside Alwir's grasping hand with his staff.

"No one, of course," the wizard replied, widening his eyes at Alwir in surprise. "But surely my lord the Emperor knows that in times of trouble many things may come about."

"Indeed he does." Stiarth got to his feet and salaamed gracefully in the direction of Alwir, Ingold, and Minalde. "Had I known that the match was so repugnant to my lady, I would have hesitated to trample her sensibilities by even the suggestion, nor, I am sure, would our gracious lord the Emperor. It is true that, having heard tales of her loveliness and gentle breeding, he earnestly desires such a union; indeed, the federation of our two Realms has long been a scheme close to his heart."

A voice from the back of the Gettlesand rangers muttered, "I bet it has."

"I am desolated to have been the fomenter of such difficulties. My lord—my lady—I await your convenience." He bowed again; in a whispering cloud of layered silken capes, he turned and minced from the room.

Vair sprang to his feet like a tiger. From among the Gettlesand rangers, Rudy could see him overtake the lithe Ambassador in the doorway, catching the petaled edge of Stiarth's sleeve with his hooks. "Are you mad?" he demanded. "The Emperor said—"

"My Imperial Uncle entrusted this matter and all others to my judgment," Stiarth replied softly. With two fingers, he disengaged his fragile ruffles. "And believe me, Com-

149

mander, I would far rather deal with the brother than have the sister and the wizard come to power in the confusion that would follow schism. I trust you concur?" Then he was gone in a rustling of perfumed silk, the click of his high heels audible for some moments as he retreated down the long hall.

It was Alwir's voice that broke the silence. "My lord wizard," he said quietly, "I would have a word with you— alone."

"I should never have let him go." Alde spoke without raising her head, her chin resting on her crossed wrists upon her drawn-up knees. On the other side of the common room hearth, Rudy put aside his long-silent harp.

"It had to happen," he said softly. "Oh, Christ, Alde, what are we going to do?"

She shook her head despairingly. "I don't know."

It was midmorning and the common room was empty. Voices murmured among the complex of cells—Dame Nan's yapping curses, Tomec Tirkenson's rumble of protest, and Kara's patient "Mother!" The only light was the honey-gold glow of the hearth. The room smelled of rising bread and of the braided strings of herbs and onions that hung from nails on the walls. Tad the herdkid had brought word that Tir was still safe in concealment among the Keep orphans. If Alwir was looking for him, it had not occurred to the Chancellor that he would be hidden there.

How do I manage to do stuff like this? Rudy wondered miserably, looking across the hearth to the girl who sat folded so compactly in the inglenook, staring unseeingly into the fire. *All I want is to love her and to be happy. Why is it that all I've managed to do is comprehensively screw up her life and bring her nothing but pain and disgrace, excommunication and exile, and loss? Was Ingold right? Are mages born damned?*

"Alde, I'm sorry," Rudy said wretchedly. "I never meant for it to turn out this way."

She looked up at him, tears shining in eyes that looked almost black in the shadows. "It had nothing to do with you, Rudy," she murmured. "Really," she added, seeing the weary denial on his face. "Don't you see? It would have come to fighting between Alwir and myself whether I—I loved you or not. It's just that—I thought for so long that he cared for me." She shifted her position, the white brocade of her skirts polished by the firelight as they rippled down over the hearth bricks. She was fighting to keep her mouth steady. "He could be so kind to me in the old days, but maybe that was because he knew I—I respond easily to kindness. I suppose he'd say Ingold knows that, too. I always thought he was a very contradictory person, but he's not. I—I'm only sorry you had to be caught in it, that it had to spoil something that was—that you—"

Rudy cried miserably, "Alde, nothing could hurt my love for you! Not time or distance or politics or the Void . . . Nothing."

For an instant neither of them moved, but only looked at each other, separated by the glow of the hearthlight, as one day the brighter light of the Void must stand between them. Then, with swift impatience, Rudy swung to his feet, crossed the light with his great shadow sprawling across the walls behind him, and dragged her to her feet and roughly into his embrace. She clung to him, her face buried in the rough fleece of his gaudily painted vest, her hands locked behind his back. He whispered desperately, "Alde, if I had a choice, I'd never leave you. I'd always be here."

She whispered back, "It doesn't matter. I'll love you no matter where you are or what becomes of you."

They clung to each other in the dim glory of the topaz light, as if they felt already the currents of their separate universes turning to drag them apart.

Then a deep, rusty voice intruded upon Rudy's consciousness. "My children?"

"You're all right!"

Ingold caught Alde by the shoulders, halting her impulsive rush to embrace him, and smiled into her flushed, anxious face. "Did you conceive that your brother would stab me the moment we were alone?"

"The way he looked, yes!" Rudy put in. "What—" His voice failed him, and he stood uncertainly, looking into his master's face. He swallowed, but still could not speak.

The wizard reached out gently and laid his hand upon Rudy's shoulder, warm and very strong. His eyes went from Rudy's face to Minalde's, a kind of wry sorrow in their deceptively bright blue depths. "Do you love each other so much, my children?"

Neither spoke, but Rudy's hand sought Alde's, the twined shadows of their fingers a closing knot in the firelight.

Hesitantly, Alde said, "If it were lawful . . ."

"If I—if I could stay . . ." Rudy stammered.

Ingold sighed. "Indeed." In the fitful lambence of the fire, his lined features looked sad and a little resigned. "I fear I had the temerity to point out to your brother, Minalde, that there are worse things than your permanent alliance to one who is forbidden by Church law and the code of the Council of Wizards to rule those who are not mageborn. And I reminded him that you are strong-willed and stubborn, and that you have, in fact, a power base among the outland chiefs. For a woman such as yourself, it is not inconceivable that at some future time, if driven to desperation, you might ally yourself to some landchief whose realms come only nominally under the sway of the Lord of the Keep of Dare. Your brother was neither pleased nor gracious—but he agreed with me."

"What?" Rudy whispered, after a long, uncomprehending silence. Then understanding penetrated to his brain, and a feeling like an electrical shock to all the cells in his body.

"My children," Ingold continued, "walk very carefully. You still flirt with scandal—perhaps you will do so all your lives. But, by the laws of the Realm, there is nothing illegal in your union, no matter that Alwir may have said . . ."

His words purled over Rudy's consciousness like the unintelligible voice of a river, barely audible through what felt like a fountain of blazing joy welling up from the depths of his being. He wanted to whoop, to dance, to sing songs and embrace everybody in sight; but as it was, his hand only tightened on Alde's. Looking across at her, he saw answering oceans of happiness in her quiet face.

Ingold's voice went on about Church law, the position of the individual Bishops, the need for utterly circumspect behavior, and the mutability of all human conditions, but to

152

them it was like the voice of a lawyer reading the fine print on a contract already signed in blood and galactic dust. Through the whirling vortex of his thoughts, Rudy was conscious only that he had never been so absolutely happy since he was a very small child; he was wishing illogically that he were Fred Astaire, so that he could swing this woman who held his hand so tightly through all sorts of crazy, improbable dance steps up and down the walls and over the furniture of the dark, shabby common room.

The old man seemed to realize how little he was being attended, for he smiled and withdrew, leaving them to their unspeakable joy.

Ten minutes later Gil emerged from the corridor that led to her own tiny cubicle, carrying a couple of wax note tablets and wearing an abstracted expression that turned to sudden and appalled guilt at the sight of the lovers embracing before the hearth.

"Oh, hell, Rudy, I'm sorry," she said, to the back of his head and to Alde's white hands that grasped his shoulders so fervidly. "I got tied up in my research. Was your flame thrower demonstration to be this afternoon, or was it yesterday and I missed it?"

She could not understand why, at her words, the two lovers broke apart and collapsed into whooping paroxysms of laughter.

CHAPTER TEN

"The old King is dead
  And he's lying on his bed,
  And the snow is a-falling all around . . ."

The voices of the Keep children drifted through the corridors, blithe as the sound of sleigh bells. From her seat by the hearth of the common room fire, Gil heard them, and in spite of her exhaustion-grated nerves and her oft-declared detestation of the young of the species, she smiled. Every child in the place had been pelting around in a state of self-induced frenzy for the last two days.

Tomorrow was the Winter Feast.

The gay carol faded into the winding distance of the maze. Gil's hand strayed to the parchment roll of notes that lay on the bricks at her side. Then she leaned her head against the stone of the chimney and closed her eyes. *This time tomorrow,* she told herself tiredly, *I will be back at the simulated-ivory towers of UCLA, explaining—or trying to explain— how come I left without notice in the second week of Fall Quarter and where I've been since.*

Tomorrow.

Other voices echoed in the hall outisde. Vair na Chandros, his tone harsh and acid, demanded, "What do you mean, missing?"

The light, fluent voice of Bektis replied, "He set out from the caves before I did, my lord. Surely he would not have strayed from the road. If the Dark Ones have taken to moving about in the dusk, before full darkness falls . . ."

"That's ridiculous," the Alketch Commander rasped. "For one thing, my lord Stiarth had a talisman that protected him, in some measure, from the notice of the Dark. He boasted of it to me."

The Court Mage's tones were apologetic. "True, the Rune of the Veil is a general protective device, but hardly guarantees . . ."

"Gil?" There was a rustle of robes in the shadows beside her and the smell of herbs and woodsmoke. "Not sad?"

She shook her head without looking at him. After a moment's silence, Ingold's light, strong hands touched her shoulders and drew her back into the comforting circle of his arm.

"It will all be a tremendous mess when you get back, won't it?" he asked quietly. "Another black mark to me. Will they believe you if you tell them that you were spirited away by gypsies?"

In spite of herself, Gil laughed. "I'll tell them I was doing research at the bottom of the Hollow Hills," she murmured. She leaned her head back against the strength of his shoulder. "That's even the truth. I said once I was going to do my Ph.D. thesis on the coming of the Dark. And there it is." She moved her fingers toward the rolled parchment with its long columns of dates and years. "It was a scholar's answer, wasn't it?"

"Indeed," Ingold whispered, and his arm tightened around her shoulders. "Gil . . ."

She opened her eyes and looked up to see the struggle in that lined, nondescript face and the naked unhappiness of his eyes. Then he sighed, as if he were putting away some impossible dream, and said, "Be happy."

"Will you?"

"I shall be happy," Ingold said quietly, "knowing that you are safe."

Light began to stir in the room as the other mages came in, a clear, sourceless brightness that sparkled like unfamiliar dawn over the familiar furnishings. The members of the Wizards' Corps began to take their places around the long central table. Dakis the Minstrel flirted outrageously with the weatherwitches Grey and Nila; the haughty Shadow of the Moon was discussing astronomy with the diffident Ungolard. The gaggle of the younger mages down at the far end of the table—not all of whom were young in years by any means—kept a wary eye out for Thoth, who had taken it upon himself to act as their tutor. Brother Wend came in, worn and hagridden, like a man being eaten from within by slow cancer. As Ingold handed her to her feet, Gil saw that Kta had been in the commons all the time, dozing in his nook by the fire.

Rudy and Alde appeared, handfast like children, as if they still could not believe their good fortune. They almost sparkled with happiness, and Gil had to smile.

Here are two, at least, who have gotten what they wanted, even if they are stuck in a world without hope.

Then Bektis entered, still stroking his milk-white beard, nattering on about the mislayment of the Imperial Nephew; and behind him came Alwir, kingly in his dark velvet, telling Bektis in a rich, melodious voice to shut his blithering mouth. The Chancellor stopped before Ingold, and there was a bleak and ugly hatred in his handsome, sensual face.

"I hope, my lord wizard, that this is not another piece of your—renegotiation—of the terms of the alliance. The armies are, after all, departing the day after tomorrow—if it pleases you," he added sarcastically.

"I am afraid," Ingold said, "that that is what we must discuss." He led Gil to one end of the long table and seated her to the right of his own place at its head. She put down her things—the roll of parchment, two or three wax note tablets, and a small wash-leather bag—and turned back, to see the Chancellor's face darken with anger.

"Really . . . !"

"Perhaps, my lord," Ingold continued in his mildest tones, "you had best sit down."

Two of the junior wizards brought up the carved chair that was usually reserved for Thoth and put it at the far end of the table. Alwir seated himself in it stiffly, the folds of his black velvet cloak spreading about him like a royal robe, suspicion as visible as a back brace in every line of his big, powerful body.

Do him justice, Gil thought. *It was only yesterday that Ingold kicked the props out from under his plans to settle down into a nice, cozy Regency here, with Alketch troops at his back and the Inquisition to keep people like Rudy in line. And after he drove out the Dark Ones from Gae—after he'd given people even the illusion that things were on their way to returning to what they used to be—he'd hardly have needed to dispose of Tir. His own prestige would have made him King by acclamation. It's no surprise that he views Ingold as a malicious meddler in affairs that hardly concern him.*

But the stubborn set of Alwir's mouth and the sullenness smoldering in his eyes made her stomach sink with dread.

Ingold took his seat at the head of the table; with a glance he commanded silence in the room around them. It always surprised Gil how the wizard, usually the most unobtrusive of men, could dominate any gathering he entered, merely by walking into the room and choosing to do so.

Alwir's voice was rough, "There's a rumor going about that you've found the key to the defeat of the Dark. If this is true, why wasn't I told? And why do you say—"

"It is to tell you of it that we asked you here tonight," Ingold said, folding his hands upon the table before him. Behind his head, against the blotched brick and soot-stained plaster of the wall, Thoth's mathematical and astrological charts formed a kind of tapestry, half-obscured by braids of drying herbs. On the hearth, the marmalade tom, the biggest of the Corps cats, was licking his paws and studiously ignoring the pans of bread which Kara had set to rise among the warm ashes.

Gil could see Alwir's gaze travel over that homey and unprepossessing room and over the faces of those who sat around the table—old men, young girls, foreigners, heathens, and vagabonds—before coming to rest on his sister. His nostrils flared with contempt.

"Then you have a damned queer way of going about it. But after yesterday, I don't suppose I have a right to be surprised by anything you choose to do." He did not trouble to hide the bitterness in his voice. "Suppose you tell me, then, since you are my Chief of Intelligence. How did humankind defeat the Dark? Or is that going to stay one of the things that only you know?"

Ingold sighed. "Often, my lord," he said after a moment's pause, "when an answer seems impossible to find, the best thing to do is to see if the proper question was asked. In this case, the question should not have been: How did humankind defeat the Dark? It should have been simply: *Did* humankind defeat the Dark?"

Alwir seemed to rear in his seat. "Of course it did! Else why did the Dark depart?"

"Another very good question, my lord—and one closer to the heart of the matter. Perhaps the real question should be, not why they departed, but why they rose."

Ill-concealed anger grated in Alwir's words. "Of what earthly good would it be to know that? It doesn't matter why they rose! If that was all you asked me here to tell me—"

"That," the wizard said quietly, "and other things. I believe I was the first human to see the Dark Ones begin to hunt on the surface of the earth, the year I was hiding in the deserts of Gettlesand, playing spellweaver and astrologer in a little farming village, with the High King's price on my head. I followed the Dark One back to its city—not a paltry hive of a defeated remnant, but a teeming metropolis of creatures to whom humankind was of no more moment that wild cattle."

Gil shivered as Ingold told of it, his voice casting its spell over those who listened. His words dislimned the shabby common room around them and drew them into the frozen blueness of that starlit desert night and to the smothering blackness of underground. Even the mulish look about Alwir's mouth faded somewhat as the old man drove home to them the horror of what he had first realized then—that the Dark did not live in that fashion because they had been driven to it, but because they had chosen it for their own.

"I had lived for five years in Gae," Ingold went on, "for three of them in the Palace, as tutor to Prince Eldor, the High King's son. I knew of the stairway in the lower vaults—more than one, some said. They were thought to be part of the old Citadel of Wizards that once stood upon the spot or part of some heathen temple out of bygone years. All that the Masters at Quo could tell me was that there were other stairways in various parts of the world, that they had the property of distorting magic, so that no mage who had ever descended one could communicate with others after he was out of sight, and that no one who had ever gone down had returned. They were thought to be curiosities, like the gray lands in certain parts of the world where time is unaccountably distorted or like those spots in the mountains where you can stand and hear voices speaking in tongues unknown to the West of the World. But no more than that.

"Yet after I had seen that unspeakable city, I was frightened; and in the years that followed, years in which I learned and read and traveled, I heard an occasional tale that frightened me still more. A chieftain of the White Raiders told me of a man who had vanished in open country on a moonless night. In a village close to the ice, there had lately been a wave of superstitious dread of the night—people could not be induced to leave their houses after dark, though they would not say why this was. I began to investigate any story that came my way of mysterious disappearances or of certain things seen or felt."

Alwir said bitterly, "So you always knew of the Dark."

"Indeed I did," Ingold replied mildly. "And I told anyone who would listen, with the result that King Umar had me imprisoned, publicly flogged, and exiled from the Realm, ostensibly for treasonously alienating the loyalties of his only son. Prince Eldor hardly needed my aid in despising his father—and he had inherited the memories of the House of Dare. He remembered the Time of the Dark. To him, my warning came like the fulfillment of some dreadful prophecy. He trusted me," Ingold finished simply—an epitaph, Gil thought, for the man who had given him his son and sent him from the final battle. "Without that trust and the preparations he made because of it, we would have been utterly lost."

Across the table from her, Gil saw Alde suddenly bow her head, staring down at her tight-clenched hands as if taken unawares by the memories of those last days.

Ingold went on. "Even then—and it was twenty years ago that the stories were first circulated—it struck me that most of them came from a small area around Shilgae in the far North, and a few from the lands of Harl Kinghead, near Weg. But even though I knew this, I did not understand what it meant until a few weeks ago, when I spoke of it with Gil-Shalos. Since that time, she has searched far and wide for knowledge of the Dark. In her own country she is a scholar and a teacher. I believe that the answer that she has found to this riddle is the true one, though she has read it, not from any man's writing, but as a hunter does, from the tracks of the game that he seeks."

He held out his hand to Gil. She took a deep breath, glanced automatically behind her for a nonexistent blackboard, and stood up. In the clear, rosy brightness of that long room, she was conscious of nothing but watching eyes and silence.

"Any historian can tell you," she began, in her best doctoral orals voice, "that *why* is probably the most slippery of all questions to answer, so for the moment I'll start with the things that we do know for sure—when and where the Dark rose.

"Ingold is our first source on when—which puts it twenty years ago in Gettlesand. Tomec Tirkenson tells me that there have always been stories about haunted caves in the Flatiron Mountains in that part of the country, of the 'way back in the days' variety, but when he was younger he said there was at least one incident of a child who disappeared in that part of the hills at night. It was put down by her family to dooic—but as he remembers it, there were no dooic around the Flatirons for a stretch of several years. Three of his rangers who come from that part of the country bear him out on this. This was when Tirkenson was twenty-seven or twenty-eight, just before he succeeded to rulership of the lands . . ." She consulted her notes. "That puts it around eighteen years ago. This was at the same time Ingold was in the North, investigating other rumors of disappearances around Shilgae.

"Now, as close as I can date them, all these disappearance stories seem to center, not only physically around

Shilgae, but chronologically in a span of three or four years. Coincidentally, that time period is better known for the failure of the wheat crop three years running, for the 'drowned summer' of the seventeenth year of Umar's reign, and for the failure of the sugar crop in Kildrayne. According to Maia, sugar has never been grown north of Penambra since. Maia knows, because his father was a sharecropper in the cane fields near Kildrayne and had to remove to the deep south because of it.

"After that four-year span, there were no disappearance stories until—" She checked her notes again. "—the winter before last. And those never reached anyone because they were in the country of the White Raiders. I've only heard of them recently, from Shadow of the Moon."

The Raider shaman inclined her head, and the strings of bleached, ancient bones twined in her snowy braids rattled faintly with the movement.

"Last winter there was a disturbance among the dooic of the Northern Plains, rumors of Night Ghosts that ate stragglers. Kta says several bands left their traditional runs near the hills. At the same time, several bands of the Raiders started shifting away from their old hunting grounds. According to some of the Gettlesand rangers I've talked to, there was a lot of trouble with them that year. Disappearances of men riding night-herd were put down to the Raiders . . . and maybe they were.

"But there seems to be a pattern appearing. First in the plains and high desert and in the far North; gradually moving south to more thickly inhabited lands."

Alwir raised his head suddenly, points of fire glinting in his eyes, like the stars at the heart of a sapphire.

"Most curious of all," Gil continued, "is what appears to be a pattern of *abandonment* of Nests, following the same course. According to the Raiders who remain on the plains, Nests in the far Northern Plains were abandoned early this autumn; Ingold and Rudy saw such a Nest, not more than a few days' journey north of the Westward Road. Before he died, Lohiro of Quo told them that the Dark Ones of the plains had deserted their Nests to join the assault on Gae and, I would guess, the breaking of the cities to the south of

161

them as well—Dele and the towns along the Flat River, Ippit, Skrooch, Ploduck, and others. At the same time, Quo was broken by an unsuspected and deeply buried Nest beneath that town. In effect, at that time the Dark Ones destroyed all organized resistance in the Realm, struck at the one place where large amounts of information could be gathered and organized, and left us as we are now—fugitives in the grip of the worst winter in human memory."

Up and down the table, soft-voiced talk eddied, those who counted themselves scholars—and there were half a dozen of them—casting curious glances at one another, for this jigsaw puzzle of hearsay had little in common with the separate chronicles over which they customarily pored. Only Thoth the Scribe, once the Recorder of Quo, did not speak; his cold, amber-colored eyes brightened with interest as much in her methods as in her findings.

Alwir laced his fingers together, suspended midway between the dragon-head arms of his ebony chair. "So you believe that the Dark Ones have abandoned these northern Nests for good?"

"For a considerable time to come," Gil said.

"Why?"

"The White Raiders who captured Ingold and Rudy on the plains believed that the Dark Ones had been driven forth—or destroyed—by a ghost or spirit mightier than they," she said after a moment's thought. "But when Rudy and Ingold descended into the Nest, they found nothing—only the bodies of the herds, all dating from a single time, as if they had all perished together. Yet I think that—that ghost—was in the Nest with them all the time they were down there.

"The ghost's name is Cold."

"Cold?" the Chancellor snapped. "Be serious, girl. The Dark have attacked on nights colder than what a man could survive."

"The Dark can deal with the cold," Gil agreed. "Maybe they don't like it—there doesn't seem to be any way of finding out." She rolled up her parchment and set it on the table before her. "But I am virtually certain that their herds can't."

162

"Their *herds?*" Alwir demanded incredulously. "What in the name of the ice in the north do those wretched creatures have to do with anything?"

"Everything," she responded quietly. "Their herds—and the moss in the Nests."

Rudy's head jerked up, as if her words had triggered memory and realization within him. She saw the wordless question that he flung to Ingold and the old man's silence that was only the echo of the answer that Rudy already knew in his heart.

"I think," Gil said, picking her way carefully over a morass that even her own world had not yet sorted out, "that the ancestors of humankind, the ancestors of the herds, and the ancestors of the dooic roamed together over this part of the world eons ago, countless ages. The similarity in their shape indicates they had a common way of living, common feeding grounds . . ."

"Common grandparents," Rudy added in English.

"Let's not broaden the Scopes of this investigation any more than we have to," Gil replied in the same language. Switching back to the language of the Wathe, she continued. "And I think that all three races alike were the prey of the Dark Ones.

"Now, at that time, hundreds of thousands of years in the past, the Dark Ones lived on the surface of the earth. If you climb the cliffs behind the Vale of the Dark twenty miles north of here, in the right slant of the light you can see the marks of buried walls, the patterns of a city that vanished so long ago that not even ruins remain; there are not even records of ruins ever having been there. The Dark tended to build in relatively stable, accessible places. You yourself have commented, my lord, on how they seem to shun high or geologically unstable ground. The Vale of the Dark is one of the few sites that hasn't been built over in the intervening millennia, and of course it is impossible to get high enough above the Nests on the plains to see whether this pattern can be detected in the country surrounding them or not.

"I think," Gil continued slowly, "that it was during this epoch that the powers of the mageborn first began to appear in humankind. It was a matter of survival. The lowest powers of the mages, the commonest even of the third echelon powers, is the calling of fire. Light, illusion, the command of the winds and storms, heightened senses, and the ability to see in the dark."

"This is all very well," Alwir said, his voice edged with suspicion, "but if what you say is so—and I am not yet convinced that it is—why did the Dark Ones abandon the surface? Why did they retreat belowground in the first place?"

For an answer, Gil searched among her things for the small leather pouch and took from it an irregularly shaped gray rock about a third the size of her fist. She rose and carried it down the length of the table to hand it to him.

He sat in silence for a time, examining the stone, turning it over thoughtfully in his gloved fingers. Without glancing at her, he asked, "And what is this?"

She took it and handed it to Thoth. The serpentmage examined it closely, angling it in the shadowless brightness of the magelight. Then he held it up between restless antennalike fingers. "How did you come by this, child?"

"Do you know what it is?"

"Not in the true sense, no," the old Scribe replied. "But I have seen ones like this before. They are found in many places, usually several together; there was a case of them in the library at Quo. Most of those were found in a stream bed in the hills behind the town, but there were some from Dele, and one—a most curious one, with imprints in it of strange insects the like of which no one has seen—that my lord Ingold brought back with him from the Barrier Hills, which border the Northern Ice."

"This one was found in the Vale of the Dark," Gil said. "In my world we call them fossils. Tell me, Thoth, do you know the plant whose leaves are printed in the rock?"

The Recorder examined the stone again and passed it across to Ingold, who shook his head. "It is similar to the ferns which grow in the swamps of Alketch," Ingold said. "But it is far larger. If such a thing exists elsewhere, I have never seen it."

"But it's a hot-weather plant; a swamp fern of the tropics."

"Undoubtedly."

Gil held out her hand, received the rock back, and returned to her seat. "Long ago," she said, "such things grew in the Vale of the Dark. Eons ago, I believe that the climate of this world was far warmer than it is now—warm enough so that tropical swamps covered most of the West of the World. But things changed, and gradually the world grew colder. Perhaps the sun became a little dimmer, or for some reason clouds thickened, year after year, cutting out most of the sun's rays. The ice in the north began to increase. The weather grew more violent.

"The Dark drift upon the currents of the air—they are not weather-wise, and are at the mercy of storms. Their retreat below the ground was gradual; the great stone pavements and stairways were the transition phase, while they themselves lived below the earth and allowed their herds to roam aboveground. The Dark did not go hunting on the surface much. Rather, they summoned their herds with spells—similar, I think, to the spell they used on you in the vaults at Gae, Ingold."

"Yes," the old man said quietly and looked down at his hands. "A—singing, is the closest I can come to describe it." He did not say more, but she saw the muscles of jaw and temple clench suddenly at the memory.

"In time the Dark called down their herds and abandoned the surface altogether. They had lived belowground themselves for a long while. I suspect the more intelligent, more deadly tribes of humankind were winning out against their herd-creatures in competition for food and territory. In any case, a long time ago, long before human beings first settled down into villages, the last of the herds were gone, and the memories of the Dark vanished from the earth. All that remained were the stairways and that indefinable aura of power that surrounded them."

She paused for a moment and shuffled through her notes, her hair falling down to hide her face. The wizards were now utterly silent; the hush in the room was as palpable as a weighted cloak upon her shoulders. Alwir's eyes burned as balefully as a plague-star above his folded knuckles. She straightened up. "Now," she said quietly, "about that aura of power.

"My first guess about the aura—the 'luck' that surrounds the Nests—was that it was deliberate on the part of the Dark Ones, to attract human settlement in the area of the Nests, thus ensuring the Dark an emergency food supply. One thing is clear from all accounts—the Nests have always been regarded as awesome places, fearsome at times, but at other times 'fortunate' or 'magic.' The records refer to some nests as 'gaenguo'—magic places. Scriptures contain references to the Old Religion and mention human sacrifice, though there is no specific reference to the stairways in the holy writings. But the word *sacrifice* itself—*clarneach*—comes from the ancient Wathe *ecl'r naieg*—literally, *to send down*. After the rise of the Straight Faith, many of the old holy places of the superseded cult were taken over. In any case, the major cities of the Times Before seem to have been built above or near the Nests of the Dark. After the Time of the Dark was past, citadels of wizardry were often built on these sites, again because of the aura that had the effect of magnifying the powers of the wizards, particularly those connected with healing.

"This leads me to believe that the power of the Dark, especially in the early days, was exerted in a positive or cherishing fashion toward their herds. The sense of dread and terror associated with the Nests was always there— hence the tendency to hide or bury the stairways themselves, which had such disastrous consequences at Quo— but the general area of the Nest enjoyed a kind of 'glow,' a by-product of the power of the Dark itself."

"This is all very interesting," Alwir murmured. He shifted his powerful weight in the carven chair. "Perhaps it is even true. But I fail to appreciate how this scholarly exposition of the history of the Dark Ones and their herds can be brought to bear upon the present problem. The past is all very fine, Gil-Shalos, but it is the present with which we are forced to deal."

"My lord is a busy man," Bektis amplified stuffily. "I hardly think . . ."

"You retain us as an intelligence corps, my lord," Ingold said quietly. "We have compiled a report of our findings, and you might at least listen to our conclusions."

"My lord has no need of intelligence . . ."

"Be quiet, Bektis." Alwir leaned forward, the opals that starred the dark velvet of his doublet catching the light like points of fire. "Continue, Gil-Shalos. Am I correct in assuming that these—these herds of filthy things that the Dark feed upon—feed themselves on the mosses that your friend Rudy found so flammable?"

"They do," Gil said. "They have done so, time out of mind, to the point where I think they can eat nothing else—or thrive on nothing else. You can keep a cat alive for a while on nothing but cereal, but in a short time it will fade and die. In the far South, I've heard about animals—little bears—that can live on nothing but the leaves of a single kind of tree; and if the tree should die, they would perish.

"Moreover," she went on, "we all know that you cannot grow good apples in Alketch or decent melons in Shilgae and that a wet winter or a cold summer will spread famine over half the Realm. If the cold itself doesn't kill a plant, there are parasites—some of them too small to be seen—that can only start growing once the temperature gets down below a certain point."

Gil paused, then picked up the scroll of her notes. There was total, mystified silence in the room. Even Kara's mother had ceased her low-voiced spate of commentary—*no mean accomplishment,* Gil thought. They were all watching her, puzzled and yet drawn. Historical methodology was not a subject taught at the School of Quo.

"I'm going to backtrack for a minute," she said, "and talk about the weather."

Alwir let out a short, harsh yelp of laughter. "The *weather?* Really, this ends all . . ."

Gil frowned, deeply affronted. "The weather," she repeated. "That's what I've been doing for the last week or so—compiling, as well as I could from the Church chronicles and the books that Ingold retrieved from the library at Quo, a tally of good and bad winters, and as much information as I can about the ice in the north."

"I've never heard such useless—" the Chancellor began indignantly.

"It has a bearing," Gil said. "Believe me, it has a bearing upon the Dark.

"I assume everyone knows that the ice in the north is spreading—very slowly, supposedly. Everyone uses the expression 'as sure as the ice in the north' to mean something that cannot be stopped. But according to Ingold, the ice is moving southward at the rate of several inches a year. Kta and Shadow of the Moon both say that some years it's more than that.

"On the oldest maps of the Realm there's a range of hills called the Barrier Hills, clearly marked, twenty or thirty miles south of the ice. Well, they're just about covered now. The Raider legends speak in their earliest records of how the ice moved back to uncover the Northern Plains, which was their first home. By backtracking the generational lists that I got from Shadow, I'd put that time between twenty-five hundred and two thousand years ago—just about the first time records were being maintained here at the Keep after the Dark Ones had vanished for good.

"Now, the reason we don't have any Keep records much before two thousand years ago is that literacy had fallen to such a low level that few records were kept and records—or anything else flammable that wasn't in use as furniture—ended up being burned. That allows us to date the end of the record-burning period at least approximately—and it falls right around the time of the last retreat of the ice from the Northern Plains.

"But the Times Before weren't cold. In the record crystals you can see that the climate was very warm and that tropical ferns grew in the lagoons around Gae. The people dressed for hot weather, and you can see the kind of bright-colored birds in them that you can only find in the jungles of Alketch now. Minalde's memories—the memories that she, as a descendant of the House of Dare, inherited—are memories of snow and storm, of blizzards burying the Pass—two

168

hundred miles south of tropical Gae! The change was sudden enough that some of the refugees who took shelter in the caves on the north cliffs were still wearing warm-weather clothing and sandals. And I think," Gil said, "that the same thing is happening now.

"You see, the world I come from is much warmer than this one. So when everyone around me has been saying that this is the worst winter anyone can remember, I never knew how much worse it was. But from things I've read—descriptions of life as it was two hundred years ago—I realized that this world was probably warmer even than my own. The novels Alde brought down from Karst describe—pretty accurately, Thoth tells me—costumes that couldn't *possibly* be worn now—thin silks and muslins. In the novels, most of the people spend much of their time trying to cool off. Even people like Ingold and Govannin, who knew Gae thirty or forty years ago, say the same. Gae's a pretty temperate place now, but Karst was originally a summer resort, a place to escape the heat. They tell me Gae also used to have one hell of a mosquito problem; Alde, Janus, and the Guards who came to Gae in the last five or ten years say that's no worse than anywhere. And now this year, mammoth have been sighted in the river valleys, where they haven't been for seven hundred years. Rudy and Ingold, crossing the desert, were driven underground by an ice storm not seventy miles north of the Plains Road—three hundred miles farther south than any ice storm has ever been reported. Isn't that so, Thoth?"

"It is so indeed," the serpentmage replied.

"Sarda Pass has been snowed shut for weeks on end this winter," Gil continued, "and, according to the chronicles of both Gae and Renweth, there has never been any record of the Pass being blocked for more than a day or so, and that in dead winter. But of the times that it has been blocked, two of them were within the first hundred years of the chronicle, and four have been within the last twenty years. The first time was twenty years ago—the same year Ingold saw the Dark hunting aboveground in the deserts of Gettlesand."

"It snowed in Penambra that year," Blid the Soothsayer said suddenly. "It had never snowed there before, though it has twice since. I remember standing in the courtyard of our house, while everyone was running about and whispering and catching snowflakes in their hands. The dooic slaves were terrified. They had no idea what it was."

"Perhaps they did," Ingold murmured, "and that was what terrified them."

There was silence, as each tried to remember back to those lost years: a boy standing in the muddy court of his home in that city of palms and flowers, catching snowflakes in wondering hands; and a fugitive spellweaver lying in the darkness of a desert cave, seeing the Dark drop on an old dooic who had shuffled in for shelter from an unnaturally icy night. Rudy thought, *That was the winter before I turned five, when I began to have visions of magic.*

Kara spoke up suddenly. "There was an epidemic in Ippit then. I was only a little girl, but mother always said it was because of the cold."

"We marked the increasing number of famines and sicknesses," Ungolard said, his earrings flashing as he raised his head. "I was in the College of Astrologers in Khirsrit. These things were noted there, but not, as you have said, my fair lady, their meaning."

"Me granddad disappeared that winter," Ilae whispered, looking up from stroking the cat. "Uncle says he went out to look for t' pigs of an eve, nor never came back."

"I think what we're dealing with," Gil said slowly, "is a weather cycle, a—an alternation of hot periods and cold, governed by the growth and retreat of the ice in the north. The ice doesn't have to move very far south to change the climate. When it does, for whatever reason, when the temperature stays too low for too long, the moss in the Nests of the Dark starts to die. The herds start to die. And then the Dark Ones begin to hunt on the surface of the earth."

She rolled her notes together and rested them endwise on the table, her hands folded upon them.

"There was a short cold spell twenty years ago. I think that the climate has been gradually cooling for at least the last hundred years. The short spell affected only the most exposed Nests—those of Gettlesand, the plains, and the far North. The one we're in now—a far deeper one—has af-

170

fected all the northern Nests—at Gae, Quo, Dele, and Penambra. It will be only a matter of time before the herds in the southern Nests begin to die as well.

"And that's the answer." Gil shrugged and scanned the faces of the mages ranged around the table. "The answer is that there is no answer. We've never found anything that indicates that Dare of Renweth ever fought the Dark at all. The cold spell then lasted six to eight hundred years. This one could easily do the same. The Dark Ones will go away when the weather warms and their herds build back to strength—not before."

"That's a lie!" Alwir's voice cracked across hers like the stroke of a leaded whip. He surged to his feet, a storm of rage darkening his face. "The whole idea of the world getting colder or warmer is utter nonsense! Foolish drivel and treason against the allies of the Realm! The world is the world, the earth is the earth. It is fixed, stable. The sun is set in its orbit and the earth in its shape. Your talk of—of the sun getting colder or swamps covering the West of the World—it is impossible!"

"But it isn't," Gil protested unwisely. "Just because a thing is created doesn't mean that it's immutable. Look at a man's body. It changes and grows old, grows a beard in its proper time or loses hair, and gains or loses flesh—"

"Don't quibble with me, girl!" the Chancellor roared, towering over her like an enraged bear. "This idiocy about women's fashions and rocks and plants and where it snows and when—pah! What proof have you that these had anything to do with the first rising of the Dark?"

"Alde's memories . . ." Gil began—and stopped. She felt slow heat rising to her face, realizing that that, at least, was one source of information that could never be revealed. Particularly not now, when Alde had put herself in defiance of her brother and publicly as much as announced her intentions of wielding at least a certain degree of power in the Keep. "The record crystals . . ." she began again.

"Don't speak to me of them unless you can feel the air of those times!" Alwir sneered bitterly. "Women would parade the streets naked in a snowstorm if fashion dictated they must! And as for your memories, my sister . . ." He bent his scathing gaze upon the girl who sat, head bowed in wretched silence, across from Gil. "You know as well as I do that only men bear the memories of the House of Dare. A convenient departure from custom," he went on, swinging around to face Ingold, who had risen and gone to Gil's side. "And how well it proves your point!

"So I am to give up the reconquest of the world from the Dark and the alliance that will rejuvenate our civilization, not because you and your amorous student wish to keep the power in the Realm between you, not because you have had a price on your head in the Empire since you fled from there as an escaping slave, not because my sister scorns to marry a true man or because our allies will not tolerate seeing the likes of you in power—but because this other student of yours has foreseen that the Dark Ones will destroy Alketch—in divinations based upon ladies' millinery!"

He leaped up, moved around the table, and snatched the parchment scroll from Gil's hands. Ripping it in two, he turned and flung the pieces into the fire. "*That* for your answer. Where are the records from which you obtained these so-called facts?"

Gil moved toward him, blazing with icy rage. Her scholarly instincts were far too offended to permit her to feel fear; for the wanton destruction of her notes, she would gladly have killed him. But a strong hand caught her arm, staying her, and it was Ingold's calm, scratchy voice that replied.

"They are in the Church archives, Alwir," he said quietly. "I turned them all over to Bishop Govannin."

"You what?"

"I feared that they might come to harm," the wizard returned, unfazed by the Chancellor's crimson face. "My lady Govannin is—quite protective of her library."

Remembering the bitter quarrels between prelate and Chancellor that had punctuated all the long journey from Karst, Gil reflected that Ingold's talent for understatement occasionally bordered on the awesome. As for Alwir, he stood for a time unable to speak, the ugly rage of a man cheated of what he had felt to be his own settling around him like a cloud of noxious smoke. Shocked stillness had descended upon the common room; in it, the Chancellor's breath sounded thick and hard, as if he had been running.

"Very well," he said finally. "I was warned, and perhaps this is something that I have brought upon myself. Having taken you in—you and this wretched crew of vagabonds you call your intelligence corps—" The slash of his hand included the dumbstruck mages, who sat frozen in their places around the table. "—and having fed you out of the rations of my own household, I should have perhaps expected something better than this treason; but it seems that in dealing with you, Ingold Inglorion, one must be prepared for the unexpected.

"As for you others," he continued, glancing about him, "you are still my servants. As such, I expect you to fulfill your part in the invasion of the Nest to the letter. Afterward you may come or go as you choose. But I tell you this: if any word comes to me, from any source whatsoever, of what was spoken here tonight or if any mention is made of this— this ridiculous treason—of the Dark rising in Alketch, either to our allies or to anyone else in the Keep, I will turn you all over to the mercy of the Inquisitor. And believe me, it would be better then had you not been born."

His eyes traveled slowly over them, fraught with a rage-blistered menace that silenced even Kara's mother. Then he looked back at Ingold. "And as for you and this besotted chit of a girl—" He broke off, the words sticking in his throat.

Gil felt Ingold's reaction, like a sudden wave of smoking heat, though she would have been at a loss to describe any change that took place in the old man at her side. But the power that blazed forth from him was like a vortex of force, an Archmage's wrath like the unveiled core of some terrible energy. She saw Alwir fall back a step before it, his face yellow with shock.

"My lord Alwir," that soft, scratchy voice said, "none of these my children are your servants, nor shall you do anything against them or against this girl."

Alwir licked his dry lips, but his throat seemed unable to produce a sound. Terror-sweat stood out on his brow and cheeks, glittering in the crystalline light. Like Gil, he had known that Ingold was Archmage of the West without truly realizing what that meant.

In the utter silence that gripped the room, Ingold's low voice was the only sound. "You will act like a fool if you choose, my lord. But do not deceive yourself that I act out of any fear or regard for you or your policies. I do what I do for the good of what is left of humankind. If your quarrel is with me, then speak to me of it; for if you harm any one of these in this room, it shall be the worse for you. Now leave us."

"You . . ." the Chancellor gasped hoarsely, but his breath dried in his mouth. His face was ghastly, a grotesque contortion of fear.

"Get out."

The bigger man flinched, as if from a sword thrust. He backed slowly to the door; but in the shocked stillness of the common room, all could hear when his footfalls broke into a run in the darkness of the halls.

Like the slow fading of sunset, the power that had scorched the air in the room waned, and with it the soft brilliance of the light. Gil had not moved, frozen in awe of the man who stood beside her; now she turned to him and saw how the lengthening shadows deepened the crags of his face. A last fragment of the torn parchment in the fireplace caught, and the sudden flare of light stippled his white hair in gold.

Kta's piping voice was the first to break the silence. "He will never forgive you that."

Ingold sighed and closed his eyes. "He would never have forgiven me in any case."

Gil put a hand under his arm and steered him to the thronelike seat so recently vacated by Alwir. Thoth came around the end of the table to join them and laid a slender, ink-stained hand on his shoulder.

"You are weary," the serpentmage said in his dry old voice. "You should sleep."

The other mages were drifting from the room, talking in low, frightened voices of what had passed or debating what was to be done. At one end of the table, Rudy still sat, his bulky flame thrower in his hand, turning it this way and that in the light of the fire, with Alde silent and anxious at his side. The last glow of the magelight had been superseded by the rosy colors of the fire.

Ingold raised his head finally to look at Gil. "I am sorry, child," he said quietly. "You worked hard. More than that, I'm convinced that your answer to the problem of the Dark is the true one." He reached up and took her hands. "Thank you."

There was silence, fraught with unspoken words. Looking down into his face, Gil was overwhelmed by fear for him and by the sense of shadows closing and thickening around him. Where, after all, could he go? Within the sanctuary of the Keep was Alwir; without it, the Dark.

"And in any case, tomorrow it will no longer be your concern," the wizard murmured. "It is the Winter Feast. You are free to return to your own world, without putting it in danger of invasion by the Dark. I shall send you back through the gap in the Void at sunrise—unless you stay long enough to keep the Feast with me."

His voice was pitched low, excluding the few who remained in the shadowy common room. His mouth had a set look under the tangled forest of white beard, as if braced against some bitter emotion; Gil fought her own urge to reach out and touch his rough, silky hair.

Instead, in a brisk voice, she said, "In spite of all this—in spite of the fact that you know that the Dark are seeking you—will you still march north with the army?"

"Of course . . ." he began, and then looked more sharply up at her, catching some inflection in her voice. ". . . not," he finished. "Of course not."

Thoth's honey-colored glance flicked sideways, startled, but Ingold cut off his words. "No, I shall remain here at the Keep. Alwir has my permission to perish in his own chosen fashion, but after tonight, I see no reason to oblige the Dark by letting them strip my bones. Don't worry about me, my child. I shall be quite safe."

Gil nodded. "I'm glad to hear it," she said. "Even though it will make things rougher for the rest of us when we march on the Nest."

"There's no need for you to endanger your life!" he retorted sharply.

"Oh, come on, Ingold, you can't expect me to leave on the eve of an invasion without knowing how it will turn out."

"I certainly can, particularly when you know better than anyone else that it is most likely to turn out, as you say, with you dead. You know how little chance there is . . ."

"I know how little chance there is," she told him maliciously, "if you're staying at the Keep. The Guards will need every sword."

She intercepted a startled look from Rudy, to whom this plan was news. It was, in fact, news to her.

A dangerous glitter of annoyance shone in Ingold's eyes, which Gil met with an air of mild defiance, daring him to contradict his own lie.

More quietly, she went on. "It was you who taught me not to forsake those I love, even though their cause might be lost."

He regarded her for a long moment, at a loss for once in his life for a retort. His hands, still closed around hers, tightened slightly; had it not been both their lives at stake in this joust of wills, she could almost have laughed at the emotions warring in his face.

Then he said, "Has anyone ever told you how unbecoming it is for the young to outwit their elders?"

Gil shook her head, her eyes wide, as innocent of guile as a schoolgirl's. "No, sir."

He snorted. "Consider yourself told."

"Yes, sir."

"Now go to bed. And, Gil . . ."

She paused in the doorway, turning to see him half-risen from his chair, edged in the reflected amber of the hearthlight as if with a lingering of his earlier searing power. Behind him, all was darkness, but for the oily sparkle of Rudy's flame thrower on the table and the shimmering twinkle of the harp strings in the corner of the hearth.

"You never needed me to teach you that kind of loyalty, Gil."

"I needed you in order to understand it."

She turned and strode quickly into the darkness, feeling exhausted, lightheaded, and yet curiously at peace.

"Did Gil really mean it?" Alde hugged her black fur cloak more tightly about her; though the sun shone, pale and distant, for the first time in many weeks, the air was icy cold. She and Rudy came out of the gate passage into the open and moved down the steps, jostled by the crowds around them. From the jumbled warren of booths made of pine boughs and ragged, colored awnings that stretched along two sides of the meadow, a skiff of freezing wind carried voices and music.

"Of course she meant it." Rudy looked over at Alde in surprise.

"But she might be killed."

The path leading down to the meadow was slushy, trampled already by the crowds that had been taking that way since dawn. Rudy put a steadying arm around Alde's shoulders. Tir, wrapped up like a little black and white cabbage and tucked within her cloak, blinked about him with wide, jewel-blue eyes and gurgled happily at the noise and confusion below.

"I didn't understand all of what she said last night," Rudy went on, "but she's right about one thing. She couldn't leave without knowing if her friends were going to live or die."

"No," Alde agreed quietly. "But she's the one who wrote that report. She knows better than anyone that humankind never defeated the Dark. She knows how hopeless it is."

"That's a helluva thing to say to the man who invented our side's secret weapon," Rudy declared in mock indignation.

The path was narrow; they brushed elbows with others descending around them: Guards in threadbare black uniforms and Tirkenson's rangers in sheepskin boots; women in rainbow skirts like those of peasants, their hair twined with jewels they'd picked out of the mud of Karst; and children, scorning the careful steps of their elders, sliding down the muddy snow, waving precious bits of honey candy in sticky fingers and shrieking like little birds.

On the edge of the warren of booths, Alde put a hand on Rudy's arm, halting him; the breath of the Feast, of honey and snow and pine and music, swirled over them from the meadow in a disturbing backwash of sound and smell. "Do you still believe that Dare of Renweth defeated the Dark with flame throwers?"

"Babe, I don't," Rudy said gently. "I've never really believed it, mostly because, while you recognized this, that, and the other thing around the Keep, you never recognized a flame thrower. I think the wizard-engineers were working on them as a defensive weapon when they disappeared and the labs were sealed up. But that doesn't mean that Alwir's plan won't succeed. If we can burn out the Nest—if we can cauterize the nurseries at its bottom—it will be enough for me and a damnsight more than Dare ever did."

"You're very serious about destroying the nurseries," she murmured, her eyes searching his, sober and worried.

"I was down there," Rudy said. "Yeah, I am."

The tug of the Feast overwhelmed Tir. He struggled in his mother's arms and declared insistently, "Andy! Andy!"

Alde caught the flailing little hand that grabbed her hair. "All right, you little wretch, I'll get you some candy." She looked back at Rudy, her face grave. "Why did the wizard-engineers vanish?" she asked softly. "What happened to them?"

Tir tugged impatiently at his mother's hair and cried, "Ad!" He pointed, as Tad the herdkid and a vast gaggle of the Keep orphans went skipping past. Since Tir's concealment among them, the orphans had accepted the heir of the Realm as one of themselves; even Winna, their guardian, had knitted Tir a little stocking cap, such as she had given to all the others as their gifts at the Feast. For his part, Tir was quite happy to be included in that mongrel gang, and Alde turned him over to them. A few moments later, they could be seen out on the meadow, engaged in a wild game of frisbee . . . It was shocking, Gil had once remarked, how much cultural pollution had been going on lately.

Hand in hand, Rudy and Alde plunged into the confusion of the Feast.

The joy of the Winter Feast was the renewal of life; even the terror of the Dark and the crumbling of civilization could not wholly eradicate the celebrations of the return of the midwinter sun. In the meadow that lay between the arms of the vast V of booths, a makeshift band was playing, surrounded by eternally shifting patterns of dancers moving ankle-deep in half-frozen slush. The air was bright with the voices of children and rank with smoke; Gil would have recognized the colorful medley as a scene straight from Breughel, but Rudy felt merely a kind of awed delight in such gay chaos. Among the booths themselves, a tangled latticework of shadows lay over the faces of those who wandered there, and a babble of voices cried whatever wares could be sold for whatever the market would bear.

Resources at the Keep were slim, but with forage parties making regular raids on all the ruined settlements of the flooded river valleys, some surprising articles had turned up. There was honey enough to make sufficient candy to sicken every child in the Keep; some dried fruits had been unearthed and small quantities of sweets. There was little wine, but Melantrys and her company of Guards had been stationed at the Keep for almost a year before the Dark had risen—enough time to make enormous amounts of Blue Ruin gin, which they were hawking in their own booth. The tangled warren of pine-bough booths boasted other entertainments as well; such as a wheel of fortune, under the auspices of Impie Stooft, the stout blond widow of the late unlamented Bendle Stooft. Blid, the Penambran Soothsayer, was telling fortunes, and Dakis the Minstrel was playing his lute.

Everyone in the Keep seemed to have turned out for the festivities—Penambrans, outlanders, and refugees from Gae and Karst. The Alketch soldiery kept to their own camp, by order of Commander Vair. Rudy had the suspicion that the disappearance of Ambassador Stiarth was more responsible for this than any consideration of peace between the allies. No sign of the missing Imperial Nephew had yet turned up, and Alwir, following his rather trying evening in the Corps common room, had evidently spent the rest of the night trying to soothe and resist Vair's outraged demands that the Keep doors be opened and a search party be sent. This, of course, was impossible. Even had Keep Law been broached, which Alde would never have allowed, there were precious few men in the Keep who would have risked their lives to look for the svelte, young Ambassador's bones.

It had done nothing for relations between the allies, but Rudy was just as glad not to have to worry about a riot breaking out between Keep and southern troops.

The day was too beautiful, the last afternoon of peace too precious, to allow that.

So Rudy and Alde wandered at peace through this winter chaos, drinking hot gin and water and eating honey candy like a couple of greedy youngsters. It was the custom to give gifts to children at the Feast, and Alde was forever being stopped by small acquaintances showing off their new toys. Even among the Penambrans, who had escaped the Dark with no more than the rags on their backs, the custom had been kept, with gifts as small as painted walnuts or rag-and-root dolls. After considerable deliberation, Rudy had presented Tir with his motorcycle keys to the child's blissful delight. Rudy knew that he would never use them again.

They wandered down to the frozen stream to watch the footraces held on its surface and laughed as heartily as the rest of the crowd at the slithering antics of the contestants. Blid told Alde's fortune, amid a crowd of interested onlookers—that she would be twice wedded, the second time to a foreign man, and that she would pass through fire and peril to win both love and power. *A respectable and unsurprising fortune*, Rudy thought, *considering what everybody in the Keep must know*.

The sight of the cards troubled him, for he knew a little of their meaning: the Tower crossed by the Rose of Death; the austere sneer of the King of Swords; and the chancy promise of the impetuous Knight of Wands. But by that time both of them had imbibed enough alcohol to find deep significance in the tiniest of matters.

He could not remember ever having seen Alde so beautiful, with her dark hair escaping from its heavy braid to tumble about her face in wisps like the wings of butterflies, and the blue depths of her eyes, like the endless promise of summer pleasures, laughing into his. She had left her cloak somewhere, and the brilliant colors of the eagle on her painted vest flamed against the cherry-red velvet of her skirt.

In the meadow, the band skirled into a wild romp, and the dancers of a crazy quadrille swung back into the arms of their original partners, while all those who watched yelled, "Kiss 'em! Kiss your partners!" The men claimed this customary forfeit from tousled and blushing women.

Rudy saw Gil standing on the sidelines, watching with amusement in her eyes, and he saw the Icefalcon pause to exchange insults with her. It occurred to him that the Icefalcon had added to his collection of bones. They were all braided into the white-blond hair, Raider-style; there seemed to be about twice as many as there had been when the man had returned to the Keep. Some of them, Rudy thought uneasily, although boiled and cleaned, looked pretty fresh.

Bok the carpenter scraped experimentally on his fiddle and tightened a peg; Janus, his Guard's uniform brightened with a woman's gauze scarf knotted over his sword hilt, tortured another gargling moan out of his bagpipes. Alde tugged, laughing, at Rudy's arm. "Let's dance!"

"I can't dance!" he protested.

"Of course you can!" she replied, her cheeks bright with punch and cold. "Listen, they're going to play my favorite . . ."

All around the slushy dancing ground, men and women were forming groups of twelve, here and there yelling, "Set! Set! We need more couples!"

Rudy saw Ingold come up beside Gil, who shook her head, her sharp cheekbones reddening. He caught the drift of that mild, scratchy voice inquiring, "You aren't going to turn down my first proposal to dance with anyone in fifteen years, are you?"

She burst into unexpected giggles. It was astonishing, Rudy thought, how Gil could shift from a mean and steel-hard combination of violence and intellect to the gawkiness and fragility of a girl. Ingold draped an arm around her shoulders and pulled her, blushing, into the circle of the dance floor. Alde put her arm through Rudy's. "Come on!"

The Icefalcon led one of his numerous girlfriends into the set; a moment later, they were joined by Maia of Penambra, leading the silent, red-haired witchchild Ilae by the hand.

"Come on!" Alde insisted, and Rudy allowed himself to be dragged into the line. She waved her hand and called out, "One more couple!" Tomec Tirkenson, looming suddenly out of the crowd like Godzilla emerging from Tokyo Bay, put an arm around Kara of Ippit's waist and drew her, startled and stammering, into position.

Rudy sighed. "What the hell. You'll have to tell me what to do."

"Oh, don't be such a wet goose. It's easy."

It was not easy.

Rudy yelled over his shoulder, "You lied to me!" But he was swept through stars and figures of eight while Alde, swinging in the crook of Ingold's powerful arm, laughed at him with her eyes.

"I'm sorry!" she gasped as he released Gil and caught her hand in one flashing figure, and then she was gone.

People were yelling to him, "Right hand! Right hand! Your *other* right hand!" He went flinging off through a grand right-and-left that reminded him vaguely of a Marx Brothers movie, with the women weaving like a chain of bright ribbon among the laughing men. The music, or maybe the gin, flamed around and through him, sharpening his awareness and altering his time sense; he found himself half in love with all the women—with Kara, who moved with such surprising grace in the brief circle of his arm, and with this startlingly pink-cheeked and giggling Gil. Brief, confused visual impressions tangled in the springing flood of the music. The Icefalcon reminded him of a cheetah, cold and precise; Ingold plunged through the mazes of the game with an agility and an abandon that were alike surprising; and Tomec Tirkenson swung the tall Kara effortlessly off her feet in a frothing skirl of tattered petticoats.

The smell of snow and pines was as intoxicating as the vast quantities of gin he'd consumed; the slurp of the muddy ground underfoot was a delight. Hands caught at his—long hands, scarred hands, fine, dainty hands, or bony ones. Blond and red and black hair tangled in the whirlpool of the music, faster and faster, while the crowd laughed and cheered and faces familiar and half-familiar swirled by in passing.

Rudy found Alde in his arms once again, the light strength of her body against his, and the music circled to its close. Someone was yelling, laughing, and pressing a bottle of spiced Blue Ruin and water upon them, and Rudy took a long drink of it between his gasps for breath. Yells broke out. "Kiss 'em, men! They've earned it!"

He looked down, laughing at the girl leaning in the crook of his arm, her black hair undone and streaming over the bright colors of her painted vest. She dared him with her eyes, and he caught her tight against him, tasting the gin and candied apples on her lips and the kindling sweetness of possession. Her hands slid up around his neck, tangling in his hair. The crowd applauded in delight, and for an endless second there was nothing, no one, but the fire of the dance in his blood and the warmth of the girl in his arms.

And then there was sudden, utter silence.

Rudy looked up, startled. He saw that the crowd around them had parted. Standing out alone in its forefront was the dark, starved face and steel-gray eyes of the man he had last seen in the Nest of the Dark!

Rudy was so startled to see him there that he wondered for a moment if he could be mistaken. But a second glance showed him that the prisoner of the Dark must have just come up from the road to the valleys below. Rudy had a momentary confused impression of a skull-gaunt face and dark wolf eyes, a shaggy gray mare's-tail of dirty hair, and filthy black rags of clothing.

And glittering under the muck of those rags were the torn remnants of a gold eagle embroidered on the breast of his filthy surcoat, like the one Rudy had painted on Alde's vest.

The eagle of the House of Dare.

All this Rudy absorbed in a few confused seconds, while he felt Alde turn to stone in his arms. Then someone pushed past him. Ingold fell to one knee before the stranger, bending his head as Rudy had never seen him do homage to anyone.

The stranger reached out stiffly to touch Ingold's shoulder. But the burning eyes did not lower to him. They shifted, chill

as a mad wolf's, over the crowd, the Keep, and Minalde—
seeing all things as a stranger. Ingold rose and took the
man's hands in his.

"Eldor," he whispered.

Part Two

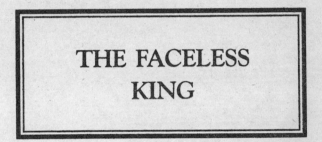

THE FACELESS KING

CHAPTER ELEVEN

"Is he himself?" Rudy asked.

Ingold did not answer at once. In the black mists that now filled the Vale like a sea of clouds, all sounds were changed, some were muffled, and others were thrown into a curious distinctness, so that the clink of a single bridle bit or the sharp *chuff!* of a horse's blown breath sounded louder than the murmur of the ranks drawn up in the meadow below them, invisible in the fog.

"Do you mean, are the Dark using him as they used Lohiro?" The wizard shook his head slowly. "No. Nor is he mad in the usual sense of the word."

Rudy shivered. He had seen the High King's eyes at the Winter Feast and again yesterday, in that terrible turmoil of reshuffled allegiances, unspoken accusations, and oaths of problematical fidelity. And one thing he knew: whatever else he was, King Eldor Andarion was not sane.

No surprise. The hideous, clammy darkness of the Nest returned to him, as it had in dreams past counting; he shuddered, trying to realize what it would be like to be trapped there, without hope of rescue . . . The fear of it had ridden his pillow through sleepless nights, ever since he himself had seen the Nest. It lurked in Ingold's eyes always, and Rudy heard it now in the disembodied voice.

"He say how he busted out?"

The hooded, shapeless head turned toward him; in the shadows between the drawn-down cowl and the gray muffler, he caught a silver glint of eyes. "He said he followed you, Rudy. He knew his way around the Nest fairly well by that time—he'd been there nearly four months."

Like a troop of ghosts, the Wizards' Corps was assembling around them in silence, cloaked and hooded as best they could manage against the wet, bitter morning. Far off in the black trees, Rudy thought he could discern the creak of leather and mail and the shrill scrunch of boots in the snow as the Army of Alketch marched down from the caves. Some distance away, before the doors of the Keep, torches burned, woolly slurs of dirty yellow in the mist.

Ingold went on quietly. "We had left the rope, of course. I don't know why no one suspected it. No one ever saw his body. By all accounts, the Icefalcon and his company rescued only half of those taken by the Dark from the final battle. The finding of Eldor's sword in the hand of a corpse was really very poor evidence, when you think on it."

"Maybe everyone preferred to think him dead rather than—than where he was."

The hooded form nodded. "I did." Ingold spoke slowly, his words slurred, like a man tired to death. It was the first time Rudy had seen or spoken to the old man since that hideous afternoon and he doubted whether Ingold had found sleep or rest in all that time.

Rudy wondered if any returning king had ever walked into such an utter bummer of a homecoming—to find his wife all pink and giggling in some other man's arms; to have his son reach out to that other man, shrieking, "'Udy! 'Udy!" in terror of that gaunt, mad wolf of a father.

Probably not, he decided. *Books were full of wives who stayed loyally celibate for twenty years . . .*

Alde! What the hell had he said to Alde when they were finally together alone?

He's her husband, Rudy thought desperately, *and that is none of your goddam business.*

But he hurt for her, with terror and grief.

He had not seen Alde since she'd twisted from his arms and fallen to her knees at her husband's feet. He remembered her dark hair spilling down over the gaudy, painted vest and her red skirts like blood in the muddy snow. He remembered Alwir, materializing as if out of nowhere at her side, holding out his gloved hands and saying, "My lord, I told them you could not be dead."

And in those somber eyes had been no more expression than in a couple of ball bearings, set in a mask of clay.

Drifts of fog blew about Rudy. He saw the Guards move down the steps to their places in the line. They would be the shock troops of the invasion, spearhead and rear guard of the Darwath companies. Vair na Chandros had his own storm troopers for the companies under his command.

Of Stiarth of Alketch nothing more had ever been seen.

Rudy caught a glimpse of Gil's face, looking sharp and odd in the frame of the mail coif she wore. She was joking with Seya and the Icefalcon, her hands hooked loosely in her sword belt, as if she had never known any world but this one or any life but that of a warrior. The shy, gawky UCLA student seemed to have vanished in the smoke that had consumed her notes in the common room fire. For her the coming battle would be her last, to die or to return afterward to California, having fulfilled her vows in the Guards.

Other companies were passing, Melantrys and the fire-squad, with the yellow torchlight of the gates slipping like water over the bulky weapons of glass and twisted gold, and grim, ugly Tomec Tirkenson, walking beside Maia of Penambra to where the outland troops were drawn up beside those of the Church. In the sudden slit of yellow light that appeared in the passage of the opened gates, Rudy saw the gaunt, spiderlike form of Bishop Govannin silhouetted, her red cowl drawn up over her head; beside her, drowned in pious gloom, was Inquisitor Pinard.

A voice barked orders. The tread of marching men sounded suddenly close. Through fog and darkness, Rudy distinguished them, rank on rank, moving out of the trees. He made out the bulkier forms of the mounted officers, the dull sheen of gold on burnished mail, and the upraised flash of curved metal hooks. Against the matte charcoal backdrop of the predawn fog, Rudy saw the prick of the horse's ears and the single stabbing spike of the Commander's helmet. Horns blew, a distant groaning. Like a serpent sluggish with the cold, the columns of the South poured on down the Vale, to take their places in the line of march, while their Commander halted by the doors of the Keep.

He was within yards of the Wizards' Corps. Rudy wondered if he was aware of them, standing like a troop of wraiths in the fog; if he was, he gave no sign of it. But Rudy glanced nervously from that chiseled, black profile, framed within its gilded mail, to the cloaked and hooded silent old man who stood at the Commander's side. He was aware that, since Stiarth's disappearance, Vair had spent a good deal of time with the Inquisitor.

The Inquisitor raised his hand now in formal blessing. The dark Commander removed his spiked helm and bowed his head. ". . . to save you from all darkness, to trample your enemies beneath your feet."

Nice, Rudy thought. *Let's have a prioritized list and a dictionary definition of enemies.*

Red-liveried servants were bringing another horse to the steps of the Keep, a black mare with flames of scarlet silk braided into the mane. In the spreading bar of gold thrown by the torchlight, a shadow lanced down the steps, rippling long and black like an arrowhead; the troops murmured like the distant surge of the sea. Alwir stood for a moment at the top of the steps, gloved hands resting on his hips, surveying the army as if it were still his to command. Then, with a curt nod of satisfaction, he strode down, the dirty slush scrunching beneath his boots, and mounted the waiting steed.

A little snuffle of wind stirred in the mists. Rudy sensed the darkness graying, like watered ink; around him, he could distinguish the faces of the Corps. Another horse was brought up, white trapped in black; someone in the ranks cheered.

Then two more shapes appeared, backlit by the glow of the passage light, at the top of the Keep steps. More cheering sounded, rank on rank taking it up. The tall, rawboned man turned his head, the light glittering like silver dust on close-cropped gray hair. The slender woman at his side hung back, jewels tangled like stars in the embroidery of her gown, and Rudy felt his heart turn over in his breast. Against the light he could see neither the face of the woman he loved nor that of the man to whom she belonged, but what was between them was starkly implicit in the distance between their two bodies, in the formal handclasp of farewell, and in the way the King turned from her briskly and surveyed the obscure army before him in the fog-shrouded dawn. Alde stood, head up, chin set, as the King strode down to join the commanders with never a backward glance.

The horns blew again, the rawness of the sound muffled oddly by the fog. Banners unfurled in the smoky dawn—the gold eagle of Darwath, the black stars of the House of Bes, the unrelieved blood color of the Church. Like distant thunder, the kettledrums boomed farther down the Vale. Eldor reined his horse from the Keep and moved on down the road between the ranks, his commanders following behind. Beside Rudy, Ingold pulled his shabby mantle tighter about him and led the wizards after them, leaning on his staff like a half-frozen beggar in the snow.

The army had begun to move. As he turned to follow the Corps, Rudy looked back, his eyes seeking the lighted doors of the Keep once more. The Bishop and the Inquisitor had gone; someone had shut one side. In the long, narrow rectangle of saffron light, a single form still stood, proud and slender and shivering in its black fur cloak. He looked back twice more, and each time she was still there, until the road, the fog, and the army hid her from his view.

It was a bitter road to Gae. Rudy had scouted it, going and coming, on their first reconnaissance of the Nest, and even then he had found it terribly changed from the way taken by the refugees from Karst. In the low ground, the original road had been flooded out, and leaden marshes or the still sheets of pewter lakes covered the land, their silver ice prickled with the rotting limbs of drowned trees. Where the road hugged the foothills closer to Renweth, the going was not as bad. But as they progressed north, through what had been the green heartland of the Realm, the land was a desolation of waters, and the army sought the path that the wizards had marked, over what had been the summits of tall hills.

The days were gray and freezing; by night, blinding storms howled down from the mountains, surrounding the camp in a whirlwind of spitting rain and snow. The bitter cold of these storms was made no easier by the knowledge that the wizards themselves were responsible, using the storms as a shield against the Dark. Once, after such a storm, they came upon a little family of beggars, gypsies in the pitiless land, dead of exposure in the lee of a hill.

"They would have died in any case in this cold," Thoth judged, standing on the road above the huddled bodies and surveying the dripping rags that covered the blue, emaciated flesh.

"All things die in any case," Ingold replied quietly. "Nevertheless, the thing was our doing."

Brother Wend, who was with them, turned away in tears; Rudy was silent, confused and unable to speak. Most of the army passed by without even seeing what lay in that hollow by the road.

Rudy saw very little of Gil during that journey, for she stayed with the Guards. Twice, crossing the camp at night in the black fury of the winds, he thought he glimpsed her bony figure with its trailing scarf pacing along at Ingold's side as the wizard made his restless rounds of the camp. But Ingold did not speak of it; indeed, the wizard spoke very little these days at all. By day, he kept among the wizards, and Rudy found himself thinking that it was odd that he did not ride with the commanders of the expedition. By night, as he had done on the road down from Karst, he wandered the camp through the rising gales, doing what he could with his spells of ward and guard. Between grief and terror of what he knew was to come, Rudy often sat awake far into the night in the outer cubicle of the two-room tent they shared, playing his harp in the darkness. But he seldom was awake when the old man came in.

The armies pitched their tents in the fields before the gates of Gae, in the shadow of Trad's Hill. The stump of the cross that had once surmounted its summit had been broken and eroded away, yet none pitched their tents in the place where it had been. As the sun bloodied the torn western clouds, Maia of Penambra held battle services there, with his sword belted at his waist. Northern or southern, the troops darkened the frosted ground in all directions as they knelt. As an excommunicate, Rudy did not attend, but the prelate's voice, oddly carrying for one so soft-spoken, could be heard wherever Rudy walked in the camp. He passed Kara and Tomec Tirkenson—another excommunicate—hand in hand on the fringes of the crowd around the cart-tail altar and saw at a distance Brother Wend, his face like a dying man's, watching the rites from the shelter of the tents.

The sun set and the winds rose. Endless as the winter nights were, it would be only a short time until dawn.

Rudy lay in the darkness of his sleeping cubicle, prey to a horrible case of funk.

It was not that he doubted the ability of the flame throwers—*our side's secret weapon,* he reminded himself wryly—to wreak havoc in the Nest. Nor did he doubt the necessity of the invasion itself. As far as he knew, the Dark Ones were still taking live prisoners to supplement their dwindling herds. If the Nests were not burned out, cauterized one by one, there was always the lingering chance that someone he cared for—Alde, Gil, or Tir when he got older—might end up there, exiled from light. He noticed the Eldor had not questioned the invasion.

Yet Rudy was mageborn enough, artist enough, to bear the curse of a vivid imagination. The thought of going into battle at all terrified him. To fight in the lightless mazes underground, to descend willingly into that hell of fire and darkness . . . Sweat iced his face at the thought.

He knew their losses would be high. The counterspells of the Dark Ones could damp magelight—maybe kill it entirely. And most of the mages were half-trained, their power weak. *We could be trapped down there . . .*

He shoved the thought away. *We ain't gonna be trapped and we ain't gonna be killed,* he told himself stubbornly. *We'll do what Dare of Renweth never did—attack the Nests of the Dark and wipe out their whole ecosystem so, even if we haven't the forces to reoccupy Gae,* they *won't have, either.*

Lohiro, dying, had whispered of the moss, the herds, and the ice in the north. He had known then what Gil had puzzled out: that they were all bound together. Sleepily, Rudy's mind groped at the remains of his high-school biol-

193

ogy class, ten years in the past and not much attended at the time.

Gil was right, of course. The moss was the—what had she called it?—the nitrogen fixer of the whole Nest ecology. It was dying already, and flammable nitrogen compounds remained in the brown, dried decay. Burn off the moss and you'd knock the base out from under the whole food chain, just like those vaguely recalled diagrams of grass, antelopes, and lions . . .

Rudy drifted toward slumber.

Ironic that the basis of the Nest ecosystem would be its destruction. The whole Nest must be saturated in nitrogen compounds, Gil had said.

What the hell was a nitrogen compound?

Just before he dozed off completely, it floated through Rudy's mind that the secret weapon was perhaps not as secret as he'd thought.

The Dark knew they were going to be attacked with fire.

Then he slept.

The cold drift of wind woke him as the outer door of the tent was opened on the other side of the separating curtain. Werelight flickered through the chinks. He heard the creak and clatter of battle gear, the clinking of buckle and spur. It was later in the night, he could tell—though nowhere near dawn. Eldor's harsh, rasping voice came to him, and Alwir's melodious drawl, along with the sinister purring of Vair and Ingold's scratchy, flawed, unmistakable tones. Their talk was of flame throwers and maps and guides, of where the companies would divide to cover the two main segments of the Nest, and of which mages would lead them down. Vair said stiffly that he would rely on maps, rather than on the directions of any servant of Satan; Ingold replied mildly that he was welcome to do so, of course, but unless he was planning to dispense with the wizards who would cover his advance with such light as they could summon, he might as well include one more as a guide. Alwir told the Alketch Commander not to be a fool.

Shortly after that, another blast of cold air seeped through the tent curtains; Rudy heard the voices saying good night.

194

Feet scrunched on the frosted ground, and Vair cursed a slave for dropping a torch. From the other chamber, Rudy heard the thick rustle and creak of the curtain falling and the rattle of the outer leather flap in the wind. Beneath the dividing curtain, the bluish light moved.

Ingold's voice said softly, "So you are determined to do this thing?"

"Don't start on it," Eldor's voice grated.

"What are you trying to do? Alwir's hoping for his own aggrandizement—at your expense, I should add—and that soulless Alketch tiger is out for whatever's left of the Realm, but you are King already. You have no need . . ."

"We all have a need." Rudy heard the creak of the chairbraces under shifting weight and the soft, restless crunch of frozen ground under pacing feet.

"You were down there, Eldor. You know what you're leading these people into. Alwir thinks the Nest is something like a slightly larger version of his own wine cellars, but you know how much hope we have of . . ."

"Do you think I fool myself about it?" Rudy could almost see the taller man rounding on Ingold from the shadows. "After lying in the muck and eating wet moss and raw fish and fearing every second for my life, don't you think I know just how hopeless it is?" There was something akin to satisfaction in the voice—a pleasure in the justification of despair. "You forget, Ingold, that I *remember*. I remember—everything."

"I had four long months to think, in the dark of the Nest; and, as they tell me is the case of—my sweet wife, I had new sights to stir old memories. Dare of Renweth did lead a force down the stairways—twenty thousand men. The men of the Times Before were not more wise or foolish than they are now, and they could foresee what we have all foreseen—that their empires would not last five years. They had their flame thrower corps—oh, yes!—and other things besides. They had their wizards to cast light about them, for all the good it ever did. I know what happened to them down in the Nests. In the darkness I remembered it. When I returned to Dare's Keep, I could have laughed aloud to see how proudly our

195

Alwir strutted his feathers like a dunghill cock. Dare's army was three times the size of this one. Do you know how many of them survived?"

For a long moment there was nothing, only that blazing, shocked, terrible silence. Lying in the darkness, Rudy knew that Ingold stared into the face of the man who had once been his friend and saw there only a stranger's hate.

When the wizard spoke, his voice was a whisper. "Why?"

The sound of pacing resumed, along with the click of scabbard buckles and the slurring whine of a cloak. "I remembered other things down there, Ingold. The Dark took none of it from me, though I prayed they would. I never forgot that I was High King of Darwath." As that harsh voice rose and fell, the long, light tread of the pacing increased, the shadow under the partition whirling and moving, as if with the unseen motion of an arm.

"I remembered how I used to sit up nights sweating out a judgment over which nobleman had what rights over the souls of his people," Eldor went on, in that low, harsh, terrible voice. "I remember endless councils and dickerings with the Church, with the Empire, with the merchants—going without sleep over the Raiders in the plains and the Alketch pirates in the Round Sea. And for what? So that I could end up squatting on my hunker-bones, chewing roots in the dark, with all the Church and Raiders and merchants scattered like the fragments of some meaningless dream. What was the use of it? Why had I bothered to sweat and worry at all? If I'd lived like my father and wenched and drunk and taken all the sweet pleasures of life, I would have ended up in exactly the same position. I had been King, and for what?"

"So what do you want?" Ingold demanded, his voice suddenly very angry. "Do you want to go out in a blaze of honored glory so that people can make songs about how great the last King of Darwath was? Do you want to die and take thousands of your followers with you, to make your death look a little more like heroism and a little less like suicide? Are you choosing to leave your people leaderless and defenseless, because you would rather die with an army at your back than demean yourself to look after a few thousand peasants huddled in a stone blockhouse who lock themselves in every night out of sheer terror of the Dark?"

"Yes." The word came soft, ugly, as if its speaker stood inches from his listener, towering over him like a lightning-blasted pine. "Yes, that's exactly what I want."

"Then you're a coward."

There was the ringing slap of a blow, backhand and then forehand, and the slight scrape of some piece of furniture as Ingold caught his balance. Then there was only the fast, shaky breathing of a younger man's trembling rage.

"Do you feel better for that?" Ingold asked quietly.

"We're lost, Ingold," the King whispered. "And I know it—in some sense I have always known. There is nothing left, only fear and darkness. Every person who follows me knows it, too. Each has lived in the world before the Dark; and the comparison is not a nice one. Death in battle is not pleasant, but it has the virtue of being quick, and I know, in the marrow of my bones I know, that slavery to the Dark Ones, in fact or by fear, is infinitely worse. Why would any have followed me on this fool's errand if they did not all, in some sense, seek death?"

"They follow you because they have always followed you, Eldor—because they love you."

"It's their misfortune, then," the King said, in that voice of soft hate. "Let them desert, if it suits them. I will die alone, if I must."

In the long silence after these words, Rudy could feel the strain of will against will, like a terrible tension in the air. There were no sounds from beyond the partition but the thick draw of breath and the rising cry of the gale winds surrounding the camp. In his blankets, Rudy shivered, feeling that hideous striving as if it were a vibration, sensed through the skin. As if with physical effort, Ingold was forcing the King to see what it was that he was doing to the last of his people; and the terrible thing was that Eldor saw it clearly and did not care.

When Eldor spoke again, his voice was quieter, but it tasted of poison more bitter than the acid of the Dark.

"You were my tutor," he said slowly, "and I followed you and adored you and trusted you, even when my father had you driven from the city like a criminal. Had you called me, I would have gone with you, forsaking everything I knew. I loved you that much. You made me what I was, Ingold; you made me love justice and law and you made me know my duty to my kingdom. You made me everything my father was not, and my love of you and hatred of him shaped my every action. There was a time when I would have died for you, Ingold, do you know that? I trusted you that much."

Then there was another long and terrible silence, with no sound but the sobbing of the wind. The harsh voice spoke again, jagged and bitter, like a broken thing. "You knew about them," he rasped. "You knew about them from the first. He is your disciple."

In the even longer silence that followed, Rudy knew that the wizard could not meet his accuser's eyes. When Ingold spoke, his words were almost inaudible. "Not from the first. It was done before I learned of it."

"But you never spoke."

"What would I have said? You were dead, Eldor, and she was alone and very frightened. She needs love, and at that point even the illusion of love would have served. He was good to her. I feared for them, yes. But I have never commanded anyone as to what they could and could not do."

"Then don't command me now!" Eldor shouted furiously. "You were swift enough to command Alwir to let her and her lover be!"

In the bitter pause that followed, a thousand other things could have been said—and possibly were understood.

"After tomorrow he may have her, for all of me, if he survives. I shall see you at dawn."

Footsteps retreated suddenly; there was the scrape of icy ground, the swift, muffled whisper of robes, and Rudy was reminded of how quickly Ingold could move. Then icy, terrible silence was broken by Eldor's cold, grating voice. "Let me go."

"For God's sake, Eldor—" Ingold pleaded, and was cut off by a harsh bark of laughter.

"God!" the King choked. "God! Do you know how many times, my dearest, oldest, most loyal friend, I called upon

God, squatting in the moss in the darkness? How I pleaded and prayed for a deliverer?"

"And you were, in fact, delivered," the wizard returned quietly.

"By whom and to what? By the man who had been tumbling my wife within two weeks of my reported death? I suppose you could call it just payment, if you had a sense of humor."

"Maybe. But no one could call it sufficient reason to lead loyal men and women deliberately to their death, when you know the nature of the danger that will destroy them."

"No?" There was a sudden crack to that voice, a faint sliding up the scale onto the edge of shrillness, that brought sweat to Rudy's face. "But life is very unjust, is it not, Ingold Inglorion?"

Cold and the wail of the wind streamed briefly into the tent in the wake of the King's going. A moment later Rudy heard those quick, striding steps retreating in the direction of the royal shelter. He lay awake waiting for Ingold to come in to sleep, frightened of tomorrow and frightened of that cracked, mad note in Eldor's voice; but when he drifted into sleep a few hours before dawn, he had still heard no sign of movement in the room beyond.

CHAPTER TWELVE

The armies of humankind entered Gae at first light.

Though the icy mists thinned away before them, revealing broken walls and flooded pavements, the ruined town still lay in the grip of that brooding desolation; there was not a man or woman of the ranks who would dare to speak above a whisper. The echoes of voices rang too hollowly in those dripping streets. Those who had known Gae in its prime or those who had spoken loudest of reoccupying the town, once the Dark had been driven forth, spoke not at all.

Among them Rudy trudged, sick with apprehension and terror, close enough to Eldor's nervous white mare to see the thin, unpleasant smile that curved the King's harsh lips as he looked around him at what had been the most beautiful city in the West of the World.

Rudy found himself thinking how easy it would be simply to throw a cloaking-spell over himself, find a comfortable seat on one of the ruined benches in the stinking swamp of the Palace courtyard, and sit this one out. But he saw Ingold break ranks and go to speak to a thin, gawky Guard; and though the dissolving mists still hung about the great courtyard of the Palace, he saw her shrug and shake her head.

Coward and quitter, she had called him once.

It didn't do any good to tell himself that he knew for a fact their cause was lost. He suspected that Gil knew it, too.

Ingold certainly did.

How the hell come I always end up associating with maniacs? he demanded despairingly, watching as the forces separated in the vast, half-frozen morass of the court. The sappers moved up to lead position with their cleated ladders; directly behind them, Eldor took his place on foot among a squad of Guards. The other prong of the strike force drew aside, a glittering serpent of Alketch forces, with Vair like a deadly, jeweled idol at their head. Rudy recognized Maia and his Penambrans among those ranks, along with Kara, Kta, a dozen or more of the other wizards, and half the firesquad.

Ingold joined the ranks at the head of the line near Eldor. For a moment his eyes met the King's; then Eldor's lips twisted in a sneer, and he turned away and gave the signal to descend.

The creeping horror of that descent was like the prelude to an evil dream. Through the vine-choked upper vaults, through the forest of pillars whose straight, inky shadows reeled and turned to the movement of the white magelight, Rudy could feel the watchfulness of the Dark Ones growing upon him. Like the warning prickle of hot breath on the nape of his neck, like a soft footfall in a room that should be empty, he could sense the touch of counterspells on the magic of the light he had summoned. In the narrow confines of the ancient stairway itself, it was a thousand times worse. He was aware of the Dark as he had never been aware of them before—the probing of that monstrous intelligence at the edges of his magic, the greedy nibbling at its weak points.

The stairway seemed to descend forever. The witchlight around him etched the faces of the Guards in harsh chiaroscuro and glittered on the weapons of the firesquad. Far below him, Rudy could see that Ingold's drawn sword had begun to burn with a chill, white light of its own.

Though there was no sign of the Dark, he could feel the pressure of their minds, their power, and the haunting evil of their presence. He scanned the gnawed rock of the walls, smooth as glass below eye level, where millions of jostling bodies had polished it over uncounted years, rough and sparkling with stray glints of quartz above. It was unbroken by crack or fissure. They would not be attacked from above.

Would the Dark lie in wait for them, he wondered, in the huge cavern below the drop-off of the stair? Or would the

Dark give way before them, luring them on, to circle around behind them in the uncharted mazes of the passages?

The grip of his flame thrower felt clammy in his hand, and he found himself wishing he'd spent the backbreaking hours that Gil had spent in learning to use a sword. Unless he planned to cut off the army's retreat by prematurely starting fires in the moss, he couldn't even use the damn thing until they were deep in the Nest. He cursed his stupidity. And still they descended.

Wind licked his cheek, startling him almost to death. A murmur went through the crowding ranks that hemmed him in. Sweat ran from the faces that looked suddenly gray in the hard, pitiless glare, and he heard the faint whispering rattle of weapons gripped in tightening hands. But of the Dark themselves there was no sign.

The tunnel walls widened before them. The stair abruptly ended. From the cavern below, a faint breeze soughed, thick with the harsh stink of the Nest. As the white light streamed forth, revealing the world that had been hidden since the founding of the Nests, Rudy heard the whisper of awe that wound back and back through the ranks on the stair behind. Pillars and chasms and hanging teeth of stone glistened wetly with acid and nacre; dark pools in the carpets of brown, rolling moss caught the light in hard onyx surfaces. The putrid air seemed to press into Rudy's skull, weighted with the malice of unseen watchers. But in all that shadowy vastness, nothing moved.

The sappers flung down their ladders, and the hollow booming rang like a cannon shot, the echoes dying slowly amid the mazes of stone. The vanguard hesitated, looking about into that horrible, alien realm. On the brink of the ladder, Ingold paused, the vagrant winds stirring at the heavy folds of his mantle, his sword glinting like lightning in his hand. Then Eldor strode forward, and his footfalls sounded, each as distinct as the tap of an iron bell, upon the separate rungs. The cynical amusement in his eyes as he gazed about him filled Rudy with chill terror.

Yet Rudy followed, as they all followed, stumbling in the crumbly mosses of the cavern floor. Against the darkness that seemed to crowd so thickly around them, Ingold's sword gleamed as he pointed the way toward the tunnels he and Rudy had taken in their earlier exploration of the Nest. The smell there was intolerable, fetid and sweet. Powder from the decaying mosses clogged Rudy's nostrils. In the open cavern, the magelight did not penetrate the darkness of the ceiling, but it threw horrible leaping shadows of the warriors among the knobbled pillars and across the inky pits of the floor.

In the descending tunnel, Rudy felt the awareness of the Dark, stronger and stronger, like a thin sound sawing its way through his skull. In the cavern beyond, it was worse. Blind, squeaking things fled before the light, their chittering echoing down the tunnels. In spite of the coolness of the air, Rudy's face was wet with sweat; he could see more sweat gleaming on the faces of the Guards packed so closely around him. As he stumbled over the soft wetness of the floor, he could feel and taste the malice of the Dark, pressing on him like the millions of tons of earth and rock above his head.

Ingold stopped in the black mouth of the next tunnel, swinging around as if startled by some noise or movement. At first Rudy thought that the old man's foxfire sword had begun to burn brighter. Then he realized that the soft, white magelight around them was dimming.

Alwir looked up into the shadows of the cavern ceiling. "Can we use the flame throwers?"

"Not unless we wish to risk cutting ourselves off from the lower Nests," the wizard whispered. In the fading glare, Rudy noted how pale he looked and how the sweat glittered on his face. "We have some three miles of tunnel to cover from here."

All about him, Rudy could hear the fearful murmuring of the Guards. Swords flashed in the graying light as the column moved into defense formation. He put out his strength into the light-spell but felt it sapped, drawn by what he knew to be magic, yet was incapable of comprehending enough to fight. As the light waned, he could see that some of the mosses were palely phosphorescent—*more of Gil's nitrogen compounds,* he thought—and moreover, there was a kind of a smell in the air, bitter and metallic, that he had never smelled before, overpowering in the enclosed spaces of the caves.

Eldor barked a hoarse command. The column moved on again, down a half mile or so of tunnel where the air seemed clearer, though the light continued to weaken. By the glow of Ingold's sword, the King's face looked harsh and terrible, a thin little smile playing about his lips.

He knows what's coming, Rudy thought, shivering with the effort of maintaining even a feeble glow. *He knows . . .*

Then blackness slammed down over them all like the fall of night. Screaming burst along the tunnel, the echoes drumming into Rudy's ears. All his strength was put into the light, yet darkness covered him; he heard the sudden, roaring buzz that the Dark Ones made when they flew underground and he felt the hissing slash of a sword that just missed his ear. He flung himself against the rock wall, the acid in the moss stinging his bare hands, and spread a cloaking-spell over himself.

Winds howled by him; something hot and wet splattered his face. Then up ahead, white light burst into being again around Ingold and the Guards; the colors of tunic and mail, of human skin and stripped, bloody bones, were shocking in the refulgent glare. But he himself was still in darkness. Dimly, he could see struggling forms, swords, faces, and the sinewy, drifting glide of dark shapes. He tried to call light and found he hadn't the strength for both spells.

He bent and pulled the gory sword from the handbones of a corpse at his feet. Then, in a single instant of time, he slashed at the Dark One nearest him, dropped the cloaking-spell, and threw everything he had into a burst of searing, white light that exploded with radiance into the blackness.

All around him there was shrieking, buzzing, clawing wind. The light that encircled Rudy grew and flickered, the Dark Ones vanishing before it, leaving the tunnel a shambles of bodies and bones half-sunk in trampled, unspeakable filth. Then darkness surged down on them again, and he struck at the things that came for him in it, the thin, black slime from their slashed bodies splattering his hands. The effort of fighting the counterspells against the magelight exhausted him; it was all he could do to defend himself. If he had not had his back to the wall and been ringed by the Guards, he knew he could never have stood a chance.

Eldor's harsh voice cut the chaos of noise like acid; the column moved forward, struggling against that inky tide. From the darkness, a spined cable as big around as his wrist caught Rudy's sword arm and dragged him upward toward the darkness that hid the roof of the tunnel with a force that all but dislocated his arm. He felt his feet leave the floor and glimpsed a slobbering black maw in the midst of swirling illusion . . .

He must have screamed, for his throat hurt from it as the Icefalcon pulled him to his feet from the trampled muck of the tunnel floor where he'd fallen. The whiplike tail was already disintegrating away from his arm, its cut end still pulsing faintly where the Raider's sword had sheared it. He felt weak with shock, sickened at the hideous strength of the thing that had seized him.

The Icefalcon dragged him along with the moving column until he could find his feet. As the Raider let go, he said, "Don't let that happen again. You're the only light source this part of the column has."

Even as the Icefalcon spoke, Rudy could feel the counter-spells slacking and the light growing stronger. As the Dark swirled away in clouds of illusion, he could see that an immense cave stretched before them, the slimy mosses of its walls and floor glittering faintly in the reflected witchlight and in the wan phosphorescence that seemed, in places, to emanate from the mosses themselves. The light grew as Eldor, Ingold, and the advance guard sprang down the slippery slope to the cavern floor, leading the straggling column that was like a long and tortuous snake. The darkness above them seemed to be alive with the chittering buzz of the Dark, dripping with their stench, yet Rudy felt their spells growing more and more distant. He hastened his steps, trying to catch up with the wizard and the King.

He had almost done so when a faint, hollow booming noise echoed through the cave, like a distant explosion, muffled by the twisting of the tunnels. The ground jarred beneath his feet, and all around him rose an outcry of doubt and terror. Men stopped, looking about into the inky vastness, as if to see the source of the sound, though Rudy could tell it was some distance off; others cried out that they must turn back and were cursed by those who said that the only hope lay forward. Ahead of them, Rudy could see the faint glimmer that was Ingold's sword as the old man scrambled up a rockfall to the mouth of the next tunnel. He heard Eldor's commands rapped out to those around him. And there was something wrong . . .

That smell, Rudy thought. *Stronger now, much stronger . . .* He looked around him, seeking a source, but he saw nothing—only the emptiness of the high-ceilinged cavern, the magelight stretching to its farthest ends. *Where the hell are the Dark?*

The ground shook again, farther off, and Rudy decided that whatever the hell the smell was, he didn't like it. There was movement in the air, not the directionless swirling of the Dark Ones, but a kind of steady draft, although, now that he looked, he could see no other entrances into the cavern except the one that was still disgorging troops and the black hole where the Guards stood grouped around their commanders. On the cavern floor, confusion was spreading— Rudy could see already how badly the column was straying. *Most of 'em must still be back in the tunnel,* he thought as he ran for the knot of Guards. *Hell of a place to get off.*

He stumbled on the slope up to the farther tunnel. He was gasping, his head feeling strangely light. The air was clearer here, blown by the faint drafts from below . . .

Gas, he thought. *Of course—the Dark Ones can use gas in an enclosed cavern.* Looking back, he could see the isolated, straggling knots of warriors, the dull gleam of swords, and the flash of glass barrels and gold among the dozen or so firesquad members still down there. Those who scrambled up beside him toward the tunnel mouth seemed to sense it, too; he saw the Icefalcon stagger and half-fall through the dark hole beyond. He remembered Gil's words about nitrogen compounds. *Was nerve gas some kind of nitric . . . nitrous . . .*

Or was the gas for something else?

He stumbled through the tunnel entrance, his hands slipping in the black, squishy moss as he fell. He heard Ingold's voice, farther back in the darkness. Then, out in the cavern, he heard someone scream.

Past the entrance he saw it—a wall of darkness falling on the column. He blinked, watching the faint lights left in the cavern die before it . . . wondered what was wrong . . .

There were no Dark Ones in the cavern!

Rudy knew it, felt it. The massive storm of blackness that rushed like the sea over the straggling line of defenders was purely illusion. Yet those Guards still standing around Eldor at the top of the slope cried out in terror or warning; two or three of them crowded back into the safety of the tunnel mouth. Deep in the ground, another reverberating earthquake shook the Nest, and Rudy lost his footing. He fell face down in a pocket of squishy moss, just as he glimpsed the red-gold glint of the flame throwers from the darkness of the cavern.

The air in the cavern exploded.

An impact-wave of heat slammed Rudy into the softness of the moss, the force of it rolling over him like a thunderclap of death. For a moment, wrapped in wet blackness, he wondered if he had been deafened as well. Then, in the tunnel around him, cries and curses began; far off, across the distance of that suddenly silent cavern, he heard distant wailing and the clash of fighting. But from the vast snake of charred and twisted bodies that littered the seared moss of the cavern floor there came no sound at all—only the sudden, hurricane rush of the winds of the Dark.

Rudy stared out into the utter blackness, fascinated, watching as the Dark poured down through the fissures in the cavern's roof in a kind of slow motion. They were truly the Dark Ones, not merely the illusion that had drawn someone's panic fire in the gas trap. A welling wave of them built into a falling wall that he watched with a kind of drained detachment, too numbed with horror at the carnage below to feel terror or surprise.

Someone shoved him aside and threw himself from the shelter of the tunnel to where Eldor's body lay crumpled in the protection of the broken rocks. Rudy saw that it was Ingold, blue rags of witchlight fluttering around his head as

207

he bent down, oblivious to the storm of darkness descending upon him like a giant black wing. Rudy saw the wizard's scarred hands press the sticky ruin of the King's face and the bony breast that heaved suddenly with the gasp of returning life.

Gil and the Icefalcon reached Ingold instants before the Dark Ones did. The old man never looked up at them; his whole strength was bent to holding and tying the life of his friend to the burned body. Other Guards crowded out of the tunnel's refuge; belatedly, Rudy gathered a handful of his strength and made a feeble attempt to call light.

The earth shook again, nearer this time. Melantrys caught her balance and raised her flame thrower to fire into the darkness. Rudy screamed, *"Don't use it!"* in a voice that hardly sounded like his own. With his calling of the light, he had laid himself open to the counterspells of the Dark; he could feel them drawing on him like leeches.

Dimly, he could hear Alwir yelling, "Come back, you fools!" He knew that panic had set in among those who had made it to the tunnel before the explosion. They were breaking and fleeing foolishly into the darkness. Other voices cried that the tunnel was blocked and that the Dark had exploded the ceiling on them.

Alwir grabbed Rudy by the arm. "Is there a way around?" He looked ghastly with strain and shock; the jewels that he wore even in battle glinted like blood through the slime that covered his armor. "We can use the flame throwers to fight our way to the bottom . . ."

"No!" Rudy yelled desperately over the rising din of the battle in the tunnel mouth. "If we use the flame throwers, we'll have another explosion! The Dark Ones are using explosive gas!"

"Gas?" the Chancellor shouted furiously. "What is this *gas?* Talk sense, boy!"

For the first time in his life, Rudy wished he had some understanding of Aristotelian physics. Gil seldom had problems coming up with flat-earth answers. "Uh—it's a vapor. Fiery vapor." He had to shout the words over the clashing of swords, the screams, the curses, and the harsh, echoing buzzing of the Dark. "It explodes in the air—it's invisible!"

Seeing the mulish set to Alwir's jaw, he cried, "For God's sake, you don't think just the flame throwers exploding could have wiped out everyone in the cavern!"

Another earthquake shook the ground, jarring them almost off their feet; the noise of it seemed to vibrate in the bones of Rudy's skull. A choking cloud of dust rolled from some passage nearby, and he heard the dull clatter of falling pebbles . . .

He felt the hold of the counterspells slacken, and light blossomed more strongly in the tunnel and around the defenders at its mouth. The cries and curses turned to cheers, and over all he heard the bass roar of Tomec Tirkenson's voice. White light surrounded them. Men dragged Eldor's gasping body back into the shelter of the tunnel. Ingold was still gripping the twisted remains of one of the King's hands. Behind them, others poured up the slope, and the landchief of Gettlesand clutched Alwir's hand in sticky greeting, heedless of their earlier enmity.

"We've got to get the hell out of here," he rasped. "They're blowing down the roofs of tunnels behind us. We've been cut off in two places already. If we stay, we'll be trapped like pigs in a slaughtering pen."

"Ingold?" Alwir said.

The wizard lifted fatigue-blackened eyes.

"Could you get us to the center of the Nest from here?"

The old man wiped at the blood that trickled into his beard, his sleeve leaving a smear of charred slime on his cheek. "I could," he said quietly. "But not out again. The tunnels get fewer as they descend. I can take us out of here—I think—from where we are now. Deeper in, it would take very little to trap the entire army."

Alwir appeared to be considering.

Rudy added. "And it wouldn't do any good, anyway, I tell you! The Dark Ones can make the air explode!"

"Don't be stupid," Alwir snapped irritably.

"He ain't being stupid," Tirkenson put in unexpectedly. "That's just what it looked like happened. The flame throwers went off, and it looked as if all the air in the cavern caught fire. I lost my eyebrows; if I'd been two steps closer, I'd have lost my life."

The Chancellor's mouth hardened. Before he could speak, however, another explosion shook the ground, a hollow roaring followed by the rending crack of stone and a ground wave that jerked Rudy's feet from under him and threw him, staggering, into the Gettlesand troops in the cavern below. Wet dust and fumes rolled from the tunnel's darkness, and from the warriors in the cavern came another cry as the Dark Ones streamed down upon them again.

The retreat from the Nest was a nightmare. Dazzled by the blinding alternation of light and darkness, his smarting sword arm aching and weak where it had been wrenched, Rudy clung to the little knot of Guards that surrounded the fallen King's makeshift litter as it crawled through that chittering storm of malice, acid, and death. He recalled what Ingold had said once back at the Keep—that he had no hope of defeating the Dark, but would go and hazard his own life once again within the Nest in order that as many survivors as possible might be saved. It was only now that Rudy understood fully what this meant.

It was Ingold who held the blazing barriers of light against the pressing darkness, Ingold who, when the light was swamped, stood foremost in the line of defenders, his sword a chill splinter of brightness in the smothering murk. He left them twice, taking squads of men back into the deeper tunnels to reunite pockets of warriors who had been cut off from the main column, and it seemed to Rudy that their forward progress slowed to a crawl until he returned.

In the tunnels, the going was worse, and the ground was choked with the bodies of the slain. The battle had spread, as rockslides and explosions had cut the column; out of winding, crossing shafts in the blackness, Rudy could hear the din of voices and see the white magelight flaring, reflected in the unspeakable muck of the floors and against the dripping walls. In some places the way was blocked by fires, as pockets of the brown moss burned with a searing, yellow glare; in other places Rudy could see the evidence of the gas traps—shattered, twisted corpses and weapons melted in the heat. Once Ingold vanished, to come back up the tunnel at the head of a column of black-skinned warriors from the deepest jungles of Alketch, their eyes glaring whitely through the charred blood that covered their faces.

And always there were the Dark, tearing at the edges of the column when it passed through open spaces or streaming down from the fissures in the roof to swamp the light of the wizards in the close-pressed confines of the tunnels. Rudy wondered dully why he didn't simply hide himself in a cloaking-spell. The mere effort to maintain even a grayish light exhausted him and slowed his reflexes, so that he could barely lift the sword. Yet somehow he never gave in to the temptation.

He saw Gil go down when the Dark Ones blew the roof of the tunnel almost over their heads and saw the other Guards pick her up, with blood streaming from her snarled black hair. In another seared-out gas trap, he recognized the body of the Raider shaman Shadow of the Moon, but only by the bones tangled in the crisped remains of her braids. He wondered how many other mages had perished.

Exhaustion blinded him and confused him; how Ingold kept his sense of direction in the black mazes of the tunnels, Rudy could not imagine. Rockslides and cave-ins turned them aside. They scrambled over broken boulders still hot from the shattering violence of the explosion, through the streaming mud and filthy water of half-flooded tunnels, and through screaming hells of the dead and dying. The counter-spells of the Dark Ones tugged at Rudy's mind and seemed almost to weight his limbs, dragging him farther and farther back.

Then somehow they were on the stairs. The King and the wounded were carried up; the wretched remnant of the army streamed past Rudy, staggering and gray-faced with shock. The Dark Ones harried them in the steep and twisting seam, and men and women who had fought their way to the limit of the human penetration of the Nest and back again died on the road to the earth's surface, their crumpled bodies or half-melted bones tripping the feet of their erstwhile comrades. Rudy hung back, staying close to Ingold, for he sensed that the wizard was near the end of his strength. As they battled to get out, step by step up that endless flight, he could see how wan the magelight that surrounded the old man had grown, how again and again the Dark killed the light altogether, and how the intervals of fighting in blackness grew longer before the light flickered into existence once more.

Rudy found himself among the rear guard, a mixed rabble of rangers, Church troops, and a handful of the Alketch halberdier corps, fighting in darkness on stairs clogged with the fallen. The Dark Ones were everywhere. Light had failed utterly, and his wizard's sight showed him slashed, dirty faces, eyes staring with fatigue, and the blades of swords striking almost at random in the moving storm of darkness and air. Above him, he could see only the straggling line of the column, fighting as it retreated up the choked steps; below was only the blackness of the shaft, the single flashing sliver of white light that was Ingold's sword, and a glimmer on the squamous backs of the things that surrounded him.

They turned a corner. Something from the darkness tore at Rudy's cheek; he heard the whine of a badly aimed sword from the steps above and behind and ducked as a flailing blade struck him on the back of the head. Heavy arms caught him as he staggered and dragged him up and backward over the broken stairs, the bodies, the treacherous, sliding footing, and the dropped weapons of the slain. There were more stairs—endless stairs. The Gettlesand rangers who half-dragged, half-carried him quickened their pace as the fighting around them slacked. Faintly, far up the inky shaft of the stairs, he heard someone cheer.

Then, up ahead of him, he saw Alwir, filthy with the mess of battle. The dim reflection of distant daylight glittered in the jewels he wore. Rudy gasped, struggling through the press of men and women, all of them fighting toward that dim promise like drowning men striving toward the air. It was still dark all around him, but the Dark Ones were falling back . . .

Then swirling wind struck his face. Behind and above him, he glimpsed the Dark, pouring down like smoke from a ceiling shaft. The warriors who hemmed him in redoubled their efforts toward the light; the Dark were behind them, and, after what the defenders had been through, there were few who would turn back to risk re-entering Hell.

Rudy twisted around, pulled backward by the mob. He yelled, *"Ingold!"* But he doubted that the wizard heard him. The Dark Ones had cut off the rear guard. Only forty feet or so of stairway separated them, but the little knot of Alketch troops around the wizard was barely visible through the shifting turmoil of darkness. The Dark were all around them. Rudy saw the wizard get his back to the wall as, one by one, the men around him fell. The white flame of his sword flashed in the smothering blackness. Still the Dark Ones streamed down from above. Rudy fought against the tide of flight that bore him along with it, his head buzzing and his hands empty of weapons, determined that the old man should not fight alone.

At the turn of the stairway, Alwir still watched, unmoving, looking down into the pit of the deeper shaft at the trapped figure against the wall. Then he glanced back at the guard of his own red-clad troopers who stood around him and said, "There are too many. Pull back."

Sobbing, Rudy fought against the tide. Hands gripped his elbows. Someone said something to him about being off his head with shock; he was dragged back by an iron grip. Through a momentary gap in the ranks, he could see the light of Ingold's blade like a misty white fire; by its reflected brilliance, he glimpsed the wizard's face, cool and filled with determination to sell the flesh off his bones at the highest possible price.

Rudy saw before Ingold did the sinuous whip of tentacle that lashed from the shadows, wrapping the wizard's two wrists where he held the sword. Ingold made a desperate attempt to pull free; another whiplike tail snagged his ankle and pulled him off his feet and away from the wall. The gleaming sword rang on the stairs as it fell, and the light of it died.

The picture was retreating, dreamlike, as Rudy was pulled back up the stairs and the darkness below him thickened. He saw Ingold twist in another futile effort to break free of the things that caught at him now from all sides. Like a half-heard, strangled cry, he felt the wizard's last, desperate attempt to call light.

A spark flickered in the darkness and died. In the daylight at the top of the stairs, Alwir, in his dark velvet cloak, looked down and watched as Ingold was dragged out of sight into the darkness.

CHAPTER THIRTEEN

"Gil?"

Rudy let the tent flap fall, shutting out the whining howl of the wind. He spoke softly, his voice barely audible over the rattle of the rain on the leather roof of the hospital-tent, so as not to wake the others lying there. He knew that Gil would not be sleeping.

He saw the gleam of her open eyes. She was regarding the tent ceiling dispassionately, as she had done all of yesterday, after she had wakened there and Brother Wend had told her as gently as he could that Ingold was dead.

Then the gray eyes shifted and met his. "Hi, punk," she said in a perfectly normal tone, as if she were meeting him by chance in a parking lot, and Rudy's heart sank within him.

"You okay?"

She shrugged. "Compared with about half the people who went down that hole, I'm fantastic." She folded her arms across her chest, and the little light that leaked from under the shade of the glowstone showed him the side of her face all streaked with rock-splinter cuts and a grimy black bandage torn from somebody's surcoat covering the abraded wound on her temple. By the look of her eyes, he could not see that she had shed any tears—which was more than could have been said of him.

After a moment she returned that flat, cool gaze to the ceiling. "They say Eldor will make it, too," she added conversationally. "Which is damn ironic, when you think of it."

Rudy shut his eyes against the burn of tears and looked away. The shattered chain of bodies across the floor of the gas trap seemed to be etched into the backside of his eyelids. "Gil, what are we gonna do?" he whispered.

"Depends on your priorities," she said, her light voice half-drowned by the torrential roar of the rain. "I'd say the smartest thing to do is send an expedition to the Nest in the Vale of the Dark for moss and make some kind of nitroglycerine-based defensive weapons against the White Raiders. You could probably also use the nitrogen base for fertilizer for the hydroponics gardens—"

"Goddam it, Gil!" he sobbed out of a blinding vortex of grief. "How can you just sit there and—and talk about defensive weapons and—and fertilizer . . . ?" The light, sexless, reasonable voice sickened him. "I always knew you were the most heartless woman I'd ever met, but . . . He's dead, Gil! Can't you understand that?"

"Sure," Gil said cheerfully. "Just because I don't shove my pain off onto you doesn't mean I don't feel any."

He was silent, his face burning with shame.

She moved her head a little on the bundled cloak that served her for a pillow. In the reflection of the half-drowned torches outside the tent, her eyes looked as gray as weathered ice and about as feeling. "You asked me what we're gonna do," she pointed out in a milder voice. "I'd say, just offhand, what we better do is settle ourselves down for a nice, long stay."

It was the beginning of the most hideous time that Rudy had ever endured.

The weeks that followed the decimated army's return to the Keep of Dare ran together in his mind into a single, endless hell of misery, grief, and fear. Rudy kept for the most part to his own cell or to the desolate Corps commons, and the surviving mages knew enough to let him be. Gil occasionally brought him news of what passed in the rest of the Keep—of Eldor's slow recovery, of the Alketch troops that occupied most of the second level, of the bitter infighting between the King and the Church—but Rudy heard it all without caring.

Gil had changed. Rudy often wondered what had happened to her when Ingold died. The gawky shyness, the scholarliness, the sensitivity, were gone. Now and then he heard her refer to the old man's death in passing without so much as a change of inflection in her light, sarcastic voice. But there was a fey quality lurking in those frozen eyes that frightened him.

Alde he saw only once.

Gil said that she never left the Royal Sector, though whether by her own choice or Eldor's compulsion, Gil did not know. Kara, who helped Thoth and Brother Wend nurse the King in the days after his shrouded litter was brought back from Gae, said that Alde kept much to her room after her first interview with Eldor when he regained consciousness. Kara said that Alwir and Bektis—the only mage who did not participate in the invasion of the Nest—were much with the King.

Even had Alde been free to go about the Keep, Rudy would seldom have seen her, but the lethargy that had settled around his heart alternated with a longing for her of a desperate intensity that nothing would allay. It was a desire he fought against, knowing the depths of Eldor's jealousy. Even to be caught trying to see her might trigger retaliation upon them both. Yet the longing grew on him, like a junkie's cravings for a drug, to the point where he was toying with the notion of slipping past the Alketch troops by means of a cloaking-spell and chancing a meeting when Eldor, who Gil said was able to get about now, was gone.

That night he waited until the start of the deep-night watch and called her image in the crystal.

The filtered pink glow of the night light showed him the room they had shared so many nights, the tumbled shadows of the bed, with her dark braids lying like tasseled black ropes against the iridescent gleam of the starry quilt, the soft, waxy sheen of the table, and the thin edge of gilt on the strapwork of her jewel box. The spindle-carved foot of Tir's bed had its heavy curtains looped back to reveal the downy, dark head on the pillow within.

Rudy's mind traced the murky ways of the Keep and considered how he could reach that perfumed, sleeping sanctuary in peace.

Then a thin sliver of light stabbed into the image as the door of the room was pushed slowly ajar. A tall shape blotted the dim glow from the hall, a momentary shadow of a man who pushed the door quickly to behind him—soundlessly, Rudy thought, for on the bed Alde did not stir. The intruder stepped carefully forward, a cautious movement marred by the man's horribly staggering gait, like that of a badly wielded marionette. The roseate light slithered across the soft black leather of the mask that covered his whole head and glinted on the gold eagle embroidered on his breast.

Rudy felt his breath stifle in his lungs.

Yet Eldor made no move toward his wife's bed. Instead, he stole, with that limping, awkward hobble, to the shadows that flanked Tir's cradle and stood for a time looking down at the child within. The silence of it, the clarity of those tiny images prisoned in the crystal, sent a prickle of horror down Rudy's back. The fact that this was occurring now, close to half a mile away at the far end of the Keep, and that he would be a helpless witness to whatever happened exerted a kind of terrifying fascination over him, so that he could not turn his eyes away.

At length, the King moved away; with that same stealthy limp, he returned to the door and was gone. As the door closed quietly behind him, Rudy saw the silken bedclothes stir, and Alde raised her head to look at the fading crack of light that marked where Eldor had gone. Her eyes were wide, plum-colored in the darkness—and wholly awake.

His hands shaking, Rudy laid the crystal aside. In time he fell into a fitful sleep, prey to other visions more terrible than that—and to one in particular, a recurring horror that he had begun already to pray was only a dream.

In all that wretchedness and despair, the one thing that he clung to was the music of the harp Tiannin. He had salvaged the instrument from the ruins of Quo, the city that he had felt instinctively should have been his home; Dakis the Minstrel and Minalde had both taught him the rudiments of Tiannin's art.

Now, through the dark winter days, it was his only company, the magic of its music the only outlet for his longing and grief. For hours on end he played, sometimes straight through the long nights, his hands clumsily shaping the songs he had learned, or following their own inclinations into long, melancholy improvisations. He sensed, as he had always sensed, the presence of a crystalline beauty within the harp that lay far beyond his striving. The notes seemed to rise toward it, as flocks of marsh birds rose toward the sun at dawn. But because Ingold had once teased him about how badly he played, he was not aware of how close to that beauty he came. The other mages, some of the Guards, and those in the Keep who had their own losses to mourn in that bleak dead of winter often came to sit in some room of that thin-walled, half-deserted complex to hear those clean and shining strains.

It was thus that Gil found him, the night that the Church finally struck.

So engrossed was he in the shimmering sounds that he did not hear her swift feet in the hall. The first he knew of her presence was when the door was flung open, and she strode with light and terrible urgency into the room.

She paused, blinking in the darkness, but she was moving toward the bed where he sat by the time he had called a feather of light to the air above his head.

"What the—" he began.

She removed the harp from his startled hands. In the pale glow of the witchlight, her brows were two black slashes above eyes that were coolly impersonal. "I just got word," she informed him briefly. "All the Alketch troops up on the second level are being sent down here. Their orders are to put all the wizards under arrest."

Rudy gasped. *"What?"* And then, rather incoherently, he protested, "It's the middle of the goddam night!"

She paused on her way back out the door, the harp tucked under her arm, its strings glimmering like quicksilver against the darkness of her voluminous surcoat. With cool scorn, she asked, "You think they'd pull a bust like this if there were likely to be witnesses?"

"But . . ."

She was gone, her black clothes mingling with the shadows. Rudy was still standing in the doorway of the cell when torchlight flooded the corridors, followed by voices, curses, and the clatter of boots. A squad of Alketch troopers turned the corner and barged toward the cell door—flat-faced, mahogany-dark men in scaled armor that glittered like an oiled rainbow in the light.

Confusion had slowed Rudy's reflexes. He slammed the door instants before they reached it and made a dash across the room for the flame thrower that was holstered beside the bed. The door was kicked open and men poured in, surrounding him before he reached his weapon; it occurred to him, as heavy hands slammed him against the wall, that he could have used a cloaking-spell instead.

His arms were twisted behind him, and he was searched, not gently; it came to him for the first time how civil and pleasant the San Bernardino cops had been.

"Listen . . ." he gasped—and collected a slap from a mailed hand that took his breath away.

He was jerked away from the wall, stifling a cry as his arms were all but wrenched from their sockets. Something sharp pricked his ribs, and someone said, "You make a noise, mage, and it will be the last one you ever make." A hot thread of blood trickled down his side.

They dragged him into the corridor, past the door of the commons. Dark figures passed back and forth across the flaring light of the hearth, their shadows huge on the walls. Firelight glittered on armor; the soldiers were smashing glowstones and record crystals, ripping to pieces Thoth's mathematical notes, and dumping books and phials of medicinal powders into the fire. He heard a groaning crash as one of them stamped his boot through Dakis the Minstrel's lute and realized belatedly why Gil had taken his harp. Then he was shoved on into the darkness and cuffed when he stumbled, his arms aching and the knife point grating against his ribs. They passed the main stairway that led up to the second level and turned aside.

It was only then that he grasped fully what was happening. Gil had known it, when she said there would be no witnesses—her quicker mind must have leaped to the truth in

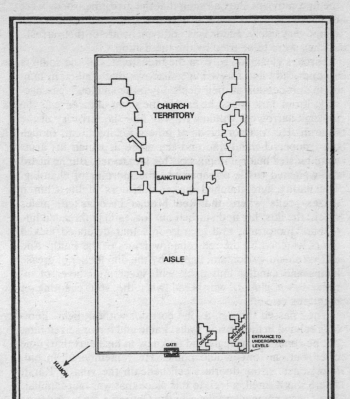

CHURCH
TERRITORY

SANCTUARY

AISLE

GATE

GRANDO

WIZARDS'
CORPS

ENTRANCE TO
UNDERGROUND
LEVELS

KILLION

NOTE:

Royal administrative and residential quarters occupy roughly ½ the area of Church Territory, directly above it on the 2nd level.

The Penambran refugees occupy most of the 4th, and all of the 5th, levels.

The Keep of Dare

the first moment she had seen that the arresting troops were from Alketch. The wizards would not be tried by the High King; very likely, Eldor was not even aware of their arrest.

They were to be tried by the Inquisition.

Torches gleamed redly on the breastplates of the soldiers around Rudy and threw huge shadows that stalked in lumbering procession at their heels down the shadowy passageway. From dark doors, he caught the scent of incense as the passage narrowed, winding its way into the territory of the Church. He was conscious of others joining them, though the troopers behind him and the angle at which his arms were twisted made it impossible for him to see. But he heard the weighted rustle of robes and the murmur of chanting. The flaring light touched darker corridors of the Church mazes—cells where the Red Monks bivouacked, aisles where the dust lay undisturbed but for a single threaded line of bare footprints, and guardrooms that defended locked doors watched by the red-robed warriors of the Faith. And all that shadowy domain, lighted by the dim flicker of grease lamps and candles and thick with layer after layer of incense-laden gloom, whispered with the soft chanting of nightlong prayers.

They passed through a long corridor without light. Footfalls echoed in the closing walls. Panic and terror seized him, but he could not struggle and he knew in his heart that, if he cried out, no one would come. He remembered Ingold, imprisoned in the doorless cell beneath the villa at Karst. There was a smell, a feel, to this place that was half-familiar. They were somewhere deep in the Church's maze, far from any inhabited section of the Keep at all. Dust rose about their feet, glimmering in the fitful glare of the torches. The smell of the place was vile, disused, and damp.

Someone pushed open a door in the dark wall. Rudy stumbled over something on the threshold and was thrust through, his cramped arms failing to break his fall. He landed hard and lay for a moment, breathless, aching, and terrified, listening to the inhabited silence in the room.

In the darkness, a bell rang. Rudy rolled painfully over, feeling the cold scratchiness of a floor long given over to dust and dirt beneath his palms. He half sat up, his wizard's sight showing him dim shapes: the weatherwitches Grey and Nila, holding hands, their voices soft and fearful; Dakis the Minstrel, unconscious, his bleeding head pillowed on Ilae's lap; Ungolard, his face bowed despairingly on his hands; and Kara, her black hair rumpled down her back, flushed with anger and working at untying and ungagging her mother.

He looked around him, frowning into the darkness. He had found that in certain times and places—in the Nest of the Dark or among the twisting Walls of Air that circled Quo—his dark-sight was less clear, and so it seemed here. He could make out the shape of a double cell, black-walled and cold, some twenty feet by forty. Its ceiling he could not see, hidden as it was in shadows. He could see only one door. The place had a fusty smell to it, sterile and somehow at once disgusting and frightening. He shivered at the half-forgotten memory that it stirred and called a sliver of witchlight . . .

. . . and nothing came. It was as if he had dropped his spell of summoning into a dark well and had seen the water swallow it.

This was a cell where no magic would work.

Dame Nan's shrill voice slashed into the terrible silence of that leaden room. "Filthy, rotten, fish-eating Southerners, to manhandle an old woman!"

"Mother!" Kara whispered, frightened, and the old witchwife scrambled to a sitting position, rubbing her skinny wrists.

"Don't you 'mother' me, my girl! If they're listening, so much the better! Curses of itches on them, from that yellow-bellied lefty on down to the last drab's bastard of a foot soldier's catamite of 'em! May piles like the warts on a drunkard's nose decorate their—"

"*Mother!*"

And in the darkness, someone gave a cracked, hysterical laugh.

Half-crouched, as if he feared to be seen by some unknown watcher, Rudy made his way to the scar-faced spellweaver's side. "Where's Thoth?" he whispered, and she shook her head.

Rudy looked around him. There was no sign of Brother

Wend or of Kta. Knowing Kta, Rudy figured that the old guru had probably been in his usual seat by the common room fire when the Alketch troops had sacked the place, and they simply had not noticed him. That was two free . . . maybe three.

Free for what? he wondered. *To rescue us? From the middle of Church territory? And where the hell will we go if we are rescued? Away from the Keep? To the Dark?*

He buried his aching head in his hands. It became suddenly, terribly, clear to him what had happened to the wizard-engineers who had built the Keep. They had vanished without a trace . . . their labs had been sealed up . . . gradually the light had died out of the glowstones, and the memory of the building of the Keep had disappeared from the minds of all but those few, like Dare, who had volunteered to carry the knowledge on in their bloodlines. If they'd kept records, the Church had most likely destroyed them.

The Devil guards his own, Govannin had said. Only there was no Devil and no Archmage—no Ingold. *Govannin would never have been able to touch us when he was alive.*

Thoth, Rudy thought. *Where's Thoth? And Wend? Or did Govannin have something special in mind for them? Thoth, as the most powerful of us left, and Wend, as the traitor to the Faith . . .*

Despite everything he could do, Rudy's too-vivid imagination began to conjure all the things that could happen to those who simply vanished.

The bell rang again, clear and cold in the darkness. The door opened, an orange bar of light falling over the frightened faces of those within; more Alketch troopers entered, jeering and laughing at the tall, elegant old man whom they shoved, stuttering with rage, in their midst.

"This is an outrage!" Bektis was gasping. "Infamy! You dare to lay hands upon . . ."

He was greeted by obscene laughter and a flurry of brutal horseplay before he was flung among the other mages, choking with terror and indignation. He made a move to rise, trod on the flowing hem of his robe, and stumbled to his knees; the room shook with the soldiers' merriment.

"You're better on your knees praying, grandpa," the captain jeered.

"You might start by praying for all those you sent to their death with them exploding weapons," said another trooper, whose burned face still bore the livid marks of the battle in the Nest. "And finish praying for yourself when the Devil gets back his own!"

"I had nothing to do with . . ." the Court Mage began, attempting to get to his feet. With the sense of timing of a trained athlete, the captain reached out with his spear butt and hooked the old man's supporting hand out from beneath him, knocking him in a sprawl to the floor once more. The other soldiers howled with laughter.

Bektis' white cheeks were stained red with anger, and his rumpled, silken beard was trembling with fury. "I demand that my lord Alwir be informed of this! He would never—"

"My lord Chancellor knows where you are, Bektis," a new voice said, a voice as soft and chilling as poison in the cold, sterile air of the black room. The troopers fell silent and bent their heads in reverence. Almost involuntarily, the mages moved back into the shadows, away from the lighted door.

Against the torchlight in the hall, two cowled forms stood framed, their faces hidden by the shadows of their hoods. But even if he had not guessed who was behind it, Rudy would have known the voice of the Bishop of Gae.

Red Monks filed into the room, their faces likewise hooded, the hands on their sword hilts white, brown, or black, strong or dainty. They moved along the walls until they surrounded those who huddled in the gloom of that long chamber. The last to enter bore candles; when the doors were shut, those two tiny slips of light were the only illumination in the pitlike darkness.

The steady, saffron glow showed Rudy the face of the left-hand man with the candle—the tortured, hagridden face of Brother Wend. As the two cowled inquisitors moved past the tiny flames, Inquisitor Pinard was seen to wear the expression of a man regretfully doing a distasteful duty; but Govannin's lips curled with a demon triumph.

They stood ranged before the doors with their light-bearers behind them, so that their faces were hidden in darkness. Only an occasional gleam of a shifting eye or the red-purple glint of the Bishop's ring as she moved those white, skeletal fingers betrayed them as living creatures, and not simply embodied voices from a nightmare of despair.

The Inquisitor spoke, his hands in their white sleeves folded, composed as those of a statue, his voice deep and rather low. "You stand convicted of heresy, of the willing sale of your souls to the Devil in trade for the Devil's powers of illusion. You stand convicted of causing the death of hundreds of good men, by weapons of evil and by the evil counsel that caused them to be used against the Dark. You stand convicted—"

"Convicted?" Rudy gasped indignantly. "Who in the hell convicted us? We haven't had a goddam trial!"

"Your life has been a trial," Govannin's dry, spiteful voice snarled, "and you convicted yourself the first day you went to the mage Ingold Inglorion and asked him to teach you the ways of power. Your trial began the day you were born, with the Devil's shadow upon your face."

"The hell it did!" Rudy surged to his feet, shaking off Kara's urgent, snatching fingers from his sleeve. "I no more had a choice about that than I did about the color of my eyes!"

The Bishop's thin voice bit across his. "Be silent."

"You know as well as I do that the invasion was doomed to failure from the beginning!" he stormed on heedlessly. "It was Alwir who wanted it, Alwir and Vair—"

"Be silent!"

"And you know yourself that it's no more against civil law to be a wizard than it is to be an actor . . . "

He barely saw the finger that Govannin lifted. But he heard the heavy stride of the Red Monk behind him and whirled to take the stunning blow from a leaded spear butt across the side of his jaw and neck instead of on the back of his skull. He was only vaguely aware of falling through oceans of roaring blackness to the floor.

For a long moment, the uproar in the room seemed to come to his ears from some vast distance, blurred by the buzzing murk that appeared to surround him. Distantly, he saw Brother Wend's face behind Govannin's shoulder, rigid and white, as if he were going to be sick. Dame Nan's screeching voice rose, screaming accusations of perversions that he had never imagined possible. Then he heard the sound of booted feet scuffling, and blows, and Kara's voice crying, "*Don't!* Please, she's only an old woman!" Bektis' whining and other sounds faded unidentifiably back along an endless corridor of muzzy pain.

Sometime later he heard Govannin's voice, spitefully triumphant, reading the formal sentence into a silence broken by Kara's muffled sobs. He felt the stickiness of blood all along the side of his face and tasted dust on his lips. As the Bishop droned on, he wondered why she bothered, unless it was to get back at someone who wasn't even there—someone who was perhaps long dead. Through the ache in his head and the growing nausea, he thought he heard the words "sentence of death" pronounced, but could not be sure. His consciousness was beginning to fade again.

Other footsteps approached from outside the door. Rudy heard the soft, measured tread of scores of feet and the muted clink of chain mail. The heightened senses of a wizard that operated to a degree even in the null spaces of that terrible room told him that there must have been over twenty of them, and he wondered with a weary disinterest why they thought they would need so many. Then the door was thrown open, and the torchlight from outside was mingled with the white brightness of the glowstones carried by the Guards of Gae.

Eldor Andarion, High King of Darwath and Lord of the Keep of Dare, stood silhouetted in the doorway.

A sudden, hideous silence fell upon the room. Though the movement brought the sour taste of sickness to his mouth, Rudy crawled to a sitting position, and his heart quickened with fear at the sight of the King.

"My lady." The King's voice was shrill, edged by the cracked suggestion of suppressed screams.

The white light pouring into the shadows of the Bishop's cowl outlined high, hard cheekbones and threw into prominence the sudden blackness of the grooves that bracketed the full, ungiving lips. "My lord King," she greeted him stiffly.

Eldor turned his head, scanning the room, taking in every detail of that chill, hushed tribunal. The light of the glow-stones caught the sheen of the black leather mask, puckered grotesquely with the draw of his breath. Behind the eye slits lay only a horrible, enigmatic darkness.

"My lady Queen tells me that you hold court."

Rudy bowed his head, weak with sudden relief. *Trust Gil,* he thought, *to know to whom to go and what to say.*

The rasping voice went on. "It seems that the invitation that you must surely have sent to do capital justice in my own Realm has miscarried, for I received none."

Govannin raised her head, her words bitter and harsh. "Since the days of your grandfather Dorilagos, it has been given to the Church to do its own justice."

Eldor linked his hands behind his back, the scarred mess of the left winding like some red, knobby growth around the strong, slender whiteness of the right. The mask rippled as his head turned, pulsing slightly as he spoke again. "Are these, then, the Church's own?"

"They are heretics," Pinard's deep voice replied, "as you know, my lord. They are seducers of innocence. To have truck with them is to share their crime."

Rudy guessed dizzily that the words probably referred to Ingold's metaphysical seduction of Brother Wend, but he could see the King's broad, flat shoulders stiffen and he felt the mad gaze brush him like the tip of a soldering iron.

Govannin went on slowly. "This is a new age, my lord King. The hope of salvation through wizardry has perished, and with it many good warriors of this Keep. The might of the Church shall work for the salvation of those who are left, whether they will it or no. We will not be stopped from this."

The shrill edge of Eldor's voice cut the air like a flint knife. "Nor will I have the Church passing sentence of death or of anything else without my knowledge, my lady Bishop. How-ever many warriors you may have been lent by the Emperor of Alketch, however much he would like to establish his rule and his pet Inquisition in the North, I am still the Lord of the

228

Keep of Dare, and justice and the power of life and death are mine and mine only. Whoso does not recognize that power in me is a traitor to me, to the Keep, and to humankind. Do you understand?"

Within her cowl, the Bishop's face was white and rigid with fury. She spat the words at him. "Do you, then, ally yourself with these—traitors? Traitors to God and to humankind, whose defenses they have murdered—and to you?"

"My lady," Eldor said softly, "to whom I ally myself and why I choose to do the justice that I do are none of your concern."

"They are my concern where they touch the Church!" she shrieked.

"But as these are all excommunicates, they are outside the realm of the Church entirely, are they not?"

He might be mad, Rudy thought, *but you get him into the kind of Church-State hassle that Gil seems to understand so well, and he can handle himself better than a sane Alwir ever did.*

"Don't chop logic with me, my lord!" She strode forward, and for all her small size, against the gold haze of the torches, she seemed suddenly taller, a dark, thin spider in an aura of flame, holding the center of a steel web of Faith that stretched throughout the Keep. "You are master of their bodies and their lives, but I am the master of their souls. I have said that these here are damned and have passed sentence of death upon them. Will you go against that and let them free to do what evil they will? It is because of their doing, my lord, that you wear a mask today."

The silence that followed these words was so long, so intense, that Rudy could have sworn that everyone in the room could hear the hammering of his heart. He sensed Eldor's gaze upon him again and his soul twisted, like a beetle trapped under the concentrated glare of a burning glass. He felt that his guilt stood out all over him, like the sweat that trickled down his face. The other mages watched them from the shadows as if frozen, knowing that whatever happened, their fate would be tangled with his.

The shifting of Eldor's eyes was like the removal of a heated needle from a nerve point.

"You have passed sentence upon them, my lady," the King said, and the jewels on his sword hilt and the gold embroidery on his breast glittered like fire in his sudden movement. "But because of their healing, which has enabled me to be upon my feet today, I commute that sentence to banishment. Let the Guards take them to the head of the Pass at sunset tomorrow; and after that, let them go where they will, as long as none return ever to the Keep of Dare, under penalty of death. I have spoken."

He turned to go.

Govannin's voice jeered at him. "You mean because your lady wife pleaded for the lives of—wizards?"

The faceless head swung back. The hard, white gleam of a glowstone caught an answering glint from within the eyeholes. "Even so." He strode from the room.

Rudy felt blackness closing over him again and groped for the solidness of the floor to lean on. Instead, someone took his arm and helped him to his feet, and he briefly felt hard, bony hands gripping his elbow like claws. Blinking through a thickening haze, he recognized Gil—that cold, impersonal, frightening Gil, her black hair braided back from a face as thin as bone and as closed and forbidding as a sealed door. He tried to get his feet under him and couldn't feel the floor; his head throbbed with every jolt of his body as she half-dragged, half-carried him toward the dark arch of the door. As they passed over the threshold, he stumbled, as he had done when the Alketch troops had shoved him in. This time he could look down and see what had tripped him.

It was a pile of bricks. There were enough there, stacked to one side of the doorway, to fill it in three or four layers thick. Beside them, mortar glittered fresh and wet in the white light of the glowstones carried by the Guards.

CHAPTER FOURTEEN

The dream returned to Rudy, as it had haunted him time and again. But his fever gave it the clarity of hallucination, and he could not, as he had so often done, waken himself by screaming. His cries stifled as stillborn moans in his throat.

His dream was of darkness, thick as smoke, hot, damp, and clinging. He knew he dreamed of the Nest, for he could smell the wet, black moss and taste the powdery choke that came from the disintegrating patches of brown that spotted the leprous walls. He was deep, deeper than he had ever gone in waking exploration, and the black weight of the earth crushed down on his consciousness like a burden of hopeless grief with the knowledge that there was no escape.

No herds came here. Only the Dark covered the walls, ceiling, and floor in a squirming swarm of blackness. The chittering scratch of their claws was like the faint, steady gnawing of rats at his nerves. He could see them, though there was no light to throw even the smallest gleam from those pulsing backs. And he could see what it was, stretched upon the rocks, that they swarmed over. Horribly, he could not see the man's face. But he recognized the hand, thick, and strong, and blunt-fingered, nicked with the old scars of swordsmanship, and he saw it grip the rocks as if in sudden agony.

He woke sobbing, drenched with terror-sweat. The room around him was pitch-black, but the darkness was familiar; the weight above him was only the weight of the Keep. His wizard's sight showed him his own cell in the Corps complex. He had a vague sense that he should not be there, but

231

could not, for the moment, recall why. He could only lie there, crushed by the memory of an unspeakable horror, telling himself over and over again, *Ingold is dead. He's dead. He's got to be dead.*

And, like an answer, he heard the echo of that calm, scratchy voice, above the memory of the grasslands wind. *I would know it if Lohiro were dead.*

Rudy rolled his head back and forth on the pillow, trying to clear it of the sticky cobwebs of the dream. *Ingold is dead,* he told himself again, sweating, frightened, and desperately fighting a growing conviction that this was not entirely true.

Vaguely, he knew he had slept for a long time—days, by the weak hunger he felt and the scratchy growth of his beard. Cloudy images of voices and of people sitting near him swam like specters to his mind, then swirled away again like mist. He wondered if Eldor had changed his mind and if, when he got to his feet and tried to open the door, he would find nothing but a brick wall.

But that's stupid, he told himself tiredly. *The walls of this cell are so thin I could damn near kick my way out.*

He wondered what Eldor had said to Alde when she'd told him that the Inquisition was trying the wizards for heresy.

A dim, white gleam appeared under the door, and he recognized Gil's light, cautious tread. The gleam shifted; he heard the quick spatter of spilled water and realized that he was parched with thirst. He managed to sit up when she came in and took the cup she gave him. His head still ached, but the sickening dizziness had passed. The water tasted very cold to his dry mouth.

Gil regarded him with pale, disinterested eyes. "Think you'll live?"

"Are they placing bets in the barracks?"

"Five to seven against."

He fished clumsily in the pocket of his painted vest and found a few coppers. "Put these against." He sank back onto the rumpled pillow. "Where are the others?"

She seated herself casually at the foot of the bed. "About fifteen miles the far side of the Pass."

He sat up with a jerk, so quickly that the motion almost made him sick. "What?"

Cold as ice, her bony hand pressed him back. "You had a long nap, punk. Kara sat up with you most of yesterday, but she had to hit the road with the rest of them at sunset last night. You were in no shape to go anywhere. Neither Eldor nor Alwir nor Govannin bothered to see the mages off, and if they were one short, Janus wasn't going to say anything about it."

Her bony fingers traced the fold of the blanket under which he lay—a gesture, Rudy thought, that she had picked up from Ingold. "Officially, Janus knows nothing about your being here," she went on, "but he did mention to me that he hoped any wizards who might have lingered would remember that if Eldor sees one, that order of banishment could just as easily get switched back to death."

Rudy nodded, the slight movement bringing on a pang of nausea. "Nobody will see me," he said faintly. "A cloaking-spell isn't invisibility; but, as long as I move quietly and don't call attention to myself, it should amount to the same thing. People might have the impression there's somebody else in the room, but they'll also have the impression it's somebody they know and that everything's okay. It should take care of me long enough for me to collect supplies and get out of here. The only person who could see me when I'm being quiet and moving slowly is another wizard, and that," he added bitterly, "doesn't seem to be much of a problem around here anymore."

The shadowy gleam of the glowstone Gil had set beside the door made her eyes look frost-colored as she turned them toward him. Her voice was neutral and uninflected. "Not anymore," she agreed.

He was silent for a moment. Then he whispered, "He did let them all go, then?"

"Oh, yes," she replied calmly. "Govannin wasn't happy about it, but Janus kept an eye on them, as much to make sure they left safely as for anything else. I was with the Guards who escorted them to the Pass. We left about two hours before sunset, actually; it's a long way to the top of the

233

Pass. On the hill of execution across the road, Kta met us—the Inquisition's soldiers never caught him at all. It was a bitter climb," she said, still in that cool voice, "freezing cold, with the wind keening down off the rocks like the screaming of the damned."

Rudy remembered that road—it was the way he has taken with Ingold, the first steps of the road that led to Quo. But Quo no longer existed; the ashes of its Archmage were long ago scattered by the wet winds of the sea. Only that black-walled Pass remained with the rocky, snow-covered road running through it, leading nowhere.

He closed his eyes, as if he could blot out the vast sensation of wretched exile that swamped him—first exile from his own world, and now from this one as well, as soon as he was strong enough to be on his feet and away.

The soft, colorless voice went on. "We stopped to rest—Kara's mother was about done in. The Red Monks roughed her up pretty badly. It didn't shut her up much. The things she said about Govannin would have made a construction worker squirm."

He clenched his teeth, remembering the struggle and Kara's voice begging mercy for her mother when she herself could have been beaten to death without a sound. "Damn them for turning her out," he whispered tiredly. "Even if she is a vicious old biddy. Besides," he added, "I kind of like her."

Gil chuckled dryly. "She'll make out. It's Tomec Tirkenson I feel sorry for."

"Who? What?" He opened his eyes and blinked at her, confused by this non sequitur. "What the hell does it matter to Tomec Tirkenson?"

Her wry grin broadened without becoming any more relaxed. "Well, we reached the foot of the Pass, as I said, when the last light was going. Most of the Guards turned back; a couple of us stayed to bid the mages good-by, though none of us had any idea where they'd go. There was me, Seya, Melantrys, the Icefalcon, Gnift, and Janus. We'd smuggled them some food—they were turned out without rations, you know."

Rudy looked away. "Goddamnit," he whispered.

She shrugged. "It doesn't matter. Because about fifteen minutes later, when we were getting ready to leave, Kta pointed back down the road, and we could just see, coming through the woods, Tomec Tirkenson and his people—the whole caravan of them, all his troops, his horses, and what supplies he could browbeat out of Eldor. All of them were heading back to Tirkenson's Keeps in Gettlesand. He drew rein by us and sat looking down from the saddle for a long time at Kara, with the strangest expression on his face. Then he reached down and offered her his hand."

Something seemed to stir under the ice in Gil's eyes at that memory; the bitter, too-sensitive mouth relaxed. "He didn't look as if he thought she'd take it," she went on in a gentler tone. "But she did. Then he kissed her fingers and picked her up, to sit on his saddlebow, like that, in the curve of his arm. And he turned to one of his retainers and sort of growled, 'Get my mother-in-law a mule.' And, by God, they did, with Dame Nan gazing up at him with those wicked, sparkly eyes, as if she were looking forward to playing hell with him for the next forty years of her life.

"Then he said to the rest of them, 'The Keeps in Gettlesand aren't as sure and strong as this, but for the likes of you and for a damned magelover excommunicate the likes of me, they're a damnsight safer. If you want it, you've a home there, until we're all devoured by the Dark.' And they rode off up the Pass, with Kara on Tirkenson's horse, Nan behind them on a mule, and the whole bobtail rabble of mages and Gettlesand cowboys following behind them, down into the West."

Rudy closed his eyes again, tasting the snow-winds and seeing in his mind the wintry gloom closing on the Pass, with the blown snow slowly covering the tracks as the last creak and jingle of harness faded. *At least they survived,* he thought. *At least there was somewhere for them to go in this bitter, dying world.*

"Did they ever find out what happened to Thoth?" he asked quietly.

Gil sighed. "I have a theory," she said, "about what happened to Thoth. You know Wend's gone back to the fold?"

Rudy nodded wearily. "He was at the trial in Govannin's suite."

"Don't judge him too harshly," Gil said. "She's been at him night and day since he came to the Keep—something that cost him all his peace of mind to begin with. It was only a matter of time until he broke. They had a big ceremony this afternoon—you were still sacked out like the proverbial log—sort of a formal exorcism of evil-minded people from the Keep. The Church was packed with people all up and down those little stairways and hanging chapels. And Brother Wend and Bektis formally renounced wizardry . . ."

"Bektis?"

"Wearing a hair shirt with ashes in his very beard," Gil mused reminiscently. "It's the first time I'd ever really seen a hair shirt. I understand now why they were considered such a penance in the Middle Ages."

"What *is* a hair shirt?"

"Basically, it's a tunic made of industrial-weight burlap."

Rudy writhed at the mere thought.

"Anyhow, Bektis pulled a sentence of bread and water and a hair shirt for the rest of his natural life and reassignment, in a menial capacity, to Alwir's household."

He looked up and caught the cynical glitter of her eyes. "Wonderful." He sighed. "So as soon as the stink dies down, Bektis gets his old job back."

"You got it," she agreed. "Maybe somebody's twigged to the fact that they may need a wizard around here later in the winter—if the Raiders should attack, for instance—and Govannin would rather have it be somebody like Bektis than someone as powerful as Thoth. Or maybe it's just a bribe to Alwir. I don't know. For the moment, Bektis is scrubbing floors." She shrugged disdainfully.

"And Wend?" The utter misery of the little priest's face came back to him as he had seen it above the candlelight in that dark, clamoring room.

Gil removed an invisible speck of dust from the frayed sleeve of her surcoat. "Wend was allowed to take a vow of lifelong solitary contemplation," she informed him in a colorless tone. "And was readmitted to the Church, in view

236

of—'services rendered,' was how Govannin phrased it, I think."

Rudy was silent.

"You see, Thoth was a damn powerful mage," Gil continued in that same quiet, almost casual voice. "He was the only survivor of the Council of Wizards, and I guess he'd been one of the most powerful people on the Council. I'm told the only way to handle a wizard like that is to slip him a Mickey Finn and take care of him while he's asleep. And I don't think," she concluded, "that Thoth would have let anyone other than another mage that close to him. Wend was his student, too, in the arts of healing. He'd have had the opportunity."

For a time Rudy said nothing, and Gil folded her bony hands in silence. Faintly, the measured tread of the Alketch patrols in the halls came to him; the Alketch troops now garrisoned most of the Keep. He thought of Alwir and the hook-handed Commander Vair, but they had little meaning to him now. He felt crushingly weary, as if, like the tortured figure he had seen in his dreams, he lay beneath the rock weight of all earth and all darkness, without hope of rescue or chance of escape.

He glanced up at Gil again. Her lips were folded in a very slight, cynical smile; veiled behind fatigue-bruised lids, her gray eyes were cold and unsurprised by this sordid tale of treachery and tyranny. Rudy found himself thinking that she had become very much like Melantrys and the Icefalcon, as ruthless and impersonal as the edge of a sword.

Yet she'd put herself in danger to save the music of his harp.

He did not want to ask the next question, but knew that he could not bear not knowing. "And Alde?"

The long fingers pleated the edge of the blanket restlessly. "Eldor may not have both oars in the water," she said after a moment, "but he's smart enough to know that Alde wasn't pleading for the wizards' safety out of regard for Kara's mother's health. I knew it would backfire on her," she went on, her voice muffled as she turned her face from him, "but I literally couldn't think of any other way to stop the trial. The Church's high-handed use of power has been a sore point with Eldor all along. I was betting he'd let you go just to black Govannin's eye."

Rudy seized her hand impatiently. "What about Alde?"

The delicate nostrils flared with scorn. "What the hell did you expect?" she snapped. "He'll let her out eventually—he can't keep her a prisoner forever."

What the hell did I expect? he wondered dully. He had known in his heart that she was Eldor's prisoner. *I did this to her.* And yet in the beginning it had all been so easy, had felt so right. From the first moment he had met Alde, that last golden afternoon at Karst, and had mistaken her for Tir's junior nursemaid, he had had no doubt that their love was right.

"We should never have started," he whispered softly, his bleak gaze shifting to Gil's face once more. "All I've done for her is screw up her life, and I wouldn't have hurt her for the world, Gil."

Gil shrugged and toyed with the hilt of her sword. "I don't suppose you could have hurt her," she observed, not meeting his eyes, "if she didn't love you—not that that's any excuse. But it just might be that loving you saved her life."

Rudy frowned, startled.

Gil went on in that almost absent-minded voice. "When you have lost the only person you loved—whether he ever loved you back or not—when you have lost your world and everything you ever had and are fighting your way forward without even a goal to fight for, it's tremendously easy to die, Rudy."

She got to her feet and adjusted her sword belt around her narrow hips. Her eyes met his, forbidding, defying him to reply or say anything to her of love or loss. "If you get on the road tomorrow, you can probably catch up with the Gettlesand party," she added prosaically. "I'll send you a birthday card when spring breaks."

But dawn brought a messenger to the gates of the Keep, a thin, brown boy on a winded horse, his crimson tunic sewn with the emblems of the Empire of the South. Janus sent one of the day watch running to fetch Vair from his quarters in the Royal Sector. Rudy, persistently unnoticeable in the cloak of his spells, had made his silent way down to the gates to sniff the weather and he saw at once that something was badly amiss.

Black clouds buried the peaks that loomed over the Vale; the distant Pass lay invisible under a gray roil of vapor and snow. By the direction of the wind, Rudy guessed that the weather would break sometime late that afternoon—very cold but clearing, he thought. If he left as soon as the gates were opened at daybreak, slipping unobtrusively out with the woodcutters and hunters, he would still be able to catch the Gettlesand cavalcade within a day or so.

From the shadows of the gate passage, he watched Janus talking to the messenger while the herdkids swarmed around them. None of them so much as glanced at Rudy. Behind him in the tunnel, Alwir's deep, beautiful voice sounded, with Eldor's breaking in like a screeching counterpoint. The dark Alketch Commander walked silently between. Rudy stood very still. Perhaps due to their preoccupation, perhaps due to his spells, none of them happened to be looking in his direction as they passed within a foot of him, though Eldor's cloak brushed his shoulder.

He remembered that one of the mages—Dakis the Minstrel?—had once recounted to him how, by judicious use of such cloaking-spells and his own native caution, he had lived for three weeks in an enemy's house without anyone's becoming aware of his presence. Rudy doubted the story was true, chiefly because Dakis could never have kept his mouth shut for three weeks. But throughout the interview on the steps, neither Janus not Eldor nor anyone else ever looked in Rudy's direction. It was as if he were simply not there.

The messenger fell to his knees before Vair, his words a quick liquid babble in the southern tongue. Rudy saw the black Commander's eyes widen and his face grow ashen, as if he had been struck suddenly ill. The cold, yellow eyes flickered to the sky, the weather, and the road; an electric tension seemed to galvanize his body. Rudy knew what the message had been before Vair turned back to speak to the Lord of the Keep.

Gil was right, he thought without surprise. *Gil was right, after all.*

The Commander said, "The Dark have risen in Alketch."

Alwir's mouth opened in a quick gasp, as if he had taken an arrow through the throat. But Eldor flung back his head and let out a long shriek of wild laughter. He could not seem to stop himself; the weird, distorted cackling went on and on, until Janus took him by the arm.

"My lord . . ."

The King choked, gasping behind the black, faceless leather of the mask. "I knew it!" he cried. "We are doomed, after all! The earth is doomed! God, what a jape!"

"My lord . . ." the Guard repeated worriedly, and Alwir seized Eldor's other arm and shook him angrily.

"Is that all you can do?" Alwir demanded, his face livid. "The only Realm remaining whole and stable, the only seat of true civilization, falls to the Dark, and you laugh?"

Eldor was cackling to himself again; but, from his unseen post in the shadow of the dark walls, Rudy saw how the long white fingers of his good hand dug to the knuckles in the flesh of Janus' arm. "Civilization?" he gasped, fairly rocking with unholy mirth. "You call that bloody welter of intolerance and slavery in the South civilization? I laugh, my dear lord Chancellor, because our friend here—" He waved his twisted red claw at the rapidly purpling Vair. "—has been strutting about the Keep like a dunghill cock, for pride that the Dark did his conquering here for him. Fate seems to spread her favors with an even hand, my friend," he said, inclining his head to address the hook-handed Commander. The quickened draw of his breath flattened the soft leather into weird and terrible patterns over the disarranged points of his features. "Who knows what you will find upon your return?"

Alwir's gaze whipped from the rage-engorged face of the Alketch Commander to the invisible one of the King. "The treaty stated that a garrison would be left us for defense until such time—"

Vair opened his mouth to disagree, but Eldor cut him off with a kind of unbalanced delight. "Not when the scramble starts, my lord Alwir. Not when our left-handed friend here has the only stable, standing force in the land and when all

240

Alketch is stricken in panic, with wealth and power there—"
He held out one strong white hand, the fingers crooking and
curling like claws. "—for the seizing." The face was gone,
but the whippy restlessness of that agile body was like the
lift of an eyebrow, the quirk of sardonic lips. "Going to take
your chances at becoming Emperor is a lot more entertain-
ing than helping the Inquisition slaughter poor little wizard-
lings—isn't it, my lord Commander?"

Vair said stiffly, "The question does not arise." The ice
winds ruffled in the ribbons of his gorgeous costume, its gay
embroideries flashing like a rainbow against the drab obsid-
ian wall of the Keep. "We have been ordered back to our
homeland with all speed. The Dark rose in all places at once,
on a night some three weeks ago. I do not know what has
happened by this time, but my lord the Emperor has said
that he needs every sword."

He turned again to Eldor, who stood rocking a little on his
heels with a swaying motion like a serpent's, the scarred
root of his left hand stuck loosely in the jeweled buckle of his
sword belt. "Our undoing amuses you, my lord," he said
bitterly. "But what you see is the ruin of humankind—the
death knell, not only of our civilization, but of all hope for
refounding your own."

"Indeed," Eldor said, shrill mockery edging his voice.
"That is what amuses me."

"You're mad," Alwir said quietly, and there was no
question now in his tone.

"No, no, my darling," Eldor crooned, laying a long,
soothing hand upon Alwir's quilted velvet shoulder. "Not
mad. Hell has merely altered my sense of humor. There was
once a man, they say, who could raise the dead—he was
killed out of hand."

Alwir jerked his arm free of that mocking caress. "You're
mad," he repeated, and Eldor laughed.

"Not as mad as you are, my friend, to lose your foreign
troops." The King turned on his heel and went striding off
into the Keep, his wild, metallic voice echoing into the dark
vaults with the news that Alketch had fallen and the Dark
Ones had overrun the face of the world.

Vair started to follow him, but Alwir reached out to stay the Commander, grasping the puffed and pearl-embroidered blue sleeve. A glance passed between them in the bruised dawnlight. Then they both went after the mad King, into the rising chaos of the Keep.

The day was one of utter confusion, as if the Keep, like a scientist's nest of ants, had been upended and shaken. As Rudy flitted here and there, hidden by his cloaking-spell and collecting provisions for his own departure, he was conscious as he never had been before of the perils of any sudden change to such a small and precariously balanced community.

The departure of the surviving troops of Alketch meant more than just two thousand fewer mouths to feed. It meant the collapse of power structures and the hasty rebuilding of provisional alliances; it meant fights over foodstuffs, and the Guards ranged *en masse* with hundreds of armed volunteers around the gates of the food compounds, forbidding the departing soldiers to take so much as a stale piece of barley bread for the road home.

"You've fed off us long enough!" yelled Melantrys, who had appointed herself captain of the defenders. "You can forage for yourselves when you get to the river valleys, as we did!" She brandished one of the handful of remaining flame throwers left in the Keep.

There were other fights, wicked, dirty scuffles with the Alketch troops in the passageways of the Keep over possessions stolen or alleged stolen and over old grudges. Vair was furious over the reports from his captains of men ambushed and murdered in the back corridors, but he could do nothing. Any soldier of Alketch who left the Keep doors was pelted with snow and garbage by the growing mob on the steps and refused readmittance.

Once, late in the afternoon, Rudy thought that he glimpsed from the Keep gates the shadowy, wolf-colored forms of White Raiders, watching the preparations with unconcealed interest from the hill of execution across the road.

The Army of Alketch marched away through the stinging

swirls of snow about two hours before sunset, the cursory notes of their horns a brief echo of the brave fanfares that had heralded their coming. Rudy could have told them they would be bogged down by snow in the lower Pass and lose many more men to the cold that night, had anyone known he was there to be asked. Even Bektis could have told them that. But Bektis had begun to serve his penance and was absent from the steps where the crowds watched the Southerners on their way.

Bektis was one of very few to miss the sorry spectacle. All the Guards were there and all the Red Monks, ranged with Govannin, steel-eyed and disapproving, at their head. Maia stood there with all his Penambrans, Rudy himself took the risk—a small one—of being seen and recognized despite his cloaking-spell, in order to stand like a ghost on the fringes of the crowd, picking out faces that he knew he would never see again after he left the Keep at tomorrow's dawn: Winna and the Keep orphans; Bok the carpenter; that skinny little old man who kept chickens in his cell despite all Alwir's injunctions about livestock in the Keep; Gil, standing between Gnift and the Icefalcon; Alwir, the black velvet wings of his cloak stirring in the bitter winds; and Eldor, faceless, somber, his thrawn body taut with barely contained amusement.

There was no sign either of Minalde or of Tir.

She would be back in her room, Rudy thought, *alone. Unguarded.*

The thought of her seemed to kindle all his flesh, like fire in dry wood. Between his fear for her and the longing that had tormented him for these aching weeks, he scarcely stopped to think; it seemed impossible to him that he would leave the Keep forever without once more hearing her voice. For months, in good times and bad, he had lived with the reality of her love, the comfort of her presence, her sweet seriousness and good-natured teasing, and her boundless capacity for affection. It seemed to him that no matter how painful their parting would be, he could not forgo speaking to her one more time.

It was tricky to pass through the crowd—tricky to go

243

within a few feet of Eldor, who, he devoutly hoped, had no idea that he had remained at the Keep, contrary to the order of banishment. He pulled the illusion of a kind of gray facelessness about him. If asked, any one of those Rudy jostled would have been reasonably certain that he had been brushed against by someone he knew, only he could not quite recall by whom. In any case, everyone was far too preoccupied with watching the troops of the South to care.

The corridors of the Keep were empty, echoing eerily with his hurrying feet. Rats scurried out of his way; cats paused in the darkness, turning flat, feral heads to observe him with their insolent eyes. Only when he passed the hallways that led into the mazes of the Church did he sense movement in the vast, dark hollowness around him—a dim suggestion of chanting somewhere far off and a vagrant breath of incense.

The corridor outside Alde's room was dark and empty. A thin line of candlelight showed beneath her door. His hand brushed over the door bolts as lightly as a passing breeze.

He paused, listening, extending his senses and stilling his mind, as if he could see into the room through the shut and bolted door. The soft creak of the carved chair came to his ears, the tiny sibilance of skirts sliding over a shifted knee. A breath of beeswax mixed with a hint of new bread and butter. Alde's soft voice was singing, as she did to herself when she was alone.

"You were the love that I should have met,
Had the roads we walked on crossed—
But time and the stars forbade it then
And the days of the summer were lost.
Now the white snow covers the hillside,
The wedding chimes are rung,
And my harp strings mourn the music
Of a song that was never sung."

He heard her voice crack a little. There was a long, desperate silence, her breath fighting sobs. Then she whispered to herself, "Don't do this. He's gone, it's over. Don't torture yourself. He's safe, and that's all that matters."

Tir's voice spoke, babbling and unintelligible, and Alde

replied with a forced and broken lilt. Rudy turned away from the door, feeling as if nails were being pulled from his flesh.

If she thinks I left with the wizards, he thought, *so much the better. She's taken the worst impact of the hurt already. It would be senseless cruelty to make her go through another farewell.*

He stumbled down the black hallways with an ache in him that he had never dreamed possible. *You wanted to hear her voice,* he told himself bitterly, *and you did.* It was the last time he would hear it, the last time he would walk these halls. And Alde would remain, virtually a prisoner of a mad, twisted husband— He shoved the images from his mind, as he had shoved those other dreams of the crushing weight of stone and darkness. There was nothing that he could do. Tomorrow he would slip quietly from the Keep and take the long road for . . .

Where?

Gettlesand was the logical choice.

People had begun to drift back into the Keep; he heard the footsteps of patrolling Guards and drew around himself the protective veils of illusion long before they came into sight. Against his will, other possibilities formed within his brain of where he might go when he took the road.

Quo? He saw Ingold's hands again as they passed reverently across the gilded bindings of the books in the ruined library. Like the harp Tiannin, they would lie sleeping, sunk in a lake of timeless stasis, until they could be brought to safety. The thought of braving the Walls of Air again chilled him, but he realized that only he and Kara of Ippit, in all the world, had ever been through those terrible roads. All the others were . . .

Dead?

There was another choice, and he turned his mind from it, shivering as if with fever. He hastened his steps down the murky corridors, passing an occasional servant like a ghost in his cloak of illusion. He barely noticed the old man he walked by, a thin old creature in a grubby burlap tunic lugging water in a pail. He certainly did not see the smoldering resentment in the dark eyes that followed him down the thick gloom of the hall or the spiteful curl of the lips in the hacked-off remains of what had once been a very splendid, white, silken beard.

In spite of—or perhaps because of—the unnatural silence of the Keep, Rudy's sleep was fitful, tortured by feverish dreams. He had searched for Gil since the closing of the great gates, but had not glimpsed her among the Guards, and had not liked to reveal himself to anyone by asking. He had an idea that some of them knew that he had not left the Keep—those who had gone up the Pass with the other wizards certainly knew—but he did not know whom he could trust. The sensation of being there and not there was beginning to prey upon his nerves. To walk unseen in the Nest of the Dark was one thing; to walk unseen among people who had been his friends was quite another.

He had returned to his cell in the deserted complex, made his final preparations for tomorrow's departure, and fallen into a restless sleep in which his terrible dream of darkness alternated with the vision of the rain-slashed ruins of Quo, the mewing sea birds, and the possessed Archmage's empty, soulless eyes.

It was from this sleep that he woke in the hour before midnight, to feel the sudden warmth of a woman's body pressed to his, a silken river of unbound hair across his cheek, and warm lips clinging frantically to his. He caught Alde's body in his arms and crushed her to him, half-awake, feeling her sobbing against him in the dark.

"My love, my love, you're all right? Rudy, tell me you're all right. They said you'd gone—all the wizards had gone—that you'd be killed if you stayed. Then they said . . ."

"I'm fine, babe," he whispered back and pressed his lips to hers to stop the flow of her muffled, half-hysterical words. "Christ, I thought I'd never see you again. I wanted to come to you . . ."

Her arms clung more fiercely around his neck. "I was so afraid," she moaned.

"Here . . ." His hands stroked her hair and her shoulders, trying to soothe the violence of her tears. She turned her face against his shoulder; in the darkness, his wizard's sight showed it white, tear-blotched, and thin, as if she had not eaten in days. He clutched her to him again and wondered how he could possibly have thought of going without speaking to her one more time. "Babe, I'm all right," he murmured. "I'm fine, I'm safe. It's you I was worried about. Are you okay?"

She moved back a little from him, her midnight-blue eyes enormous in the gloom of the cell. She nodded, the tendrils of her hair swinging down over her face. Her voice was trembling as she lied, "I'll be all right."

Rudy felt his heart contract in his chest. "Does Eldor—" He broke off, knowing that he had no right to ask it of her. She looked away, and he saw the tears glittering on her face.

Softly, he asked, "Do you want to come with me? To Gettlesand, to the Keeps of Tomec Tirkenson?"

Until he spoke the words, he had not so much as thought of it. But in her silence and the sudden tremor that passed through her body, he could feel the possibilities of that solution. Her lips parted a little, her eyes wide and filled with a sudden flare of desperate hope.

Then she looked away and said in a small, flat voice, "I can't leave my son."

"Bring him, then. I can get both of you away from here under a cloaking-spell. We could go to the Keep at Black Rock . . ."

"No." The violence in that low-voiced denial told him how fierce was her temptation. Against the dark red velvet of her gown, her face was dead white in the darkness, her hands trembling in his. "If I had our son, do you think he'd ever let us be? He would follow us, Rudy. Then Tirkenson would have to decide which one of us to betray, me or his King. We'd be fugitives wherever we went, Rudy," she whispered. "I wouldn't do that to Tir—or to you."

"Does Eldor care that much for you?" he demanded angrily.

"I don't know!" Her voice cracked over the words. Unbidden, to Rudy's mind rose the grim scene he had witnessed, the grotesque shape of the mutilated King looming in the shadows, looking down at his sleeping son. Was Tir the only one Eldor had looked upon? And was the single incident that Rudy had seen but one of a series of stealthy

247

visits? Did Alde have to lie there, feigning sleep, every night?

In a strangled voice, he said, "You've got to get out of here, Alde. God knows what he's likely to do. I'll go back for Tir . . ."

"No," she said, soft but unyielding.

"We'll find some place . . ."

"No," Alde repeated. "It isn't only for Tir." She shivered, and he drew her down to him again, warming her in the circle of his arm.

She went on softly. "Rudy, I may be the only person capable of bringing Eldor back to his senses. I can get through to him somehow—I know I can. I can't leave him."

"He might kill you!"

She was silent, but he felt the shudder that passed through her flesh.

"Do you love him?"

"I don't know," she whispered. "I don't know."

He felt the warmth of her tears through the coarse fabric of his shirt and cradled her head against his shoulder. She sighed, her bones relaxing in his grip, and for a time it was as if she had fallen asleep. He turned his head, and her scented hair tickled his nostrils.

"Alde," he said quietly, "I think I'll always love you. I only want to see you happy." He spoke slowly, the words difficult. "If you ever need me—no matter for what—don't let anything keep you from asking."

He sensed her nod, and her arms tightened about his body.

"Send Gil for me," he went on, though he knew in his heart that, because of his love, she would never call on him for help. "If anyone can find me, she will."

"Gil!" Alde pulled free of his arms and sat up with a gasp. "What about Gil?"

"Gil sent a message to me." She shook back her rumpled hair with fingers that trembled. "That's why I came here. She—she said you were dying."

"What?" Rudy pushed himself up to a sitting position. "*Gil* said that?"

"She sent me a note."

"Tonight?"

"Just now. Just . . ." She fell silent, her eyes staring, huge and frightened, into his. There was the sudden reflection of torchlight under the door, the tramp of boots in the hall.

"Oh, Christ." Rudy made a move to roll off the bed, to do something—anything—when the door was hurled open with a crash, and the glare of torches and the whiter light of glowstones stabbed into the dark heart of the room. Alde stumbled to her feet, her face blanched with terror, and hurried to meet the man who came striding out of that blaze of brightness.

Eldor did not so much as look at her. With terrible strength he hurled her aside, and the Guards who filled the doorway and crowded the hall beyond caught her and held her when she tried to run back to the King.

For a long instant, Rudy and Eldor faced each other in silence. Behind the eye slits of the featureless mask lay nothing but darkness, but Rudy could feel the King's bitter gaze resting on him in smoking hatred. Then Eldor stepped forward and knocked him to the floor with a backhand blow.

Rudy caught himself on one knee and forced himself to stay down in spite of the consuming wave of rage that went through him. It would help neither him nor Alde to return the blow. As he knelt there, his head ringing with the force of it, he looked at the Guards in the doorway and saw that the man who held Alde back, the man who stood foremost of them with a slight, scornful smile on his full lips, was Alwir.

He knew then who had sent Alde the note that had brought her here.

A shadow fell over him, and he looked up into the blackness behind the slits in the mask.

"You love an impatient woman, young man," Eldor said softly. "It would have been better had you waited until I was away from home."

There was a hypnotic quality to that featureless face that dried Rudy's voice in his throat. He stammered, "It's not—not how it looks."

The King laughed bitterly. "Is it ever?"

"Eldor!" Alde pulled desperately at her brother's grip. "It

isn't his fault. I came to him. He told me to leave. Eldor, listen to me! I had to speak to him . . ."

He faced around on her, and she shrank from the demon glitter that she saw deep behind the mask-holes. He took a step toward her with that swaying gait that was so oddly terrifying, and she pressed back against Alwir's immovable, velvet bulk.

"If you went to him," Eldor whispered, his voice poison-soft, "he had more than time enough to send you away. I understand your whoring after him when you thought that I was dead, and perhaps even now, when you wish that I might be." He reached out to touch her face, and she flinched from the deformed hand.

There was a kind of amused satisfaction in his harsh voice. "I suppose that even in the dark, you would know that you shared the pillow with this face. But you are the Queen and the mother of my heir. There are ways of making sure of the paternity of my other heirs."

He loomed so close above her that his shadow seemed to cover her; her eyebrows stood out like streaks of ink against a face chalky with terror. But her voice was steady as she whispered, "Let me talk to you. Alone. Please, before you do anything."

The twisted fingers caressed her tousled hair, then her cheek, and this time she did not pull away. "There will be time," he replied, "for you to plead your case at leisure. As I said, I understand your desire for a young and well-favored lover, with time on his hands to entertain you. You are young, and the young bore easily. But I will not have all the Keep saying that the King is a cuckold, not even to oblige you, my sweetest of queens."

"It's not like that."

His voice hardened suddenly. "Then perhaps you can tell me what it is like when a woman bribes and suborns her way out of her room, to creep in darkness down to join her lover."

"He is not my lover!" she cried, and the King laughed, a high, wild, screeching laugh, as he had laughed that morning when word had reached them that the Dark Ones held sway now over all the earth. He laughed on and on, the sound harsh and terrible but not hysterical, and Rudy felt his flesh creep.

Eldor choked himself silent at last, the gasp of his breathing pulling the mask flat over the twisted remains of nose and lips. "If he is not your lover, my sweeting," he rasped, "he is at least a mage who has defied my order of banishment and remained behind in the Keep when ordered to go. And since he has—for what reasons we can only surmise—chosen this fate, let him have the death that my other sweet lady, my lady Govannin, would originally have meted out."

He turned to the Guards. "Take this man out and chain him on the hill."

"Tonight?" Janus asked uneasily. "But the gates are shut . . ."

"I said tonight!" the King shrieked. "Let the Dark Ones take him, if they'll have him! And count yourself fortunate, my lady, that I do not give you leave to bear him company as well!"

CHAPTER FIFTEEN

The Rune of the Chain hung roped to Rudy's right hand. In the vague dreams of his half-conscious state, it took on other shapes and other meanings—visions of horror and disgust, vileness and pain. At other times, as his mind cleared briefly, he saw it as it was, a round lead seal marked with that terrible Rune, turning slowly on its black ribbons. The aura that flowed from it was a corruption that smothered all magic. In its presence his mind felt blotted; the hope and knowledge upon which magic was founded were swallowed in fetid pits of despair.

Rudy wondered where the Dark Ones were. The night was dead still and brutally cold, and the moonlight shone through the breaking clouds to turn the snow into a hard, brilliant crust of diamonds. It was the kind of night they loved. Their darkness could smother the moonlight; their illusion could stretch out the long, hard shadows of the black Keep to creep toward him across the buried road. He wondered if having the flesh pulled off his bones would be any more painful than the slow soaking away of his life from the cold, and found that he couldn't much care. His shoulders ached, half-wrenched from their sockets by the drag of his body weight against the chains that suspended him between the pillars. Now and then he tried to stand to relieve the drag on his arms, but exhaustion, cold, and the numb dizziness from the blows he'd received when he had fought against the Guards robbed him of strength. Then he fell, and was brought up short by the agony of his arms again.

In the silence of the Vale, he could hear the wolves

howling, as they had howled out on the plains. Without the rushing of the wind in the dark trees, it seemed to him that he could hear everything in the night around him; his senses spread like the great blazing net of the Milky Way over the blackness of the earth. The smell of his own blood on his wrists was very clear to him, as was the scent of the glaciers moving inexorably down from the high peaks. He felt that he could hear the faint, crinkling music that the stars made as they moved and all the sounds of the night world. He could hear the distant groan of the ice in the north, advancing a few inches every year, and the rippling of the wind in the curtain that separated universe from universe. And far below the earth, he sensed the clatter and whisper of claws in the dark and Ingold screaming.

He came to suddenly, to a shock wave of pain. In the brightness of the moonlight, he saw a grim, pale face close to his and felt the warmth of a hand on his frozen arm through the rags of his torn shirt. He must have cried out in pain, for a voice whispered, "Shut up, punk." Thin, scarred fingers worked at the key.

The release of his left wrist was like a lightning bolt of agony. Gil caught his body as he sagged on the remaining chain and eased him down as gently as she could. Her breath was a steam cloud of diamonds in the moonlight, her eyes frost-white under the thick shadows of curving lashes.

To hell with all the movie pin-up girls and even Minalde, Rudy thought groggily. *At this moment Gil Patterson is absolutely the most beautiful lady I have ever seen.*

"What the Sam Hill is this?" she whispered, drawing back in sudden revulsion from the dangling seal.

He managed to say, "The Rune of the Chain. What they used to imprison Ingold back at Karst. Govannin brought it out for me, special."

"Sweet of her." Gil wiped her palm instinctively on her breeches. Then she drew her sword, as Rudy had done when he'd first come in contact with the thing, and gingerly cut the sable ribbons. The lead seal fell with a little scrunch into the snow; Gil kicked it aside, as far as she could. Then she set to work with the key again.

Rudy's breath felt dry and burning in his lungs, the numbness of his body broken only by fiery shoots of agony at the slightest movement. When the chain fell away, he crumpled like a soaked blanket into the snow, and darkness gathered him and warmed him.

From several miles away, he felt his body being shaken and heard Gil say, "You pass out on me now, punk, and I'll kill you."

He tried to explain to her that he was perfectly all right and he'd feel fine after he woke up again, but somehow the words never made it past his throat. Every muscle in his back screamed in red agony as he was jerked to a half-sitting position against a bony shoulder. Someone threw what felt like a ratty old army blanket over him, tipped his head back, and dumped several gallons of napalm down his throat.

Rudy came to gasping. "What the . . ." He struggled, trying to break clear of Gil's cloak and recognized the taste in his nasal passages as guardroom gin.

"Shut up and lie still," Gil ordered briefly. She pulled off her surcoat—it had been inherited in the first place from some other poor soul who was currently feeding the worms and was far too big for her—and threw it over the cloak. "Think you can make it as far as Gettlesand? I brought some food, but I couldn't carry much. I'll let Alde know you got away safe."

"Thanks," Rudy whispered. "Gil, thanks. I don't know how you managed to do all this, but . . ."

"I pinched the keys from Janus," she replied. "I suspect he knows—or anyway, he won't ask. The Icefalcon's on gate guard tonight."

Rudy tried to move one arm and was rewarded by what felt like a terminal case of cramps. "You'd better get on back, then," he whispered. "You'll both be in trouble if someone comes by and finds the gate open."

"The gate's not open," Gil said, shocked at the suggestion. "You think, after all we've been through, I'd leave the gate open?"

"But the Dark . . ."

She shrugged. "The Icefalcon lent me this." She pulled a little token of wood from her belt, hand-carved and old, on which Rudy could make out the carven Rune of the Veil. There seemed little point in asking how the Icefalcon had reacquired it from the late Imperial Nephew. "It should be plenty warm in the cattle pens, and I know how to get in past the wolf traps around them. Don't worry about me, punk."

He looked up at her face, as chill and aloof as marble, and wondered that he had thought of her as a mere bookworm spook when he'd met her in the warm dream world of California. He rolled up onto his side, the effort bringing blinding pain.

"Gil," he said softly, "listen to me. You've saved my life—I'll never be able to pay off that debt. But I need your help. I need it bad."

She frowned, puzzled. Stripped to her shirt sleeves in the deep cold of the night, she had begun to shiver.

Rudy sighed and tried to pull himself to a sitting position. He sank back with a stifled moan, the packed snow buckling suddenly under the hand that he dropped to catch himself. He was only barely aware of the cold of it. "Gil," he went on, "I can't go to Gettlesand just yet. There's something I have to do first, and I can't do it alone. I . . ." He fell silent, his eyes going past her to the moon-washed steps of the Keep.

Alwir stood there, as dark as the shadows of the Dark Ones, his great sword gleaming naked in his hand.

He came lightly down the steps, the moon's sheen like pewter on the folds of his velvet cloak. As he crossed the road and came up the path that Eldor's Guards had trampled to the top of the execution hill, Rudy could hear his boots squeak on the dry powder snow. Gil stood up as he came near, clots of snow clinging to the darkness of her worn breeches and tattered gloves.

Alwir stopped. "Get away from him, Gil-Shalos," he said, his voice deep and musical in the hard, crystal air. "I may even be willing to pretend that I never saw you. But I am afraid, Rudy, that I cannot allow you to leave Renweth."

He took a step nearer. Gil's sword hissed from its sheath and caught the moonlight like a flicker of pale lightning. Faint contempt glinted in Alwir's eyes.

"What the hell does it matter?" Rudy demanded, struggling unsuccessfully to rise and slipping suddenly on the icy, treacherous surface. "I thought you *wanted* me to leave the Keep, for Chrissake! Eldor will never know the difference."

"There are risks that a wise man never takes," the Chancellor replied smoothly. "Allowing for the possible return of a mageborn royal lover who holds a grudge against me is one of those risks." He moved the sword. Light slithered along the blade like luminous blood.

"But I won't ever return!" Rudy argued frantically. "You don't have to . . ."

"Unless Eldor dies." Gil's light, cool voice held no trace of cynicism. Her body swayed with the slight movement of the armed shadow before her; there was a tautness in her, a tension that all but crackled the air around her, a readiness that had nothing to do with either anger or fear. "Isn't that right, Alwir?"

Rudy looked from one to the other, seeing the comprehension and shared knowledge between them. "I don't understand," he stammered.

"Come on, Rudy," Gil said roughly. "A King who's lost his Realm and his honor and everything he ever knew— wouldn't you think he'd have had enough after he found his wife in the arms of his best friend's disciple? What did you give him, Alwir? Poppy juice? Or did your pal Vair slip you something a little stronger before he left?"

"You've grown quick," the big man said with a thin, ironic smile. "His Majesty has taken poppy to help him sleep every night since his return from below the ground. Bektis always mixes it for him. And it is well known that the dosage is a chancy thing. Stay where you are, Rudy." He shifted, as if to counter Rudy's clumsy effort to rise. He took another step forward, his footing cautious on the packed and slippery snow. A brief gleam of silvery moonlight caught in the jewels he wore and along the killing edge of his poised sword.

Gil moved forward to meet him, the tip of her blade raised and thinly glittering. Rudy saw that her face was calm; her eyes were as expressionless as snow water—and as cold.

Alwir sneered. "As you will," he said. "I can no longer afford to deal with a madman or with the whims of a love-struck chit of a girl. It has become necessary for me to clear my way of them, once and for all."

Like an avalanche, he struck. Steel whined on steel as Gil caught his blade on her own, parried it in a single whipping motion, and slid from beneath its burning arc, her arms half-numbed from the force of his blow. He was both heavier than she and more experienced—he knew how to use his weight against a lighter opponent. Nevertheless, she squared off, gauging the dark bulk of his massive shape against the cruel glitter of the packed snow of the path. Curiously, she felt no fear, for she had neither the hope nor the intention of saving her own life, and this freed her. She was fighting purely for the pleasure of revenge.

"My dear child," Alwir said pityingly, "I was killing men with a sword before you were born."

He rushed her with a great swinging blow like an ax stroke, driving her back before him. Her feet skidded on the powder snow that lay fresh and unbroken beyond the trampled ring about the pillars. As she ducked and sidestepped she felt the hot trickle of blood down her face and the stinging burn of the air in the opened flesh. She sprang back again, parrying, and Alwir floundered, his greater weight breaking the snow beneath him and all but throwing him to his knees. But as Gil swept in, he was up again, parrying, striking, driving. The weight of his blows jarred the bones of her wrists and grated on all the old wounds she bore in shoulder and collarbone. He struck at her again, his rushing drive slowed by the depth of the drifts. The snow creaked under Gil's boots as she sprang back, but it gave no more than an inch.

Her breath rasped in her throat like an icy saw. *In and out, before he has time to touch you,* Ingold had said. It was her only defense against the driving strength that smashed her sword aside and razored a gash several inches long in the flesh of her side. The blades sang against each other, moonlight searing down their stained edges, and Gil drove in, bringing blood from the big man's thigh.

Alwir cursed, lunging after her, hard specks of snow whirling about him as he surged free of the drifts and foundered again. He came after her nevertheless, slowed by the snow but never faltering in the treacherous footing, hacking at her with heavy cuts that crumpled her lighter attacks. She felt his blade rip her flesh like a talon of fire; as she twisted clear of him, she was struck by the sick weakness of blood loss and shock. She danced back, her feet slipping in the icy drifts, with darkness closing around her vision as she skidded and stumbled.

Wet cold bit her knees. Aching, she staggered to her feet, propelled by the memories of thousands of hours of Gnift the swordmaster's drills; her eyes cleared as she ducked and spun away from Alwir's floundering stroke. In spite of the intense cold, she saw how his face glittered with sweat in the moonlight, saw how the breath rolled from his mouth in great steaming clouds of white.

She thought, *He's rusty. He's breathing like a bellows.* She herself was exhausted by fighting for footing; Alwir must be half-dead with it.

As she backed, she saw the dark, splattering trail of her blood on the snow. Alwir was driving her, knowing her to be weakening; she saw his mouth twist with ugly fury and frustration as the ever-deepening snow underfoot slowed him down with his own weight. She sprang back before his cuts, then in, sweeping his blade aside, the metal whipping in a tight circle before he threw hers off and cut, floundering in a drift. She angled for position. He blocked her feint, surged up out of the drift in a flying storm of crystals, and slashed in great whirling strokes. Back again, then in, parrying and striking, faster and faster, their feet sliding on the hard crust. She retreated, cutting, her muscles burning with fatigue, watching for the one opening in his guard that she would buy at the cost of her own life.

Feint, parry, dodge! Her wrists were numb with the force of his blows. The roar of his breath and her own filled the night around her. Strike and counterstrike! The world narrowed to the dark bulk of his body. Flounder, slip, recover, and counterattack. Move back, drawing him toward the deeper drifts—dodge under the staggering force of his blows—back, then in! She was conscious of nothing but the burn of air in her lungs and the light, cold joy of battle.

He struck her blade aside, floundering clear of a drift, his sword cleaving the darkness as he fell upon her. She sprang back, then in—and kept on moving in.

His blood erupted out over her hands, unexpectedly hot in the freezing air of the night. For a moment, impaled on her blade, he simply stared at her, incredulous. Then the astonishment fixed on his face as his eyes turned back, and his body began to slump. She jerked the blade free and stepped back, crimson-handed, to let him fall at her feet, and he lay dead before her in the trampled drifts, a great black shadow of spread velvet and pooling blood.

The night silence seemed for a time to fill the earth. Gil stood above him, looking down at that still form and the black puddles that were already seeping into the snow, lost in a kind of detached wonderment. She had won a fight which she had not even expected to survive. She was avenged and alive. For a time it seemed to her that she felt nothing, neither joy nor gratification, only a deep, impossibly brilliant consciousness of how beautiful the night was, how the moon edged each footprint in the trampled snow with a transparent fringing of diamonds, and how clear was each single star above the ice-edged glimmer of the black mountains. Chill sweat was already freezing on her face, but the blood still warmed her hands; in them, the weight of her sword seemed suddenly immense. It was a quick-burning ecstasy that left her detached, relaxed, and filled with an indescribable sense of peace.

Rudy's voice broke that magical stillness. "Hell," he said rather shakily. "I wanted to do that."

Gil drew a deep breath, as if she were waking up, then expelled it in a tremulous laugh. She bent and cleaned her hands in the snow, wiping her blade on the corner of her dead foe's cloak. By the time she reached Rudy, she was trembling uncontrollably.

"Can you walk?" she asked him.

"Christ, lady, I should be asking you that!"

She pulled him to his feet, staggering a little at his weight against her. He drew the cloak around both their shoulders; under the sweat-drenched, blood-daubed shirt, he felt her flesh like ice. A moment ago she had been almost terrifying to him, a coldhearted, deliberate killer; but now he felt protective of her as she nestled gawkily against his side beneath the warmth of the cloak.

"How long has it been since I was put out here?" he asked.

Gil frowned, her concentration bent on negotiating the slippery snow of the hill. "Three hours or so."

"Then I might still be able to save Eldor, if I can get hold of some medicines."

She looked up at him, startled. "But the gates won't be opened until dawn."

"You think so?"

Color rushed into her bone-white cheeks. Keep Law was knitted into her nerve endings. It had never occurred to her that Alwir would have violated it. But she didn't even need to follow Rudy's gaze to the darker slit among the shadows of the Keep's western face to know the truth. "That—" she began, and continued at length. Rudy noted that swordsmanship wasn't all Gil had learned in her training with the Guards. Looking back toward the prostrate body, she delivered the final, crushing judgment. "It figures. Let's go, punk. We've been lucky so far. If . . ."

Her words stuck in her throat. At the same instant Rudy turned, knowledge and awareness like a chill smoke twining around his heart. Around them, the moonlight failed.

Gil's arm tightened around his body, not in fear, but in a businesslike effort to drag him toward the Keep before they were overtaken. Rising wind whirled at their hair, and it seemed that all the trees in the Vale began to toss and whisper. As they stumbled across the road, the sense of the awful numbers of the Dark Ones rose like the rising tide. Over his shoulder Rudy could see the river of illusion and death pouring down from the somber trees that hid Sarda Pass; unguessable numbers of the Dark Ones swirled the snow in glittering eddies, killing the light.

His feet caught on the edge of the lowest step and he fell, bringing Gil down with him. His every muscle cried out at the jarring blow. After that fight, she wouldn't be in much better shape than he was, he thought as they both struggled to rise. The winds stung his face, the smell of them harsh, acid, metallic . . .

. . . and looking up, he saw the Dark Ones turn aside.

Within a dozen yards of the half-open gates of the Keep they flowed, filling the earth, covering the sky like a cloud. But they paused for nothing, howling past the silent fortress and away like an elemental storm.

"What's happening?" Gil whispered, kneeling on the snow-covered steps above him, her fingers nerveless on the hilt of her sheathed sword. "I didn't know there were that many Dark Ones in the Nests of Gettlesand. You don't think the—the wizards—had anything to do . . ."

"No," Rudy said softly. "No wizard in that group, or all of them together, could touch the Dark."

"Then what is it?" she murmured as the directionless winds tore at the cloak they shared and stung their faces with blown snow. "Where are they going?"

With a wizard's understanding, Rudy knew the answer, though he shuddered to think of the reasons for what he knew. He glanced sideways at Gil and replied unwillingly.

"They're going to Gae."

"Christ, I wish I knew more about healing." Rudy stood against the light of the banked glowstones, looking down at the fevered body that writhed on the narrow bed. Without the mask, Eldor's face was hideous, not only from the sunken masses of shiny, twisted scars but from the marks of the last extremities of suffering. "I'll tell you one thing, though—poppy wouldn't do anything like that." He knelt beside the King and felt the racing pulse under the hot flesh of the wrist. Eldor regarded him unknowingly, the glazed eyes half-hidden under lashless lids. His breath came in a fast, steady whine through his teeth.

"Where did Alde go?"

Gil shook her head. "When I told her what was going on, she stuck around only long enough to wrap up Tir before she took off at a run."

"Can't say I blame her," Rudy muttered. He dragged the covers away from the restless body. "You know where Bektis keeps his medicines?"

261

She glanced up from the hearth, where she had been setting a kettle of water to heat. The firelight glittered on the half-dried blood on her drawn face. "The Inquisition destroyed everything of his," she said, and Rudy muttered something savagely about the Inquisition. She added, almost shyly, "But I have all of Ingold's stuff. It's—it's under my bunk, where I stashed your harp. I'll go get it." She rose to her feet, brushing ashes from her hands.

Rudy slung the covers back where they had been. Outside the closed door, the Icefalcon's cool voice could be heard, turning away servants, clerks, and Guards who had been drawn by the commotion. Rudy tried to think, his mind clouded by the long exhaustion of that horrible night. "I think you'd better stay with Eldor, Gil," he said at last. "I'll see what kind of purgatives I can find in the commons and stop by the barracks on my way back here." He shivered, realizing for the first time how damp his own clothes were. He couldn't look much better than Gil did.

From the darkness of the hall came the sudden, muffled tread of many feet and the Icefalcon's light, warning voice. "It's Govannin!" he called, and Rudy groaned.

"Christ, that's all we need," he said. A hoarse, dry voice rapped out an order, and he heard the rattling of scabbards and mail. A moment later the door opened, and the Bishop of Gae stepped into the room.

Bitter, dark eyes under those graceful, curving brows studied him, like a gardener contemplating a snail. "So you returned, mage."

He stood up, conscious of the smarting of his bruises, the ache in his shoulders, and the sting of the life returning to his frostbitten fingers. The weariness of the eternal night seemed to be grained into the flesh of his body, but anger stirred in him, like a swig of fiery brandy. In a shaking voice he said, "I was told there was a man sick here, my lady."

She gave a single dry sniff of contemptuous laughter. "I should think he is the last man you would aid."

"Yeah, *you* would think so," Rudy said tiredly. "And considering he's tried to break your power over the people of the Keep, he might be the last man you would aid. But whatever else I am, I'm a wizard; and though we don't make any vows and we don't preach about what people ought to do, there's an understanding among wizards that we hold our power as a trust and we help whoever needs it, whether that person has just got done cursing us, or whether it would be more convenient for our love lives if he died, or whatever. Now, if you're not going to help me, lady, you get the hell out of my way."

Govannin glanced over her shoulder at the Red Monks who filled the doorway at her back. "Arrest him."

There was a thin metallic whine as Gil pulled her blade free of its scabbard, and the light of the glowstones sang along its edge. The Red Monks hesitated visibly.

Govannin's vulture eyes never shifted. "Arrest them both. Eldor's illness is a judgment upon a man who would choose to deal with magic and the work of wizards."

Rudy shouted, "For a lady who'd use the Rune of the Chain, you talk mighty big about magic!"

The monks, startled, looked curiously at their Bishop, and her flat black eyes narrowed dangerously. "Silence me this liar."

"Is he a liar?" a soft voice inquired from the corridor. The warm white light of the room reflected off a shaved skull in the darkness, and Govannin swung around, her lips growing tight with anger.

"What affair of yours is this, you peasant upstart?"

"Peasant or not," that gentle voice replied, "I am duly ordained and chosen Bishop of Penambra, and if you, my lady, have indeed tampered with a thing as God-cursed as the Rune of the Chain, it is fully within my powers, both sacerdotal and actual, to place you under arrest for heresy."

Maia of Penambra, followed by half a dozen of his ragged warriors, limped into the brightness of the room. In his shadow walked two others who were not warriors: a slender, dark-haired woman, the black smudges of exhaustion like bruises beneath her eyes; and a stocky young man, barefoot and shivering in a dust-streaked hair shirt, carrying a little bundle of medicines under his arm.

Even a few days ago, Rudy knew he would probably have thrown his arms around Alde and kissed her—not only for locating Brother Wend but for having learned enough of

Gil's political savvy to get a military backup first. But now their eyes only met, and she turned hers away. Though he was bruised and aching in spirit as well as in body, Rudy understood. She had made up her mind, and there was far too much at stake now to confuse the issue. They each had a clear duty, though it would destroy forever whatever chance they might have had to rejoin their love.

Govannin's eyes flickered from one to the other in baffled hate, then to Brother Wend, who bent over Eldor's bed. "Heresy!" she jeered. "You talk of heresy to me, you ignorant butcher! What shall we say of a prelate who deals with mages? Or of a monk who has sworn himself to lifelong solitude, but who cannot wait three days before violating his vows?"

Brother Wend flinched at that, as if at the flick of a whip, but he did not look up from the sick man.

Maia turned back from helping Alde to a chair in the shadows of the hearth and replied calmly. "We shall say, my lady, that neither the prelate nor the monk can be proven to have tampered with black magic—as the Rune of the Chain, according to the unanimous ruling of the Bishops at the Council of Gae, undoubtedly is."

"All magic is the same!" she snarled at him furiously. "It is all the dealings of the Devil!"

"Not," the Bishop of Penambra said, "according to the Ecumenical Councils."

"Solipsistic hairsplitting!" she cried. Looking at her eyes, Rudy was reminded of a rattlesnake about to strike.

Brother Wend glanced up, his sick, dark eyes filled with misery. "It was not she who drew the Rune on the door," he said wretchedly. "It was I. She isn't mageborn; she could not have drawn and spelled the Rune of the Chain . . ."

Govannin whirled on him. "Be silent, you filthy heretic!"

"What door?" Gil asked suddenly. "The Rune of the Chain was on a seal. It was hundreds of years old, by the look of it."

"Be silent, on penalty of eternal hellfire!"

Gil gripped the young monk's sleeve, and there was desperate urgency in her voice. "What door did you draw the Rune on?"

264

But Wend was looking up at Govannin, confused. "Seal? What seal?"

Rudy supplied the answer. "Govannin had the Rune drawn on a seal—and it wasn't the first time she'd used it, either. Alde can testify to that. Your Bishop gave it to Alwir at the place of execution tonight."

Wend's eyes grew huge, staring up at his terrible preceptress, the sick man on the bed before him momentarily forgotten. "You used it yourself, then," he whispered. "The door that Bektis and I sealed— It wasn't the first time that you tampered in black magic."

"What door was this?" Gil demanded. "Where?"

"If you speak," Govannin whispered, and her eyes held Wend's like a snake's, "I swear to you, by my power as Bishop of Gae . . ."

"Get her out of here," Maia said. There was not a Red Monk who moved in protest as the Penambran soldiers surrounded the enraged Govannin. "Where is this door, Wend? What cell did you seal? It could be Eldor's life or death."

Wend shook his head helplessly. "I don't know. It was on the first level, in the Church territory. We were blindfolded and taken there. The cell had been spelled before. It was a small one, but no magic could be used therein. Bektis and I only renewed things that were already there."

Maia glanced over at Gil. "Gil-Shalos? You know the back corners of the Keep. Will you take my men and search?"

Gil nodded briefly and stood up. Though it was hot in the royal bedroom, with its fur rugs and braziers of coals that burned redly in the shadows about the bed, the door let in a draft of icy air from the hall. Rudy stripped off the shabby black surcoat Gil had lent him and threw it to her. She pulled it on loosely over the slashed and blood-smutched shirt and headed for the door.

"Gil-Shalos?" Maia stayed her and turned her face gently to the light with one crippled hand. "Are you all right?"

"I'll be fine," she said. Most of the wounds Alwir had dealt her had stopped bleeding, probably including the biggest one, which was in her right side and which Rudy had patched crudely before starting to examine Eldor. It had surprised him a little that Gil literally could not remember receiving most of the wounds—only the first one, which was on her cheek. By the look of it, Rudy could tell already that she'd be scarred for life.

The few Penambrans who had remained after Govannin's removal followed Gil silently into the dark hall, accompanied by the Bishop's confused and whispering monks. Brother Wend looked up from his patient, his hollow eyes tortured by doubt.

"Who is it?" he whispered. "Whom do you seek?"

"Yeah," Rudy said, confused. "Who do they have sealed up?"

The Bishop of Penambra raised an eyebrow, and wrinkles laddered all the way up his high, narrow forehead. "You have not guessed?"

The sensitive hands resting on Eldor's wrist trembled. In a shaken voice, Wend murmured, "She told me that he was dead. I killed him. I . . ." He bowed his head, unable to go on.

"I sincerely doubt," Maia said, bending down to touch the priest's shoulder in a faint rustling of patched brocade, "that with your small skill you would be capable of concocting a poison strong enough to kill Thoth the Scribe. Nor do I believe that my lady Govannin would permit any wizard simply to die painlessly— It was painless, wasn't it?"

Wend nodded wretchedly.

"To die painlessly or quickly, if it were in her power to make it otherwise. So take courage, Brother—her spite may well have been her undoing in this." He straightened up and moved back toward the door as Wend returned shakily to his task. Only to Rudy did Maia turn a worried face, in the shadows that shrouded the doorway. "By the look of my lord Eldor," he said in a low voice, "it will take all Thoth's great skill to save him. I pray that he can be found."

But the night hours wore into morning, and Gil and her squad did not reappear. Rudy and Brother Wend did what they could, using Wend's stock of herbs and Ingold's medicines and working with their combined magic to hold soul and body together, but Rudy could feel Eldor's life slipping away.

266

His own mind and body were numb, and his hands fumbled at their tasks. He was barely cognizant of the passage of time or of his surroundings, scarcely aware of hunger or thirst. All he knew was the task before him and a weariness that became a dull torture. The golden flicker of the fire on the embroidered hangings around the bed began to swim before his tired eyes, and his occasional speech with Wend grew less and less connected. He wondered that it had been only yesterday morning that the messenger had ridden to the steps of the Keep—a little over twenty-four hours since the Army of Alketch had departed.

Alwir must have begun to plan it then, Rudy thought, and he had been mere bait, the ostensible trigger for the larger trap. With what feeling remained to him, he felt a dull anger at Alwir, lying stiff with cold and rigor mortis in puddles of frozen blood on the hill. *He would have stamped me out like a cockroach, disgraced—maybe killed—his own sister, and slain Gil more or less in passing—all as a cover-up for the real thing.*

And yet, beside the silent passing of the Dark Ones toward Gae, Alwir, Eldor, and even he had already begun to seem very small and insignificant. His suspicion had strengthened to virtual certainty; he knew in his heart what was awaiting the Dark there. And he knew what would have to be done.

He sank, exhausted, down on a bench and leaned his head against the mingled colors of the tapestry behind him. The bullion stitching of it scratched his cheek; distantly, dark against the shaded glow of the banked white lamps, he saw Brother Wend wiping his hands, his dark eyes weary and defeated. Eldor had ceased to toss and rave. Exhausted and broken from repeated purgings, he lay with his half-open eyes sunk into skull-like sockets, staring blindly at the ceiling above him. Rudy's glance crossed Wend's, and the little priest shook his head.

Rudy sighed, mumbled a curse, and tried to find the energy to stand. "Maybe if we . . ."

"No," Wend said. "I do not think there is anything we can do for him now." His head and face had been shaved anew for his return to grace, and the razor burns stood out red and ugly against his pallor.

"There's got to be," Rudy said doggedly. "Where the hell is Gil?"

"Perhaps she could not find the sealed door." Wend moved stiffly to a carved chair and slumped down on its yellow silk cushions. The coarse burlap of his sleeves had been rolled up over his elbows; he continued to wipe his hands, slowly and mechanically, as he spoke. "Perhaps Thoth is dead, as my lady said. The poison—I—I did not mean . . ."

"Hell, I know Govannin." Rudy sighed. "I'd hate like hell to try and stand against her will on something I *was* sure of, let alone something I wasn't." He tried to remember how long it had been since the arrest of the wizards, but the days slipped from his mind as the pestles and tubes and herbs had slithered from his nerveless fingers. He ran his hands through his long hair, as if trying to clear cobwebs from his brain. "There's got to be something . . ."

Wend shook his head. "We have done what we can," he said quietly. "Eldor has been weakened by his wounds and by the long debilitation and undernourishment in the Nest."

"And it may be," a woman's soft voice added, making both men turn in surprise, "that he has no further desire to live."

Alde rose quietly from the corner where she had been sitting so silently that neither of the mages had remembered her presence in the room. She still wore the dark red velvet dress that she had worn when she had come to Rudy the night before. Within the frame of her dark hair, her face looked haggard. Rudy tried to recall what he had been saying to Wend at intervals during the last few hours. He knew he had described Alwir's death, and, although Alde had long since ceased to believe in her brother's love, she need not have heard of his death so callously. Her eyes and nose looked raw from weeping, but he could not remember having heard a sound.

As she came into the brighter light and sat on the edge of Eldor's bed, Rudy could see the glisten of two white threads among the unbound blackness of her hair. She took the King's good hand, his unburned one, in hers. When she spoke, her voice was low and tired. "They are much alike, you know—Gil and Eldor. Having lost everything, they are too stubborn to die. And they are both the kind of person who would rather die under torture than admit their true feelings or ask anyone for anything." She turned Eldor's hand over in hers, stroking the fine shape of the fingers, the split and bitten nails, and the scars left by the hard mastery of the sword. "I never knew what he did feel for me," she went on quietly. "Maybe it was that he didn't trust Alwir and feared I would be his pawn. Maybe he just did not trust himself."

Rudy sagged back against the embroidered hangings and looked up into her still, ravaged face. "Maybe he just didn't know how to show love. There are people like that, too. It's hard to tell the truth, even when you want to very badly."

The long white fingers clenched suddenly over Alde's. Looking down, she saw the gun-metal eyes blinking up at her, heavy and sardonic and half-asleep. "Alde?" the King whispered.

It was the first time that Rudy had heard Eldor address his wife by her name.

"I'm here," she said.

"Are you well?"

She touched the tops of his protruding knuckles with gentle fingertips. "Yes," she murmured. "Yes, I'm well."

"It is true, as they said?" he whispered. "Alwir is dead?"

"Yes," Alde replied softly. "The girl Gil-Shalos killed him in a duel."

There was silence, and then the faint, creaking breath of a laugh. A sliver of the old, amused malice gleamed in the sunken eyes. "He must have been surprised."

The corners of Alde's mouth tucked in, very slightly. "Perhaps," she said and transferred her light touch to his forehead. "No one else was. Rest yourself, my lord. Later . . ."

"Rest." The hideous features twitched in a grimace. "Rest indeed." His breath was coming in thick wheezes through half-uncovered teeth. "No later," he whispered, "no light. Only dreams. Tir?"

"Tir's asleep." In the grate, the log broke and crumbled, the sudden spurt of golden light showing Alde's lashes beaded with amber tears. "I'll send someone to Maia's church to fetch him if you want."

The King moved his head slightly, dissenting. "No. Look after him. Ingold promised me he would."

"And so he did," she murmured.

His hands moved restlessly, then stilled again in hers. "Ingold—where is he?" he muttered.

She hesitated and cast an agonized glance at Rudy.

"He's at Gae," Rudy said softly.

"Ah." Eldor frowned suddenly, as if at something forgotten. The effect on the rucked, scarlet flesh was horrible. "I struck him," he murmured finally. "Tell him—I am sorry."

"He knows."

Eldor sighed and shut his eyes. "You spoke of love," he said at length, "and of truth. A man may love a kitten, or a child, or a woman. My kitten, do you love this boy?"

"I love you," Alde whispered, and the burned, red fingers twitched, waving her back from him.

"You need not kiss this face to prove it."

"A woman never loves a man's face, Eldor." She leaned forward and touched his lips with hers.

They twisted into the ghastly mockery of a grin. "A brave kitten. A brave woman, maybe . . . Do you love this boy?"

Alde was silent for a long time, holding his hand, listening to the slow drag of his laboring breath. She finally said, "Yes. I do. I don't know how it's different, but—I love you both."

"A woman may worship a hero," the King whispered, "and love the man whom she was born to love. I was fond of the kitten and I might have loved the woman. But I never met her. I wronged her—and perhaps myself as well."

"There is time," Alde said softly and bent to kiss his lips again.

The door opened quietly, and Gil entered, the wizard Thoth leaning on her shoulder. The old man looked weary and ill, his hairless face and head as white as a skull's above the black folds of his grimy robes, but the gold eyes had lost none of their haughtiness. Silently, Wend bowed his head. The Scribe of Quo had a bitter turn of invective when he chose.

But Thoth only shook off Gil's supporting arm and moved to the side of the bed. His light fingers searched Eldor's wrist, then his forehead, the deep-sunk eyes narrowing to slits, as if the old man listened to the King's dreams. Then he said, "Leave us. No—" He shook his head as Wend rose thankfully to go. "I'll need—" He paused. The chilly amber eyes widened, resting for a long moment on his betrayer's white face. Then, without change of inflection in his harsh voice, he said, "I would like your help, little Brother. But not," he added acidly, "if it means an unseemly display of redundant contrition."

Wend blushed hotly and wiped his eyes.

Thoth turned his enigmatic gaze on Minalde, who had risen likewise. "Perhaps, my lady, you had best stay as well."

The Icefalcon was waiting for Gil and Rudy in the hall. "If he dies," the Raider commented callously as the door was closed behind them, "he shall have none to thank but himself." His glance rested briefly upon Gil's scabbed, discoloring face, filthy tunic, and crusted boots. "Good work," he added. "You have bones to braid in your own hair now, my sister."

"He was out of training," Gil commented, and winced as the bandages on her side pulled when she moved her arm. "Christ, I'm tired."

The Icefalcon moved her gently into the light of a solitary glowstone in a niche and looked critically at the cut in her arm. "That should be seen to," he said, and she nodded.

"Gil—" Rudy caught at her sleeve as she turned to follow the Raider back to the barracks. She looked back at him, and he saw again how bad she looked, cut up and exhausted from the fight and from the long night of searching through the Keep. *It's a helluva thing to do,* he thought, *to somebody who's just about running on empty; and poor thanks to her for saving my life.*

"Gil," he said, "I have to talk to you."

271

"If it's to thank me, don't worry about it," she said fretfully as he drew her into a deserted cell near Eldor's chambers. "He sure as hell had it coming."

Rudy shook his head. "I can't thank you enough," he said simply, "so it would be stupid to try. If I knew what to say, I would. It's—Gil, I'm leaving the Keep tomorrow morning."

She shrugged tiredly. "I don't think you'll have to."

"Not because of Eldor."

She frowned, brushing the hair out of her eyes, wincing again at the pain. "The Dark," she said, picking that single memory from the tangled events of the night. In the faint, grubby light that leaked into the room from the passage, Rudy thought she looked like a couple of teaspoons of warmed-over death. "You said they were headed for Gae. You know why, don't you?"

Rudy swallowed. Absurdly, he remembered a cartoon he'd once seen of a wife removing a Band-Aid from her husband's hairy arm and asking, "Do you want it in one agonizing rip or in a series of excruciating jerks?"

He knew that Gil was of the one-agonizing-rip school.

"I think Ingold's still alive."

Gil closed her eyes, took a deep breath, then opened them again and asked conversationally, "What makes you think that?" Only her worn, sharp face got whiter, and her mouth tensed, as if against the agony of a wound.

He went on, stumbling painfully over words. "I told you about what happened at Quo—about Lohiro. Well, all the way across the plains to Quo, Ingold kept saying that he didn't think Lohiro was dead. He said he'd know it. Partly because of the Master-spells and partly because there's a—a link between student and teacher. I think it's a link that works both ways.

"Ingold made me a wizard, Gil, and I love that old man like a father—more than any father I ever remember. I know he's alive. But the Dark have had him for weeks now. When he comes back—if he comes back—it won't be him."

She was crying without sobs, the tears sliding like ice water down her still face. She started straight ahead of her for a long time, only the rigidity of her mouth betraying the wrenching grief within. When she finally spoke, her voice was even, detached. "But he still has the Master-spells over you, doesn't he? And over every other wizard in the world. And his are the spells that bind the Keep gates against the Dark."

Rudy nodded miserably, thanking God for Gil's brutal quickness of mind that made it unnecessary for him to explain what had to be done or why.

"And what's more," she went on, as if she were speaking of a stranger, "you and I are probably the only people who would be able to detect anything wrong."

"Yeah," he agreed in a strangled voice.

Gil pressed her hands briefly to her face, so that her scarred fingers covered her mouth. From behind them, her voice was muffled and thin. "Oh, Rudy," she whispered, and was silent then, gray eyes gazing blindly into space.

"I'm sorry, spook."

She shook her head. "He was afraid of it all along, you know," she told him quietly. "He said something about it to me once, but I didn't understand. He said that they didn't want him because of something he knew, but because of what he was. With him on our side, we could fight a defensive war. With him on their side—we're gone."

Rudy said nothing. Outside in the hall, the day's traffic bustled back and forth, voices of the people calling anxious rumors to one another, feet hurrying on errands, far-off children's voices crying. With all its smoky air and endless, lightless mazes, its bleak, grimy cells and inescapable odors of unwashed clothes and cooked cabbage, the Keep of Dare was the last sure sanctuary humankind had.

"You think they're mustering for an attack, then?"

He looked back at Gil. Her hands were hooked in her sword belt again, her face like rain-streaked bone. "I think so." He paused, then said, "He's a helluva wizard, Gil. I'll need someone who can handle a blade."

She nodded as if it were something long agreed upon between them. Then she wiped her eyes with the back of her hand and tossed the end of her braid over her shoulder. "I have to go get patched up," she said, still in that flat, calm voice. "I'll see you in the morning, punk."

Rudy followed her out into the corridor, wanting to offer

some comfort, some apology, some mitigation to the hurt of her grief. But she brushed him off and strode away without a word. The white emblem of the Guards on her shoulders bobbed out of sight in the shadows, passing the black-robed figure of Thoth, on his way to give Rudy the news that Eldor was dead.

CHAPTER SIXTEEN

They were not able to leave the Keep until some forty-odd hours had passed.

Eldor's body was burned at sunset the following day, on the great meadowland where the dancing had been held for the Winter Feast and where he had first seen Alde in Rudy's arms. Supplies in the Keep did not permit much extravagance in the way of grave-goods—the embroidered coverlet that had been drawn over his body for his lying in state was removed before Thoth called the flames to life within the pyre. Burned at his feet upon the same pyre was Alwir's body, still crumpled together as Gil had left him. With the cold, the rigor had stayed in the corpse. As the flames rushed over both bodies, it was almost as if the Chancellor had prostrated himself to the ground at the feet of the man he had murdered.

Standing in the crowd between Thoth and Brother Wend, Rudy glanced up at the makeshift dais that had been built for the flame thrower demonstration and saw how composed Alde's features were in the scarlet light. Her son was weeping softly in her arms, more from cold or fear of the fire or from the solemnity of the occasion than from any real understanding of what took place. Watching her, Rudy saw something that he had observed with his many sisters: there was a moment when a girl's face changed, took on the indefinable quality of a woman's, and was a girl's no more.

The woman with whom Eldor had barely become acquainted turned from the ashes of his pyre and walked back to the Keep in the deepening gloom. Bishop Maia walked at her side—he had traded his grubby conglomerate of salvaged brocades for the blood-crimson of the official Church and looked for the first time like a Bishop of the Straight Faith instead of a refugee from the Haight-Ashbury. Between them her son toddled, an unrecognizable bundle of furs, and her people walked in solemn silence behind.

Govannin Narmenlion had gone. She had slipped out, some said, at sunrise and made off with a few retainers after the troops of Alketch. Bektis was gone, too, and Rudy suspected that the Bishop had coerced the mage with visions of a double trial for conspiracy and black magic and had gotten him to throw a cloaking-spell over them both.

Politics makes strange bedfellows, and conspiracy even stranger ones. He wondered what the Bishop and the Court Mage would find to talk about on the long road south.

That evening he went to bid Alde good-by.

She was in her cell, sitting at the table which she'd cleared as a kind of work space, surrounded by wax tablets, glow-stones, rolls of scribbled palimpsests, and an abacus. She'd tied her hair back in a thick bun at the nape of her neck, and wore the gaudy ski vest he'd made for her over the worn white gown that she'd first had on when he'd met her in Karst and mistaken her for her son's baby-sitter. He paused in the doorway, watching how the lamplight flickered on the jeweled stylus, on the splinter of silver that gleamed in her hair, and on the little worry wrinkle between her brows that, like Gil's scar, would forever mark her face. He did not know quite how to speak to her, for there was no mistaking her for anything but a Queen now.

Then she looked up and saw him, and happiness kindled in her eyes like the coming of spring. She held out her hands to him, hesitantly, as if she, too, were uncertain of where and how they stood.

"I wasn't sure I'd recognize you," he said.

She smiled. "I'm not sure that I recognize myself."

Gently he drew her to her feet and kissed her lips. It was the kiss of a friend, but she held him from parting from her and returned the kiss of longtime lovers whose love had gone deeper than passion or change or grief. There was rightness and magic in it, like coming home to warm firelight after a sleet-ridden night journey. The sheer joy of being with her again mingled with and magnified the knowledge that whatever happened, he would always have a loyal partner in this odd, quiet woman who ruled the Keep of Dare.

"I've come to tell you I'll be leaving in the morning."

Her hands tightened where they locked behind his back, but she only nodded, accepting, as women who loved wizards must do.

"We should be gone three weeks, maybe a little more."

"We?"

"There's something that Gil and I have to take care of in Gae."

She nodded, her brows deepening slightly over eyes that had grown suddenly grave. "You would not be going all that way," she said softly, "if the cause were not urgent. Is there anything you'll need?"

"Only supplies for the journey. I don't think we'll need a pack animal. With the wolves in the river valleys, it would be more of a hindrance than a help."

"All right."

Looking down into her eyes, he could see there her weariness and confusion, the tangled emotions of mourning men who had long ago died in her heart. He kissed her again, and this time she clung to his warmth, her face pressed to the woolly collar of his vest. For a long time the scented silence of the room enfolded them, broken only by the faint sounds of the embers on the hearth.

"Will you be all right?" he asked at last.

She nodded, standing still in the circle of his arms. "The work is good for me," she said. "Gil says that a tough project is the best drug the soul can take—and I think she's right. Thank God, Alwir's chief clerk kept the books decently."

He chuckled a little in spite of himself at this matter-of-fact epitaph for the Chancellor. He saw that Alde had her own work now, her unschooled hands picking up the reins of responsibility and power. He could no more understand it,

277

no more have done it, than he could understand or have emulated Gil's cold and rational violence; but he saw that, like Gil, Alde was going to be very good at what she did.

He wondered, very briefly, what would happen to her—to Tir, to all of them—if he and Gil were slain. He pushed the thought from his mind. *Time enough for that later,* he told himself. *If there is a later.*

"Rudy?"

Her doubtful voice called him back with a start.

"You aren't—you will be back, won't you?"

He felt an impulse to wipe the troubled fear from her upturned face with a heartening assurance, to protect her from unhappiness as he had often, not very successfully, tried to protect her from harm. But he owed their love more than that; and he could not drive from his mind the memory of the rain-slashed ruins of Quo and the knowledge of what he was going to Gae to meet.

So he bent to touch her lips again and whispered miserably, "Babe, I don't know."

The journey to Gae was wet and bitterly cold. Rudy and Gil followed the track the armies had left, through slushy bottom lands, iron-gray in the frozen grip of winter, or over the stumpy summits of submerged hills. On the fringes of the vast, pewter-colored meres, they found evidence of bands of White Raiders; and once, in a hollow between three rocky hills, Gil found signs of some other large band of what she thought might be dooic, over a thousand strong. One night wolves attacked their spell-cloaked camp, and Gil killed three of them before they drew off.

"Pity about the skins," she said regretfully. "I always did want a wolfskin rug in my study. It would impress the hell out of my Ph.D. advisor."

It was one of the few times she referred to the life before her exile, and it already seemed incredible to Rudy that Gil had attended UCLA; or indeed, that she had ever been anything but a Guard. When they were on the road, she didn't speak much at all.

When the nights closed over the gray, crow-haunted land, Rudy spelled the camp against the Dark Ones, against wolves, and against bandits, while Gil built a hidden little fire to cook their meager rations of pan-bread and salt meat. Afterward Rudy played the harp, or they talked—of their journey, of the small doings of the people they knew at the Keep, of the possibility of Alde's restarting the hydroponics gardens, or of Maia's changes in Church policy. They plotted scenarios for Raider attacks, or what they would do in the event of another major assault by the Dark. They seldom referred to California, and then only in passing, as of a mutual childhood, half-forgotten.

"You'll be staying at the Keep now?" Gil asked one night as Rudy sat softly weaving the glimmering strains of a haunting, half-familiar melody that Dakis had sung.

He nodded. Neither spoke the same thought—that a week from now they might both be dead, the Keep shattered, and Tir's and Alde's bones mixed with the bloody snow that blew in through its broken walls. "I'm going to get in touch with the Gettlesand wizards and see if maybe some of them could come back to help out Thoth and Wend."

Gil made a noise of assent, not looking up from the dagger she was whetting. She did not ask what good all the wizards in the world would do if Ingold returned to the Keep.

Rudy was silent in thought. Now and then he touched stray notes from the harp strings that dropped like silver coins into the dark well of the night. Across the shallow lakes of the valley, the wolves howled, and winds stirred the mists that curled from the waters' dirty surfaces.

"How long have we been here?" he asked at last.

"Six months, or a little longer," Gil replied, turning her dagger edge to catch the light. "It's round about the middle of March, though you wouldn't guess it from the weather." It had snowed last night, a thin, icy scum on the ground.

Rudy sighed. "As soon as the weather breaks, I'm taking the road."

She looked up, startled.

He went on. "I'm going back to Quo." He put his hand to stop the quavering of the harp strings and looked across them at Gil. "Ingold always said that he was the only person alive who understood how the Void works and how to create the gates from one universe to the next. But he had to have learned that from somewhere. I'm going to have a look at the library of Quo and see if I can find something about how to bridge the Void and get you home."

The knife whined once more against the whetstone, then stilled. Gil did not look up. "Don't knock yourself out over it, Rudy," she said. "We wouldn't have had any more luck returning than Eldor had."

"Eldor?" Rudy frowned. "But Eldor was nuts when he came back. It wouldn't be the same if you went back to your own world . . ."

Gil sighed and looked up at him. "Punk, there was nothing wrong with Eldor that a couple of years with a good therapist wouldn't have taken care of. But as for going back . . ." She shrugged. "They ever teach you about the old Greek myths in school?"

"Some," he assented doubtfully.

"You remember the one about the Goddess of Spring, who was carried off by the King of the Dead? She wouldn't eat or drink anything while she was in Hell, but just before she got bailed out, he tricked her into tasting a pomegranate. And because she'd eaten something in his domain, she had to stay there, at least part of the time.

"We're the same way, Rudy. We've eaten the pomegranate. Even if Ingold had lived, neither of us could have gone back."

He folded his hands over the curve of the harp. "I knew from the start that I never could," he told her. "I didn't know you felt the same."

She wiped the dagger and slid it back into its sheath with a vicious little snick. "I was afraid when we couldn't go back right away," she said softly. "And after that . . . It does something to you when you kill someone, Rudy. And you improve with practice. I knew I was going to kill Alwir, weeks before it happened. I just didn't know how or when. But I'm not the same person I was." She looked across the fire at him, the shadows dancing over the half-healed sword cut on her face.

She picked up a stick and began to rearrange the fire, the light reddening to blood the white emblem of the Guards on her surcoat. Rudy's hands returned to their music, shaping hesitantly, like a long and flashing chain of diamonds, the air of a dance. After a time he asked her, "Why did you decide to kill Alwir?"

The reflection of the flame sparkled in the tears that flooded her eyes as she raised her head. After two false starts, she said, "I loved Ingold, Rudy. I loved him with all my heart, from the moment I first saw him."

"Yeah," Rudy said softly. "I knew that."

Her breath came raggedly as she fought to calm her trembling voice. "I told myself it was stupid, but it didn't do any good, you know. I told myself I had my own life, my own plans, and they sure as hell didn't include falling in love with a man who was forty years older than me and a wizard in another universe to boot. I told myself he'd never look twice at a skinny, ugly, crazy weirdo like me . . ."

"You were wrong about that one," Rudy said quietly.

Gil sighed. "I told myself all kinds of stuff. It didn't matter. I loved him. I still do," she added brokenly. "I still do."

"Were you lovers?"

She shook her head. "I think we would have been from the start, you know, if he hadn't been afraid of—of doing just what happened, of tying a part of me to this world. And then, he knew that his love would make me a target of the Dark, too." Tears were still streaming down her face, a torrent of all the wretched grief that had been pent behind her cool, ironic facade.

Her sorrow hurt him as sharply as his own, for he recalled how it had felt to know that he must lose both love and magic forever. But she would not tolerate his touch, so he only said, "I'm sorry."

She shook her head. "It's all right," she said in a calmer voice from which all that flat, cool, conversational tone had vanished. "I know why you asked me to come. If the Dark have taken his mind, we can't let him live. It sounds crazy, but I'd rather it was me who did it. And you don't have to worry about my bursting into tears and refusing to hurt him or anything. I'd hate you if you killed him."

"Lady," Rudy said softly, "there's damn little chance that I could even touch the guy."

Her fingers shook as she pushed the straggling hair away from her face. In the aftermath of the storm, her features were more relaxed than he had ever seen them, the odd beauty of that thin, overly sensitive face emerging from behind the glacial reserve. "I don't hold a lot of hope that I'll be able to," she admitted, brushing the tears from her long lashes. "You may have seen him fight—but I've fought him. He's stainless-steel lightning, Rudy."

She lay down and drew her cloak and worn blanket over her. In a few minutes, Rudy heard her breathing even out into the dreamless rhythm of deep sleep. He himself sat awake far into the night, a prey to unwilling memories, playing bits and pieces of music on the harp.

The quick touch of Gil's hand brought him out of sleep into the black pit of predawn darkness. He tapped her arm soundlessly, signaling his wakefulness, then sat up in his blankets and looked out toward the beaten paleness of the road. Mist had risen from the nearby lake, swathing the world in damp, intense darkness that even his wizard's sight was hard put to penetrate, but he could hear a kind of slipping, shuffling tread as someone or something hurried furtively south. After a moment's concentration, he made them out—twelve or more men and women, pale, unhealthy, and stinking, their faded silk rags glittering with jeweled embroidery.

In a subvocal whisper, he breathed, "Ghouls."

Gil was kneeling beside him; he felt her hair brush his arm as she nodded. Even to one not mageborn, there could be little question when a shifting of the air brought their fetid carrion stench up to the camp. "But why are they leaving Gae?"

As softly as she had whispered, one of the ghouls halted, raising his head, weasel eyes glinting in the gloom. Their utter filth and the greed in those slobbery faces angered Rudy suddenly, and he drew to him a breath of illusion, a suggestion of directionless wind in the fog and the metallic, acid stink of the Dark Ones.

At this, the ghouls flinched and fled down the road,

squeaking like spooked rabbits in the darkness. It seemed for a time that their reek lingered in the vaporous air.

"I don't know why they left Gae," Rudy whispered, settling down into his blankets again. "But I can guess."

In the two days that followed, his guess grew to certainty as every step brought them nearer to the haunted city of Gae. The louring consciousness of the Dark Ones was everywhere, like a sickness of the air that had spread from the city to engulf the gray desolation of the country around. Rudy sensed their presence, far off but in unthinkable numbers, and the dread of them seemed to stalk the sodden road at his elbow, even in what passed for daylight under the thick boil of wet, low-hanging clouds.

When they reached Trad's Hill before the gates of Gae in the vile darkness of early evening, Rudy looked down from its bare crown to the city. Horror congealed in his heart, not at anything he saw, but at things felt and half-seen. The presence of the Dark was like a marsh mist that hung over the whole town, and the shifting ripple of their illusion made the broken towers and groping, matted trees quiver in his wizard's sight, like a heat dance. Evil, violence, terror, and the lust to suck dry the squeaking rind of the human body rose to his senses like a reek from that dark cloud that seemed to hang above the slimy streets. Peering through the darkness, he sensed the maggotlike movement that teemed in the city's cellars, even before he noticed the flickering white shapes that wandered in the murk, picking vainly for forage among the frozen weeds—the herds, of course. He and Gil had found their stripped bones or frozen bodies everywhere in the surrounding countryside. But he barely noticed them. Over all the city seemed to lie a hideous doom, a waiting darkness, a terrible vortex of unspeakable malice and power.

At the center of that vortex, he knew, was the man whom he and Gil must kill.

Even the next morning's daylight could not dispel the murky horror that filled and covered Gae like a sour, dismal swamp. The sunlight strove weakly against the whitish overcast, brighter than it had been in days. But in Gae it was

283

filtered, as if through a mist, into a dozen hideous perversions of unknown color. By that ghastly light, the city seemed foully unreal, its walls and towers sinking to the earth under the weight of unnaturally riotous vines, as if the stone itself were softened or had the life sapped from it by those obscene roots. The snow that lay in the streets appeared to have melted, though it was piled thick outside the limits of the city, and it was pulped by the churning of thousands of crooked little feet.

The bones of the dead herds were everywhere, fresh or in varying stages of depredation by the petty carnivores of the deserted town—wild dogs, cats, and bold, red-eyed rats. The cold killed the smell of them, but Rudy felt queasy with a nausea compounded from stench and revulsion.

Almost as bad as the dead and the hideous feeling of being watched was Gil's remote calm. She waded through the putrid muck of Gae's overgrown streets with scarcely a batted eyelash, and the queer, leaden light of the vaporous sky lent a terrible expression to her frost-hard features.

After her single outburst of tears on the road, she had not mentioned Ingold or the upcoming battle to Rudy again. As he watched her in the Palace courtyard, methodically stripping off her cloak and surcoat and hanging them on the limbs of a burned tree, it came to him why this was.

Grief or pity would have blinded her, weakened her. She had made up her mind what she must do, Rudy realized; she had sealed whatever chinks in her defenses she could. There would be time enough to think after Ingold was finally dead.

The two remaining palace buttresses, stabbing like skeleton fingers into the white air, cast watery shadows over Gil's face as she removed her scabbard from her sword belt and turned to Rudy with the sheathed weapon in her hand. Wind flattened her shirt sleeves over thin, hard-muscled arms. "You ready?"

Rudy nodded and tightened his grip on his staff. He'd used it to help himself over the rough ground, all the way from Renweth, but its pronged, razor-edged crescent could serve as a weapon as well. Ironically, it was the very weapon Lohiro had used against Ingold at Quo.

Which didn't do him a helluva lot of good, Rudy thought

dryly as he followed Gil over the blackened, sunken remains of the steps and down into the vaults.

The explosions that had torn the roofs from the underground tunnels and trapped the invaders had shaken the Palace above. Through riven roofs and crumbling beams, wan sunlight lay in bars and streaks of fallow gold. The upper level of the vaults was a smeared ocean of ash and muck, cracked stone and fallen groinings wallowing up through the mess like half-sunk hulks. The lower level, though foul with the stink of the herds, was empty, except for places where the clinging, ubiquitous vines had taken root in some fallen heap of stone and dirt overhead.

Through the gaping vaults, wan light checkered the floor, showing the crisscrossed tracks of the herds, like a spattering of clay on the black smoothness of the unbroken pavement. In spite of the miasmal light that slatted across Gil's figure from above and in spite of the cloaking-spell that lay around them both, Rudy found himself looking uneasily over his shoulders, waiting for the Dark Ones to attack.

Walking ahead of him, Gil seemed to fear nothing, feel nothing. Rudy could see that the hand that gripped the worn leather of the scabbard she carried was relaxed; when he glanced sideways at her, her face, surrounded by the ragged wisps that escaped from the thick braid of her hair, was calm. The shiny places in the hilt of her dagger winked in the occasional glints of sunlight. She never looked back at him, never hesitated, but wove her way through the broken forest of the limitless pillars and arches as if her feet had known that route from the beginning of time.

They emerged into a sort of clearing in the vaults, and Rudy recognized the red porphyry stair before them, down which the army had descended to the black stair of the Dark. Mud, dead leaves, ashes, and bones lay all about the place now. From a broken ceiling two levels above, a great aisle of straw-colored sunlight streamed, like an imperial carpet, to within ten feet of the utter blackness of the gaping pit.

Between darkness and light, crumpled on the pavement at the very lip of the abyss, was the body of a man, face down. The hooded brown mantle that covered him was streaked and bleached with the slime of the Dark, frayed by battle, and stained with smoke and blood. One reaching hand lay in the bar of light—a scarred, blunt-fingered warrior's hand.

He was unconscious and unarmed.

Gil sighed. "Stay here," she ordered and pulled her dagger from her belt.

There was something horrifying in her businesslike calm as she crossed that bright bar of light. *It's better this way*, Rudy thought hopelessly. *If he had a chance to fight us, it would be all over, not only for us but for everyone in the Keep. It's our only hope of taking out the most powerful mage in the West of the World, whose mind is the mind of the Dark.*

But tears blurred his eyes and ran, stinging, down his face.

Gil knelt beside the body, drew her sword, and set it aside, the hilt ready to her hand just in case. She shifted her grip on the hilt of the dagger, reached out to touch Ingold's shoulder, and carefully turned him over. Rudy saw the old man's face outlined against the light as the hood fell back from it, scored and shadowed with the tracks of sixty-odd very rough years. The light glinted in the rough, dirty silk of the white hair. He looked at peace, sleeping as Rudy could scarcely remember having ever seen him sleep—the profound sleep of exhaustion.

Do it, Rudy thought, fixing his gaze on the shining blade of the dagger. *If he is what Lohiro was, a prisoner in his own body, let him go before he wakes to become what he fought so hard to escape!*

But Gil made no move. She studied the sleeping wizard's features for an endless time, and Rudy saw the bright glitter of tears on her inhumanly still face. Light skated along the edge of the knife with the sudden trembling of her hand.

Do it, he cried silently, *and for God's sake, have done!*

At that moment the old man's eyes opened and looked up into Gil's.

The razor edge that lay against his throat did not move. He looked worse than he had in the desert, the horrible pallor of his face blotched and discolored with bruises and the small, vicious wounds of the Dark Ones' claws beneath a layer of bloody grime. He made no move; he only sighed, closed his eyes again, and said something softly to Gil, something that Rudy did not hear.

A stray beam of sunlight sprang from the blade as Gil's body was suddenly shaken with a convulsive shudder. With an abrupt movement, she hurled the dagger against the red stone of the steps that led up toward the light, her shoulders bowing as sob after sob racked her body. To Rudy's utter horror, he saw Ingold half-rise and reach out to her and Gil crumple forward into the wizard's arms.

With an inarticulate cry he sprang forward, the pronged gold of his staff flashing in the wan sunlight as he drove its points toward Ingold's unprotected back. Gil cried out a warning, and the old man twisted away from the blow, thrusting her out of danger as he staggered to his feet and raised his arm to shield his eyes from the unaccustomed glare of the light. Gritting his teeth, his own eyes half-blind with tears, Rudy drove the razor edge of the crescent on the end of his staff toward Ingold's throat.

Rudy had not reckoned on Gil. A pair of bony knees scissored his legs viciously from under him and he fell, the staff clattering on the stone floor. He groped for it, and Gil kicked it out of his hands. He looked up in time to see her scramble to her feet, snatch up her drawn sword from the floor, and fling it, glittering, into Ingold's waiting hands.

Sobbing, Rudy grabbed for the staff again, and this time Gil stepped back, tears pouring uncontrollably down her face. With a cry of frustrated fury, he took a step toward her, his own mind unclear as to what he intended.

Ingold rasped, "Touch her, and I swear you will never leave this city alive."

Rudy stopped, blinking, wondering for a dizzied second whether Ingold had placed some kind of spell of *gnodyrr* upon Gil with those few words he had murmured to her when he lay with her dagger at his throat. The old man's ragged breath was the only sound to pierce the uncanny stillness of the cellar. His blue eyes, pale and bright within the rings of cut and blackened flesh, went warily from one to the other.

Then in a strained voice, Ingold said, "Neither of you

should be in this city. Get out of here. Get as far away as you can."

"I won't leave you," Gil said quietly.

He rounded on her, his eyes widening with sudden and blazing fear. "You'll do as I say! Get out! Get out now!"

"The hell we will!" Rudy yelled, and Ingold swung back toward him, his borrowed sword flashing in the pale light. "You've been a prisoner of the Dark . . ."

The wizard moved back a step into the bar of sunlight, his long, matted hair glistening like seaweed. The light around him dimmed. Looking up, Rudy could see, through the crazy tangle of broken timbers and charred stone, the soft coils of white fog beginning to blur the day.

"And what?" Ingold asked softly.

Rudy cried out, "Why did they want you?"

"You'll learn that in time." The wizard retreated another step, the blade poised before him, orienting himself, his red-rimmed eyes growing used to daylight again. Rudy took a hopeless step toward him, and Ingold shifted a little, readying himself for an attack, his body moving with the old, deadly lightness.

Then Gil cried, *"Rudy!"* Her voice was sharp with terror. He whipped around and saw her blink in surprise, like someone just waked from a trance . . .

. . . and turning back, he saw that Ingold was gone.

Cursing, he plunged up the red stone steps toward the waning daylight. Gil hurried at his heels, stammering, "I'm—I'm sorry. I don't know why I yelled . . . "

"You yelled because he wanted you to!" Rudy stormed at her, his voice rough with anger that was three parts fear. He stopped and caught her arms, facing her in the mottled shadows of a broken doorway among leaf drifts and rotted bones. "Christ, Gil, why did you stop me?" he whispered. "I understand how you couldn't do it, but—"

"No," she interrupted quietly. Her eyes were swollen but perfectly calm. "If he had been possessed by the mind of the Dark, I would have cut his throat. But he wasn't."

"Fantastic!" Rudy sighed in disgust. "That's all I need to—"

"I don't know what's going on," she continued, unruffled, "but his mind is his own. I know it."

"How the hell would you know it?" Rudy yelled passionately. "He's had you wrapped around his finger from day bloody one! The Dark have had him. He's been their prisoner. There's no way they would have let him go—not after they hunted him from one end of the continent to the other!"

"I know it because I know him!" she lashed back at Rudy, jerking her arms free of his grip and striding on ahead of him up the stairs. Above their heads, the broken vaults of the Palace showed the sky a chill and smoky white, and Rudy could see that Gil was shivering with the cold seeping through her frayed homespun shirt.

He stormed after her. "And just where the hell do you think you're going?"

"I'm going to find him, you jackass!" she flung back over her shoulder. She slipped through a half-fallen arch, her boots slurring thickly in the knotted mats of half-burned creepers that swamped the halls. "He wants us out of town because he's in some kind of danger himself."

"He wants us out of town so we won't stop him from heading back to the Keep and opening the gates some dark night!" Rudy's foot snagged on a coil of vine, and he fell sprawling. Cursing, he scrambled to his feet again. "It's up to us—"

Gil whirled so suddenly he all but impaled himself on the dagger that appeared like a splinter of ice in her hand. "You harm a hair of his head, punk . . ."

Cold stirrings of wind blew a thin mist over them and muttered in the blackened tangles of half-dead vegetation. The air felt suddenly weighted with the presence of the Dark. Even in the daylight, both of them looked around, as if expecting to see blackness stealing from the murky shadows of the fallen Palace. It occurred to Rudy how very alone they were.

Through dry lips, he managed to say, "We can't split up, Gil. We've got to stay together."

Slowly, she lowered the knife. "All right," she said.

It was on his lips to say, "If we meet him, don't kill me

from behind," but something in those gray, cool eyes forbade it. He remembered that she had given Ingold her sword.

Though it was almost noon, the light was graying. Fog was rising from the scummed marshes of the drowned lower town, spreading clammy, ubiquitous tendrils throughout the dripping streets. Gil and Rudy moved cautiously through the broken, silent Palace, past empty chambers teeming with eruptions of mosses or slithering with vines, and over crazy, tilting pavements where the rotting tapestries whispered with a horrible suggestion of rodent life. Skulls grinned at them from under chairs, veiled in the white stirring of ground fog. Through the broken barrel vaults of one chamber, gray mists leaked like some kind of heavy gas, to flow like water around their feet.

Rudy paused, feeling the touch of a counterspell on his mind. Heart hammering, he looked around the empty hall and out past crumbling archways to the buckled and subsided pavements of a courtyard flooded with brown, filthy pools.

"Gil," he whispered. "Gil, listen to me, please. You know what's happened to him."

She stopped for a fraction of a second, then turned her face away and moved on.

"Dammit, Gil, if you can't help me, at least—at least stay out of it," he pleaded. "I need your help, for God's sake! I'm not a warrior and I'm not a hero! I can't do it."

"Can't," Ingold's soft voice chided from the smoky deeps of the mist. "If you say *can't* enough, you will end up convincing yourself of it, Rudy."

Rudy whirled, his throat seeming to tie itself into knots. It took him a long moment to realize that Ingold was standing beside the arch that led into the court, his hoary rags stirred by the faint winds that moved the mist.

For an instant they faced each other, and Rudy felt as if he were trapped between love and death. His feeling for the old man struggled against his terror of the wizard's power, his memories of another battle in a ruined city against another Archmage, and his knowledge of what would happen to Tir and Alde if Ingold lived. With a wrench of almost physical pain, he broke the hold that seemed to be closing over his mind and hauled his flame thrower clear of its holster and fired.

The column of flames roared glaringly bright into the dull grays of that monochrome world. Ingold made no move to avoid the blast; the fire splattered against the wall a few feet to his left. Steam hissed and curled from the damp stone. Cursing his aim, Rudy fired again and heard Gil's frantic footsteps running toward them. He missed again, the lichens searing from the ruined pillar of the arch beside which Ingold stood. Just before Gil's hands tore at his wrist, he fired a third time and realized what was happening.

Never fight when you can pass unseen, Ingold had said to him out in the windy plains. He wouldn't put it past the old man to fox his aim. In fact, there wasn't much he'd put past the old man at all. As Gil hung panting on his unresisting arm, his eyes met the wizard's. Under the weedy tangle of beard, Ingold's smile broadened. He lifted Gil's sword in salute and walked out into the mist-enshrouded court without another word.

With a strength born of desperation, Rudy shook Gil off him and slammed the useless flame thrower back into its holster. With his staff held before him like a spear, he plunged into the milky vapors of the court. He stopped, panting, scanning the wall of mist before him, his hair hanging wetly in his eyes. Some sign—some clue . . .

Steel whined, and he barely parried as the sword whipped down from behind. Ingold had merely stepped to one side of the arch, letting Rudy pelt out past him into the open. The blade snarled thinly against the metal of the staff's sharpened crescent, brushing it aside. Rudy moved back, staggering in the icy water and narrowly avoiding the loss of his staff. He attacked the sword, trying to catch it between the crescent's points and wrench it from his opponent's hands, as he had seen Lohiro do. But he had neither the former Archmage's timing nor his precision of eye. The sword flicked away. Rudy sprang clear of its slash and sank to his knees in something under the surface of the waters that shifted and bubbled horribly.

Parrying frantically, he backed to higher ground. Ingold

had a far better sense of footing than he and drove him relentlessly, exhausting him in a defensive battle that left him no opportunity for riposte. Slimy things clung to his ankles as he scrambled to a ridge of dry pavement. The wizard cut at him out of the darkness of the fog. He felt the staff parried, the prongs knocked aside, and heard the sheering whisper of the descending blade. In desperation he caught the sword on the iron-hard shaft, up close to the hilt. For a split second of locked strength, he stood almost breast to breast with the vagabond specter he fought and found himself looking into those blue, brilliant, disconcerting eyes.

There's something wrong, he thought suddenly. *Lohiro . . . Lohiro . . .*

Then Ingold smiled, though his face was white with strain. An instant later, he reached out one heel to hook Rudy's braced foot from beneath him. Rudy toppled backward with a sickening *plouf!* into the squishy waters of the slough, and Ingold was gone, flitting like a wraith into the smoky darkness.

Gil emerged from the fog a second later and helped him to his feet, dripping and shivering and utterly filthy. She picked up his fallen staff and handed it to him. "There," she whispered, pointing into the murk. "Can you see him?"

Something moved in the opaque mists that filled a broken gateway. The mists stirred, as if brushed by the torn hem of a mantle.

Rudy picked a rotting weed stem from the matted fur of his coat collar, streaming dirty liquid at every move. "Let's go," he muttered.

At times in that horrible pursuit, Rudy remembered bitterly that Ingold had originally led the reconnaissance to Gae because of his knowledge of the alleys and byways of the ruined town. He hunted the old man through broken and abandoned mansions, filled with the rotting loot of the city and stinking of ghouls and foxes, and along streets and courtyards where the thickening veils of fog wreathed impassable tangles of rope-tough vines. Sometimes Rudy found the mark of the wizard's boot in the smeared mud by a cracked marble cistern or printed in the frost that furred the broken cobbles. He traced his quarry in the stirring of water, in the slurred track of Ingold's cloak over the dew that beaded the greenish mats of filthy mosses like silver carpets of diamonds, and in the matted, overgrown bushes broken by the passage of his body. And always Rudy thought, *There's something wrong here. I'm missing something important. Lohiro . . .*

A rustling sound caught his attention, the slip of feet over stone. He stopped, his eyes struggling to pierce the cloudy miasma that seemed thicker there than it had appeared elsewhere in the ruined city. He thought he saw a dark doorway in a wall, set between molded pillars leprous with moss and festooned with the brown, knotted cables of clutching vines.

Beside him, Gil paused, her boots scrunching softly in the twisted mats of half-dead vegetation. She caught his sleeve as he stepped toward the door and whispered, "Can't you feel it?"

All around them, the nearness of the Dark Ones was like a buzzing heaviness in the air. The day was far spent. In the dense, gray mist that shrouded the city, it was impossible to guess the hour, but Rudy knew that the light would soon fade. In darkness, Ingold would be utterly beyond his power.

Cautiously, he advanced toward the door. The crescent end of his staff began to burn with a pale, smoky light, blurred by fog. By it, he could see the peering gargoyle faces carved in the pillars and the darkness of a broken stairwell beyond them, its walls bulging under the thrust of young tree roots. A drift of warmer air touched his face and stirred the fog around him.

A footfall rustled; a heavy boot crunched in the dried snarls of the ubiquitous vines. Rudy whirled, and the white glow of his staff, barely penetrating the slaty darkness that engulfed them, showed him Ingold standing a few feet away.

Rudy's nerve snapped. White light streamed from the tip of his staff as he lunged at the wizard. The old man parried the thrusts, casually sidestepping the whining steel that missed his eyes by inches. The cold phosphorescence of the staff illuminated the honed steel, but Ingold himself was all but invisible in fog and darkness. Rudy pressed his attack, sobbing, exhausted, his chilled muscles cramping, and the

– 293

wizard faded before him. Somewhere in the boil of vapors behind him, he could sense Gil moving, keeping on the fringes of the fight.

Vines seemed to knot themselves around his ankles, and he tripped, barely keeping hold of his staff as he fell. He heard Ingold retreating through the tangles of foliage and scrambled hastily to his feet, wading after the wizard through the oddly persistent creepers. Darkness hid Ingold from him, but he heard the old man pause.

A paving-stone tilted under Rudy's feet, pitching him into the rubble that choked an abandoned gateway. Hands lacerated, heedless of anything but his frantic need to finish his quarry before darkness permitted Ingold to take on the form of the Dark Ones, Rudy plunged after the wizard, down a long tunnel of black fog and shadows.

In the open ground outside the city walls, the darkness seemed less pressing. The leaden mists cleared a bit, showing Rudy the wizard moving off downhill, his stain-mottled mantle blending into the colors of the fog. Rudy threw all of his strength into a clearing-spell, a wind to scatter the mists, and felt on his mind the cold grip of counterspells that strangled his power into silence. The mists wrapped tighter around him, a dun burial shroud, and he broke into a run, feverish with terror at what should happen if he met Ingold and what should happen if he did not.

He found himself stumbling blindly through a gray, steaming world, his way blocked at every turn. The stunted corpses of dead trees loomed before him in the darkness. Roots snagged at his feet, pitching him headlong into slimy patches of mud and scum. The skirts of his sodden coat slapped wetly at his thighs, his streaming boots felt weighted down with mud and water, and his body was chilled and aching to the bone. Lost, half-frozen, and gummed to the eyebrows with mud, he stumbled on alone through a nightmare of darkness and fog.

Then, wholly unexpectedly, he burst into a clearing in the mists. He staggered to a halt, the flickering light of his staff casting a wan illumination over the scene before him.

He saw Ingold and Gil standing, facing each other, close enough that the magelight mingled their two shadows into a single pool of indigo blue on the rock-hard ground. The sword Ingold held gleamed in his hand as he turned it and offered its hilt to Gil.

She took it and tested its familiar weight. Her long hair was half-unraveled around her face, and her eyes were gentler than he had ever seen them; for the first time since Rudy had known her, he could understand how a man could find this scholarly, violent, and entirely contradictory woman fascinating.

Ingold stood before her for a long moment, his hands empty at his sides. Framed by the long, dirty mane of white hair, his face was haggard, the bones seeming to stand out through colorless flesh, but for an instant Rudy found it impossible to believe that this man was anything other than the charming old wizard that he and Gil loved in their separate ways.

He wondered suddenly if that was why the Dark Ones had wanted Ingold—for his charm, which made it impossible for anyone to close the gates against him for long.

Numbly, Rudy made a move toward them. Ingold raised his head, and for an instant his eyes met Rudy's—exhausted, driven, and yet curiously serene. Mists blew between them, momentarily obscuring Rudy's vision; when they cleared, only Gil stood on the barren hillslope, her sword in her hand. Not so much as a track marked the rocky ground.

She sheathed the blade as Rudy stumbled toward her. In their search of the Palace, Gil had long ago recovered her cloak and surcoat, but they were damp from the mists, and she shivered.

Quietly Rudy asked her, "Why, Gil?"

"He might have needed it."

Rudy wiped his numbed, stiffening fingers on his soggy coat. "You're crazy, do you know that?"

"Probably," she agreed.

He looked around him at the shifting wraiths of fog that hemmed them in. "So what do we do now?"

Gil shrugged. "Wait. If he survives whatever danger he's going to meet tonight, I think he'll be back for us."

"Oh, come on!" Rudy exploded, the calmness of her voice putting the finishing touches on the day's cold, terror, and exhaustion. "You don't still think he's out to have his final confrontation with the Dark tonight, do you? More likely he's hotfooting it back to the Keep. . . ."

She folded her arms, huddling the cloak tighter about her thin shoulders. "If that's so, why didn't he kill me?"

Exasperated, he retorted, "Probably because you were more use to him alive!"

"Then why didn't he kill you?" she pointed out hotly. "And don't tell me he couldn't have carved you into *hors d'oeuvres* half a dozen times in the course of the day. Why did he let us track him—"

"That's it!" Rudy said suddenly. "Why *did* he let us track him, Gil? Ordinarily, nobody could track Ingold across a black floor sprinkled with flour. But if he was trying to lead us out of the city, why didn't he lead us the shortest way from the Palace, to the land gate opposite Trad's Hill? Why did he take all day and work us out to wherever we are now?"

Gil frowned. "Did he want to keep us away from that end of town?"

"Or from Trad's Hill? It's the biggest landmark outside the city."

She looked quickly around her. Rudy had begun to sense it, too—an uneasiness in the air, an electric dread, as if earth and fog had begun to stir with the power and malice of the Dark. For no reason, he looked behind him, half-expecting to see a shadow forming there, and felt his heartbeat quicken.

Gil whispered, "You think Trad's Hill is where he's going to meet the Dark?"

"Yeah," Rudy murmured. "But the question is: Why?"

It was full night when they reached Trad's Hill, black and icy, thunderous with the overwhelming sense of the presence of the Dark. Rudy had quenched the light that came from the end of his staff and, in the black overcast, he led Gil by the hand, picking his way cautiously over the rough ground of the plain. In spite of the cloaking-spell that covered them both, he felt smothered by the dread of the Dark. They were too close to Gae, he thought—they had followed its broken walls, barely visible in the fog—too close to the horrors that he sensed were welling from every cellar, every vault, and every passage of the endless, twisting mazes of the half-burned Nest. He felt almost stifled with fear and was shivering in the deep cold of the night.

Sudden and chill, wind whipped them, chasing the last wet rags of fog from the landscape. It flung his long, damp hair around his face and stung his abraded hands. He felt Gil's fingers tighten over his arm. The smoky veils cleared, revealing the long, irregular darkness of the walls of Gae and the paler shape of the land beneath the eerie glow of the stars.

Then he heard Gil gasp. Looking back at Gae, he saw the Dark. They rose above the broken roofline like the funnel of a monster tornado, a swirling column that spread to blacken the air. Their faint, chittering hum buzzed in his brain. The illusion they spread engulfed the cloud-splotched sky, drowning the world in stygian, all-encompassing darkness; the wind from them rushed like a hurricane over the sightless earth.

In the darkness, light flared at the top of Trad's Hill, white and strange, its reflection picking out the lines of Gil's temple and jaw, giving Rudy a brief, terrible impression of a skull within the whirling mane of her ragged hair. The mounting clouds of darkness loomed higher, blotting the invisible towers of Gae; the little spark of whiteness burst again, and this time Rudy could see, outlined in its thin glow, the black form of a man at the top of the hill, with the billowing rags of his torn mantle falling back to bare the sword-scarred, muscular arms.

Light sprang from Ingold's upraised hands, its reflection flickering in the blowing halo of weedy white hair and on the claw-cut, upturned face. The white spark broadened in the heavy air and lengthened to a twisting thread of fire that jerked and wavered in the sudden winds that swept down over the hill in a bitter, stinging wave of the smell of acid and stone. As the Dark poured down toward him, the light expanded to stretch from the hilltop to the louring blackness of the overcast sky.

Then Gil screamed, *"No!"* Turning, Rudy saw in those

shock-stricken gray eyes a blinding understanding, horror, realization, grief—and the knowledge that she had, after all, been betrayed.

Torrents of cold brightness rained over them as the streak of light opened into a fluttering gap. It was as if earth and sky had been painted upon a curtain, and that curtain was pulled aside, drawing everything with it. Beyond lay only the misty whiteness, the colorless fires, and the vivid darkness of the Void.

Toward that enormous gap, all the assembled Dark Ones of the world swarmed in a howling river of doom.

CHAPTER SEVENTEEN

California, Rudy thought numbly. *All the world that gave me birth. That was their target all along.*

He did not know why he had not seen it earlier. They had all known that Ingold was the sole guardian of the secrets of the Void. The Dark Ones must have known it as well. It was to prevent just this thing from happening that he and Gil had voluntarily submitted to exile all those long and frozen months.

And for nothing, he thought. *For nothing.*

Though there was no possible way Gil could have stopped the wizard or closed the blazing wound in the fabric of the Cosmos, she flung herself up the hill at him, the glaring light of the Void bursting like nova fire from the edge of her drawn sword. Ingold swung around, a black, swirling shape framed in that blinding aura, and raised his hand; Gil fell to her knees in the muddy snow. He towered on the hillside over her, blazing with an Archmage's terrible power. Still near the foot of the hill, Gil bowed her head to her hands, and her single, hoarse cry of bitter despair splintered the spinning darkness of the night. Then she was silent.

Above her, the Dark ones poured around Ingold, through the gap in the Void, and to the world beyond.

They seemed to have no fear of the weird brilliance that streamed from the Void. Indeed, Rudy was aware that, while it had the appearance of light, it was not truly light as it was known in this world. Its cold brightness stabbed through those sleek and dripping bodies and showed that the Dark Ones were not dark at all, but as transparent as spring water, beings of crystal protoplasm threaded with clear ruby veins. From the millrace of shadows, a single creature detached itself, shrinking in size as it drifted down, to alight like some grotesquely beautiful glass insect upon Ingold's shoulder. Others followed it, pulsing, glittering, and sinking vicious, delicate claws into the folds of his mantle and his sleeve, their long, whiplike tails hanging like sparkling ropes down his back. The chill nonlight threw into stark prominence every line graven into his ravaged face, every protruding muscle and bone, and the tortured exhaustion of his haunted eyes.

It had been known from the beginning that Ingold was the strongest and the cleverest of them all, Rudy thought, his tired mind stumbling over the realization of what he witnessed. Gil's love for the wizard was his ideal cover. Dead, damned, or enslaved by the Dark, he knew she would never have harmed him. Loyal, brave, and single-minded, she had not truly conceived in her heart of hearts that he would ever be defeated.

And the knowledge that she could have killed him and saved our world from the destruction that has encompassed this one is the price she has to pay for that blind trust.

Like a shimmering at the edges of his mind, Rudy heard a kind of singing, a music made without sound by creatures without ears. The spell of it drew at him and cast over him a confused and frightened longing. He looked quickly away from the blinding brightness of the gate to which he had felt a sudden, irrational urge to run. As he turned his head, he saw movement in the darkness near Gae, a shuffling, sluggish stream of almost-humanity, following the music with wide, unblinking eyes toward the Void.

They passed within a few feet of him, close enough for him to see the round faces, the chinless, slobbering mouths, and the white arms that clutched heavy burdens of moss. *Of course,* he thought. *The Dark would take what was left of their herds, to pasture on the ruins of their new world, in the windowless high-rises of New York and in the sewers of Paris.* There were thousands of them, far more than Rudy would have imagined could have survived in the cold under the cellars of Gae. The fetid, flabby smell of them filled his nostrils as they ambled by, their squeaking chatter grating on his nerves. They moved around Gil, jostling and shouldering one another, the light glaring out over them, unbearably bright.

Standing among his glittering masters, Ingold gazed at them expressionlessly as they were swallowed in the cold glory of the light.

Through the endless horror of that freezing night, Rudy watched the setting forth of the invasion of the Dark. Their limitless numbers and the vast size of the herds lost all meaning in his mind; he had not thought that there could be so many of them on the face of this earth.

He had learned too much about politics, power plays, and the confusion of crisis to believe that his own world would be able to take the necessary kind of concerted action against them quickly enough to stem the first tide of destruction. *If there was some kind of general crisis in the U.S.,* he thought, *its enemies would take the opportunity to bomb the daylights out of it first and ask questions later.*

I never intended to go back—but I never believed that it would be destroyed behind me.

In numbed grief, Rudy let his eyes return to the tattered, silent form of the gatekeeper of the Cosmos, standing alone at the conjunction of worlds, rimmed in searing light.

The clouds overhead broke shortly before dawn. The dazzling radiance of the Void narrowed to a slit as the fabric of the torn universe was allowed to heal itself, and the slit shortened to a single flame and vanished like the paling stars in the blue darkness.

The Dark and their herds were gone; the road by which they had traveled had vanished, too. At the end of the trampled track of churned slush, there was no mark; the huge spoor ended abruptly, as if it had been chopped short with a pair of scissors. Beyond it, pale and untouched, frost gleamed on the bare ground.

Ingold stood like a marking stone on that vanished road, his head bowed, alone beneath the vast, cold darkness of the empty sky.

The Dark had left him, Rudy thought, to account for what he had done.

Faint wind stirred through the dawn stillness, and the old man raised his head. Shining thinly in the predawn light, a sword stood, stabbed upright in the earth, just beyond where the gate had been. Ingold walked toward it, the hem of his robe sweeping damply across the glittering ground, and pulled it free. Rudy saw that it was the wizard's own sword, the one that had fallen from his hands on the dark stair beneath the Palace. The Dark had returned it to him.

The silence that filled the earth seemed to stretch unbroken to the fading hems of the sky. Ingold turned the blade in his hands, looking unearthly in the underwater blueness of dawn, as if he had absorbed some of the Void's blinding light. As Gil and Rudy came slowly up the hill toward him, he turned. The sword glinted as he sheathed it in the empty scabbard he wore at his belt.

He faced them empty-handed.

"If it would do any good," Rudy said quietly, "I would kill you for what you have done."

The old man regarded him in silence for a time, swaying slightly on his feet with weariness. In their bruised and darkened hollows, his eyes were heavy with fatigue, yet still serene. Rudy had not seen such peace in them since he and Ingold had set forth to seek the Archmage at Quo.

"And just what is it, Rudy, that you believe I have done?"

Rudy blinked at him, his face blank with surprise.

The wizard faltered unsteadily on his feet. Gil, who had stood in taut silence, stepped quickly to catch his arm. Their eyes met, and Rudy thought he saw a lightening, like a smile far back in the drugged blue depths, answering Gil's look of tormented doubt. Then Ingold sighed and turned to Rudy.

"You were very fond of your world, Rudy. But, given the infinite number of parallel universes, the Dark would hardly choose a place so—relatively—chilly and so extravagantly over-illuminated." His hand tightened suddenly on Gil's supporting shoulder.

"Come," he said quietly. "I am dying of cold and, at the moment, I doubt I have the strength even to call fire."

In the hollow below Trad's Hill, Rudy removed the spells of ward from their hidden camp and kindled a fire there. Gil brought out the walking staff that she had used on the journey from Renweth and returned it to Ingold as he sat beside the blaze.

"I saved it, along with your other things," she explained.

He smiled up at her as he took it. "You couldn't have known you would have the opportunity to return it to me," he said.

"No," she told him matter-of-factly. "I planned to bury you with it, after I killed you."

An impish lightness flickered for a moment in his eyes, and, rather to Rudy's surprise, he took her hand and lightly kissed her fingers. "That's my Gil."

Then Rudy realized what had been wrong. In all the battle and pursuit through the slimy, fogbound ruins of Gae, he had never seen in Ingold's eyes the inhuman emptiness that had characterized Lohiro's. Throughout that day and through the eerie horrors of the night, the wizard had been frightening, but he had never been other than Ingold.

"That's why they wanted you, wasn't it?" Rudy asked softly.

"Yes," the old man murmured and held out unsteady hands to the warmth of the blaze. "They—wanted to talk to me. I think they would have come and fetched me eventually, wherever I was."

Above the trampled crest of Trad's Hill and the broken skeleton of Gae, the sky was now stained with lavender, a soft dove color that infused the earth from horizon to horizon and lent an ashy pallor to the old man's white face.

"Did they take over your mind?" Rudy asked.

Ingold kept his eyes steadily on the fire. "In a manner of speaking," he replied. "They are not exactly one being, but they speak from mind to mind in a fashion that we would find—rather horrible. It was only when Lohiro, in an act of foolhardy desperation, gave his mind to the Dark that they realized communication with us was possible in any fashion at all." The lacerated flesh around his eyes puckered suddenly as he closed them, as if to shut out some hideous vision. "I fought them endlessly," he went on. "I don't know how long." A shiver racked his body, and he bowed his head, his forehead resting on suddenly clenched knuck-les. "Of course it was stupid," he whispered. "They knew they had only to wait until I tired."

Gil's hand gently touched his bent shoulder, and gradually the shivering ceased.

At length he raised his head again. "The Dark were in desperate straits, you see. They are a farsighted race, with understanding of things whose mere existence we ourselves have barely guessed. You were only partially right, Gil, when you spoke of a—a weather cycle. The deep cold spell of three thousand years ago was only a small fluctuation in a much longer, deeper cycle. This one—the one that began this autumn, after what I suppose could only be called a warning flutter twenty years ago—will last uncountable years of time. The Dark Ones said that the ice in the north will spread until it covers much of the world. It may be possible for humankind to survive the cold, they said—but the herds of the Dark would not last another two years. The famine in the Nest had already reached proportions far more severe than ever in the past, and there was no hope of salvaging the herds in the deepest caverns and waiting for the cold to pass. In a very short time the Dark Ones would have cracked the last citadels of humankind, devoured its final representatives—and themselves perished."

"Could they have?" Rudy asked doubtfully. "They tried to break the Keep at the beginning of winter . . ."

"They could," Ingold said somberly. "Believe me, Rudy, they could. I know the Dark—now.

"They saw no alternative to the annihilation of both races until this autumn, when I crossed the Void to speak to you, Gil. Then they became aware of the Void. When I rescued Tir from the destruction of the Palace at Gae, one of them crossed it . . . And they have hunted for me ever since."

He folded his hands and sat gazing into the fire. Around them, the wet, slushy plain was emerging from obscurity, gray sheets of ice lying in all directions, pricked with black friezes of branches and sedge. The mournful cry of rooks grated faintly into the dawn air.

"They wanted me to find them a new world," the wizard

went on softly, as if scarcely aware now of either his surroundings or his listeners. "A world such as this one was eons ago, when the Dark first built their eldritch cities in swamps whose very memory is no more than stratum of pebbles in the bed of a desert stream. A warm world, dark and marshy, where they could tend their herds, build new cities, and dream."

Against the paling sky, the broken walls of Gae were clearly visible, a black crenelation against the gray of filthy waters. It was a city wholly empty now, except for the rats that fed on jewel-circled bones. As if in a vision, Rudy saw again the mists rolling back from the ruins of Quo and heard the dim boom of the breakers at the foot of Forn's shattered Tower. Dull anger burned in his heart for the greedy callousness that had crushed and wasted this world and then passed on, unscathed and unavenged.

"So they made you their slave," Rudy said quietly, "and left the rest of us to pick up the pieces."

Ingold glanced sideways at him. Life seemed to be stirring back into the wizard. The sunken, corpselike weariness was passing from his face. "Oh, I was never their slave," he murmured. "Merely their—collaborator."

Rudy looked up sharply.

"The Dark Ones never took over my mind," Ingold explained gently. "They couldn't do that—not if they wanted me to retain the knowledge of how the Void operates. If I were their slave, do you think I would have tried to get you out of town before you were caught up in the spells of the Dark and drawn along with the herds through the Void?"

In a dull voice, Rudy said, "Then after all they did— destroyed your world and murdered your friends—you helped them willingly."

Annoyance sparkled deep in the azure eyes. "Hardly willingly."

When Rudy still sat in smoldering silence at the unfairness of it, Ingold asked, "If you are in a fight and your opponent knocks you down and then walks away, do you call him back to hit you again, in the hope of defeating him?"

"Well—" Rudy said grudgingly. "Some people do."

"And that, Rudy, is how some people get noses like yours," the wizard retorted. "As for the rest—it is finished."

"You know they rose in the Alketch?" Gil said, after a moment's silence.

"I was informed when it happened."

"Did you know Eldor is dead?"

The wizard sighed, and it seemed that his broad shoulders sagged a little, as if at bad news long expected. He shook his head wearily. "But it hardly surprises me. He did not want to live very badly. As you yourselves have no doubt found, the world into which we have all been thrust is a poor trade for the security and comfort of civilized life." He looked up from the fire, the cool pallor of dawn now clearly visible about them. "And that, my children," he said, "brings us all to the time that I have come to dread. We are where we should have been many months ago, had not politics and the chances of fortune intervened."

He took Gil's hand and rose haltingly to his feet. Behind him, the first warmth of the sun infused the neutral landscape with color, tinting the rocks that protruded through the dirty snow with the richness of rust and indigo, edging the broken ice in burnished gold. Looking down suddenly, Gil could see in the protected hollows of the rocks that surrounded their camp the first green threads of grass and the hardy green weeds of the coming spring.

Deep and scratchy, Ingold's voice came to her ears. "You are free now to return to your homes," he was saying, "wherever those homes may be."

The hush that filled the morning world was so profound that Gil could hear the far-off whistle of a chickadee in the willows that fringed the river. She became conscious that she was hungry and cold, as she had always been since coming to this world.

Rudy was the first to speak. "I thought you didn't believe in the chances of fortune, Ingold," he said quietly. "You know I could never go back. It almost seems I always knew that, even on the first day we were in Karst, before I'd met Alde, or understood about magic, or—or anything."

Ingold smiled. "And that is why I do not believe in the chances of fortune. My dear . . ."

306

Gil looked up, to see grief and gentle regret in the old man's eyes.

"I know there were times that you hated me for robbing you of what you had and what you sought in your own world. There is little scope here for your scholarship. In the years to come, humankind will be reduced to fighting for its bare survival. And due to my carelessness, you have been kept here against your will, and in your absence that other life that is waiting for you has become badly disrupted. Forgive me, Gil. I think you shall find, when you return, that nothing is irreparable."

"I'm not so sure about that," Gil said shakily. "I don't think I'll ever patch up the break in the wall that I'd built around myself there. And maybe other things besides."

The glacier wind from the mountains burned her scarred cheek. Through her mind floated a host of trivialities— movies, the stereo, coffee, hot showers, her parents, and the peace of a soft bed. She realized how badly she ached with lack of sleep and how icy were her hands in that light, sword-scarred grip.

She raised her head again and held his gaze with hers. She asked, "Do you want me to stay?"

She saw his eyes widen, all the serenity in them put to flight by sudden, springing hope that was resolutely crushed before they turned away from hers altogether. His low, grainy voice was carefully neutral, but she could feel his fingers tighten over hers.

"Gil," Ingold said quietly, "I told you once that I am a dangerous person to love. I have tried very hard not to love you—without success, I might add—and if you stayed, I would not want to be parted from you. And that, my dear, would bring you nothing but disaster."

"You don't think that, after all that's passed, I can't cope with disaster?"

He looked back at her, taut misery on his face. "You don't understand," he said. "From the time I was your age, my power, my damned curiosity, and my infernal meddling have brought danger and horrible deaths to those I have loved and to those who have loved me. I have never loved a woman as I love you—God only knows why, for I've never met such a stubborn and hardhearted woman as yourself. I have never before loved a woman so much that I would rather lose her than see her come to harm."

"If it comes to that," Gil replied mildly, "I've never met any man—any person—whom I'd risk my neck to stay with—until you."

"I cannot allow it . . ."

"That wasn't my question."

Something very close to anger darkened his face. "I can't let you do this to yourself," he told her roughly. "Aside from being pointed at as an old man's folly—"

"Old?" Her brows shot up. "*You?*"

Under the scrubby beard and long, unkempt mane of hair, his scarred cheeks colored. "Gil, you have no idea what you are asking," he pleaded.

She put her hands on his shoulders, and the coarse folds of his mantle were damp and cold under her fingers. "I know what I'm asking," she said in a low voice. "Now forget your responsibility to everyone else for once in your life and give me a straight answer. Do you want me to stay?"

She saw the struggle on his face, his love and protectiveness toward her fighting against a wholly selfish desire to keep her at his side as his woman and his friend. She thought that he would lie, as he had often lied, to keep her from harm, retreat behind a smoke screen of words, send her away from him, and meet his own doom in his own way.

But after a moment he reached up and took her wrists, a half-amused, half-regretful wryness in his eyes.

"I want you," he said softly. "You know perfectly well that I have always wanted you, my love."

Rudy looked consideringly at the two cloaked forms, locked in a sudden and crushing embrace in the pale, heatless sunlight. He shook his head. "And I thought *I* was involved in a relationship I didn't understand," he remarked.

"The only thing in *that* relationship I never understood," Gil commented judiciously, when she and Ingold broke apart at last and she pushed the tangled hair back from her face, "is Alde's taste in men."

"You're coming real close to spending the rest of your life as a frog, spook," Rudy warned her.

"A rash threat," Ingold said, "considering that her true love is on the spot and yours is a week's journey away at the Keep of Dare."

Rudy sighed, realizing that he was outnumbered. But then, he thought, eyeing that curious couple, Gil and Ingold together were capable of outnumbering almost anything.

"Why do I put up with this?" he demanded rhetorically.

"It's very simple," Ingold replied, draping one arm around the frayed shoulders of the awesome and intellectual warrior at his side. "Since nothing is fortuitous, you yourself chose this world over the one that you were born in. Perhaps, since we do not know the reasons for all things happening as they do, you chose it long before you ever came here. Even a cursory comparison of the two worlds proves that you are out of your senses."

"Thanks." Rudy sighed. "I wondered about that."

"It explains why you're always surrounded by lunatics," Gil offered hopefully.

"No," Rudy objected. "Even a plea of insanity wouldn't explain that."

Ingold laughed. "Come," he said. "Your lady at the Keep will be growing anxious. It is time we were bound for home."

Pale sunlight glimmered on the ice in the flooded valleys before them, turning the trampled mud of the plain into a flashing carpet of diamonds. Though cold winds blew the scent of barren rock and glacier ice down upon them from the mountains to the north, it could already be seen that the pools were edged with the vivid green rushes of a late and chilly spring. The shadows of the wanderers rippled hard and blue about their feet as the three moved off down the hill to take the southward road.

About the Author

At various times in her life, Barbara Hambly has been a high-school teacher, a model, a waitress, a technical editor, a professional graduate student, an all-night clerk at a liquor store, and a karate instructor. Born in San Diego, she grew up in Southern California, with the exception of one high-school semester spent in New South Wales, Australia. Her interest in fantasy began with reading *The Wizard of Oz* at the age of six and graduated in natural stages through Burroughs, Tolkien, *Star Trek*, and Heinlein, and she has been writing fantasy almost as long as she has been reading it.

She attended the University of California, Riverside, specializing in medieval history. In connection with this, she spent a year at the University of Bordeaux in the south of France and worked as a teaching and research assistant at UC Riverside for two years, eventually earning a Master's Degree in the subject. At the university she also became involved in karate, making black belt in 1978 and going on to compete in several national-level tournaments.

Ms. Hambly currently resides in Riverside, California. In addition to writing and karate, her hobbies include sewing, painting, Regency dancing, and reading Tarot cards.

Enchanting fantasies from

Dear Reader,

Your opinions are very important to us so please take a few moments to tell us your thoughts. It will help us give you more enjoyable DEL REY Books in the future.

1. Where did you obtain this book?

Bookstore	☐1	Department Store ☐4	Airport	☐7	5
Supermarket	☐2	Drug Store ☐5	From A Friend	☐8	
Variety/Discount Store ☐3		Newsstand ☐6	Other_____		

(Write In)

2. On an overall basis, how would you rate this book?

Excellent ☐1   Very Good ☐2   Good ☐3   Fair ☐4   Poor ☐5   6

3. What is the main reason that you purchased this book?

Author   ☐1   It Was Recommended To Me ☐3   7
Like The Cover ☐2   Other_____

(Write In)

4. In the same subject category as this book, who are your *two* favorite authors?

_____   8
_____   9
_____   10
_____   11

5. Which of the following categories of paperback books have you purchased in the past 3 months?

Adventure/		Biography	☐4	Horror/		Science
Suspense	☐12-1	Classics	☐5	Terror ☐8		Fiction ☐x
Bestselling		Fantasy	☐6	Mystery ☐9		Self-Help ☐y
Fiction	☐2	Historical		Romance ☐0		War ☐13
Bestselling		Romance	☐7			Westerns ☐2
Non-Fiction ☐3						

6. What magazines do you subscribe to, or read regularly, that is, 3 out of every 4 issues?

_____   14
_____   15
_____   16
_____   17

7. Are you: Male ☐1   Female ☐2   18

8. Please indicate your age group

Under 18 ☐1	25-34 ☐3	50 or older ☐5		19
18-24 ☐2	35-49 ☐4			

9. What is the highest level of education that you have completed?

Post Graduate Degree ☐1	College Graduate ☐3	Some High	20
Some Post Graduate	1-3 Years College ☐4	School	
Schooling ☐2	High School	or Less ☐6	
	Graduate ☐5		

(Optional)

If you would like to learn about future publications and participate in future surveys, please fill in your name and address.

NAME_____

ADDRESS_____

CITY_____ STATE_____ ZIP _____   21

Please mail to   Ballantine Books
DEL REY Research, Dept.
516 Fifth Avenue — Suite 606
New York, N.Y. 10036

F-10